Praise for W

Movie Rogue

'*Movie Rogue* is the third novel in Coles's Rogue series, and they just get better and better. I haven't read a funnier book all year. Coles knocks it out of the park again with a comic humdinger. What an arresting conceit it is to base a novel around Stanley Kubrick's last film, *Eyes Wide Shut* – and yet, this book is based on a true story.'

TUNKU VARADARAJAN, THE WALL STREET JOURNAL

Eton Rogue

'A delicious tale in which class, politics, and a toxic press all jostle'

TUNKU VARADARAJAN, *THE WALL STREET JOURNAL*

Palace Rogue

'This charming tale of secrets and love is a must for royal fans.'

HELLO MAGAZINE

'A plump and cheerful romp through royal corridors and bedrooms.'

TUNKU VARADARAJAN, *THE WALL STREET JOURNAL*

'This rom com is packed full of love, laughs and scandals, and is well worth a read.'

HAMPSHIRE CHRONICLE

'A right royal romp through one of Buckingham Palace's shadier moments.'

SHAUN BYTHELL, AUTHOR OF THE INTERNATIONAL HIT *DIARY OF A BOOKSELLER*

The Eton Affair

'Charming, moving, uplifting. Why can't all love stories be like this?'
TUNKU VARADARAJAN, *THE WALL STREET JOURNAL*

'This is a charming and uplifting book.'
PIERS MORGAN

'An outstanding debut novel. A wonderful story of first love. Few male authors can write about romance in a way which appeals to women – but Coles has managed it quite brilliantly.'
SUNDAY EXPRESS

'Elegantly structured, tinglingly evocative of the passion and brutality of first love – a wonderful read.'
LOUISE CANDLISH

'What a read! Every schoolboy's dream comes true in this deftly-written treatment of illicit romance. A triumph.'
ALEXANDER MCCALL SMITH

Dave Cameron's Schooldays

'A cracking read... Perfectly paced and brilliantly written, Coles draws you in, leaving a childish smile on your face.'
NEWS OF THE WORLD

'A fast moving and playful spoof. The details are so slick and telling that they could almost have you fooled.'
THE MIRROR

Dearest Matt,

MOVIE
ROGUE

*So this is the
result of your*

WILLIAM COLES

*great stories!
Thank you!
lots of love Bill x*

LP

Legend Press Ltd, 51 Gower Street, London, WC1E 6HJ
info@legendtimesgroup.co.uk | www.legendpress.co.uk

Contents © William Coles 2025
The right of the above author to be identified as the author of this work has
been asserted in accordance with the Copyright, Designs and Patents Act
1988. British Library Cataloguing in Publication Data available.

Print ISBN 978-1-91716-343-9
Ebook ISBN 978-1-91716-344-6
Set in Times.

Cover design by Ditte Løkkegaard

William Coles has been a journalist for over 30 years and has worked for a number of papers including *The Sun*, *The Express*, *The Mail* and *The Wall Street Journal*.

William's novels, *Palace Rogue* and *Eton Rogue*, are the prequels to *Movie Rogue*, and were published in 2023 and 2024.

Visit William at
wcoles.com

and follow him
@WilliamColes1

For Mike Hamill, stalwart

PREFACE

In the late autumn of 1996, the world's most pernickety film director, Stanley Kubrick, started filming his last great project. *Eyes Wide Shut* would ultimately enter the *Guinness Book of World Records* – though not, perhaps, for the reasons that Kubrick might have hoped for. While most movie shoots last around three months, *Eyes Wide Shut* garnered the world record (a record that has still yet to be touched) for the longest continuous shoot in history. Kubrick's gargantuan shoot lasted 400 days and took its toll on every single person involved. When filming finally wrapped, the entire crew – who'd not had a holiday in over a year – were close to suffering from post-traumatic stress disorder.

Naturally enough, the world's media was absolutely fascinated by this super-secret squillion-pound shoot. The only thing that was really known about *Eyes Wide Shut* was that it starred the hottest Hollywood couple of the decade, Nicole Kidman and Tom Cruise. There was also talk of a searingly graphic orgy scene. But beyond that: nothing. No one even knew the name of the book that the film was based on.

This naturally led to the most feverish tabloid speculation: eye-popping tales of Harvey Keitel storming off set because he couldn't stomach Kubrick's OCD levels of perfectionism; talk of Kubrick constructing a whole chunk of New York City right outside London; endless chatter about Tom and Nicole's rocky marriage. There was even a weird whisper that Kubrick was only surviving the brutal film schedule because he'd hired a body double.

One little-known story from *Eyes Wide Shut* was that the film set was infiltrated by a reporter from one of the British tabloids. The hack not only worked as an extra on one of the most outlandish orgy scenes in movie history, but also, it's believed, became friends with both Cruise and Kubrick.

It is perhaps one of the better stories that's told about *Eyes Wide Shut*.

It is the story of *Movie Rogue*.

CHAPTER 1

On this night of nights as the rest of Britain is all but abed, Tom Cruise steadies himself and readies himself to walk through a doorway for the 79th time. His mercurial director, Stanley Kubrick, forever thirsting for something more, but never quite knowing what it is that he wants, sips lemonade as he lounges behind the camera. Kubrick's Assistant Director, Glenn, who does the donkey work, sucks it up, just as he's done for the previous six months; above all Glenn tries not to wonder how many times Cruise will be made to walk through this doorway before Kubrick is finally happy (though that in itself raises the fatal question of whether Kubrick can ever be happy). Nicole Kidman – Nic to her husband – is not on the set, and instead continues with her project of general self-improvement, which this year includes learning Italian.

On the newsdesk of Her Majesty's *Sun* newspaper, the night news editor seethes as her booziest reporter, one Kim by name, sips "Ribena" as he languidly leafs through the first editions.

And meanwhile over a hundred miles away in Manchester, Nina, our topless heroine, cavorts around a pole and ponders that insuperable problem that comes to all of us in the end: how the hell am I going to get out of this fix?

For reasons which we may yet come to, Nina has been working in the Red Coat strip club for four years now. She is a beautiful and accomplished pole-dancer, bringing in more than enough money to fund her impossible dream: writing a bestseller. To date, she has written four manuscripts and has had one of them published; so far it has sunk without trace. But Nina is resilient and she continues with the project. Nina has adopted as her personal mantra the heart-warming words of the late great Iain Banks, whose sage advice continues to inspire writers the world over: the first million words you write are shit.

Roughly speaking, including first and second drafts, Nina has now written nearly 700,000 words, so only another 300,000 pieces of faeces to get through, and then, truly, she will have paid her dues – and perhaps, just possibly, might have written a book which actually brings in some money. Until that happy day, Nina will continue to grind out the Red Coat hours for four nights a week – and although some might see her work as demeaning, exploitative, Nina's glass is half-full. She's got two good friends, one of them a keeper. She gets loads of material for her writing. And, despite considerable pestering, she hasn't yet become a prostitute.

Nina and Mandy are entwined round adjacent poles on the podium in the middle of the club. Nina has a rich sense of humour and can indeed see the ridiculousness of the song they're dancing to – one of the hits of 1997, 'Barbie Girl' by a band called Aqua. The song's utterly banal, of course, but because they're pros, both Nina and Mandy are giving it everything they've got. Certainly for Nina, her smile is genuine.

Since it is altogether possible that you have never been inside a strip club – leastways not a 1990s strip club – we'd best describe it. The Red Coat is fairly dark, the better to obscure the dark deeds that occur behind the pillars and in the nooks and corners. The walls are grey, the carpet is dark blue and dotted about the room are a scattering of chairs and little round tables. At one end, a large bar, and at the other, lounging in a booth next to the entrance, is Ali the pock-marked manager.

While Nina and Mandy are the main draw on centre stage, a number of their colleagues prowl the floor, traipsing around the tables, weighing up the punters for their looks and their wealth and, indeed, their general cheeriness. Most of the clientele are besuited menfolk, and those that are deemed not overly offensive are accosted with a smile and a question about their hometown or their business in Manchester.

If the answers prove satisfactory (or at least not wholly unsatisfactory), the girl will sit down and join the man, and with luck will persuade him to buy her a drink; with a little more luck, she will entice him off to one of the curtained booths for a private lap dance, for this is where the real money is to be made. (The rules state that there is to be no touching in these private booths, but shall we just say that the strippers have a certain degree of latitude.)

What these beautiful women are offering up is a fantasy, and one of the most common male fantasies is – perhaps regrettably, perhaps not regrettably – to have a threesome. (That is one man and two women; two men and one woman does occur, but is less common.)

Now – it's during these threesomes that the spats occur. You might imagine that strip club fights are usually between the menfolk. Not so. Most fights are between the girls and are usually sparked by a perceived unfair distribution of the spoils. For instance... suppose that a beautiful girl, Linda, has taken the interest of a rich middle-aged whale, whom we shall call John. Now Linda may have invested some considerable time in buttering John up, teasingly asking him about his wife and his dreams, and getting him to buy a bottle of the expensive but disgusting house champagne. At length, John may decide that he'd like to go to a booth for a private lap dance with Linda, and then, what the hell, he decides to have another girl join them, and the girl who just happens to have taken his fancy is Bambi, a Russian (her real name was Svetlana, but that was deemed too much of a mouthful). Now Bambi is certainly beautiful, but she is no friend of Linda's. The girls have previous. But still – both Linda and Bambi are both thoroughbred professionals, and professionally go about their business of lightening John's wallet.

The altercation starts when it comes to the dividing of the spoils. John has given Linda and Bambi some £600 in cash, but the money itself had actually been handed to Linda. And the moot question is this: is Bambi deserving of half of the spoils, some £300, or should she have a lesser cut, say, £200, or even, a stingy £150? On the one hand, it's Linda who's put in all the hard yards chitty-chatting with John; but on the other hand, Bambi more than did the business with John in the private booth.

If only a handy lawyer was available to make some Solomon-like adjudication on how the money should be divided, but as it is, there is no such lawyer in the Red Coat (or at least one prepared to declare himself), and so Linda and Bambi decide to sort out their differences in the old-fashioned way: with a cat-fight.

There is clawing, there is hair-pulling, and there is slapping and grappling, and the whole thing is all most unedifying. The punters, however, cannot take their eyes off the extraordinary spectacle – all save one, Leon, and since we will be returning to Leon, he shall have the benefit of a description: Leon is quite a slight man, not above 5' 7", and is wearing a rumpled suit and yellow-tinted glasses. He has longish shoulder-length hair which is both thinning and receding. What makes him stand out from the rest of the punters is that, on his round table, alongside his dirty Martini, is an A4 notebook, into which he jots the odd note with his Montblanc pen. He also occasionally draws a picture.

Though all the rest of the Red Coat clientele are watching Bambi as she writhes around on top of Linda, Leon only has eyes for Nina and Mandy, who continue their slick performance at the poles. And the look on Leon's face? He has a smile of wry amusement as he wonders just how much longer these two girls can ignore the unignorable screaming scrap that is occurring right on the floor in front of them.

Now – as to the catfight, after a minute on the floor, Linda has realised that she is being bested by the younger and more agile Bambi. What she needs is a weapon – and, useful tip here, if you're in a catfight then there's only one real weapon in town: a stiletto heel. She hurls it as hard as she can, but instead of connecting with Bambi's face, or even her throat, it whistles clean over her head and straight at Nina.

Nina, still doughtily dancing with Mandy, is doing what she does so very well and that is to zone out, thinking about what she'll have for dinner that night. From out of nowhere, she suddenly becomes aware of the stiletto zeroing point first straight towards her head. She catches it, pure reflex, and now she's still dancing away but she's got Linda's stiletto shoe in her hand. But… what to do with the stiletto? Place it neatly on the stage for Linda to retrieve whenever the security goons have dragged her off Bambi? Or perhaps… pretend it's a phone? Or a microphone?

Nina happens to glance at the guy with the yellow-tinged glasses and the straggly hair, our friend Leon, who has already sized up the problem. He makes a little gun with thumb and two fingers and shoots her.

Nina, smart as paint, immediately cottons on. As the cat-fight is brought to a close by two security goons (final result? Probably a score draw), Nina channels her inner James Bond to start shooting people with her new stiletto. In her mind's eye, Nina is the gorgeous Maud Adams, the only woman to have featured in three Bond films. First, she shoots Mandy (who then handily mimes being shot, staggering against her pole before slow-mo collapsing to the floor), and then picks off various punters. In the classic 007 stance – feet wide, knees bent – she shoots Leon, and he, pleasingly, takes the shot full in the chest, before (and this is what especially won Nina over) upending his chair and throwing himself backwards, as if hit by the full force of a Magnum .45.

The end of the song also brings an end to the shoot-out, and Nina and Mandy saunter off the stage, ten- and twenty-pound notes being teasingly tucked into their red suspender garters. Nina deposits the stiletto on Linda's dressing table.

'Nice catch,' Mandy says. 'I thought the shoe was going to hit you.'

'So did I!' Nina laughed.

'Fancy a chat with Mr Yellow Glasses?'

'Why not?' Nina says. 'He looked fun.'

* * *

The girls put on their bras again for the fifth time that evening, and after slipping on their red silk kimonos (hence the club's name, the Red Coat), they sashay over to Leon, who has now righted his chair and is contentedly scribbling in his notebook.

'I hoped you'd come over,' Leon says. The notebook is snapped shut. 'Nice bit of improv. Care to join me?'

Mandy pulls up a chair. On a whim, Nina turns the chair round and straddles it, legs brazenly akimbo, and leans forward, forearms on the back of the chair – seductive, powerful, the iconic pose of Christine Keeler, the woman at the heart of that great 1960s scandal, the Profumo affair.

'So what are you writing in that notebook of yours?' Nina asked breezily. 'Is it a novel?'

'I'd love to write a novel,' Leon said. 'Sadly, I do not have the skills.'

'I'm on my fifth,' Nina said. 'I used to think I was quite good. And sadly for me, I now know I'm still in the foothills.'

'Truly?' Leon said.

'Truly.'

'Is this gig funding your writing?'

'It is,' Nina said.

'Good for you,' he said.

It was Mandy, of course, who cut to the chase. 'You gonna buy us a drink or what?'

'What would you like to drink?'

'Normally they want us to buy a bottle of champagne – they make more money on that. But I fancy what you're having.'

'And you?' Leon said.

'I think I'd also like a Martini,' Nina said. 'Dirty.'

Three dirty Martinis were ordered, and after a pleasant pause to exhale and to settle, Nina asked the question that still lingered in the air: 'If you're not writing a novel, what are you writing?'

Leon smiled to himself, and, hand on chin, reflected on whether he was yet ready to share his secret.

'That is the question.' He plucked the stick from his third Martini of the evening and ate the olive, and because he was enjoying himself and liked the cut of Nina's jib, not to mention her cat-like catching skills, he decided that the secret could be revealed in all its great glory.

For what Leon possessed was two golden tickets out of the strip club – and two tickets, mind, which would offer so much more than the usual passport out of the Red Coat, which was, generally speaking, a life of being a paid-up mistress.

'I've been making notes on all you dancers,' Leon said. 'I particularly liked the way that you weren't fazed by the fight.'

'Really?' Nina said.

'Yes really.'

'Prove it,' Mandy said.

The notebook was opened. Leon riffled through the pages. It appeared as if every girl in the club had her own page. 'This is you,' he said to Mandy, swivelling the pad so that she could read his black ink notes: 'Yellow polka-dot bikini, 5' 10", blonde shoulder-length hair, supple, brassy, in your face, might work.' Beneath the words, Leon had drawn a remarkably accurate picture of Mandy, legs wrapped around the pole, with smoking eyes and pouting lips.

'What does "might work" mean?' Mandy said.

'You might work,' Leon said simply, before turning a page and pushing the notepad towards Nina: 'Red bikini, 6' 1 ½", long brown hair, statuesque bordering on Amazonian, magnificent shoulders; potential.' The line drawing was of Nina shooting her stiletto pistol.

'I've got potential?' Nina said. 'That better than "might work"?'

'Marginally,' Leon said.

The three Martinis were delivered – though not by one of the usual waitresses, but by the pocked Ali, our oh-so frustrated manager.

'Three Martinis,' Ali said. 'Looks like you're having fun.'

'We most certainly are, thank you very much indeed,' Leon said.

'See you've got a notebook,' Ali said. 'What you been writing?'

'Nothing of your concern.'

'Mind if I have a look?'

'I do as it happens.' Leon didn't even bother to look at Ali.

'That's not very friendly,' Ali said. He leant on the back of Mandy's chair.

'I didn't realise friendliness was a prerequisite for entering your club.'

'But you didn't mind showing your notes to the girls.'

'I didn't,' Leon said. He stretched over the table to pick up his fresh Martini and took a sip before admiring the two new girls on stage. They were good, but just not quite as silky smooth as Mandy or Nina. 'But these girls were more polite than you.'

'Were they now?' Ali said.

'Tell me – is this really the best you've got?'

Ali turned to Nina. 'Is he telling the truth?'

'Yes,' Nina said. 'Why's it any skin off your nose? I couldn't care less what he writes in his notebook.'

Mandy chipped in. 'What's the big deal, Ali? Who gives a stuff?'

'It's a security issue, girls.'

'He can write what he likes!' Mandy said. 'Why do you have to be so nosey?'

'Customer security.'

'You know what, it's fine,' Leon said. 'I've got what I'm looking for. I'm leaving.'

'And just you pay your bill!' Ali said.

'Do I look like I'd do a runner?' Leon asked, though his words were lost on Ali, who was already bustling to his booth. 'Perhaps I do,' he confided to Nina.

He fished out a silver card case from his jacket and tapped it with slim fingers. 'I am recruiting girls for a major motion picture,' Leon said. 'You'll be topless but wearing masks. Rehearsals start next week and they'll last for at least four months.' He took two cards from the case and slipped them to Nina and Mandy. 'After that, you'll be filming – could take two months, though probably more. It's near London. We'll put you up. The pay will be a little less than what you're earning here, but it'll be a sight more interesting.'

'That'll be Kubrick's new film,' Nina said.

'The one starring Tom Cruise and Nicole Kidman?' Mandy squealed. 'I saw the pictures in the *News of the Screws*!'

Leon laughed. 'How did you know it was Kubrick's film?' he said.

'He's the only director who spends that long on a shoot.' Nina tucked Leon's card into the pocket of her kimono.

The girls watched as Leon settled his bill at the bar.

'Think he was genuine?' Mandy said.

'I so hope so!' Nina said.

And to the girls' very slight amazement, Leon was the genuine real deal. His name was Leon Vitali – and for the previous two decades, he had been the right-hand man and indeed first lieutenant of the world's most tricksy film director, one Stanley Kubrick. Vitali did absolutely everything for Kubrick – and that included hiring all of his strippers.

CHAPTER 2

There are two types of people who work on film shoots – those who take good care of themselves, and those who let themselves go.

Most of the time it doesn't make much difference. As most shoots don't last more than a hundred days, it's no big deal if you put on a few kilos. On the longer shoots, it starts to make a difference. And when you happen to be on the longest shoot in world history... then look out!

Glenn, the first assistant director on *Eyes Wide Shut*, is the type who takes good care of himself. In the morning, he goes to the gym and does stretches and press-ups and pull-ups, and then, after a double espresso, goes for an hour-long walk. On set, he allows himself just one more coffee and then drinks only water. He never touches any of the biscuits, pastries or sumptuous slices of cake that are offered up to him, though on Fridays, as his one and only treat, he will have one small *pastel de nata*. As he savours the delicate custard and the flaky pastry, he closes his eyes and, for a few golden moments, he's back with his mother and his brother on a sultry Saturday in the café of the local bookshop.

That, then, is Glenn.

The second assistant director, Roddie, falls into that second category of people who work on a film shoot: in the six months since filming started he has put on more than ten kilos. Not for Roddie any morning stretches or physical jerks, or indeed bracing walks – no, Roddie just rolls out of bed, puts on the previous day's clothes that are lying on the floor and, without brushing his teeth, and certainly without looking in the mirror, he heads straight to the set canteen, where Molly the cook has been up since 4 a.m. He always orders the complete works, link sausage, black pudding, white pudding, bacon, eggs, fried bread, beans – all that tasty stuff that so wonderfully clogs your arteries. He dulls the tedium of the day by never refusing any of the cakes or biscuits that the runners constantly waft beneath his nose.

And that is Roddie.

Today, during the union-regulated hour-long meal break, both Glenn and Roddie are true to type. Glenn helps himself to a green salad, a piece of cooked salmon, a wholemeal roll and, for pudding, an apple and a satsuma. In front of Roddie is arrayed the full smorgasbord: chicken soup with two slices of white bread and butter, beef stroganoff on rice, a bowl of trifle, a slice of orange chocolate cake and a plate of biscuits and stilton.

The canteen is, as yesterday, relatively empty, because there are no extras (by that we of course respectfully mean 'supporting artists'). The scene that Glenn and Roddie have been repeatedly shooting consists of just the star of the show, Tom Cruise, walking down a New York street in the middle of the night. Since they're inside a studio, the scene could be shot in the daytime, but as the director Stanley Kubrick prefers night-shoots, then night-shoots it's got to be.

Tom and Kubrick have retired to their trailers, so in the canteen that evening it's just Glenn, Roddie and the core crew – the cinematographer, the first assistant camera operator (Kubrick often preferring to wield the camera himself), four grips, including the key grip (who fiddles with the lights), the gaffer (more of a light technician) and the boom operator, whose job it is to hang the sound boom over the star's head. Oh, and perhaps there's one other person in the canteen we should touch upon: Sven, the Steadicam operator. The Steadicam had revolutionised Hollywood film-making, allowing a cameraman to walk around as he follows the action – though instead of the rushes coming out shaky and blurred, they were unbelievably steady and smooth. Kubrick loves the Steadicam. But his Steadicam operator – not so much.

It's a tight team who have been working together for a solid six months without a single day off. Saturdays and Sundays off? You have got to be joking, sailor! Directors like Kubrick are not people to leave expensive sets and costumes and equipment going idle over the weekend. No – when we say that this team have been working six months straight, we mean they have worked for 180 days without a break. All of them are entirely at Kubrick's beck and call. It is Kubrick who determines when the day begins and when it ends; it is Kubrick alone who decides on every last detail of the multiple sets and costumes; and of course it can only be Kubrick who decides when there have been a satisfactory number of takes. No detail whatsoever is too small for Kubrick to be involved with. The colour of a supporting artist's lipstick? Kubrick's on it! The pleats on some bystander's trousers? Kubrick's on it! The selection of every single one of the 200-odd supporting artists? Kubrick. Is. On. It. This guy is all over it like a rash. Kubrick is the living embodiment of obsessive compulsive perfectionism, and Warner Bros, who are funding the whole show, have given him free rein to do just about whatever he wants. His films always come in under budget, and they always make money. As far as Warner Bros are concerned, Kubrick is the golden goose, and if he wants to make the world's biggest star, Tom Cruise, walk through a damn doorway over a hundred times then… Tommy, we sure hope you like turning doorknobs!

Just as in the army, there is a strict hierarchy on this film set. At the top, jostling for position, are Kubrick and his two stars. Kubrick is of course the man who calls the shots, and Tom and Nicole, absolutely desperate to work with him, have signed the most unbelievably stringent contracts which even forbids them from signing up for any other projects until

Kubrick has 100 per cent finished with them. But though Tom and Nic have to do just about everything Kubrick wants, they've still got a few cards. They can get 'sick', or be bolshy, or turn up late. Kubrick is the boss. But he still needs them.

Though everyone else involved with the film is chicken feed, there is still a solid pecking order, with Glenn and Roddie up at the top with the cinematographer, followed by the gaffer and the grips, and the costume and props people, as well as the teasers on hair and make-up. Down near the bottom of the pile are the runners (effectively gofers, earning beans, dreaming dreams) and the stand-ins, who stand in for the stars as Glenn tees up the next scene. Right at the very bottom of the pile are the supporting artists. They're paid even less than the runners and they have no clout whatsoever – but they are thrilled beyond belief to be working, *dahhling*, with Tom Cruise and the legendary Stanley Kubrick.

The *Eyes Wide Shut* hierarchy is most evident when it comes to food. Cruise and Kubrick, ensconced in their ivory tower trailers, get to eat anything that takes their fancy. The rest of the crew eat in the Pinewood canteen, but even then, just as in a pride of lions, the big cats eat first; as for the supporting artists, they very much eat last, and if there's been a run, say, on the chicken chow mein, they'll have to take what they're given. Supporting artists are rarely offered pastries or biscuits, and are usually grateful just to have an urn so that they can make their own lukewarm tea. They are the worker bees, life's mild-mannered toilers, diligently going about their business without a single word of thanks.

In the canteen, presided over by chef Molly, the top dogs stick with the top dogs and the underlings joyously mix with the other underlings. It would be inappropriate, say, for a supporting artist to join the senior crew – though if the crew care to unbend themselves (usually because they fancy one of the supporting artists), they will sometimes slum it at the underlings' trough.

At this meal break on the 181st day of the shoot, Glenn

and Roddie are all talked out. They are too far gone to be depressed. They are like incarcerated prisoners of war, not a word of news from the outside world, not a sight of friends or family, no end ever in sight, and every day so identical they wouldn't know if it was a Monday or Thursday.

Glenn cuts a tomato into very precise quarters. Between thumb and forefinger, he sprinkles on a few flakes of sea salt. He forks a quarter-slice of tomato into his mouth, chews and swallows, and for a brief moment he is in that moment – he is eating a tomato, and his full focus is on that tomato.

Roddie is not so circumspect. He takes a glutton's solace from his food, though there's precious little thought going on as the meal is mechanically shovelled into his mouth.

'Ever think about what you'll do when the shoot's over?'

Roddie looks at Glenn through smudged round spectacles, bits of bread and rice sticking to his beard. 'Dunno,' he says. 'We're not halfway through yet.'

'You must have some idea.' He sprinkles two flakes of salt onto the next quarter of tomato and puts it into his mouth.

'Dunno,' Roddie says. 'Never thought about it.' And that is the end of that conversation.

'How many takes did we get through this morning?' Glenn doesn't normally dwell on these sorts of matters. Better to busy yourself counting the stars in the sky than attempt to count the number of takes in a Kubrick film.

'Dunno,' Roddie says. 'Don't care.'

Glenn scratches at his neck with the back of his fingers, and allows himself to say the unsayable. 'I sometimes wonder what's the point of all these takes. I mean obviously Stanley's a perfectionist, and he's always looking for that special something.' Another quarter of tomato is popped into his mouth, he chews and he savours.

Roddie's not even listening – there's stilton to be eaten. He has not the slightest interest in talking about why their mad director demands so many hundreds of takes.

'Could it be as simple as Stanley getting off on this huge

power trip with the most powerful couple in Hollywood?' Glenn muses. 'Or have I missed…'

He happens to glance over at Sven the Steadicam operator. Sven is tall and gangly, his skin waxy white from six months without sunshine.

Sven has chosen to sit apart. He's at the far end of Glenn's table and is methodically pushing his food around his plate.

'What's going on with Sven?' Glenn says.

'Dunno.'

Glenn takes his glass of water and walks over to Sven. 'Mind if I join you?'

'Come into my garden.'

'Er – sure.' Glenn sits down.

Sven has a large mound of plain white rice on his plate. He has smoothed it flat with a palette knife and is now tracing over the rice grains with a fork. 'It's called *Karesansui*.'

'Yes?'

'I've got a Zen garden at home.' Sven said. 'It's got sand and gravel.' He returned a grain of rice to the plate. 'A few rocks and some shrubs. The shrubs will all be dead. I haven't been home in six months.'

'Oh,' Glenn said. 'I'm sorry.'

'So I've made my own Zen rice plate.' He smoothed a ripple of rice with the knife. 'Would you like to try?' For the first time he looked at Glenn. He looked completely unhinged.

'I would,' Glenn said. He trailed a fork over the rice. 'How you doing, Sven? You all right?'

'Yeah, I'm good, Glenn.' Sven smiled. He looked like he'd stopped brushing his teeth.

'Really? You really OK?'

'Yeah, I'm great, man! I'm terrific!'

'That's good.' Glenn stood up. 'I'll be getting on.'

Glenn mooched back to the set, this New York street that had been so meticulously constructed at Pinewood Studios. Kubrick had given so many reasons why this street had had to be built in Britain, when it might have been easier just to film on an actual street in New York. He had said that his street was not meant to look like a real New York street, but rather a street that you might recall in your dreams. He'd also claimed it was much more expensive to be filming in New York City – you could hire the whole Pinewood studio, equipment, everything, for months and months, and it would still turn out cheaper than filming in Manhattan. But Glenn couldn't help but think the main reason Kubrick had built this enormous set was because Kubrick was absolutely terrified of flying. The only possible way that Kubrick could ever have made it to America was on a boat.

A couple of the grips were moving the lights. Glenn had lost count of the number of times they'd filmed Cruise walking down this street. They'd done about fifty or sixty takes with the camera set up in front, then another fifty with the camera behind, and today they'd had about twenty tries with Sven walking around with the Steadicam. Glenn thought that Sven and Cruise had nailed it on the second take, but what the hell did he know? Kubrick just sat there in his director's chair, small delicate hands on his plump tummy, and muttered his three-word mantra: 'Do it again.'

These three words, repeated over and over again for the past six months, had cast a great grey fog of depression over the entire cast and crew. No one has the faintest idea why Kubrick wants scenes to be shot over and over again – and to have asked Kubrick what the hell he *did* want would have been an act of the most gross insubordination. One did not hector the world's greatest director with demands for explanations. No – one's job, and most especially the job of his assistant director, was to make it as easy as possible for this manifest genius to go about his craft.

It might have been easier for the crew if, at the start of each scene, Kubrick had given them some idea where he was heading. Just a quick heads-up as to what he was looking for. But it had begun to dawn on Glenn that Kubrick didn't have the first idea what he wanted. He was just making it up as he went along! Hey guys, let's just do it again. We'll see if I like it any better. Do it again!

At 11 p.m. exactly, Tom Cruise was on his mark, the crew were attending to their equipment and Kubrick waddled onto the set. Had he been anywhere else, Kubrick would have been mistaken for a hobo. (Indeed, during the recent shoot at the Lanesborough Hotel in London, Kubrick had looked so shambolic that the doormen wouldn't let him in.) The great man was wearing a blue boiler suit and a grubby tunic that he'd kept from his previous film, *Full Metal Jacket*. His hair and his beard looked singularly unkempt and, judging by the badgery smell, neither Kubrick nor his clothes had been washed in a while. He nestled into his director's chair, and when he was properly settled, one of the runners, Olivia, proffered a double espresso in white china cup and saucer. 'Ah, thank you, Olivia,' he said and, after taking a noisy sip, to no one in particular, 'Shall we begin?'

This is Glenn's cue. As the assistant director, Glenn is the guy who does the heavy lifting, and it is he who translates Kubrick's "vision" (such as it is) onto the set. A little while later, the cameras are rolling, Cruise is walking down the night-time New York street and Sven is walking next to him with the Steadicam.

'Cut,' Kubrick says. 'Sven, a word please.'

Sven takes off the bulky harness and Steadicam and, hands loose by his side, stands in front of Kubrick.

'It's not quite what I'm looking for, Sven,' Kubrick says.

'Yes, Stanley.'

'Tom moves with such graceful fluidity.'

'Yes, Stanley.'

And then, the fateful words. 'Do it again.'

It takes about ten minutes for the scene to be reset, Tom Cruise dutifully at his mark, the make-up girl patting his nose, the hair guy combing his hair. Glenn notices how Sven is visibly shaking as he straps the harness back on. And it's roll camera again, and it's action time again, and Tom Cruise is walking, and Sven is walking in front of him but walking backwards. There's another 'Cut!' from Kubrick. He finishes the last of his double espresso, languidly handing the cup and saucer to the runner before beckoning Sven over again.

'It's good, Sven,' Kubrick says. 'But somehow… the magic just isn't there. Do it again.'

As the scene is reset, Glenn remembers the one man who'd rebelled: Harvey Keitel. Keitel, who'd been given an absolutely plum part in *Eyes Wide Shut*, had left the shoot in under a week. Harvey's first scene was to have been at a big New York party, but in the usual Kubrick fashion, Keitel had been left to cool his heels on set for a few days without any direction whatsoever. Keitel's instincts had somehow kicked in, suddenly realising the bottomless abyss in front of him. Without having said a single line on camera, Keitel summarily quit – leaving Kubrick to once again go through the immense rigmarole of finding himself a new star.

Several times a day, Glenn wonders whether, even now, it might be better to for him to quit. The one thing he knows for certain is that for every single one of Kubrick's films, the shoots have got longer and longer. When he'd started out in the 1950s, Kubrick had been punching out film shoots in under three months. On his last film, *Full Metal Jacket*, the shoot had taken over a year (albeit with a three-month hiatus after one of the stars was injured in a car crash).

But this film… this film had all the hallmarks of lasting well over a year. God, it was tempting to do a Keitel and say sayonara to all the madness. But the big difference between Keitel and Glenn was that Keitel had become a superstar after his standout role as Mr Wolf in *Pulp Fiction*, whereas Glenn was just another jobbing assistant director. If Glenn left mid-shoot, he'd become a pariah. No one would touch him – he'd be lucky to get a job as a runner! And that, sadly, would be the end of his twenty-year dream to direct movies. Not that it would be *that* devastating. But he'd been in the game for fifteen years since leaving school, methodically working his way up the ladder; kind of a shame to throw it all away just because he couldn't stomach working with Mr Hundred Takes. Though in fact… it was pretty funny. When he was a kid, his lovely mum Frances – hadn't seen her in six months! – had used to chide him for his lack of patience. And as a result, the universe had decreed that Kubrick should give him a proper learning. Frankly, he only had himself to blame! He'd certainly never ever complain again about having to queue or being stuck in a traffic jam.

Do it again!

Without even being aware of it, another take was over and Cruise was ambling back to his first position. Kubrick beckoned to Sven. 'Much better, Sven!' the great man said. 'Really much, much better. As smooth as if you were on castors. Do it again!'

Another take, another take, and Glenn is – for the moment – in that moment, but he is becoming aware that the man with the Steadicam is looking anything but steady. As he peels off his harness for another pep talk, Sven is pulsing with this crazy energy.

'Beautiful, just beautiful, Sven,' Kubrick says, delicate thumbs tucked into his two breast pockets. 'Do it again!'

Sven shakes his head and whispers, 'I can't do it again.'

'Beg pardon?'

'I can't do it again!' Sven said, and a shockwave ripples through the set.

'But, my dear Sven, you've got to do it again. I am the director of this film. I want you to do it again.'

'We've had enough takes.'

'That's not how things work on a movie set.' Kubrick shook his head and smiled. Complete pin-drop silence. 'I am the captain of this ship – and it is me and me alone who decides when we have had enough takes. It is you, the Steadicam operator, who must accede to my wishes. Do it again!'

'I won't.'

'You're not hearing me, Sven.' Kubrick was suddenly

white with rage, eyes flashing to the most vicious black. 'I've asked you to do it again. Do. It. Again.'

Sven was standing about five yards from Kubrick, fingers flexing, unflexing. 'I'll do you!' He whipped out the palette knife and charged at Kubrick. He was holding the knife straight out in front, as if to spear it through Kubrick's windpipe.

Glenn was the first to move. He took two smart steps and tripped Sven up. Sven sprawled onto the floor, practically ending up at Kubrick's feet. 'Let me do it again!' He lunged at Kubrick's ankles. Glenn sat on him.

Four security guards were called. Sven, still screaming, was dragged off the set. All was silence.

'Time for a tea break,' Kubrick said as he levered himself out of his chair. 'Thank you for that, Glenn.' He was just wandering back to his trailer, when he turned back. 'Find somebody for the Steadicam.'

'Maybe the third assistant director?'

'He'll do,' Kubrick said. 'Then after tea, we'll do it again.'

CHAPTER 3

And into this Elysian idyll is about to be inserted what Prince Harry so fondly refers to as "a piece of scum-sucking pondlife". Though us *Sun* reporters do have a certain amount of self-respect. For we are not just Prince Harry's scum – we are *la crème de la scum*.

Though I am so, so much more than a mere *Sun* staff reporter. I am a mischief-maker. Above all else, I am a match-maker.

I only have the very fondest memories of working with dear old Stanley: rubbing shoulders with a dozen of the most beautiful women in Britain, and barely a stitch of clothing between them! On first-name terms with my great pal Tom Cruise – "Tommy" to his mates! And, no swanks but... on perhaps even more familiar terms with Tom's delectable wife Nicole!

So that was a lot of the good stuff about Stanley. Though there were, of course, his innumerable takes, and for someone with the attention span of a goldfish (*moi*, your humble narrator), it did on occasion become just a teeny bit boring. Gosh, he had everyone hopping!

Maybe one of the reasons why he insisted on having hundreds of takes was that he never wanted it to end. He just loved having his own little fiefdom – and as soon as the shoot wrapped, well that was going to be the end of Stanley bossing people around. Certainly no more getting Tom Cruise to ring a doorbell a hundred times over just for the sheer hell of it.

Now that I think of it, movie directors are not so very different from tabloid newspaper editors. They are each sole rulers of their own little kingdoms; they have an entire army of minions who can be sent hither and thither on the smallest pretext whatsoever; they have status and they have a coterie of bootlickers whose job it is to make the boss's life more congenial. Above all: they and they alone call the shots.

A few differences, too. Tabloid newspaper editors, though prone to tantrums, are for the most part congenial fellows who adore making the most of their limitless expense accounts. Movie directors, on the other hand, tend to be tortured souls who believe themselves creators of high art. The big wheels like Stanley are obsessive compulsives who demand nothing less than perfection.

Editors, on the other hand, must content themselves with, at best, a solid job. They've got that wonderful thing called an honest-to-God deadline! And when that deadline arrives, as it does, every day on the dot, then they have to press the button and put the paper to bed, and though the paper won't be even close to perfection, it will be that first beautiful draft of history. Come the next day, the slate is wiped clean, and all those hard-spun stories are fit for nothing more than fish-and-chip paper. But the very concept of having hundreds of takes on a story would be anathema to a newspaper editor. Editors – like their star reporters – are easily bored, and even after just three days of a story, they're ready for something fresh. They fancy a nibble at a new story. And they surely as hell wouldn't be able to stomach Stanley bawling, 'Do it again!'

I, however, being mere lowly cannon fodder, am well used to being told to do things again, and in fact it was really rather refreshing to hear those three special words from dear Uncle Stanley; he was always very polite and never once swore at me. Spike, on the other hand, my venomous deputy editor, just lived for swearing. As I fondly look back on my days at the soaraway *Sun*, I can hardly recall a single conversation with Spike that was not pungent with four-letter words.

But enough of my musings! We've got a story to tell – and this is how it all started, on a fragrant spring morning in 1997, with not overly much going on at Fortress Wapping. The chief reporter, John-Henry, was out lunching his very best contact from the Ministry of Defence and had invited me along for the ride.

Now – where oh where in London would the super-smooth chief reporter of the *Sun* take his best contact for lunch? Perhaps some quiet Soho bistro, or a discreet pub on Fleet Street? Not one little bit of it.

When John-Henry wined and dined his contacts, he almost always took them to one of the very smartest clubs in London, the Royal Automobile Club on Pall Mall. He'd taken me there before, and I knew the drill and was wearing my smartest suit (Prince of Wales check, very natty).

I'd come direct from some boring press conference, and John-Henry was already *in situ* in the RAC's magnificent dining room. I haven't been back into that room in years – indeed, after that particularly frenetic luncheon, have not been *allowed* back. But as I remember the dining room now, it was huge, the size of a ballroom, with high ceilings, light oak panelling, discreet tables with starched-linen tablecloths, sparkling silver cutlery and cut-crystal glasses that were just begging to be filled with rich red wine. The moneyed bluebloods just loved to lunch there.

John-Henry was alone and sitting at his favourite table in the corner, back to the window, perfectly positioned to survey everyone who walked into the room. To look at him, with his thinning hair and white beard and waxed moustache, you might have taken him for a diplomat, possibly the director of a private bank. The very last thing you'd have taken him for was the *Sun*'s chief reporter, the King of the Scoops.

'Young man!' he said as I ambled over. 'What are you drinking?'

'Thank you, John-Henry,' I said. 'I'll have what you're having.' (Typical journo trick – drink and eat what your guest is eating. It creates an instant affinity.) I clapped him on the shoulder and sat down. 'How are you?'

'Never better!' he crowed, pouring me a chilled glass of Churchill's favourite, Pol Roger. 'Christine can't wait to meet you,' he said and looked up, and immediately got to his feet. 'And here she is and as always, her timing is impeccable. Christine!'

Christine was a petite bird-like woman in her forties who I think probably had a large crush on John-Henry. She obviously adored the way he fussed over her, taking her cashmere coat and nestling her down and pouring her a glass of champagne. She giggled as they chinked glasses: 'You spoil me!'

'The pleasure is most entirely mine,' he said. 'Drink up, my dear, for we, today, are drinking a magnum of your favourite red.'

'Chateau Musar?'

'What else?'

'You dear thing.'

They chatted about this and that, bits of MoD gossip that had been in the news, and – at least until the main course arrived – I behaved impeccably, the loyal and trusty lieutenant who's watching his brigadier's back. I listened intently, laughed at John-Henry's jokes and, when called upon, eased the social wheels with a modest little anecdote of my own.

How very civilised it all now seems – the pleasant clatter of the soup spoons and John-Henry guffawing and Christine shyly smiling at her genial host. Funny to think that just a few short years later, they'd both be in the dock at the Old Bailey, one of them ending up completely broken and the other ending up in jail. Risky business being a *Sun* reporter.

Even more risky selling stories to the *Sun*.

After a bit more shilly-shallying, Christine gave John-Henry the bone he'd been hoping for: a married army captain, Angela Jackson, had been caught having a fling with a colour sergeant.

John-Henry drooled over Angela's photo. 'It's an absolute

belter!' he said. 'A three-tugger! What a piece of crumpet!' Angela was blonde and pretty, which would have some bearing on how the story played out in the *Sun*. Stories in the British tabloids get much bigger licks if they involve a pretty woman. If she's also been caught having illicit nookie, then it's absolute catnip for editors.

I laughed as John-Henry handed me the photo. 'It's Captain Crumpet!'

'That's what she is – Captain Crumpet!' John-Henry said. 'That's the splash headline!' (As indeed it was.)

John-Henry affectionately patted Christine's hand as he tucked the photograph into his breast pocket. The story would run for at least three days; it'd be billed as a 'World Exclusive' and he'd be getting not just a front-page byline, but a picture byline. Even though he'd been on the *Sun* for over twenty years (with a short stint in a lunatic asylum, though that's another story), when it came to front-page bylines, John-Henry was like a rookie reporter: he absolutely loved them.

As John-Henry poured the Chateau Musar, I left the two of them billing and cooing and took myself off to the RAC's lavatories. They were sumptuous Edwardian, built to last a thousand years, filled with creams and unguents and fluffy towels; they'd even got a couple of armchairs with a selection of the day's papers, which included, naturally, a copy of the *Sun*.

I am an absolute sucker for newspapers. I adore their smell, their crisp, clean feel, and in those days I was reading at least six or seven a day. I picked up a copy of the *Evening Standard*, and since I was in no hurry to rejoin John-Henry and Christine – and since they most certainly weren't champing for my return – I settled myself down in the furthermost cubicle for a read of the paper.

There was some stuff on the front page about Princess Diana going on tour to America on an anti-landmines tour. I think that in those last few weeks before she died, she had never looked more beautiful. She had a fresh sense of purpose too – right ahead of the curve, she was championing the victims of both AIDS and land mines. Her front-page picture had become the classic default of every tabloid editor in Britain.

I'd been in the cubicle for about a minute, when two men came into the toilet. They were mid-conversation. I didn't make a sound.

The first to speak had a well-oiled patrician voice, the chairman of the board addressing his shareholders. '…by some Viennese chap called Arthur Schnitzler, contemporary of Sigmund Freud, dontcha know – though I'd never heard of him until Stanley told me. Some little book called *Dream Novel*.' I heard the sound of flies being unzipped. 'I had a flick through. It was the most boring tosh imaginable. But Stanley's been raving about it for over forty years, though God knows why.'

Toilet man number two spoke next. He sounded crisp and suave, and had more of a politician vibe. 'So how they getting on with the shoot?'

'Stanley's been at it for over six months without a break – he's a madman! God knows how Tom Cruise is putting up with it, but he does.'

The mention of Tom Cruise's name was like a dog whistle. I was all attention.

'How much longer filming at Pinewood?'

'Maybe a month or three,' said the Chairman of the Board. 'Then they're off to Elveden Hall to film – you wouldn't credit it – a ruddy great orgy, and I can tell you that, if ever there were a time to drop by the set, it would be then. Some absolute stunners – I've seen the pictures.'

'A good time to be an extra.'

'Maybe if I'd been thirty years younger!' The Chairman was by now washing his hands. 'But if your boy Josh is interested, Stanley's hiring, all super hush hush…'

My infernal phone went off. I hauled it out of my pocket and stabbed at the off button, but the damage had been done.

'What!' said the Chairman of the Board. 'We've got an eavesdropper!' He hammered on my cubicle door. 'What are you doing in there?'

'*Che?*' I said in my best Italian. '*Italiano!*'

'The pillock's putting on an Italian accent!' he said – which wasn't strictly fair, as not only did I have an O-level in Italian (C grade), but I had actually dated an Italian girl for six months, and I can tell you there is no greater spur on earth to learning a new language than having linguistical diligence rewarded with a lover's kisses.

'*Mi scusi, non capisco!*' I said.

'*Non capisco*, my arse,' he said, giving the door a hefty kick. 'You know what you are? You're a five-star turd.' He gave the door another kick that practically took it off its hinges. 'Well, you know what, Anthony, I'm in no hurry to get back for pudding. Get one of the waiter wallahs to bring me a large Armagnac. I'll make myself at home in one of these chairs and read the papers.'

'Really, Sir James?' said the smooth politico who went by the name of Anthony. 'Don't want to leave it?'

'I'm going to smoke him out.' I heard the sound of an armchair being moved, followed by a gentle creaking sound as he settled himself down.

'I'll order your Armagnac.'

The sound of the lavatory door closing and then the crackle of a newspaper being opened.

Well, this was all very mildly aggravating. There was me, in my mild-mannered, mousey way, just trying to have a read of the papers, and – through no fault of my own whatso-goddamn-ever – some nutcase was out for my blood.

So, doing exactly what any sensible person would have done if they'd been caught in similar circumstances, I settled myself down onto the throne, feet up against the cubicle door, and started to do the crossword. If Sir James was happy to wait, then so was I. I could outlast him any day of the week! My specific nickname at the *Sun* (along with "mild-mannered Kimmy") was "the ever-so-patient Kim", and though some might have taken this as sarcastic, this was definitely not the case. I was so patient I could have given Job a run for his money!

We continued like this for about ten minutes. Sir James's double Armagnac was delivered – 'Thank you, Patrick' – and I discovered that my throne was getting more and more uncomfortable. The problem was the pipe connecting the cistern to the toilet. It ran right down the middle of the wall, which meant that when I leaned back against the wall, my whole body was askew. No matter – us *Sun* reporters don't mind uncomfy. Along with patience, it is one of our (many) virtues. After another five minutes, my back went into spasm, so I gave up lolling against the wall and leant forward, *Evening Standard* crossword across my knees.

My phone went off again.

I stabbed it off.

A minute later my pager started to vibrate. A pager? I know it's hard to believe, but although we had mobile phones in 1997, there was no such thing as phone-to-phone texting. If you wanted to text someone a message (if, say, they were wilfully refusing to answer their phone), you had to do it via their pager, and it was quite a caper too. You had to call up the pager service and dictate your text message to an actual human being, who would type it out and ping it into the ether. Five seconds later, and with a bit of luck, it would end up on the recipient's pager.

The message was just as terse as they always were when they came from my mad masters: "Call Deputy Editor ASAP."

So I did what any sane human being would have done and completely ignored it. Spike could go boil his head.

I got fed up with the crossword and, in search of something else to allay the tedium, I moved onto the business pages. (In my defence, I was absolutely desperate.)

My phone went off again. I stabbed the off button.

Sir James spoke up from his armchair. 'You're very popular this afternoon,' he said. 'I do so hope it's not your boss.'

I gave him another '*Non capisco*' and then cunningly switched my phone off altogether.

The pager went off again. 'Call Deputy Editor IMMEDIATELY,' followed by another text from John-Henry, 'Are you OK? What's happened?'

Unfortunately, it being 1997 and still in the technological Dark Ages, I was unable to respond to these messages, as that, obviously, would have meant making a phone call.

So, like the easygoing dormouse that I aspire to be, I continued to sit tight. Things were so bad with the *Evening Standard* that I'd even moved on to the sports pages.

My pager started beating a tattoo in my pocket, one message after the next – Spike must have tasked all three news desk secretaries with tracking me down. 'Call Deputy Editor MOST IMMEDIATE!' plus more in the same vein, along with a rather plaintive note from John-Henry which read, 'Where are you, dear boy?'

What the hell to do? Leave Spike stewing? It was probably just some sub's query on a piffling piece of copy that I'd written a week ago. I mean all that nonsense about "ASAP" and "MOST IMMEDIATE!" – well, from anyone else it might have meant something, but all of Spike's messages sounded just exactly like that. He probably even paged his secretary with peppery notes such as, "I WANT A BLACK COFFEE! IMMEDIATELY!", or even, "BRING ME MY BISCUIT! ASAP!'

In the end, it was the *Evening Standard* that did for me. By now I'd even tried the *Standard*'s yawnola leader column. I thought about taking off my jacket and curling up round the toilet for a kip on the floor, but after half-an-hour stuck in the men's cubicle of the RAC, I was feeling a mite tetchy; besides – how bad could this ageing oiler be? I'd be out of that cubicle faster than a greased piglet, and then it'd be just five smart steps to the exit. Sir James, stupefied on his double tot of Armagnac, wouldn't even be out of the starting blocks.

In absolute silence, I eased back the lock on the cubicle door. Deep breath in, deep breath out – my pager went off again, another blood-curdling imprecation from Spike to call him – and I smoothly opened the door, stepped out into the toilets, and walked swiftly towards the exit. I'd caught Sir James absolutely napping, his glass of Armagnac still halfway to his lips.

Unfortunately, Sir James had positioned his chair so that it directly blocked the exit. There was no way round him.

Sir James was a huge bloke, at least 6'4", in his mid-fifties, and looked like the sort of chap who'd once been in the Second Row of the England Rugby XV. He was bald, but rather than going for the full skinhead, his skull was dotted with a few sparse tufts of baby hair. He was wearing a grey double-breasted suit, and I particularly remember his hands, which were huge and covered in black hair. (I believe there was more hair on his fingers than there was on his head.)

'Ah,' he said as he put down his glass of Armagnac and lumbered to his feet. 'The eavesdropper reveals himself.'

'*Non capisco?*' I said, giving him my most winning smile as I edged to the door.

He unleashed a torrent of fluent Italian, something about the weather, and, giving as good as I got, I told him that it was particularly mild for the year and that I hoped the rain would hold off at the weekend.

'*Sei Italiano?*' he said.

I assured him in my very best Italian that not only was I an Italian but that I didn't speak a word of English; not that I looked very Italian, but I made up for it with a lot of florid hand gestures.

We continued to chat in the most familiar terms about the weather and about Italian football, and it was all going absolutely swimmingly. Sir James had levered himself out of his chair, and was standing by the door. I felt that we'd had enough chitty-chat and decided to take my leave. '*Arrivederci*,' I said.

He smiled. 'Buy you a drink?'

I smiled and shook my head – and immediately realised the size of my blunder. I'd forgotten that I was supposed to be a monolingual Italian.

'I knew it!' he shouted. 'You must take me for a complete mug!'

'*Scusi!*' I said. '*Non capisco! Non capisco!*'

'Well, how do you comprehend this, my fine fellow?' he said, and took one smart step forward and gave me a thundering slap to the cheek.

I cannoned into one of the cubicle doors. Sir James had hit me so hard that he'd almost unbalanced himself.

I saw my chance and darted past him towards the door. Just as I was about to open it, the door opened of its own accord. Standing in the doorway were two middle-aged gents in suits. They looked a bit crusty – in fact, they looked like exactly the sort of people who would deplore a fight in the inner sanctum of the RAC toilets.

'Gentlemen, gentlemen,' I said. 'This man here has attacked me.'

'Has he, by God?' said one of the chaps, bit of a military gait about him, probably an ex-colonel.

'Yes, he did!' I said. 'I came out of my cubicle, and this, this ape, assaulted me!'

'You're here as a guest of John-Henry?'

'I most certainly am!' I replied with some asperity. 'I am a guest! I am John-Henry's guest!'

'He's more than a guest,' said the second chap, who from his voice I recognised as Sir James's pal Anthony. 'He's another reporter from the *Sun*.'

Sir James, who'd begun to wash his hands at one of the basins, exploded. 'He's a *Sun* reporter – you have got to be joking!'

'It's of no matter, I meant no harm,' I said. 'I didn't hear a thing – nothing at all, so help me God.'

'I don't believe a word of it,' Sir James said. 'You're a *Sun* reporter. You lie for a living.'

'Absolutely not! On my honour!' I said. 'I am an upstanding member of Her Majesty's press.'

'*Non capisco, non capisco!*' Sir James mimicked. 'Wasn't that what you were telling me?'

'Guys,' I said, hands up at shoulder height, please don't shoot me. 'I can see there's been a bit of a misunderstanding here. So shall we just leave it at that, and I will go and join John-Henry for my entrecôte steak.'

The military chap tugged at his moustache. 'I can assure you, my dear fellow, that the very last thing you'll be doing is joining John-Henry for your entrecôte steak.'

'And who the hell are you?'

'Aren't you the young Turk?' he said. 'I, for your information, am the club secretary – and it gives me very great pleasure to bar you from the RAC. With immediate effect.'

'No steak for poor little Kimmy?' I brushed a speck of lint from my lapel. 'And I'd heard they tasted like fresh shoe leather!'

'Out you go, young man, and if you ever set foot in the RAC again, I'll have you arrested for criminal trespass.'

'I can't wait to get out of here.' I made my way to the door. 'There's a McDonald's nearby which beats you on both quality and price – and as for the clientele, they knock the RAC into a cocked hat.'

Sir James had been drying his hands with a towel. The club secretary stood aside and held the door open for me. I was about to leave when I caught a slight flurry of movement. Sir James was trying to send me on my way with a savage kick up the backside. I skipped to the side and in one fluid movement caught Sir James's foot on the upswing, moving it up and up until he overbalanced and fell flat on his back with a deliciously satisfying thud that set the wall tiles rattling. The fall quite knocked the stuffing out of him.

'You, young man, are leaving this club now,' the club secretary said, and a moment later he'd got me in a half-nelson and I was being frogmarched out of the toilets on my tippy-toes.

'Get off me, you moron!' I yelled. He'd got my arm so high up my back that my feet were barely touching the ground.

'I'll get off you when you've got out of my club,' he said.

I caught a glimpse of John-Henry and Christine, eyes like saucers as I was whisked past the entrance to the dining room.

The doorman smartly opened the door, and then, with a kick up the pants, I was ejected out of the RAC. I sprawled on the steps. A genteel couple were just getting out of a taxi.

'I wouldn't risk lunch there.' I readjusted my tie as I got to my feet. 'I forgot to wash my hands in the toilets and look what happened to me!'

I walked onto the pavement. John-Henry was looking at me through the window and gestured with his palms up – What the hell's just happened?

I gave him a cheery thumbs-up and went on my way. I supposed now was as good a time as any to call up my esteemed deputy editor.

I was put through to Maria, the editor's secretary. 'Kim?' she said. 'We've been looking everywhere for you.'

'It's a long story.' I wasn't really in the mood for chatting.

'I'll put you through.'

Spike picked up the phone on the first ring. He just went straight for the jugular. 'Why don't you ever call back when I want you to call?'

'Sorry, Spike,' I said. 'Got tied up.'

'What – tied up drinking with John-Henry in the RAC?' he said. 'You've been in there for over an hour.'

(Just a small point of note. Spike's conversations were invariably larded with swear words. But since leaving the *Sun*, I have become such a delicate flower that I have decided to edit them out. If, however, you would like a flavour of how Spike genuinely spoke, you can add the four-letter words yourself. Those last two sentences, for instance, contained at least four swear words.)

'Can we please just leave it?' I said. 'I've just been thrown out of the RAC.'

Spike must have caught something in my tone. 'Fine, see me when you get back,' he said with a note of finality.

'Hey, hang on,' I said. 'What did you want to talk to me about?'

'Oh that,' he said. 'That story you filed last week about the motorised sofa that's as fast as a racing car.'

'What's the problem?'

'It's sorted,' he said. 'It was going to be the splash. We've got something else.'

'Oh, right,' I said.

The phone clicked. I was left to make my merry way back to Fort Wapping. I thought about getting a cab, but remembered that there was indeed a McDonald's just off Admiralty Arch. Having been denied my entrecôte steak, there seemed to be nothing on earth quite so tempting as the prospect of a Big Mac.

I was still coming down from the whole bizarre episode with Sir James and the club secretary. Now this may all seem richly ironic, coming as it does from a (reformed) *Sun* reporter, but I did feel that I'd had a bit of a rough ride. It wasn't as if I'd deliberately set out to eavesdrop on the oafish Sir James. Didn't he know that walls have ears? And besides – if he really was going to discuss something as sensitive as Stanley Kubrick's new film, then the onus was surely on him to ensure that nobody was listening.

There are, I know, some people who've suggested that a gentleman might have coughed when I was in the RAC cubicle, thus alerting Anthony and Sir James to the fact that their conversation was not entirely private. That is all entirely true, but in my defence I have two points to make. Firstly, Sir James had only happened to mention the hottest star on the planet, one Tom Cruise. Who wouldn't want to know more?

And secondly, well, I'm a *Sun* reporter. I absolutely adore earwigging on other people's conversations. It's in my nature.

Anyway, the rights or wrongs of how I came by this extraordinary nugget of information about *Eyes Wide Shut* are neither here nor there. The substantive point is that having been thrown out of the RAC, I was on a one-man mission to somehow, anyhow, get onto Kubrick's movie set. And once I was there, well, I'd just do what any normal, self-respecting *Sun* reporter would have done: get all the pictures, snag all the gossip, and then spill my guts over the front pages of Britain's biggest selling daily newspaper.

CHAPTER 4

Nina, former Manchester stripper, had had her tea and was sitting in the twin room that she shared with Mandy. It wasn't an especially nice room and looked as if it had been styled in the 1960s and not touched since – creamy Artex walls, pink waffle bedspreads with tassels, foam pillows and nylon pillow cases. The retro theme continued in the en-suite bathroom with the brown toilet and fittings; there were no windows and it had a long line of black mould along the bottom of the shower. But on the plus side – and Nina was always one for plus sides – the room was quite large, certainly larger than her old bedroom; it had a glorious view of the River Lark, and not just a glorious view, but windows that actually opened. Also of note: a television which no longer worked after Nina had removed the fuse on the second day; a 100-watt light bulb that hung in the middle of the room, and which had dangled so low that Nina had hit her head on the pink shade (the second time it had happened, she'd handily tied a knot in the cord, raising the shade by a foot); two small pink armchairs; and, joy of joys, a small balcony, from where she could soak up the river view as she drank her morning coffee. And the best bit for Nina? A decent desk and a usable chair, and night after night it was to this desk that Nina would retire to, sweeping aside Mandy's make-up and creams to clear just enough space for her pride and joy and her one luxury in life: an Apple Mac PowerBook 1400, purchased the previous year and which had set her back over a month's earnings.

Nina had been living in Bury St Edmunds for over four months now. She was 160 miles from home, far from friends, and she'd worked the last 130 days with just the occasional Sunday off – apparently that's how things were done in the movie business. Some of the girls had complained that the work, endlessly repetitive, was boring.

Nina loved it.

She'd found a delicious routine – getting up at 7 a.m., going to the gym and returning an hour later for her river-view coffee; then shower and breakfast and ready to catch the coach with the rest of the girls at 9 a.m.; in the rehearsal studio and ready to go by 9.30 a.m., and though it was indeed a little repetitive with Leon and his two whippers-in, she found it fascinating. An hour-long break for lunch, where she sometimes joined the other girls, but if it was sunny she usually preferred to go outside to read a book. Another two hours rehearsing, quick tea break, then on the coaches at 5.30 and back to her B & B by 6 p.m. By 7 p.m, her fingers were crackling to get to work on the Apple Mac, and most nights she usually managed a solid three hours before it was time for a read and lights out by 11 p.m. Now that she had earplugs and an eye mask, she barely even woke up when Mandy rolled in at whatever time Mandy rolled in at.

The menfolk of Bury St Edmunds had never seen anything like it. Since the arrival of Stanley Kubrick's All Star Beauty Pageant, the young men, the older men, the geriatrics, all of them had started taking much greater care of their appearance – hairdressing salons were booked for weeks; Next and Gap had had their busiest run in years; and as for Boots the chemists, they had quite sold out of Brut aftershave, Lynx deodorant and Listerine mouthwash. Why, even the shoe shops had been doing a brisk trade, as the men of Bury St Edmunds sought to get an edge over their love rivals.

The girls – all of them professional strippers, and some of them prepared to offer a little more than mere stripping – loved it. They spent their days having fun with like-minded women and they spent their nights not only being treated like goddesses, but being able to decide for themselves onto which of these mortal males they might bestow their favours. (If, indeed, they cared to bestow any favours at all.)

Most nights, they'd have supper in little clusters at any of the cheap wine bars, though if any of the girls was on a date then, obviously, they went to the most expensive restaurant in town. Later, they might meet up in a pub, and later still, they'd often go clubbing. Of a weekend, men from as far afield as London would flood into Bury St Edmunds, and the cannier club owners laid on all the champagne that the girls could drink. The next day, regardless of what time the girls had got to sleep, they would all be queuing up for the 9 a.m. bus to the studio. (Two girls had been sacked after missing the bus on the third day.) Carefree times, good times, but also with that glorious sense of purpose that came with being involved in something far greater than themselves. For they were involved in not just the creation of high art, but a Hollywood blockbuster – and they'd be acting with the biggest superstar on the planet, Tom Cruise! Oh, and it was being directed by some old guy, Stanley Kubrick – never heard of him – but he was supposed to be a big wheel – why, some of the girls had even heard he was meant to be the greatest movie director in world history.

It was a Saturday night – not that it made any difference to the girls whether it was a Saturday or a Tuesday – and they'd been given the next day off. Tom Cruise and the rest of the circus had apparently finished filming at Pinewood and the whole troupe was moving up to Bury St Edmunds. The chippies and light crew would spend the next day getting everything ready, and on the Monday, the girls would get to feast their eyes on Tom Cruise, and it would be roll cameras, action. After four months of rehearsals, and of Leon ordering them to do the same thing over and over again, they were all extremely excited.

But tonight, as ever, Nina had words to write. The novel

was going OK. It felt like she was hewing a sculpture out of a block of marble, slowly bringing it to life. It wasn't great – she could see that – but it was only a first draft. Had potential, room for improvement – though on black dog days she told herself that actually it was irredeemably awful, and it may genuinely have been awful, but that was of no matter, because the next evening, come what may, she still had to show up at the Apple Mac.

It was gone 8 p.m. when Mandy knocked and barged into the room.

'Hiya!' she said, coming over and fluffing up Nina's hair. 'Scribble, scribble, scribble – how do you do it?' She picked up the lipstick on the desk and applied it with gusto.

'How do you manage to party every night?' Nina parried.

'Practice, Nina, practice.' She tossed the lipstick onto the desk and blew herself a kiss. 'Hey you oughta join us tonight. You're allowed one night off a month.'

'No, I'm good,' Nina said, and then, because she knew her literature, she smiled. Her response had been typical of all heroines throughout history: before they set off on their quest, they must first refuse it.

'Suit yourself,' Mandy said – and that also made Nina smile, for after the heroine refuses the quest, her friend is supposed to keep wheedling away until the heroine grudgingly accepts. But there'd been no wheedling at all from Mandy – just a "suit yourself" – and in another minute she'd be out the door, and Nina would be alone again with her Apple Mac. And though Nina knew that writers had to put the hours in, she also knew that they needed new fodder for their stories. They had to embrace weirdness.

'Sorry.' Nina saved her words and switched off the Apple Mac. 'I'd love to come. Thank you very much for asking me. Just give me a second.'

Most of the girls she knew wore skimpy dresses and skirts when they were out on the tiles in Bury St Edmunds, so Nina wore the exact opposite: black trousers, black shirt and a waist-length white coat. (Though that description does not quite do Nina justice. The trousers were snug at the top, flared at the bottom, the better to show off her long legs; the black shirt was made of silk and the top two buttons were undone; the coat – given by a luckless suitor – looked expensive and was indeed expensive. And as for her shoes, which we haven't even mentioned, Nina wore a classic pair of black Tod's loafers which had cost even more than the coat.) Five seconds to put on some lipstick, ten seconds to brush her hair, and she was good to go; Mandy was still touching up her mascara.

They sauntered down the stairs, where the sour plum that was Mrs Cocker was watching television with the lounge door open, the better to espy all the comings and goings into her B & B. What particularly vexed Mrs Cocker about the six girls who'd been billeted with her for the last four months was that every one of them was a beauty; she didn't quite know what they'd all been doing before they'd been signed up for this movie thing, but she sensed that it was something sluttish and disgusting. And… why not ask them? 'Hey, you two – what did you do before you became big-star movie extras?'

'I was a librarian,' Nina said.

'You were a librarian?' Mrs Cocker swallowed her disbelief and scowled at Mandy. 'What about you?'

'Me, love?' Mandy said. 'I—'

'I am not your love.'

'Ta for reminding me, Mrs Cocker. I worked in a bookie's. We called everyone "love" in there. Particularly the people who lost.'

'I'll bet you did.'

Did they think she was born yesterday? Mrs Cocker chewed on the walnut-sized quid of tobacco that was permanently tucked in her cheek. The beauty of chewing tobacco, or so her dad had told her when she was fourteen, was that you didn't need a match, and you didn't stink of smoke. The one down side was that you built up a lot of saliva and this periodically had to be expectorated – an action which was not, Mrs Cocker admitted, very ladylike. But she was one hell of a spitter. She could nail the spittoon from three yards, easy – which was what she did now, a globule of tobacco spit sizzling laser-straight to the back of the spittoon.

'We've got the day off tomorrow, so could we have a late breakfast?' Mandy asked.

'Rules is rules.'

'What's that mean when it's at home?'

'It means no!'

'I hope you have a lovely evening in front of your television.' Mandy opened the front door. 'My nan always loved *Coronation Street*. Never missed an episode.'

'And don't bring back any men!'

'Don't you worry, Mrs Cocker – I wouldn't dream of bringing a man back to a place like this!'

Mrs Cocker listened to the girls laughing as they walked down the garden path – and then they didn't shut the garden gate, and that made her hate them just that little bit more.

Mandy amicably slipped her arm through Nina's. 'The boys won't believe it,' she said. 'They thought they'd seen the lot of us!'

'And now they're going to see me,' Nina said.

'They haven't got a hope.'

'A guy from Bury St Edmunds? How could I resist?'

'You even want a boyfriend?'

'Couldn't care less,' Nina said – and is there anything ever so beguiling for a man as a woman who is utterly indifferent? 'No, I don't particularly want a boyfriend.' She thought about it a moment and corrected herself. 'But then I don't *not* want a boyfriend either.'

'They're gonna go mad for you,' Mandy said. 'Though just keep your hands off a lad called James. And Alex.' They walked on in silence. 'And there's a guy called Isaac. Funny little chap. I quite like him.'

'I will stay well clear of James and Alex, and I will

especially remember to avoid funny little Isaac.' Nina said. 'Just let me know if there's anyone else who's off limits.'

'General rule of thumb is that if they've got anything going for them, then one of the girls will be into them.'

'I'll leave well alone.'

They went into one of the town's oldest pubs, the fifteenth-century Fox Inn, where ten of Bury St Edmunds's most beautiful women were having a drink – and as you would expect of such a gathering, they had taken centre stage, sitting around a large oval table. They were by one of the windows, the better to attract more clientele, and the bar area was infested with drooling swains who gazed at these beauties but were rarely allowed to touch. The landlord, aware that his best customers did not want to be harassed, had even erected a red velvet rope, the better to keep the hordes of pestilential men at bay.

One local lad had had the effrontery to send over a single glass of champagne to Vicky. She'd sent it straight back – with a tart message that she'd need a bottle of decent champagne, minimum, to share with her friends, and if that were forthcoming then… Vicky might – or might not – permit a few words of conversation. In consequence, there were three large ice buckets on the oval table, each with its own magnum of champagne.

There were of course other girls in the pub, most of them connected with the Kubrick film, but they were not in the same league as the girls sitting around the oval table, for even among extras there is a pecking order. The girls at the top table were at the top of that pecking order.

They had been earmarked for the most evocative scene in the entire film – and it was this one scene that Leon had had them so relentlessly rehearsing. The other extras were also involved in the orgy, but for the most part they were mere masked spectators. A few of them, it's true, were going to be featuring in the second half of the orgy, which was going to be filmed at Highclere Castle after Kubrick had finished at

Elveden Hall. But this second part of the orgy was altogether more graphic and not nearly so classy. No, it was the prelude to the orgy which was going to be the knockout.

They had rehearsed umpteen different scenarios, all deliciously enticing, but it would be Kubrick and Kubrick alone who decided which one to shoot. The only fixed certainty was that there'd be a masked man in a red cloak and that there would be the twelve girls. Each girl was to wear a gorgeous cape in shimmering blue and a custom-made mask that was a direct copy of the masks from the Venice Carnival. All of the rehearsed scenarios were different, but they all ended the same way: with the capes falling to the floor, and the girls left standing in all their most majestic glory. They'd be wearing nothing but their masks and elegant stilettoes in midnight blue and the very skimpiest of black G-strings. Tom Cruise, meanwhile, would be standing in the background feasting his eyes on the fantasy girls – though unfortunately, and much to Mandy's disappointment, the star would be keeping his clothes on.

Mandy and Nina slipped into the pub unnoticed, but as soon as Mandy unclipped the red velvet rope, an awestruck murmur rippled through the pub – another couple of stunners had joined the hotties! And there was fresh meat too – one of them, tall and sultry, had never been spotted in Bury St Edmunds before!

Vicky was the first to notice Nina. 'Look what the cat brought in!' she called.

'I believe the cat has finally arrived,' Nina said. The landlord scurried over with two fresh chairs, all but tugging his forelock as Nina asked for two dirty Martinis.

'Don't think I know what dirty means, Miss,' he said.

'It's got a dash of olive brine,' Nina said.

'I'll get one of the lads to get some olives from the corner shop.'

'It's fine, don't bother.'

'No trouble at all, Miss,' and this time he genuinely did

tug his forelock, backing away from the table and returning the red velvet rope to its golden hook.

Vicky topped up glasses with champagne. Like most of the girls, she wore a skin-tight dress, the better to show off her spectacular figure. In as much as the twelve beauties had a ring-leader, Vicky was it – because unlike most of the other girls, she had a few lines to say. Better than that, she'd be getting to pair off with Tom Cruise and would even kiss him on the lips (though not a very erotic kiss, as both Vicky and Cruise would be wearing full face masks).

'Finally!' Vicky said. 'Welcome to our party! Hear you're writing a book, Nina.'

'I'm trying.'

'Is it about us?'

'Maybe one day.' Nina, who was sitting two down from Vicky, pushed her chair back and surveyed the pub, with its ogling whippersnappers and its old codgers staring sightlessly into pint glasses, and all the crew, the men and the women, so very excited to have been given a night off. So yes, it had been a good idea to join Mandy – and she'd come again. Only a time-serving wallflower spent every night of the week chained to her laptop – though Nina did acknowledge taking a perverse pleasure in never once going out. Perhaps it was a reaction to her former life: after four nights a week at the Red Coat, she'd needed a little time to decompress with her desk and her words.

She was chatting to the girl next to her, Holly, when out of the corner of her eye she noticed two men walking into the pub.

The first guy was a shambles – blue dungarees, tatty tennis trainers, some weird army top with a lot of pockets. Coal-black eyes beetling out from round glasses, and the whole look topped off with a thinning comb-over. But for an inexplicable something, he could have been a hobo. The guy behind him: much taller, much younger. Nina couldn't quite place it, but there was also a trace of deference. They were walking towards the bar when the older man caught sight of Nina and the rest of the girls. After a brief word with the younger man, he waddled over. He then did the unthinkable. He lifted the red velvet rope from its golden hook and stepped into the pub's inner shrine.

'Hey girls,' he said, with a tang of a New York accent. 'How you been getting on?'

The pub ground to a standstill. An old man had done the unthinkable. He'd lifted the red velvet rope. He was talking to the girls.

Vicky laughed and slapped the table. 'What you say, Grandad?'

'Errr.' The smile faltered on the man's face. 'Have you been enjoying yourselves?' Now that he was up close, Nina could see food stains on his dungarees. The pockets on his tunic were all crammed with notebooks and pens. The second guy, she could see, was over by the bar buying drinks.

Nina looked again at the unkempt old man with the wild comb-over. She looked at him, wasn't quite sure.

'Leave it out, Grandad,' Vicky cackled. 'You think we're going to be interested in you?'

'I see I have made a mistake.' The man left the table, and after reattaching the red velvet rope to its golden hook, he joined his companion. Nina watched them walk to a reserved table at the far end of the pub.

'That told him!' Vicky said. 'Cheeky old bastard! Who's he think he is?'

'You're about to find out.' Nina savoured the olive of her dirty Martini; not at all bad. It was her first Martini since she'd left the Red Coat.

The tall man who'd been with the old vagrant came up to their table. 'Ladies.' He stepped straight over the red velvet rope. 'There has been a misunderstanding.'

Just as with the old man, Nina sensed the unmistakable whiff of power. The guy was just in jeans and a blue fleece. He was holding a gin and tonic and he was smiling.

'Not another one!' Vicky said. 'That rope's there for a reason – we don't want to be pestered.'

'Can I give you a tip, Vicky?' The man grinned.

'How do you know my name?'

'I know all of your names,' he said. 'I know everything about you. In fact, I probably know every single person in this pub – including Harry the publican.'

'I don't believe it.'

'Course you don't, Vicky – but for what it's worth, you're from North London. And then we have Holly from Leeds, and Patty, and Leila, and Fiona, and Isobel, and Evie…' He pointed at each girl in turn. 'And then we have Mandy, from Manchester, Annette, who's also from North London, Tara and Ruth, and then lastly we have Nina, from Manchester, and she is the writer.' He smiled. 'How's that for size, Vicky?'

'Who the hell are you?'

'I'm Glenn.' The man took a leisurely sip of his gin and tonic – and, certain of his audience, added chattily. 'My first gin and tonic in a week: ecstasy.' He took another long pull, ice clattering in the glass. 'And Vicky, about that tip I was going to give you. It is risky insulting people when you don't know who they are. That is especially the case in Bury St Edmunds, which is currently chock-full of movie people. Oh – and I'll give you one more tip – almost any one of these movie people could have you fired on the spot.'

'That so?'

'It is so, Vicky – and I know this for a fact because the director, Stanley Kubrick, is currently asking Leon Vitali, who I think you might know, to have you dismissed.'

Vicky's jaw dropped. 'That old guy wants me sacked?'

'That old guy wants you sacked,' he said. 'Grovel hard enough, you might just be able to salvage the situation – though you'll have to be quick.'

'You're having me on.'

'Sit here for another minute and you'll find out.'

'Oh my God!' Vicky said, this golden-haired goddess

suddenly realising the very great fragility of her pedestal. 'Sorry! I'm so sorry.' She leapt over the red velvet rope and hurtled to the back of the bar. The last Nina saw of her, Vicky was on her knees and throwing herself at the old man's feet.

'Sorry for the interruption,' he said as he stepped back over the red velvet rope. 'I'll let you ladies get on with your evening.'

Nina happened to catch his eye. 'What sort of movie person are you, Glenn?' she asked.

'Quite right, Nina, I should have mentioned that,' he said. 'I am the assistant director.'

'And is Vicky really going to be fired?'

'Nah,' he laughed. 'Just thought I'd put the wind up her sails.' He glanced over at Vicky, who was still writhing around on the ground in front of Kubrick. 'And I succeeded.'

CHAPTER 5

I pouted seductively and, as instructed, stared a few inches above the camera lens.

'Is that the best you've got?'

'I don't think I can do much better,' I said.

'I'm not sure your best is going to cut it.' Grubby scowled as he fired off a couple more frames. 'Just try and relax! You look like you've got chronic piles.'

'It's not very easy trying to relax when every other minute you're yelling at me to relax.'

'You're touchy today,' Grubby said, before coming out with his first decent idea of the day. 'Let's have coffee.'

'Let's.'

We left Grubby's studio, which doubled as a spare room, and went through to his galley kitchen. It was cosy and immaculate, not a spoon out of place, not a dirty cup in the sink. I realised that if Grubby was going to fill the kettle and then switch it on, it would be easier if I stood in the doorway.

'Nice pad you've got,' I said.

'Well, it's home.'

'If you don't mind my asking, how come it's spotless?'

'How do you mean?'

'It's pristine – you could eat your dinner off the floor tiles.'

'Why shouldn't it be pristine?' He scratched at his belly button. It being a Saturday and his day off, he hadn't bothered to shave; I wasn't even sure he'd bothered to dress. He might have been wearing his pyjamas, though they could also have been some unfeasibly trendy shell suit. It was difficult to tell.

'Well, you know.' I tried to be delicate. 'I mean, you're called Grubby, and I thought your flat was going to be pretty grubby too.'

'Well, it's not grubby is it – and do you want me to take these pictures on my day off or not?'

'Of course, of course,' I said lightly. 'Anyway, I was just trying to say it's a lovely flat, very light, very clean – you've even unloaded the dishwasher.'

'What are you driving at? Why shouldn't I have unloaded the dishwasher?'

'Sure!' I said. 'Absolutely!' I grabbed my rucksack off the floor and opened it. 'This is for you! Bottle of malt whisky. Small token of my esteem.'

'Thank you.' Grubby examined the bottle. 'Teacher's? You don't really know your whiskies, do you?'

'A little bit,' I said.

'It's a blend, mate.'

'Oh right,' I said. 'There much difference?'

'It's a lot rougher – and a lot cheaper.'

'Interesting,' I said. 'Never knew that.'

'How do you want your coffee?'

'Just black's great.'

'Want a slug of this gut-rot?'

Under normal circumstances I might have bridled at having my gift described as "gut-rot", but since I was trying to keep Grubby sweet, I chose the true and trusty path of diplomacy. 'That would be lovely, thank you.'

He poured two hefty tots of Teacher's into the coffee mugs and we repaired to the lounge. It was not just spotless but, dare I say it, tasteful. On the coffee table, a vase of crinkled parrot tulips; black-and-white photographs on the walls, possibly even taken by the great Grubby himself; some bookshelves that were – amazingly – full of books; and a sofa, two armchairs and plenty of pillows. And not just any old pillows – plumped pillows!

'Charming,' I said, continuing in ambassadorial vein. 'Delightful.' I sipped the coffee. It was pretty bad. It might have been the coffee, but more likely it was the whisky. 'Delicious,' I said. 'I must have it like this more often.'

Grubby sprawled on the sofa, kicked his feet up on the coffee table. He wasn't wearing any slippers. He had singularly hairy feet and his toenails looked like they needed a spell with some farrier's clippers. 'So how many copies do you want of each picture?'

'Eight of each please,' I said.

'Just remind me what look you're going for?'

'Couldn't be more simple,' I said. 'I want to look like I'm about to attend a high-class orgy.'

Grubby raised his eyebrows. 'A seedy toff?' He took off his thick Clark Kent spectacles and gave them a polish with the hem of his pyjamas/shellsuit top. 'But that's what you always look like.'

'I don't know if I'd use the word seedy,' I said.

'Just remind me what you have to do to get thrown out of the RAC.' He slurped his coffee, wiping his mouth with the back of his hand. 'Not bad. The coffee helps take the taste away.'

'They throw more than just seedy people out of the RAC,' I said primly.

'Hear John-Henry's none too happy with you.'

This was an understatement. John-Henry had had his RAC membership suspended and was having to make do with lunching his contacts in the Farmers Club. Rubbing shoulders with the horny-handed sons of the soil. Slumming it in Whitehall Court. Tough times.

'Quite so,' I said. Though I am famously mild-mannered, I was having some difficulty in maintaining my usual affable demeanour.

'Wish I'd been there!' Grubby chuckled to himself. 'Did you really get kicked all the way down the stairs?'

'Got the bruises to prove it.'

'Happy days,' he said. 'And with these pictures, you're somehow hoping to get one over on your mateys at the RAC.'

'That's right.'

'Sounds like a bit of stretch.'

'Thank you for your support.'

'Just saying it like it is. Let's get back to the studio.'

We went back to the studio to take more pictures – though I have to admit that, for once, Grubby was spot on. It was going to be a bit of stretch.

Now generally in the *Sun* newsroom I was industrious, diligent, and above all, keen. But since my altercation with Sir James at the RAC, I had become just that little bit more keen: in fact, I was hungry. I was going to do Sir James over any way I could, and if that meant worming my way onto Kubrick's film set, then that's what I was hell-bent on doing.

First, I had to find out everything I could about Kubrick and his new movie. After calling up all the cuttings from the News International library – I know, I know, who on earth these days can conceive of having an actual cuttings library, staffed by a dozen librarians? – I quickly adduced that Kubrick should have been sectioned. So many crazy Kubrick stories to choose from – here's my favourite: when Ryan O'Neal was filming *Barry Lyndon*, Kubrick asked him to have his leg amputated. Kubrick had apparently booked O'Neal into a highly reputable Swiss clinic for the operation.

'What operation?' O'Neal said.

'To remove your leg,' Kubrick explained. 'For the final scene.'

O'Neal was incredulous – 'You're asking me to get my leg cut off for this film?' he said.

'Well, I don't know what else to do,' Kubrick said dolefully. 'Maybe you have another solution.'

As I had yet to meet Kubrick, I initially thought that this story was, well, a bit of a stretch. But after I'd seen Kubrick in action, I realised that the story was not only true, but that it was the mere tip of the iceberg. Kubrick's demented perfectionism had turned him into a stark staring madman.

Also, from the cuttings library, I discovered that Sir James was Sir James Hutchison, a baronet, no less. He'd worked on a number of Kubrick's previous films and was the executive producer on the latest project which so far, it seemed, had largely been filmed at Pinewood Studios. A scum-sucking paparazzo had even scaled a tree to get some grainy shots of Tom Cruise walking around the studio. (Kubrick ordered the offending tree to be cut down, but when the council refused permission, he just got the chippies to raise the height of the studio walls.) Apart from these little nuggets, the whole shoot was a mystery; no one knew the first thing about it.

I, however, was armed with two delicious morsels of information that, applied judiciously, might yet get me onto Kubrick's movie. The first was that Kubrick was actively recruiting extras for this great orgy scene that was about to be filmed at Elveden Hall. And the second was the name of the novella that the movie was based on – Arthur Schnitzler's *Dream Story*.

I soon established that there were eight film extra agencies in London, and not knowing which ones Kubrick would be using, I had to join the whole lot – and for that I was going to need plenty of mugshots. Hence why I was spending my Saturday morning in Grubby's spotless flat having my picture taken over and over again.

Since the whole venture was such a ludicrous long shot, I'd not bothered to tell my mad masters. Mention it to my deputy editor Spike, and he'd have been pestering me every day of the week and twice on Saturdays to find out what was going on. No sirree – my mad masters would be informed just as and when Stanley Kubrick approved my application to join the Elveden Hall orgy. Until then, the only person who knew about the Sticking-it-to-Sir-James Project was Grubby.

Most extras' portfolios show people looking as glamorous as the photographers can humanly make them, with big smiles, clear eyes and sober, frank faces.

But I was looking for pictures that were much spikier. I was wearing dinner jacket and black tie, but it was a threadbare DJ that had seen much better days. Ruffled hair, scuffed shoes, glimpse of a shirt tail and tie at half-mast. I hadn't shaved, and there was, I hoped, a raffish glint to my eyes. Basically just my normal everyday Saturday self.

'You're looking like a dirty old man,' Grubby said – helpfully. 'The sort of guy that's hanging around the school gates. Look – you're supposed to have come out of a posh orgy. Can't you look a bit classier?' He fired off another frame.

'I'll try.' I glowered at the camera – less seedy, more sexy.

'Don't do that – you're giving me the creeps.'

'What do you want me to do?'

'Let's try it another way, Kim.' He gave his glasses another polish and walked round from behind the camera. 'Imagine you've just had the greatest scoop of your life. It's brilliant! It's a story that's going to go right round the world, and it's going to run for months. And then, because you've got something to celebrate, you dress up in your nicest togs and go out on the town with your mate Grubby. You've been drinking, you've been clubbing, you've lost a little money playing blackjack but not too much. You've had a great time. Can you imagine that?'

'Yes, I can.'

'At 8 a.m. you stumble home to bed. Just as you get in through the front door, you get a phone call. It's the editor. He says he's very sorry but the story's been pulled. You got me?'

'Why was the story pulled?'

'Because his mistress asked him to pull it – obviously,' Grubby said. 'So, Kim, I want you to get into that frame of mind. Fantastic night on the town. Little the worse for wear. Your great scoop spiked. Yeah?'

'Yeah.'

'Do it.'

And I did it. I imagined that world-weary hack who, after months of slaving, has delivered the most exclusive of World

Exclusives. His delighted editor tells him to have a night out, and he does just that, goes on a mighty bender and then, just at sunup, still feeling a little spangly, he gets the call to say that, in time-honoured tabloid fashion, the scoop is a bust. It won't even be fit for fish-and-chip paper.

'Better,' Grubby said. 'Much better. More crestfallen. You've been working on this scoop for years! And it's all for nothing.'

My mouth became just that little bit more petulant.

'Good!' Grubby said. 'We are liking this. Take your jacket off. Sling it over your shoulder. That's it! That's it! Now squeeze out a tear! A single tear!'

I tried. It didn't work.

'Oh no,' he said. 'You look like you've got piles again.'

'Are we done? Please say we're done.'

'Yes, we are,' he said, 'Forget Kubrick's orgy – these pictures are your passport into a genuine orgy.'

'Is that so?'

'Yes it is so,' Grubby said, and he gave me the most disgusting wink.

I went to the bathroom to freshen up. Like everything else in Grubby's flat, it was immaculate. The taps gleamed, not a stain in the bathtub, not a rogue hair in the plug-hole; one thing I did find a bit weird was that the first sheet of the toilet roll had been tucked over, like you see in the posh hotels. Was it possible? Were all of Grubby's grubby shirts and soiled suits just an act for his *Sun* colleagues? A façade to mask this house-proud neat-freak?

I washed my hands with the Jo Malone liquid soap and dried them on the fluffy white towel.

I strolled back to the lounge. Grubby was checking his watch.

'Thanks very much indeed, Grubby,' I said. 'When do you think the pictures will be ready?'

'Tomorrow morning.'

'Great,' I said. 'And I must say, coming here has been a revelation. It's… it's remarkable.'

'Yeah, thanks.' He clapped me on the shoulder and was about to wheel me out of the flat when the front door opened, and in barrelled a little round ball of a woman – sort of like Mrs Tiggy-Winkle the hedgehog, if you know your Beatrix Potter. She wore a yellow pinny and carried a plastic carrier box full of brushes and cleaning fluids. ''Allo there,' she said, quickly sizing me up. 'Don't think I've seen you before.'

'Hello,' I said – so that's how the bastard did it! He'd got a cleaner! Who even turned up on Saturdays! 'I'm Kim, one of Grubby's colleagues.'

'Grubby?' she queried. 'I'm Lucinda – pleased to meet you.' She shook my hand before giving Grubby a kiss on the cheek. 'How's my boy?'

'Coffee?' Grubby said.

'Yes please, dear.' She smiled at me. 'He always makes me a cup of coffee in the morning, don't you, Phil?'

'Yes.' Grubby shifted uneasily on his hairy-toed feet.

'Do you live nearby?' I asked.

'Live nearby?' she said. 'I live upstairs! When old Petey died, we split the house into two. Phil's got his own space but it still feels like he's home with me. I pop in every morning, clean the flat up. Otherwise it can get into a bit of a mess, can't it, Phil dear?'

'Yes mum.'

'Oh he lets it get into a bit of a state does he?' I said. 'I find that very hard to believe.'

'It's the God's own truth.' She cuddled in to her scrofulous son. 'Every year I go to the Costas for a week with my friends, and when I get back, you'd have to see this flat to believe it.'

'Bit of a pigsty, is it?' I asked.

'It's not a pigsty, it's Armageddon.'

'Astonishing,' I said. 'And to think he's such a stylish dresser.'

'Weren't you on your way out?' Grubby asked.

'I was,' I said. 'Lovely to meet you, Lucinda – and I will see the *Sun*'s best-dressed photographer tomorrow morning.'

What an exquisite piece of knowledge to have come by. I greatly looked forward to sharing it with my *Sun* colleagues.

Mind still very much on the Kubrick case, I made the short drive from Stoke Newington to Soho. I was going to a place that I'd driven past many times, but had never visited – the London Library. There was a suitably Kubrickian reason behind my trip: the London Library contained the only extant English-language copy of Arthur Schnitzler's *Dream Story*. Several years later, I discovered the reason why it had been so hard trying to track down a copy of *Dream Story*. Kubrick had been so terrified of somebody else reading this magical book and turning it into a movie that he'd bought up every single known copy. The novella had been buried in a collection of Schnitzler's other stories, and Kubrick's minions had scoured the country for copies. I often wondered what Kubrick had done with all these hundreds of books – were they burned, or did they line the walls of a special *Dream Story* suite?

I filled in the library forms and went off to wait in the café. I was half-expecting to be told that, for some quite unaccountable reason, the library's only copy of *Dream Story* had been stolen, but an hour later, I was called through, and there it was waiting for me at the reception.

It is true that I may have been missing something. All right – I'm a philistine! But as I sat in the reading room leafing through *Dream Story*, I was finding it very difficult to keep my eyes open. The story is set in early twentieth-century Vienna. Fridolin is a successful doctor who's married to Albertine. One night, they each confess to their fantasies: Albertine had once lusted after a young Danish army officer; Fridolin had been smitten by a girl on the beach. As in a dream, Fridoline then gets into various scrapes. He visits a dying patient and is propositioned by the man's daughter; he befriends a prostitute; he meets an old friend, Nachtigall, who says he plays piano at a high-class orgy. Fridolin gets a mask and cloak and joins the orgy.

The orgy scene was another big let-down. Schnitzler rattled

through it in barely 500 words – did he know nothing about milking a scene? Fridolin leaves without even a kiss, let alone orgiastic sex. There were a few more twists and turns but, as in all dreams, Fridolin eventually winds up back home, where, lying on his pillow, is his orgy mask. Fridolin confesses all and promises Albertine it will never happen again. Albertine forgives him and trots out the fat platitude that it's important not to look too far into the future.

I found the book particularly underwhelming. This was it? This was the story that had obsessed Kubrick for over forty years – and that he was turning into a multi-million-pound movie? This was the story that had so enchanted Mr and Mrs Cruise that they'd both signed up for a never-ending film shoot?

I took the book to the photocopier to copy the two-page description of the orgy. What was it about the story that had so captured Kubrick's imagination? Obviously he was Fridolin. Had one of his three wives once told him her shocking fantasies? Or was Kubrick's obsession driven by the fantastical orgy scene?

I drove back home in the rain, feeling like I'd just wasted the whole afternoon on *Dream Story*.

Cutting to the chase: three weeks later, I had a call from one of my eight extras agencies. They wanted me to send in a two-minute clip of myself – and this, I knew, would be seen by Kubrick himself. Most other directors left the choice of extras to the second or third assistant directors, but not Kubrick. When he'd made *Full Metal Jacket*, Kubrick had insisted that every one of the bit-part extras send in a short clip of themselves – and now he was doing exactly the same thing for the Schnitzler story.

I'd have two minutes to make my personal pitch to Kubrick. Hit the sweet spot and I'd have a ringside seat at the Elveden Hall orgy.

As before, I was a jaded young buck in a dinner jacket and skewed bowtie. It was lunchtime. We had commandeered one of the empty offices at News International.

'Ready when you are,' Grubby said.

I stared at the ground, channelling my inner rake before looking down the lens of the video camera.

'I've got a problem,' I said. Very casually, I lit a cigarette. I spent some time over it and allowed myself a leisurely inhale. 'Last night, I got drunk on champagne with my girlfriend. We talked about our fantasies. I dreamed of climbing Mount Everest. Her dream was much more explicit. She said she was very attracted to one of my closest friends. I paid the bill. We went home and had amazing sex, honeymoon sex. But this morning, when we got up, it was as if nothing had ever happened. I made her coffee and I went to work. And this is my problem: should I bring up this fantasy of hers? Should I mention it to her? Should I mention it to my friend?'

I blew out my cheeks, sighed. 'I don't know. Should we let sleeping fantasies lie – or should we, perhaps, try to turn them into a reality?'

I gave Grubby the thumbs-up. He switched off the camera.

'Bizarre story,' he said. 'I didn't even know you had a girlfriend.'

'I don't.'

'So why did you tell it?'

'Just a hunch,' I said. 'Thought it'd appeal to Stanley Kubrick.'

CHAPTER 6

Glenn hadn't been inside Elveden Hall in nearly a year, since those carefree days before filming had started when he and Kubrick had been scoping out possible locations for *Eyes Wide Shut*. There had been several reasons why Kubrick had picked Elveden. It was derelict and it was cheap and it had an immense and very ornate white marble hall that was surrounded by a first-floor balcony. But probably the main reason Kubrick had picked Elveden was that it was a short drive to his home, Childwickbury; after a day's filming, the homebird director could sleep snug in his own bed.

It was the Sunday after they'd finally finished shooting in Pinewood. For Glenn and the rest of the crew it felt as if, after months and months of grazing on the same muddy paddock, they'd been set loose on fresh pastures. Even Kubrick's never-ending takes were forgotten as the caterers and the cameramen, the grips and the runners, all savoured the sweetness of something new and different, and above all something that was most definitely not Pinewood Studios.

Glenn had arrived at Elveden first thing. The crew were already there, an army of ants wheeling in the tons and tons of equipment. The entire sweep of gravel in front of the hall had been turned into a parking lot. There were at least a score of equipment trucks, grips and all the rest of the crew swarming back and forth with lights and scaffolding and great coils of black cables. The caterers, at the vanguard of any film shoot, had set up shop the previous night, a large lorry for the food and two double-decker buses which had been converted into canteens. Set off to the side, with the best views of the rolling Suffolk countryside, were the two giant silver Winnebagos that were for the personal use of Kubrick and Tom Cruise. Knowing Kubrick as he did, Glenn guessed that neither the catering trucks nor the Winnebagos would be moving anywhere before Christmas.

Glenn might have lingered, but Roddie was suddenly squawking over the walkie-talkie; Glenn was needed in the hall. Coffee in hand, Glenn wended his way to the hall.

He'd forgotten how big it was. He'd forgotten quite how magnificent it was. It was an entrance hall fit for a palace – a Mughal Palace. The hall that Kubrick had picked for his orgy scene was huge, bigger by far than a tennis court, three storeys high and topped with a domed ceiling of beaten copper. Everything, but everything, from walls to pillars and arches was made of white Carrara marble and covered in the most intricate Indian ornamentation. Italian craftsmen had been shipped over to Britain to carve the latticework *in situ*.

Glenn went up the stairs, fingers drawing a dusty line on the balustrade, to survey the scene from the first floor. Roddie was already up there, bellowing into his walkie-talkie. Glenn was more circumspect about ordering the troops at this early juncture. Any decision he made would almost certainly be countermanded by Kubrick; in fact, if he were to issue any instructions whatsoever to the crew, they would inevitably be reversed by Kubrick. Although Kubrick couldn't make up his mind about anything, he certainly knew what he didn't like, and the chances of Kubrick approving Roddie's set-up were vanishingly small. Glenn had long since realised that Kubrick actually got off on saying, 'No it's not quite right,' setting the entire ant army back to work again before loafing back to his Winnebago and his copies of *House & Garden* and *Country Life*.

Roddie tucked the walkie-talkie into his breast pocket and unwrapped a Mars bar. 'It's way too cold,' he said. 'I need gloves and thermals.'

'It's colder inside than out,' Glenn said. He looked at Roddie. He'd never seen a Mars bar eaten so fast.

'Those girls are going to be mighty chilly.'

'Good point.' Glenn said.

Another obstacle to be surmounted – and the thought of this fresh obstacle did not dispirit Glenn, far from it. He actually smiled.

Roddie looked up from his crisps. 'Something funny?'

'Not really,' Glenn said – as trying to explain his smile would be to explain an entire philosophy, and that would be best done over a leisurely pint. As Glenn had long ago realised, if you did not enjoy the business of surmounting obstacles and overcoming difficulties, then the movie business was most certainly not for you. As far as Glenn could see, making a movie was a never-ending gauntlet of obstacles, sometimes big, sometimes small, and sometimes back-breakingly gargantuan. The trick, for Glenn, had been just a simple change of mindset, so that now, when a problem came along, as it did, every day, he didn't just accept it, he relished it.

It had happened after he'd been late going round to his mum's for a Sunday lunch. There'd been a pile-up on the motorway and he'd been three hours late. By the time he'd arrived, he was in an absolutely boiling temper; all the guests had gone, and all that had been left of the lunch was a carrot and a nub of cold roast beef. He'd been about twenty-one at the time, three years into the movie business, and as his mum had made him a cup of tea and a roast beef sandwich, he'd let rip – about the greedy guests, about the traffic jam, about the gawping rubber-neckers who'd caused a second crash on the other carriageway.

'Got a book you might like to read,' his mum had said, leaving him at the kitchen table eating his sandwich – which actually, with horseradish sauce and the sliced carrot, had been pretty tasty.

She came back a minute later with a thin scuffed book.

On the grey cover was a picture of some Roman guy, Marcus Aurelius. 'Who's Marcus Aurelius?' he'd asked.

'One of the great Roman emperors.' She was knocking up another roast beef sandwich, this time with a cold Yorkshire pudding. 'These are his meditations. Strangely enough, they're as valid now as they were 2,000 years ago.'

Glenn had been pretty sceptical when he'd started leafing through the book. But occasionally, very occasionally, you come across a piece of ancient wisdom that hits the mark – and Marcus Aurelius's *Meditations* hit a bullseye. Simply put, if you aspire to anything in your life, there will be obstacles in your path – little niggling glitches which make it more difficult for you to achieve what it is that you've set out to achieve. In the smallest microcosm, this might just be a simple road trip to see your mum, where the obstacle might be, say, a crash on the other carriageway.

Once confronted with an obstacle, you can – seemingly – adopt one of two separate mindsets. You can either rant and rail about the sheer annoyance of this pain-in-the-neck problem in your path, not to mention the injustice of it, and the terrible bad luck that's just been inflicted on you; or you can take the stoical path, and shrug your shoulders, and say that worse things happen at sea.

Marcus Aurelius suggested a third way: an obstacle is a means for personal growth and evolution; an obstacle is a beautiful means by which we can make ourselves stronger and more resilient; an obstacle builds character; and above all, an obstacle is to be relished and enjoyed, and the bigger the obstacle, the more you should be licking your lips, for the greater the opportunity to reach a state of serene godliness.

Glenn wasn't quite there yet. When confronted by a mighty big obstacle – such as, say, the total collapse of some project that had been months in the making – he might let slip a short sweet expletive, but pretty soon, within a matter of minutes, he'd be back to his serene best, and would be exploring if there were possible routes around this particular obstacle, thanking the universe for giving him yet another opportunity for personal growth.

So, after being presented with the obstacle of the Freezingly Cold Film Set, Glenn had speedily conjured a route around it. Two runners were tasked with going through the *Yellow Pages*, and in under ten minutes he had the manager on the line and had ordered up a dozen industrial heaters to be delivered immediately. If they had the heaters going round the clock for the next week, then the hall might just about be warm enough for the girls – and at the thought of the twelve girls, and of all the obstacles that soon enough they'd be creating, he smiled again. Gosh they were beautiful, stunning even. Not that that would have any effect on his professionalism. In the previous decade he had dealt with so many scores of beautiful people that he was now immune to beauty; he could appreciate it, could admire it, but it did not touch him. And, gross generalisation but… he had observed that great beauty did not in any way mean great character, or kindness, or wit – in fact, far from it.

Glenn went off to report to Kubrick, and gave a light knock on the Winnebago door. As with everything else on set, Kubrick had very strict rules about his Winnebago: the only person allowed to open the door of Kubrick's Winnebago was Kubrick himself.

Some sort of kerfuffle was happening inside before Kubrick gingerly opened the door. Not for the first time, Glenn wondered whether Kubrick genuinely didn't care that he looked like a vagrant, or if it was all an act.

The Winnebago was just as you would expect of a multi-millionaire movie director who was going a bit mad. It had all the makings of luxury, except it needed a thorough clean – piles of paper dotted on the sofa, on the floor, on the table, magazines littered all over the place; the entire interior looked like it had been sprayed with food crumbs.

As usual, Kubrick's heavy-duty three-kilo rock tumbler was grinding away in the corner. It was Kubrick's latest fad. He'd gathered a number of small rocks from the Suffolk beaches and had then put them into the tumbler's drum with some grit. After the stones had been tumbled for weeks and weeks, their edges had been knocked off and the stones had taken on the sheen of polished glass. A few of the choicer stones were arrayed on a shelf by the tumbler; a harmless enough activity for a child, though perhaps a little odd for a guy in his late sixties.

Kubrick poured himself another coffee from the cafetière and stirred in some sugar. 'So what's up, Glenn – when we getting the strippers in?' Kubrick cackled at the thought.

'We can get the girls in tomorrow, but they won't be stripping for at least a week.'

'Naah?' Kubrick said. 'What's up?'

'The hall is freezing. I've just ordered some space heaters.'

'So no stripping then?'

'Not for a week. We'll rehearse them, see some of Leon's routines. But they'll just have to do it with their clothes on.'

'Fine,' Kubrick said. 'Hey Glenn, ya know that pert chick Vicky who was rolling round on the floor of that pub? She's the one who's got the lines, right?'

'That's right.' Of the dozen girls in the orgy, Kubrick and Leon had decided that Vicky was the girl who would be pairing off with Tom Cruise.

'Know what I think Glenn? I think when we're filming at Highclere Castle, she can lose the G-string.'

'You want her naked?'

'I want 'em all naked!' Another lewd cackle. Kubrick gleefully rubbed his hands together.

'I'll check the girls are OK with that.'

'Hey, what's the problem, Glenn?'

'So not a problem,' Glenn said. 'We did tell the girls they'd be wearing G-strings.'

'Well, tell 'em I now want full frontals!' Kubrick said. 'But hey – they can keep the masks and stilettoes on. And I want 'em trim down there – know what I mean? – trim but not shaved.'

'Sure,' Glenn said, pulling at the stubble on his chin, sizing up this new obstacle that had just hove into view and pondering how best to tackle it. It would call for delicacy and diplomacy and a whole lot more money.

CHAPTER 7

So what is it that we *Sun* reporters do when we are in the newsroom and there's nothing much cooking? Are we hitting the phones, pummelling our contacts for stories? Are we leafing through the papers, trying to find some news item that might be worth a follow? Are we, perhaps, getting the teas in for our hard-working colleagues?

No. Most of the time when there's not much going on in the newsroom; we tend to gossip about our colleagues, bitch about our colleagues and take the utmost delight in the discomfort of our colleagues.

And sometimes, very occasionally, we reminisce about our glory days, about our scoops and our world exclusives and those rare-as-hen's-teeth times that we have contrived to cover ourselves in glory. It's not really in the nature of tabloid journalists to talk about their old stories – by definition they're just old news, to be so rapidly overtaken by whatever is the latest story *du jour*. Besides, just as the great Bard says, "What's won is done – joy's soul lies in the doing." There's very little pleasure at all in seeing your story in print; the pleasure comes from digging up the story in the first place.

But as it was a special day for Paddy, I was more than happy to indulge his trip down memory lane.

'Tell us about the Falklands,' I said.

Paddy – white hair, a sweet old grandad, absolutely nothing like what you'd expect a seasoned *Sun* reporter to look like – took off his glasses and started to give them a polish. 'The Falklands,' he said. 'Yes.'

'Did you really just go to Portsmouth to see HMS *Invincible* off?' I asked.

'Now that is true,' he said, rueful, all too aware that his best days were long behind him. 'Invincible was leading the task force, 127 ships in all.' He sighed, rubbing the back of his hand. 'I'd gone down to see them off. The next thing I'm being told to get on the boat and sail 8,000 miles to the Falklands.'

'What did your family make of that?'

'Not overly surprised – well, if you're married to a hack, then you know pretty well that the story is king, and family comes a long way second.'

'But what a story!' I said. 'Britain at war and you're at the very centre of it. You're writing stories from the frontline!'

'Not that my stories bore much resemblance to what was actually printed,' he said. 'Look at 'em.' He gestured to the far side of the newsroom, which had a wall of fame for the *Sun*'s greatest front pages, lit from behind and blown up to about five feet by three feet. These included the *Sun*'s legendary front pages like "Freddie Starr Ate My Hamster", and "Up Yours Delors", as well as two of Paddy's Falklands front pages, "Stick It Up Your Junta!" and "Gotcha!" after the sinking of the General Belgrano.

'I don't think I wrote a single word of those stories,' Paddy said.

'Your picture byline is on them though,' I said. 'You got all the glory, you had all the fun. And that was real news – as opposed to most of the celebrity gossip that we're filling the paper up with now.'

'I'll miss it,' he said. 'I'll miss you all.' He'd started to cry. He wiped away the tears and gave a hefty blow into his handkerchief.

He stood up. 'Well, I suppose this is it,' he said.

'Good luck on the outside, Paddy.'

'I'd give the world to be starting out all over again.' He shook my hand.

I started slapping my desk with the palm of my hand and the rest of the news reporters immediately followed, not just slapping their desks, but hammering with their fists. The layout guys, the subs, the news editors, the secretaries, they all broke off from whatever they were doing to bang this old war horse out of the newsroom for the last time. The noise was immense. The sports reporters were pounding their keyboards up and down on the desks, and the back bench were drumming tattoos with their fists, and some of the photographers had come out of their hutch and were humping their chairs up and down on the floor. The editor, pink and pudgy, stood at the double doors. Paddy shook his hand and gave us a wave, and then he stepped through the doors and looked up to that great call to arms above the newsroom door – "Walk tall, you're entering *Sun* country!" And now that he was leaving *Sun* country for the last time, he knew that his life would be just that little diminished, that he would be walking smaller. He gave us a courtly bow and with that he was gone. His days as a frontline newsman were over, and back he'd be going to his wife and his family, never to be disturbed again by the thrill of the midnight call telling him to hie himself off to Heathrow Airport – no longer a *Sun* staff reporter, but merely consigned to those vast ranks of ex-hacks who'd once been a newspaper somebody.

Paddy's retirement party was just up the road from Fortress Wapping at London's oldest riverside pub, the Prospect of Whitby. The pub dated back to 1520 and I loved it in there – the history pulsed off the walls as you rubbed shoulders with the shades of rum-swilling sailors. A lot of the *Sun*'s leaving-dos were held at the Prospect of Whitby, and they were the nearest we ever got to a team-bonding session. (Christmas parties were a different piece of cheese altogether, more booze and more staff looking to bring a year's worth of yearning to a fitting climax.) Forty or fifty hacks were already in the pub, mostly from the *Sun*, though there were a few hacks from the other tabloids.

John-Henry was already at the bar. He pointedly ignored me.

'Evening, John-Henry. How's it going?' I said, joining him at the bar.

He gave me a very slow inspection. I had the distinct feeling that if it came to me and a cockroach, the cockroach would win. 'Well, I was doing a lot better until you came along.'

'John-Henry!' I said, with a light touch of the elbow.

'Don't you touch me!' he said.

'Sorry,' I said. 'Look – I've apologised for what happened at the RAC. And I'll apologise again. I'm very sorry.'

'I have never been so humiliated in my entire life.' He caught the eye of the barman and ordered a couple of bottles of Rioja and a tray of glasses.

'Here, let me get these,' I said.

'You buy my drinks?' John-Henry said. 'I don't think so!'

'OK,' I said, before pacifically adding, 'Great story you had last week about that navy admiral.'

'Do they have admirals in the army – in the air force?' he asked.

'They've got red admirals down the butterfly farm,' I said.

He ignored me and took his tray of Rioja and glasses off to one of the far tables by the windows, the better to enjoy the glorious views out over the River Thames and, doubtless, the better to bitch about me.

Well, couldn't be helped. I was more than aware that I was not everyone's cup of tea, though I did think it was a little unnecessary of John-Henry to take his RAC suspension so personally. It wasn't as if I'd meant to earwig into Sir James's damnable conversation in the toilets.

I consoled myself by having a lightning-fast pint of Stella and a double Glenfiddich chaser, and then bumbled off to the toilets. I'd taken up position at the furthermost urinal and had just undone my flies when there was a bang on the door and in came my esteemed Deputy Editor, Spike, who was short and bristling – never was there such a fitting case of nominative determinism. He grunted when he saw me. It certainly wasn't a grunt of delight; it had more of the flavour of an eyeball roll – an "Oh it's you" kind of grunt. Out of the corner of my eye, I watched him take up position at a urinal two down from me. He then unbuckled his belt, unbuttoned his trousers and unzipped himself, so that the entire front of his trousers was at half-mast. He unfurled himself – so to speak – and then stood at the urinal with both hands on his hips. I didn't like to look. There was now no prospect whatsoever of me having a pee. With Spike doing his alpha-pisser impersonation, I was dry as the Sahara.

He looked over at me and sniffed. Under normal circumstances I might have said something – on the lines of 'How's it going?' or perhaps even, 'Watching the game tonight?' – but since Spike was the boss, I decided to leave the opening conversational gambit to him. Maybe he didn't want to talk. Maybe he just wanted to have his majestic pee without being disturbed by an underling.

As it turned out, Spike was in the mood for a chat. 'What have you been cooking up with Grubby?' he said.

'I'm sorry?' I said.

'What's this thing you've been doing with Grubby?'

'Err,' I said. 'How do you mean?'

'It's perfectly simple, Kim. What have you been doing with Grubby?'

'Oh, well, yeah,' I said. 'How do you know about that?'

Pee at an end, Spike tidied himself up, the zipper was zipped and the belt was buckled. 'Since when do I, the deputy editor, have to tell you, a news reporter, about my sources?'

'Of course, of course,' I said, speedily buttoning up my flies. 'Just didn't think that anyone knew. Apart from me and Grubby.'

'Start talking,' he said. Not for Spike such fripperies as soap, water or hand-washing. He adopted the same pose that he had in front of the urinal, hands on hips (though now, thankfully, with trousers buttoned up).

I washed my hands. 'It's like this,' I said. 'There's a film...' I trailed off. I noticed that one of the cubicle doors was not only closed but locked – and we just know what can happen when a conversation is eavesdropped in a toilet. I jerked my thumb at the cubicle. 'Walls have ears.'

He was grinding his teeth as if there were nothing he'd like so much as to take a large chunk out of my neck. 'Tell me in the pub.'

'Of course,' I said, and suddenly felt a desperate urge to pee. 'I just need a quick pee. Then I'll come and join you.'

'Thought you'd already had a pee.'

'I suffer from shy bladder syndrome,' I said. 'I can't pee in public.'

Spike muttered some sweary expletive to himself, and the door banged again – why was he always slamming doors, what on earth had happened in his childhood? – and I was left to make my second attempt at a pee. I undid my buttons; how on earth did Spike know what I'd been doing with Grubby? Had he bugged the News International offices? I wouldn't have been the least surprised. I had just started my well-deserved pee when the cubicle door opened behind me. I couldn't see who it was, but I could heard the man sauntering over to the washbasins. I could sense that he was looking at me, but as I was stuck at the urinal mid-pee, I was at something of a disadvantage. The steady flow turned to a trickle and stopped.

'Must be terrible having a shy bladder,' he said. 'Did it all kick off at that posh school of yours?'

I glanced over my shoulder and after the most momentary of flinches, speedily zipped myself up.

It was Bain, my opposite number on the *Sun*'s deadly rival, the *Daily Mirror*. He had the dubious honour of being my number-one nemesis. I've got plenty of other nemesises (nemeses?), all the way down to number twenty, but Bain had the top slot.

'Bain?' I said. 'What the hell are you doing here?'

'Ma-a-a-te,' he said, and that single word was enough to put my teeth on edge. 'Got a tip for you.' He started to give himself the most luxurious handwash, for all the world like a surgeon scrubbing up, sleeves back, soap between the fingers, the works. He looked me up and down. 'Best to wear dark suits in the office – the pee doesn't show up so much round your crotch.'

I looked down at my crotch and, blast him, there wasn't so much as a drop of pee on my trousers. 'How's it going with the fairy stories?' I said. 'Got yourself a kiddy book publisher yet?'

'At least I'm getting some stories in the paper.' He winked and gave me a cheery smile; he had all the charm of chewing tin foil. 'You haven't had an exclusive in over a month. Not surprised you're off on this film lark with Grubby.'

I couldn't believe it. Bain, from the *Mirror*, was busting my chops on my home turf. He was at a *Sun* leaving party! God, he had a nerve. 'At least I haven't yet resorted to wholesale fiction,' I said.

'I guess that's the reason why Spike's tapping me up for a *Sun* staff job,' he said. He grabbed a handful of paper towels.

'You really are in cloud cuckoo land!' I said.

'And offered me a handsome salary with it,' Bain said. 'He said... now what did he say?... Oh yes! He said the news team was getting a bit stale. Needed beefing up. Needed what he called a heavyweight.'

He gave me a little wave and walked out.

'Spike wouldn't touch you with a bargepole,' I called after him, but the door had already swung shut.

With much to mull over, I returned to my urinal. The toilets now thankfully empty, I was finally able to complete my pee. I returned to the bar and bought myself another pint of Stella. Spike and Grubby were at a round corner table by the window. Spike was laughing, and to my horror I saw that Bain was also at the table.

'Take a pew!' Bain said, dragging over a spare chair from the neighbouring table.

'Thank you,' I said with stiff formality.

'Charlie's just been telling us how he got that great scoop last week,' Spike said. 'He dressed up in a chicken costume!' And at that he let rip with another howl of laughter. Charlie? Charlie?? Since when had Spike been on first-name terms with Bain? No, no, no! Nobody called him anything but Bain! That was his name! Bain was his name! Bane was his nature! Another example of nominative determinism.

'Here's to you,' Spike said, chinking Bain's glass.

'Your very good health, Spike,' Bain said, chummy as can be as he got to his feet. 'I know you've got much to discuss about this movie scoop that Kim's cooked up with Grubby, so I'll leave you to it.'

'Good to see you, Charlie,' said Spike, once again toasting the scum-sucker. 'And you'll let me know?'

You'll let me know?? What the hell did that mean? Let him know about what? An icicle tip tripped down the back of my spine. Was it possible?

Spike took a quick sip of stout. 'Spit it out,' he said, quickly reverting to type.

I was still thoroughly discombobulated by what had just happened. Bain? Please God, don't tell me he was going to be joining the *Sun*. That would be just the end!

I fenced to find out how much Spike already knew. 'What's Grubby told you?' I said.

'I ask the questions.' Spike started picking his nose, his thumb delicately edging at the rim of his nostril. He inspected the crusty piece of snot, absent-mindedly rubbed it between thumb and forefinger and then – and I promise I'm not making this up – flicked it straight at me. 'Why has Grubby been filming you?'

'Gosh, you've got good sources,' I said. 'Have you really bugged the offices?'

'You better start talking, Mr Shy Bladder.'

'It's like this,' I said, looking over my shoulder to see where Bain had got to. The human oil slick had managed to insert himself onto John-Henry's table. 'The two biggest stars on the planet, Tom Cruise and Nicole Kidman, are making a film with Stanley Kubrick. I'm trying to get on the set as an extra.'

'So you want to be an extra with Tom Cruise? Is that right?'

'That's right,' I said.

'Sounds pretty boring to me,' he said, and poured more stout down his throat, eyeballs still on me as his Adam's apple bobbed up and down like a yoyo. 'Who the hell cares if we get a few snaps of Cruise making a film?'

'True, so very true.' I could have pointed out that the *Sun*'s sister paper, the *News of the World*, had just run with a whole load of grainy pictures of Tom Cruise wandering around Pinewood studios, but instead decided to play my one and only trump card. 'But it's not any old scene – it's an orgy.'

'Tom Cruise is going to be filming an orgy?' Spike said.

'That's right.'

'Will he get his kecks off?'

'I don't know,' I said. 'But what I can tell you is that there are going to be a lot of women in the orgy.' I flipped out the photocopied text from Schnitzler's *Dream Story*. It was the two-page description of the orgy.

'What's this?' Spike held the piece of paper between thumb and forefinger.

'This is from a book by the legendary Viennese writer Arthur Schnitzler—'

'Arthur Schnitzler?' Spike said. 'How the hell can he be a legendary author if I've never heard of him?'

Now there indeed was a question: could anyone on the planet be "big", let alone "legendary", if Spike hadn't heard of them? 'He was big in his day,' I said magnanimously. 'Anyway, this is Schnitzler's orgy scene – and this is what Tom Cruise is soon going to be filming in Suffolk. The women are wearing black lace masks with dark veils around their heads. But apart from that they are completely and totally naked.'

Spike pulled out some reading glasses from the breast pocket of his shirt; for some reason I was reminded of the wolf in *Little Red Riding Hood* who, having eaten the granny, settles himself in the old lady's bed and puts on her round-rimmed glasses. Spike started to read. Grubby spotted his chance and took it. 'Get either of you two gents a drink?' he said before lumbering off to buy more stout and more Stella.

Spike read it through once and then reread it. (I assume he was reading it – he may just have been a very slow reader.)

The glasses were folded up and returned to the breast pocket. 'How do you know all this?' he said.

'I overheard the producer talking about it in the toilets of the RAC.'

'So that's why they duffed you up?'

'Yes,' I said.

'Good.'

I didn't know whether he meant the eavesdropping or the duffing-up was good.

He finished the last of his stout and stared out of the window. I joined him in contemplative silence, watching the great river roll by, and thinking, I don't know, of all those thousands of great men, power exuding from their very fingertips, who had once stared out of those same window panes.

Grubby returned with the beers, and he, also, knew better than to disturb Spike's melancholic moment. Perhaps Spike was thinking about Paddy's retirement, and how, soon enough, he himself would just be another ex-hack, summarily deprived of his army of minions and only able to lord it over his pet hamster. 'People have been sitting here for nearly five hundred years,' Spike said. 'And now they're nothing but dust.'

I glanced at Grubby. He shrugged. Well, of course they were all dust – that was sort of the nature of being dead for four centuries. But I had no idea how it was even remotely connected to the matter in hand: me becoming an extra on Tom Cruise's latest film.

'Are you all right, Spike?' I said.

'What the hell's it got to do with you?' he snapped.

'Nothing, nothing!'

He drank more stout. 'So you want to get on this big-deal movie set?'

'I do!' I said. 'Get all the pictures – get all the gossip. It'll be fantastic.'

'Yeah,' he said. 'So you get these pictures, but it's still just a hill of beans. It's not like when you were a Buckingham Palace footman. Now that... that was a national security scandal. But this...' He gave a dismissive flick of his hand and looked out of the window again. That view must have really been giving him the hump. 'Big deal.'

A big deal? Excuse me – was this *not* a big deal? Digging up pictures and dirt was what *Sun* reporters did for a living. Day in, day out, this was precisely the sort of stuff that filled the pages of the *Sun* newspaper! Who cared whether there wasn't any particular scandal attached to this new Kubrick film – certainly not the *Sun*'s 10 million readers. No, what they wanted – and, indeed, what I wanted to give them – was pictures of Tom Cruise surrounded by a bevy of beautiful topless women. Was that too much to ask?

But Spike, it seemed, was having an existential crisis which made him question the very essence of what it was to be a tabloid journalist. (Answer: digging up every scrap of gossip there was to be had on the world's biggest superstar – and if there were pictures to boot, then so much the better.)

Spike continued his inner monologue. 'Apart from anything else, Kubrick will probably hit us with an injunction before we've even gone to print. He's a real litigious bastard.'

'Yeah, you're right,' I said. I was really getting into the spirit of things.

Spike's shoulders slumped – probably the effect of having

a drink with Bain. 'Well, if you get picked, I suppose you better do it,' he said.

'Great,' I said, trying to sound full of vim and vigour. 'Fingers crossed.'

'Mind taking it out of your holidays?' he said.

'What?' I said. 'You cannot be serious! I'll be sweating my guts out on this set trying to bring you a world picture exclusive and you want me to take it out of my holidays?'

Spike presciently moved onto the final matter at hand. 'How long do you think you'll be on set?'

'Don't know,' I said, before idiotically blurting out, 'Maybe a couple of weeks.'

'We can just about stretch to that,' he said – but at that stage, what did he know and indeed what did I know of the movie-making methods of that great auteur Stanley Kubrick. Two weeks? After two weeks at Elveden Hall, Kubrick had barely put film in the camera.

CHAPTER 8

Nina and the rest of the girls were picked up at 9.30 a.m. sharp, but instead of being taken back to their usual rehearsal studio, they were driven to the film set. They had no idea where they were going. Everything about the film had been so utterly secret that, despite four months of rehearsals, not one of the girls knew where they'd be filming. Nina had a hunch it was going to be Elveden Hall – Timothy Dalton had been James Bond there a few years earlier in *The Living Daylights* – but it wasn't until they were being driven through Elveden's entrance gates that she knew for sure.

The girls stared at the hall in silence as they were whisked up the drive – not only was it vast, but a vast fleet of vehicles was parked outside the front, trucks and cars and double-deckers and even a pair of silver Winnebagos. It was just a little... daunting. This was for real – a huge production, with a huge star and a slightly terrifying director. It was Vicky – of course – who broke the ice. 'Ready to get your tits out, girls?'

A runner, Olivia, checked off their names on a clipboard; Olivia was different from the other runners because she had a lot of tattoos on her arms and on her throat – not really to Nina's tastes, but nor were a lot of things. They were told to go and get some coffee and cake from the catering lorry. Mandy and Nina were far too excited to sit tamely in a canteen – there was a movie set to be explored! Despite being dressed in jeans and overcoats, they sparked quite a reaction. And thinking about it, of course there was going to be a reaction. They were going to be filming an orgy! With Tom Cruise! And not a bra between them! And since the crew – mainly men – had been filming for over eight months, it stood to reason that they were probably looking forward to the orgy. All right: salivating. Even Nina – normally impervious to a person's looks – could concede that the girls were a good-looking bunch. En masse, they were slightly terrifying. As doubtless the lads of Bury St Edmunds had already discovered.

They could have asked for permission to go into the hall, but Nina was a devotee of the great Rear Admiral Grace Hopper, who opined that if you had a good idea you should act on it immediately: it's so, so much easier to apologise than it is to ask for permission.

It was freezing inside – no wonder they'd been told to wrap up warm. A dozen space-heaters were belching out hot air, but the hall was so huge that they'd need be at full blast for a week before the girls were ready to take their clothes off. At least twenty men and a couple of women were toiling away in the hall putting up lights. Glenn, talking into a walkie-talkie, seemed to be masterminding the whole operation.

'Morning, Mandy, morning, Nina,' he said.

'Hi Glenn.' Nina quite liked this strong aroma of competence. You couldn't quite put your finger on it, yet it was unmistakable. This guy had put in his 10,000 hours; he'd mastered his craft. She'd have liked to talk – so many questions to ask – but he was already walking away.

'You'll be a little safer upstairs,' he called, and went off to confer with a plump guy.

Some of the crew were rigging lights by the balconies. Standing apart from them was a tallish man in a black cloak with a cowl, sort of like a monk's cloak.

He gave a wolfish smile when he spotted them. 'Well, hello, ladeez!' he said.

Amazing – the guy had said just three words, and already Nina had taken against him. He was smooth and cocky, hair slicked back into a black helmet. For some reason he was wearing a dinner jacket and black tie.

'Hi there,' Nina said.

The man sauntered over. 'We have been so looking forward to seeing you all.'

'Oh yeah?' Mandy said. Mandy, it seemed, had also not taken to the guy.

'They've been talking about it for weeks – even Tom's excited.'

'Well, that's nice,' Nina said. 'I hope we don't disappoint.'

'No chance of that!' The man looked them both up and down. 'Is one of you Vicky, by any chance?'

'No,' Nina said. 'Why do you ask?'

'I'm supposed to be kissing her,' the man said. 'And from the amount of takes we had at Pinewood, I reckon I'm going to be kissing her for at least a fortnight.'

'Guess you're Tom Cruise's stand-in,' Nina said.

'Aren't you the smart cookie?' he said. 'Yeah I'm Tom's stand-in. What a pro. He just gives Stanley exactly what he wants, over and over again. Like a machine.'

Mandy looked at him curiously. 'So what's a stand-in?'

'I stand in for Tom when they're fixing up a scene,' he said. 'Then when everything's set and Glenn's ready to roll, a runner goes off to Tom's truck and tells him to get on the set, and then, when everything is exactly ready, then Stanley gets the call and he comes onto the set. He's far and away the most brilliant director I've ever worked with – and I've worked with some of the best.'

'Oh yeah?' Nina said, her estimation of the stand-in dropping by the minute. 'What's so special about him?'

'He is the quintessential perfectionist,' the guy said. 'He's always searching for something extraordinary. He just never gives up.'

'I had a boyfriend like that,' Mandy said. 'Good-looking – but what a pain. Binned him after a month.'

Vicky and a couple of the other girls came up the stairs to

join them on the balcony. Nina was more than happy to take a step back. 'This is Vicky,' Nina said.

'So you're the lucky one,' he said. 'I'm Jimmy, and we are going to get very intimate over the next month.'

'Really?' said Vicky, not quite as punchy as she'd been in the Fox two days ago – perhaps she really had taken on board Glenn's advice not to insult strangers.

'Yeah,' he said. 'I'm Tom Cruise's stand-in. Half the time you're gonna be kissing Tom – and half the time you're gonna be kissing me.'

'But I thought we were all wearing masks,' Nina said. 'How do you get to kiss someone if you've got a mask on?'

'You can get pretty intimate with a mask,' Jimmy said.

'Sounds like the most unerotic kiss on earth,' Nina said. She'd had enough of the balcony, and she'd certainly had enough of Jimmy. 'Let's get some fresh air.'

They explored the house and the estate, which was barely a husk of what it had been a century before, with smashed windows and broken fences and overgrown gardens that had turned to jungles. When it started to rain, they repaired to one of the double-deckers. A few of the other girls were there. They talked for a while, and then Nina took herself off to a corner table and pulled out a book from her coat; she never went out without a book tucked in her pocket. And books looked as if they were going to be a necessity on this shoot, because unless Nina was much mistaken, they were going to be doing a lot of hanging around.

At lunch, the girls trooped out in the rain to the catering truck, where they had the option of lamb stew or baked cod, though Nina daringly had the pudding, a treacle sponge with custard. Hell – what was the point of exercising every single day if you couldn't occasionally indulge yourself?

Glenn came up to the top floor of the double-decker. The conversation faded. Jimmy was the last person to stop talking.

'Hi team,' Glenn said. 'Thank you for your patience this morning, just taken a little longer to set up than we thought it would. But it looks like we'll be on set in a couple of hours or so, when we can see what you've been working on with Leon. It will be the high point of the film.'

Jimmy nudged Vicky's arm and whispered something in her ear. She didn't try to hide her laughter.

Glenn clapped his hands together as if he'd come to a decision. 'Right,' he said. 'The director has ordered a change of plan with this masked ball—'

'Don't you mean orgy?' Jimmy called.

'We are calling it a masked ball,' Glenn said. 'As you know, half of the party will be filmed here. The second half of the masked ball is going to be filmed at Highclere Castle.' He nodded to himself, as if mentally rehearsing what to say next.

'Now, ahhh…' He tugged at his lower lip. 'There's no easy way to say this. But the director wants all the women at Highclere to be naked – and now, well, if this is not for you, I entirely understand. So if you're coming to Highclere, you can keep the masks and the shoes on, but, ummm, there will be no G-strings. You will be naked.'

Jimmy whispered in Vicky's ear and she punched his arm. 'How much extra you going to pay us?' she asked.

'Double what you're on now,' Glenn said.

'Double?' Vicky said. 'I'm in.'

'What does everyone else think?'

The girls tick-tocked. Most didn't take long to make up their minds.

'How about you, Nina?'

'I'm going to think about it,' she said. 'I'll let you know tomorrow.'

'Fine,' Glenn said. 'Thank you.' He was going down the stairs when he turned back. He had actually started to blush. 'Oh just one more thing. The director has requested that you are… you are not shaved.'

'Kubrick likes bushes, does he?' Vicky said.

'That's what he wants.' Glenn looked like he wanted the ground to swallow him up.

'Old-fashioned kinda guy,' Vicky said.

Glenn was relieved to have delivered the message. 'We'll be in the hall in an hour or two.'

The moment he'd left, the girls were abuzz with chatter. Nina was, if anything, amused. Would it faze her one little bit to be naked rather than topless? Not in the slightest. She was looking as good as she was ever going to look – so why not record it for posterity? And one day, when she was old and grey, her grandchildren would watch this film and (after getting over their initial revulsion) would exclaim, "Granny, you were a stunner in your day!" So why not sign up immediately for the nude scenes like the rest of the girls? Simple point of principle. As her mum used to tell her, there was hardly a decision in the world that wasn't the better for being slept on.

An hour later, Olivia came to collect them. All twelve girls were shepherded into the hall, which now had a large red square carpet in the centre. Leon Vitali, who was to play Red Cloak, was already there in his red cloak and his six-inch stacked heels. He was holding an incense burner and a long wooden staff, which was to be sonorously hammered into the ground. And he happened to be talking to the great man himself, Stanley Kubrick – and from the way everyone deferred to him, you could see that this was a king in all his pomp.

In the past couple of months, Nina had read three of the Kubrick biographies, forewarned being forearmed. He was mad about chess; was obsessed with Napoleon – in fact even styled himself on Napoleon, often comparing a movie set to a battlefield; had been a photographer at *Look* magazine for four years, before making the giant leap to movies; and had been married three times, the third marriage to Christiane appearing to have worked out better than the first two. There was the control-freakery and the work ethic. The love of cats and dogs. And there was his epic number of takes. Every single film he'd made had taken longer to shoot than the previous one.

And since his last film had taken over a year to shoot, that rather indicated that Kubrick had another six months to go before he was happy with *Eyes Wide Shut*.

Nina had seen three of his films. She'd seen *Spartacus* when she was a kid, bit long, actually very long. Then there'd been *The Shining*, utterly terrifying, which she'd seen with an old boyfriend, and had jumped clean out of her seat when the Grady twins appeared in the corridor. (Interestingly, according to one biography, Kubrick had used so much blood in *The Shining*'s elevator scenes that after it had all sluiced into the drains, the locals thought there'd been a murder at Elstree Studios.) Nina had also seen Kubrick's last film, *Full Metal Jacket* – it was OK, probably more of a guy film.

And now here he was on his tenth big-budget film, and here she was, now just the very smallest of (stripped) cogs in this whole magnificent machine – and to strip or not to strip, that was the question.

Kubrick was looking even more tramp-like than when Nina had last seen him in the Fox. He was wearing a rumpled blue boiler suit, grubby tennis shoes fit for the bin and one of his multi-pocketed jackets. But despite the clothes and the wild hair, Kubrick exuded this unmistakable whiff of power. It was also noticeable how everyone else on the set – with the exception of the pudgy second assistant director – looked sleek and well-groomed.

The girls went through the hall to one of the anterooms where all the costumes were being kept. For the moment, it had been decided they'd wear their masks, stilettoes and midnight-blue cloaks, but underneath they'd keep their clothes on.

There was noticeably less chatter. Over the previous four months, they'd rehearsed at least a dozen different scenarios, and now Kubrick, with a majestic waft of his hand, would decide which scenes pleased him. Or perhaps would decide that none of Leon's scenes pleased him even in the slightest, and that the girls would have to start again from scratch.

And from what Nina had read about him, there was every chance that that might indeed be the eventual outcome. He was the Goldilocks of the movie world, where everything was always too hot, too cold, too hard or too soft, too dark or too brilliantly bright white, and where nothing was ever, ever quite to his liking.

Nina put on her cloak, which was beautifully made – she'd love to keep it when the movie was over – and pulled on her full face mask. It was almost Egyptian in style. Each girl had a different mask, with Vicky wearing the most beguiling of them all, an exquisite mask that was trimmed with black feathers.

Vicky, resplendent, led the girls back into the hall, and as they walked in, the crew stopped and stared and Kubrick broke off from his conversation, and all the talk and all the noise evaporated to the most still silence. 'Perfect,' Kubrick said. He had a very soft voice with a light Brooklyn accent. 'Better than I could possibly have dared hope for.'

The girls stood in a line while Kubrick inspected them with the head of wardrobe. He walked round each girl in turn, making little comments which the wardrobe woman jotted down into her notebook. 'Hey, who are you?' he asked.

'I'm Nina.'

'Ah yes, ah yes,' he said. 'You have two lines, I believe.'

'I have,' Nina said, before trotting out a line. '"Do you want to go somewhere a little more private?"'

Kubrick chuckled. 'Very good, Nina,' he said. 'I wrote it myself. Comfy in the mask, comfy in the shoes?'

'They're fine.'

'Good, good, excellent.' He turned to Helena, the wardrobe woman. 'Nina's cloak needs another four inches at the bottom. What do we think about her mask?'

'I like it.'

'It's not quite there,' Kubrick said. 'Let's try some others.'

A wardrobe minion brought out another dozen masks, one on top of the other. Nina tried them all as Kubrick prowled around her muttering to himself. When she'd tried them all, he had her put them on again a second time. 'We'll go with this one,' he said, pointing at Nina's original Egyptian-style mask. 'Very good,' Helena said, scribbling into her notebook, so well drilled that she did not so much as raise an eyebrow.

Kubrick moved onto Vicky. 'Ah Vicky,' Kubrick said. 'Fully recovered from Saturday night?'

'Yes, Mr Kubrick.'

'Do call me Stanley.'

'Yes, Stanley.'

Nina was pleased to have her mask hide her grin. She'd never heard Vicky so submissive.

'Know your lines?'

'Yes, Stanley.'

'Try me.'

'You want to hear one of my lines?'

'Yes, please.'

'Ummm... How about this one? "I'm not sure what you think you're doing, but you don't belong."'

'Very good,' Kubrick said. 'Though is that line quite right? I'm not sure it is. Hey Glenn, can we check?'

Glenn rustled up a script and flicked through to the orgy scene. 'You're right,' he said. 'It should end, "You don't belong here".'

'Ah, there we are, Vicky,' Kubrick said. 'Now you must say the lines just exactly as they're written – just exactly. We have spent years perfecting this script. I don't want you to change so much as a single syllable. Can we try it again?'

'Yes, Stanley,' Vicky said. '"I'm not sure what you think you're doing, but you don't belong here."'

'Perfect. Very good indeed. Thank you.'

Kubrick pottered onto the next girl. Nina and the rest of the girls were left standing on the red carpet for well over an hour before, finally, Leon was allowed to put them through their paces. Leon had them in single lines and double lines, and in marching squares, and all the while this crazy music was coming over the speakers, quite creepy, very creepy, especially with Red Cloak hammering the ground with his staff. The scenarios were all different, but they all ended in the same way, first with the girls unclasping the hooks on their cloaks, and then letting the cloaks fall to the floor; in a week or two, when the hall was warm enough, they'd then be down to just their G-strings.

Kubrick just watched – first from ground level and then from the balcony. Sometimes he asked them to try another variation, but most of the time he just said, "Do it again". So they did it again, and did it again, sometimes walking, sometimes standing, and a lot of time dropping to their knees into a straight yoga position, the Child's Pose, knees on the red carpet, bums back towards their feet and torsos forward with arms extended. The first thirty or forty times they did it, it was quite fun – they were doing everything just exactly as they'd rehearsed it and now they were being watched by the great Stanley Kubrick – but after a while it got boring, and after a little while longer it was knackering. Before Kubrick called time for a tea break, Nina must have knelt down on that thin red carpet over sixty times. Her knees were killing her!

By end of the day, they'd gone through everything that Leon had choreographed for them. 'That's great,' Kubrick said. 'Lots to work with, lots to be done.'

Nina had an early night of it, and surprisingly, Mandy was also in bed by 10 p.m.; Nina went to sleep with the sound of Red Cloak's eerie music still ringing in her head, and she had a funny feeling that, over the next couple of months, it would have wormed its way into her nightmares.

Olivia checked them all off the coach the next morning, and after they'd been left waiting on the double-decker for a couple of hours, Glenn called them over to the hall.

'Hi Nina,' he said, stepping in sync with her. It was quite nice walking with a guy who was taller than her. She wondered if she'd ever get to know him, or if he would always be so icily businesslike. 'You've had the night to sleep on it. Will you be joining us at Highclere?'

'I think I will.'

'Good,' he said. 'Thank you.'

'Know why?'

'No.'

Nina smiled as they walked into the hall. 'I want to find out how it all turns out.'

CHAPTER 9

Since the debacle of *Full Metal Jacket*, Kubrick had been obsessively secret about all of his film projects. *Full Metal Jacket* had been Kubrick's last film and, as usual, he'd taken years and years to make it. Crucially, he was beaten to the punch by another Vietnam film, Oliver Stone's *Platoon*.

Platoon cost half the money of *Full Metal Jacket* and was completed in half the time. It hit the cinemas a full five months before Kubrick's Vietnam film, and went on to sweep the board, not only making much more money than *Full Metal Jacket*, but winning four Oscars, including – guttingly – best picture and best director.

It was probably just coincidence that *Platoon* and *Full Metal Jacket* were made at the same time, but Kubrick had been obsessed by it for over a decade, which was why nobody knew anything at all about *Eyes Wide Shut*. As far as Glenn knew, all that the extras and the girls knew was that they were filming an orgy. Only a handful of people in the world knew the source material.

Which was why Glenn couldn't believe his ears when he happened to overhear a conversation in the double-decker canteen. They'd spent the previous couple of days checking how the light fell on the masks of every single one of the sixty-odd extras. This level of meticulousness was par for the course on *Eyes Wide Shut*. Later that night, they'd be having their first proper rehearsal.

It was gone 11 p.m., time for their meal break. Roddie and

Glenn, being part of the crew, had had first dibs at Molly's catering truck, and were sitting at a middle table on the top deck. Glenn had gone for the fish and salad; Roddie, as ever, had gone for the works, sausage stew this time, with Waldorf salad, apple tart, ice cream and a selection of cheeses.

'How do you think it's going?' Glenn said.

'Going all right,' Roddie said, shovel-a-shovel with the food.

'Think the girls are ready?'

'Sure.' Roddie looked up, pushed his glasses back up the ridge of his nose. 'They take their kit off for a living.'

'Er, well, yeah.' The girls would indeed be getting their kit off – though Glenn wouldn't have expressed it quite like that – and at that moment, three of the girls came up to the top deck with their food trays. The girls were Mandy, Vicky and Nina, and, just as he'd been doing for the last ten days, Glenn studiously ignored them. That's what you had to do with beautiful women. You had to ignore them. Especially if you were working with them.

So after just the briefest of glances at Mandy and at Vicky, and after no glance whatsoever at Nina, Glenn immersed himself in his salad. 'What a great salad!' he said. "The vinaigrette really sets it off. Do you think Molly makes it herself?'

Roddie looked up from his sausage stew and pushed his glasses back up his nose again. 'She just buys it in, like she does all the other stuff.'

'I like it,' Glenn said – and enthusiastically too, because that was another thing you had to do when you were in the vicinity of three beautiful women.

'It's the same muck you've been having on your salad for the last year,' Roddie said.

'Oh,' Glenn said. 'Well, it's very good.'

Continuing to eat his delicious salad, Glenn was tuning in to the girls' conversation. 'What book is this film based on?' Mandy said.

'Wish I knew,' Nina said.

By chance, one of the extras, Lawrence, happened to be walking past the girls' table. 'I can tell you,' Lawrence said.

'You know the source material?' Nina said incredulously.

'I do,' Lawrence said. 'Not only have I read it, but I've seen two of the other film adaptations.'

Glenn could not believe his ears! Lawrence knew the source material? He'd watched two of the other adaptations? Glenn had only watched one of them!

'Budge up and I'll tell you all about it,' Lawrence said chattily, and Nina moved up the bench to make space for him. He plonked himself down and started peeling a banana.

'It's based on a 1926 novel by an Austrian writer who you've never heard of, Arthur Schnitzler, and it's called *Dream Story*. Took me ages to find a copy, and eventually I had to go to the London Library. It's a pretty short story.'

'So what is the story?' Nina asked.

In between nibbles of his banana, Lawrence went on to tell the girls the complete story of Schnitzler's novella. 'There have been two Italian adaptations of the book,' he said. '*Il Cavaliere, la morte e il diavolo*' – said in surprisingly good Italian – 'came out in 1983, pretty modest, and another low-budget effort which came out in 1989, *Nightmare in Venice*.' Lawrence now delved into his rucksack and pulled out a large bottle of Ribena. He poured himself a large slug – though somehow it didn't quite have the colour of Ribena. Come to that, Lawrence didn't really look like a Ribena drinker. 'The films are not bad,' he said. 'But Stanley will blow them out of the water.'

How – how – how did he know all this?

Lawrence plucked a scrumpled piece of paper out from his breast pocket. 'Here's Schnitzler's description of our orgy, in case you're interested.'

Nina took the piece of paper. 'How do you know all this?' She started to read.

'Oh – you know,' Lawrence said.

'No, I don't know,' Nina said.

Glenn was just as interested as Nina. He left Roddie to his stew and sat down at the table on the other side of the aisle from Lawrence and the girls. Ignoring the fact that Lawrence was drinking a bottle of red wine when booze on set was expressly forbidden, Glenn repeated Nina's question. 'I'd also love to know,' he said. 'Not even a dozen people know the source material for *Eyes Wide Shut*. How did you find out?'

'Oh hello, Glenn,' Lawrence said. He poured himself another glass of Ribena, transparently buying himself more time. 'It's all perfectly simple.' He took a long, long sip of the Ribena. 'Delicious,' he said, smacking his lips. 'It all comes down to having once dated an Italian girl, a real firecracker, Bianca. Her dad, Federico he was called, he worked in a winery in Puglia, and every day for lunch and dinner we'd drink his red wine. I tried it again recently, but it was never the same, and it made me realise that a lot of wines taste best when they are drunk in their country of origin – though of course it could have been the company. Bianca was great, very shouty, and her dad was a real laugh. After a couple of bottles, he'd start singing, what a voice—'

'What has Federico's singing got to do with *Dream Story*?' Glenn said.

'Just a passing detail, Glenn,' Lawrence said. 'Adding a little colour to the story. I thought that you, being a fellow artist, would appreciate that sort of thing more than anyone.'

For the first time in a week, Glenn locked amused eyes with Nina. 'Of course I appreciate that sort of detail,' Glenn said. 'Forgive my interruption.'

'So…' Lawrence then had the nerve to pour himself another glass of "Ribena", wafting it under his nose before taking a sip. 'Federico, as I mentioned, was a good singer, but it was Bianca's mother Maria who was far and away the best singer in the house, if not the entire town. Sometimes they'd do duets together, just charming. Verdi was their favourite, though they also loved Rossini, still miss them even now – and do you know what, Glenn, I've only just realised this, but Bianca was a bit of a highly strung nutcase. Had it not been for her parents, we wouldn't have lasted more than three weeks together.'

'Really?' Glenn said. 'How fascinating.'

'Yes, it is fascinating, isn't it, Glenn? What it is that keeps us with lovers who are long past their sell-by dates, along with, of course, that equally intractable question of what it is that drives us into each other's arms in the first place.' He paused and, for no apparent reason, looked first at Glenn and then at Nina. 'Now I'm sure you're wondering why I have included Federico and Maria in my story – perhaps you were imagining it an irrelevant, not to say boring detail – but as it is, Glenn, Bianca's parents are an important cog in the story. No Federico and no Maria means no *Dream Story*.'

'I'm so glad to hear it.'

'I realise Glenn that as the assistant director you possibly have better things to do than listen to shaggy dog stories from your extras, so I will speedily cut to the chase. Both Federico and Nina—'

'You mean Maria?'

'Yes, I of course mean Maria – thank you so much, Glenn, good that you were paying attention – ahhh… so as I was saying, both Frederico and *Maria* were mad about movies – they'd go to the cinema every chance they got, and along the way they had also infected Bianca with the movie bug. Tell you the truth, I was rather grateful when we went to the movies together, because it was about the only time she ever shut up.'

'I had a boyfriend like that,' Mandy said. 'Though it wasn't movies he was mad about, it was football.'

'I had a boyfriend like that too!' Vicky said. 'When the football was on, I could have been dancing around stark naked in the living room and he wouldn't have even looked at me!'

Nina, Glenn was pleased to see, was not about to share her own story of boyfriends past. Well, of course she'd have had boyfriends in the past – how could she not? More pertinently… was there a boyfriend present?

'And continuing?' Nina said.

'And continuing,' Lawrence said. 'We just happened to see both versions of *Dream Story* in the cinema – it was rather odd, actually, going to the cinema with Bianca, because not only would her parents sit directly behind us, but also her uncle Giorgio, Federico's brother, and his wife, who was also called Maria.' He sniffed and buried his nose into his glass of Ribena again. 'The films were OK – though actually there's a 1969 Austrian TV adaptation which is supposed to be a cracker. Couldn't track that one down,' he mused. 'Anyway, the films intrigued me enough to go off to the London Library to read Schnitzler's book – and there you have it.'

'OK,' Glenn said. 'I get that you saw these two films in Italy. And I get that you've read the book. But how did you make the connection that *Eyes Wide Shut* was based on *Dream Story*?'

'Oh that,' Lawrence said airily. 'The clue was our weird masked orgy. Though tell you the truth, Glenn, I didn't know for certain that *Eyes Wide Shut* was based on *Dream Story* until you confirmed it ten minutes ago.'

'What?'

'I had a hunch that Schnitzler was the source. But it was only when you came over and started giving me the third degree that I knew for sure.'

The girls laughed. 'He's got you there, Glenn,' Nina said. She looked him in the eyes again. It was the first time that she had spoken directly to him in weeks.

'You are one cheeky bastard, Lawrence.' Glenn got up. 'Please don't mention *Dream Story* to anyone else – Stanley will have a heart attack if he finds out. See you all on set in twenty minutes.'

Glenn left the bus. It was preposterous, the biggest load of tosh he'd ever heard – just happened to have watched both versions of *Dream Story* in the original Italian, and had then read the book? And had also just happened to possess a photocopy of the orgy scene? It was ludicrous!

But if Lawrence hadn't invented that hokum story, then how to blazes had he come by this extraordinary piece of information? Kubrick would have absolute kittens! They were only supposed to be working on the most super-secret movie in Hollywood history – and now even the extras were yakking about the source material!

The space-heaters had been going round the clock for ten days and the hall had finally been deemed warm enough for a full dress rehearsal. As so often with the *Eyes Wide Shut* rehearsals, Kubrick would be filming it. He found it easier to get a feel for the film if he could see the dailies.

The hall was gradually filling with extras. Red Cloak sauntered into the room with his incense-burner and staff. The girls, wearing masks and cloaks, trooped out of their special anteroom and took centre stage on the red carpet. The lights and sound were ready. The camera crew were ready. Tom Cruise's stand-in had been stood down, and the star was as ready as ever. Glenn called up Kubrick on the walkie-talkie. 'Stanley, we're ready for you.' And five minutes later, after the director had quite finished doing whatever he did in his infernal Winnebago, Stanley Kubrick decided that he, also, was ready.

'Hey girls, warm enough for ya?' Kubrick called. 'We're gonna do the scene again – sort of like a dress rehearsal. Though I like to think of it as an "Undress Rehearsal"' He was the only person who chuckled. 'We're gonna film it too, see how it looks.'

And the cameras rolled, and the background action began, and for the first time that year in Elveden Hall there rang out that succulent one-word call to arms which, even eleven months in, still sends shivers up Glenn's spine: "Action!"

All afternoon, the extras and the crew had been pulsing with this tingling electricity. Not a word was said, not a word needed to be said, as the crew diligently and efficiently went about its business, and as the extras clustered together to small-talk their time away. This tangible sense of anticipation

– this was it, this was for real, the cloaks were coming off, and for the first time the twelve girls would be wearing nothing but G-strings. Funny how the most relaxed people by far on the set were the girls themselves. Half an hour ago, when they'd been chatting on the double-decker, you wouldn't have an inkling what they were about to do. Cool as damn cucumbers.

Glenn dispassionately analysed how he felt about the cloaks coming off. He'd known the girls for nearly a fortnight now. He liked them. For the most part, he admired their cheerful professionalism. And they were, all of them, very, very beautiful.

Was he attracted to any of them?

Look, let's just get this straight: he liked them – what was so wrong with that? Above all, he tried to keep things just as professional as he knew how. His watchword was that he said nothing to the girls that he would not have said to his dear old mum Frances.

So, purely from a professional point of view, he was interested to see how the girls would look when their cloaks slipped to the ground; it would be good to see how it all fitted together. But as for the suggestion that he, Glenn, had any personal interest in seeing, say, Nina naked, that was just absurd. Now Nina – for the sake of an example – was a very handsome woman, a very bright woman, a personable, capable woman and a writer to boot – but the fact that in a matter of minutes she'd be all but naked in front of him was so neither here nor there. He was the assistant director for God's sake, a professional to his fingertips; frankly you'd get more reaction out of... out of Nelson on his column than you would out of Glenn on the set. These beauties in all their nakedness held about as much as allure to Glenn as... as a naked Stanley Kubrick! (What a thought! Yuck! Probably not the right analogy at all.) But the point was that the girls, they did not move him. They did not touch him. Further to that, he would not – could not – allow himself to be touched by them. So: keep things formal, keep things professional, and never

ever allow himself to be sucked down the seductive path of a chit-chat conversation which might then lead to… feelings that were not, well, were not as professional as he might have liked. And as for what it would be like at Highclere Castle, when even the G-strings were discarded, and when the girls really would be naked-naked (*au naturel*, not shaved), well, in the words of the Good Book, "Sufficient unto the day is the evil thereof!"

Red Cloak was weaving in and out of the girls as he swung his smoking incense burner, and Jocelyn Pook's spooky music was pumping out over the speakers. Apparently, or so Kubrick had told him, it was a fragment of the Orthodox Liturgy – though played backwards with the words chanted in Romanian. Glenn had a feeling that, over the next couple of months, he'd be getting to know this piece of music rather too well.

The girls had got up now from their child's pose yoga positions and were standing in a circle with Red Cloak in the middle on his six-inch platforms. The girls were pretty tall in their blue stilettoes, Nina especially.

Funny how you could spend a fortnight doing your best to avoid someone else's company. Yet when you were in the same room together, you found yourself instinctively seeking them out.

And there she was, almost more alluring in the Egyptian mask. She was standing in between Vicky and Mandy, head bowed like a medieval penitent. Red Cloak was hammering the floor with his staff, slow, rhythmic, thrusting…

What if… what if he'd just, say, met Nina at a dinner party. If they'd just happened to be sitting next to each other. Well, deep breath, if they'd met at a dinner party, they'd have talked about this and that, and she'd have mentioned her writing (he'd actually read her book, merely due diligence, and had thought it first-class; you could turn it into a film, no problem at all), and he might have talked a little about his life in the movies, but he definitely would not have come across as Mr hot-shot movie man, because he'd have been much more interested in learning about Nina and her dreams and her demons. But… if he *had* met Nina at a dinner party, well, they might have clicked and they might not have clicked, but would he have asked for her number? Would he have asked her out?

What on earth has got into him? Just get a grip! If he had met her, and if this, and if that, and if the other, then they might have got it together and they might not have got it together, but as we well know with "ifs", if his aunt had had wheels she could have been a damn tea trolley! What was the point in pondering these ridiculous hypotheticals when he had so not met Nina at a dinner party. She, Nina, was a professional stripper and he, Glenn, was not only her boss, but was the guy who was doing the real graft on this multi-million pound movie while His Nibs, Stanley Kubrick, swanned off back to his Winnebago and his stone tumbler and his copies of *The Lady* magazine and *Horse and Hound*. So, not only would it have been thoroughly unprofessional to have asked, say, Nina, out for lunch, but even if they had gone out for lunch, and even in the unlikely event that they'd hit it off, he just didn't have time for a relationship!

But, off on a slight tangent… What would it be like dating a stripper?

Just let's not go there! Not going to happen. Not ever going to happen.

Pook's music is coming in waves, seems to be hammering Glenn. The girls' hands move to their throats. The golden cloak chains are unclipped, and in a synchronised swoosh the cloaks drop to the floor. As one, the girls transform from bent penitents to brazen beauties, shoulders squared and masked heads held high. The rear of the G-strings were so negligible they might as well have not been there, just a thin line of black floss.

One thing Glenn enjoyed about an actual take was that, for a very short time, he could relax. In between takes, he was running around like a blue-arsed fly, sorting the lights, the actors, sorting all the million and one other things that needed to be sorted. But for that brief interlude of a take, he could enjoy the live theatre that was being conducted right in front of his eyes. And... weren't the girls looking just terrific?! They were carrying themselves like Guards officers, just a knockout, and as for Nina, she was just spectacular, like, incredibly beautiful, and with her long hair cascading over her shoulders... not that he was even remotely affected by her beauty, but more important by far was that she seemed like a really lovely woman, genuine, and wry, and—

'Cut!'

And what the hell was he thinking of – just pull yourself together, you daft mutt...

Since it had been their first full rehearsal, Kubrick was giving the team a pep talk. 'Wonderful,' he said. 'Just wonderful, better than I dared hope. Quite, quite magical. Thank you...'

He continued to burble. The girls were picking up their cloaks. What toned legs Nina had, what a gorgeous—

Kubrick was beckoning him over. 'The lights aren't quite right on Red Cloak,' he said. 'Let's do it again.'

'Absolutely,' Glenn said, daydream well and truly snuffed.

They did it again and they did it again. The other rehearsals were all very good, but for Glenn, there was nothing to touch that moment when the cloaks had first fallen to the floor. The girls had been transformed into powerful, sassy women.

At the gym the next morning, Glenn went through the usual routine. It was a very peculiar dance that they performed. He, certainly, was aware that it was a dance, and the beautiful thing about this dance was that, although seemingly oblivious, Nina was also a performer.

Not that Glenn was even remotely a man of routine, but, give or take two minutes, he normally hit the gym at 10 a.m. He then spent ten minutes warming up on the StairMaster or the running machine. During this warm-up session, Nina would arrive. She always warmed up on one of the exercise bikes. And she always had her hair in a ponytail and she always wore basketball gear, not just the long baggy shorts and the shirt, but all the way down to the socks and the shoes. She seemed to own about three different basketball shirts, and today's shirt was the Chicago Bulls. Guess she played basketball. Big shirts though. Almost man-size…

It being, he believed, a Tuesday, this was the day for his high-intensity work out. After warming up on the StairMaster, he'd pick up a couple of twenty-kilo dumb-bells and do arm curls for a couple of minutes. Then back to the StairMaster and do one minute as hard as he could. Plod to one of the machines, the lats one this time, set the right weight, start pulling the bar down and Nina just happened to be directly in front of him, over by the windows. She was holding a plank position. She could really hold a plank position, like two or three minutes. She'd beat him out of sight!

Back to the StairMaster for another one-minute pounding. He'd started to sweat now, drops popping on his forehead. Back to the quad machine, no maybe the bicep one, oh and look, there was Nina again doing the clean and jerk – superb technique.

Their movements were always perfectly choreographed, so that they never came within twenty metres of each other. If Nina was on the dumb-bells, Glenn would head straight for the pull-up bars; if Nina was on the StairMaster, he would divert to the running machine. This was how it had been for at least the last week, never once talking to each other, not a hint of eye contact, both in their own worlds, both exercising as if the other did not exist. There were other people in the gym too, and these people were also ignored; but the difference for Glenn was that he was not aware of them. They did not register. He'd barely have recognised them if he'd seen them out on the street half an hour later.

But with Nina, he didn't even have to look up to know where she was. He presumed it was mutual. You can't avoid someone for over a week without them also wanting to avoid you. And that was not only understandable but great. Gyms were sacred spaces, where people could just get on with their exercise without being pestered or having people – worse, bosses – coming over and saying hello.

And back to the StairMaster, and then, avoid going anywhere near the lats machine, because someone with a ponytail was using it, and instead head over to the skiing machine, apparently very useful for practising your cross-country skiing – and repeat, and repeat, and after a final session on the StairMaster, sweat now freely dripping off his chin, he went for a five-minute wind-down on one of the vibrating platforms, where his legs would be given a rough massage, and where he would stare straight up at the ceiling thinking about not very much… thinking about Nina. Did she think about him as much as he thought about her? While she was doing her weights or her lats, did she allow her eyes to wander over to where he was. Nah, probably not, probably dreaming up the plot of her next novel.

He went off for a shower, aware without needing to look that Nina had already left the gym.

Glenn had his shower and shaved and brushed his teeth. He left the men's changing room. In order to reach the exit, he had to walk past the café. Nina was seated at a table. She was drinking a cup of coffee and reading a paper, *The Guardian* from the look of it. She happened to look up. They caught each other's eye. Glenn smiled and she smiled. He gave her a brief nod and he was quickly on his way – out of the club and out into the sunshine, and not even remotely nettled.

CHAPTER 10

The run changed everything.

The run changed it for me – for Nina, for Glenn. Most particularly, the run changed things for Tom Cruise.

I'd been signed up five weeks earlier, getting the call-up from one of the smaller London extra agencies, and I was now going by my second name, Lawrence. It was unlikely, of course, that any of my fellow supporting artists would recognise the name of that outstanding *Sun* reporter Kim, but best not to take any chances.

We'd been on night shoots for nearly three weeks. Not that I'd ever been on a film set before, but night shoots are a real pain – though as with everything else about Stanley, our displeasure was his purpose. And since the entire shoot had so far been built around night shoots, he wasn't going to stop now that the crew had moved to Elveden Hall. Most days we'd start at 6 p.m., and if we were lucky we'd be wrapped by 2 a.m., when we would skulk back to our beds. I was always so wired that it took me ages to get to sleep. The night shoots certainly put paid to the girls' nightlife in Bury St Edmunds. Those poor local lads – all those cases of aftershave and deodorant, all those fancy rags, and all of it now suddenly gone to waste.

Anyway, Kubrick had been filming now for about a fortnight, and his sex-starved (and mainly male) crew had finally got to feast their peepers on the twelve topless beauties – and I myself had also made a quiet inspection of the lovelies, and very nice they looked too, though believe it or not, I always found them more beguiling when they wore their beautiful cloaks of midnight blue.

I had been cast in the same role as the other extras: we were all seedy old lechers perving on the girls as they stripped to their G-strings. We all wore masks and monks' cloaks in black. My mask was a particularly fetching number in red, with an angry expression and a gaping mouth such as you might find on a farmer yelling "Git orf my land!" With the masks on and the cowls up, you couldn't tell one man from the next.

The call-time was generally 6 p.m., when it was already dark, but since I was keen, and since I was a *Sun* reporter athirst for gossip, I was usually on set soon after lunch. I'd been so desperate to get out of the *Sun* newsroom that I'd actually arrived at Elveden Hall a full week before the extras were due. I tried to make myself useful – getting in teas and coffees, doing errands, occasionally driving into Bury St Edmund's to pick up stuff. I was the runners' underling. If they wanted to put their feet up, I was more than happy to do their chores. Along the way, I made it my business to be as disarmingly charming as it is possible for a *Sun* reporter to be. Within two weeks, I knew the names of every one of the crew and the extras – though with the girls one had to tread warily, because we'd all been explicitly warned that if there was even so much as a hint of harassment, we would, like Adam and Eve, be cast out of this Eden of sex. I'd occasionally talk to the girls, but I kept the conversation as straight and sexless as if I'd been chatting to my granny. Nina was my favourite – well, she was not just a reader, she was also a writer. (Us artists, we do what we can to look after our fellow creatives.) As for Tom Cruise and Stanley Kubrick, I didn't see so much of them in the first month. Glenn, the assistant director, had told us that, as regards Cruise and Kubrick, we were to treat them like royalty: we were only to speak to them if they had first spoken to us.

After a month, then, I had won round not just Glenn (by dint of being generally keen, up for it and non-whiny), the second assistant director Roddie (via a constant supply of snacks and treats that I kept about my person) and most especially Molly, the restive caterer, with whom I would sit knee to knee and peel potatoes and carrots, and would occasionally bring her a bunch of flowers with which to titivate her hatch.

One person and one person only failed to warm to my charms and that was Jimmy, Tom Cruise's stand-in. Perhaps he had divined a fellow rogue. I gave him a wide berth, easy in the knowledge that, given enough rope, such reprobates usually contrive to hang themselves.

There was a large elephant in the room, ever present, always lurking on the periphery of our senses, though which was never once mentioned: sex. Ironic to think how we were filming the world's longest orgy, but that the senior crew never talked about the main action that usually tends to occur during an orgy. The general attitude to sex was that we were all of us consenting adults, and that so long as it didn't affect our work, then we were all free to have sex with whomsoever would have us. If that happened to be with one of Kubrick's twelve beauties, then fill your boots!

As far as I knew, only one of the twelve girls had a lover, and that was Vicky, who quickly fell for that smooth hound Jimmy. Well, it was hardly surprising – Kubrick had had them practising a single masked kiss for three days straight, with Vicky topless throughout!

After a few days of night-shooting, I quickly got into a routine. All the extras were staying in and around Bury St Edmunds– though unlike the girls, we were having to pay for own board and accommodation. For the bulk of the extras, this meant staying at cheap B&Bs, but since I was going to be claiming every last penny that I spent on my *Sun* expenses, I was staying at the very upmarket Angel, which was where a lot of the crew were also putting up.

Most days, I'd get up at around 10 a.m. and go for a

run – not that I'm an exercise junkie, but being on set is so sedentary that if you didn't exercise you'd go stir-crazy and be putting on a kilo a week.

Tell you one thing about film sets: you'll never go hungry. Molly and her team were cooking enough food for a small army – starters, mains, puddings, salads, cheese boards, cakes, biscuits, muffins, you name it, they'd got it, and if you liked your food then Molly was always there with seconds or even thirds. (As for Kubrick, he, bizarrely, tended to have the same meal over and over again – liver and onions, it was, delivered personally to his Winnebago by the pneumatic Molly. She used to spend ages with him, though I could never fathom why. Perhaps she was personally spoon-feeding the liver and onions into the great man's maw.

I'd try and run about five miles, heading out on the B-roads before loping along the country footpaths. Back by 11 a.m., with time for a shower and coffee and a late breakfast. Roddie, the second assistant director, often used to join me for those breakfasts. We'd sit opposite each other in companionable silence while I read the papers and Roddie worked his way through a full English and completed the *Times* cryptic crossword. As I remember him now, I think those breakfasts were one of the high points of his day, just him and his food and his crossword, and me bringing him another latte; for a short while, Roddie was free from the demands of his demented director.

After breakfast, I'd return to my room and type up the Tom Cruise gossip from the previous day, though for the first few weeks, I'd only unearthed the barest scraps. Tom was the consummate pro who turned up on time and who did what was asked of him. Unfortunately for the gossip-mongers like me, Cruise did not tend to spend any time chatting to his fellow thespians.

Notes written up, I might mooch into Bury St Edmunds for a light lunch. Other extras and sometimes the girls would also be loitering around town, and as often as not, we'd have a soup together or a quick sandwich. By 3 p.m., I'd be back at Elveden Hall – a full three hours before our call time – there to do all the weaselly things that a tabloid reporter so loves to do: schmoozing the bosses and gossiping over a cup of coffee.

That's how it was for week after week, every day all but identical as Mondays and Sundays blurred into the same day over and over again, and that's how it would have continued had it not been for the day of the long run, and after the day of the long run, everything was different.

It was a Sunday in October. The reason I could tell it was a Sunday was because most of the shops were closed. I was off on my daily run, but this run was going to be a little longer than the usual five-milers. I'd had it in mind to run the Great North Run in Newcastle, so that morning was set on running eight miles. I'd planned the route on an Ordnance Survey map. I'd be running along the old drovers' roads and had every hope of seeing Suffolk at its most picturesque.

My running gear in those days consisted of Lycra leggings (to stop my chubby thighs chafing), baggy shorts (for modesty's sake), an orange-coloured wicking T-shirt (to avoid the bleeding nipples that come with damp cotton) and lastly my white socks and my "support" running shoes (a must for overpronators). On that day of days, it was all fresh out of the hotel laundry; for once I smelt not of stale sweat but of floral conditioner.

Glenn was already up, though he preferred the gym to my country runs. He was on the phone to his mum, so I quietly placed a triple espresso in front of him. He mouthed a thank you and I went off to a corner table to enjoy my own triple espresso. They always say the hardest part of a run is that first step out of the front door – and it's true. I would delay the moment and delay the moment, eking out the coffee to the last drop, or indeed chatting to anyone who would chat.

Glenn flopped into the chair at my table. Interestingly, he'd never have done this if I'd been one of the girls. Although he was always courteous to the girls, he kept himself as formal as the Elveden Hall butler. He never really chatted with the girls – and in that first month at Elveden, at least, he was doing his level best to behave like a human cyborg, not a drop of red blood in him. He was not in any way going to allow himself to be tempted – and I can tell you there was a lot of temptation. Swayed by all those beautiful swaying naked women – no, sirreee! When it came to the girls, he'd decided to model himself on Darcy, the stiff hunk from Pride and Prejudice.

With the chaps, however, and even with the lowest minions like myself, Glenn was positively engaging.

'I don't know many people who call their mum every day, but you do, and I think it's wonderful,' I said.

'Haven't seen her for nearly a year,' he said. 'The least I can do.'

'How is she?'

'Happy as a clam,' he said. 'She's just being taken to church.'

'She actually enjoys church?'

He took a sip of his triple espresso, decided it needed sugar. 'I can't think of anything she doesn't enjoy.'

'Wish I could be like that – there's tons of things I don't enjoy, and lots of things I hate.'

'What do you hate, then, Lawrence?'

'I hate being sworn at. I hate treading in dog shit. Worse than that, I hate getting back home and discovering that I've trodden in dog shit. I hate tripe. I hate black pudding. I hate litter louts. In fact, I hate louts in all their guises. I hate rude people—'

'I'll give you that one,' he laughed. 'Even my mum hates rudeness. Anything you hate about this movie?'

'No,' I said. 'I completely adore it.'

'Not irked by Stanley's multiple takes?'

'We, Glenn, are making something magnificent – it's a privilege to be a part of it.'

'That we are,' he said.

'Are you in a relationship, if you don't mind my asking?'

'I wish!' he said. 'Though if I was, my girlfriend might be getting just a little frustrated.'

'What if... what if...' I mused with my most pensive face. 'What if she was working on the same movie as you?'

'Yeah, that's a great idea!' he snickered. "What if she was an incredibly beautiful pole-dancer?'

'Now that is a great idea,' I said. 'Why should Jimmy get to have all the fun?'

'Away with you!' he said, getting to his feet as he hurled a napkin in my face.

'Don't tell me you haven't thought about it!'

'You're incorrigible!' he said, strolling off to his beastly weights and leaving me to ponder on why anyone would want to go to a gym when they could be outside running in the rain.

I drained my coffee to the last drop, but since my juices still weren't juiced, I reached over to another table to pick up a discarded copy of one of the Sunday papers, the *Sunday Express*. Hah – the *Sunday Express*! This once great rag is now a mere shadow of the paper it once was, but in the 1990s it still had a little clout – and indeed could still run stories that were capable of vexing Tom Cruise. They had one hell of a spicy story; even in all my *Sun* pomp, I'd never have dared run with it. The story claimed that Tom and Nicole's marriage was one of passionless convenience; that they'd either got married on the say-so of the Church of Scientology or because one or both of them was gay; that Tom was impotent or sterile and they'd adopted their two kids on a mere flight of fancy. For good measure, the story had claimed you couldn't trust a word they said unless they'd been wired up to a lie detector. Strong stuff! Why – the story made Mr and Mrs Cruise sound even more repellent than a *Sun* news reporter!

A perfectly sensational start to my day. I'd heard a couple of these Tom and Nicole rumours before, but had dismissed them as nothing more than Hollywood chatter. But to have actually run with this flim-flam? The *Sunday Express* was in it up to its ruddy neck!

Buoyed by this excellent news, I ambled over to the hotel entrance. It really was raining – raining quite hard. If I'd been a lightweight, I'd have abandoned the run and gone back to bed – but then if I'd done that, there would be no story to tell.

I started out in a slow jog, just keeping it light and easy; with not much traffic about, the town was all my own. I followed the river, and within five minutes I was so wet that I might as well have been in the river. The first ten minutes of a run is always hard work. Your body's adjusting to all this ill-advised exertion, and it spends at least ten minutes complaining before eventually it knuckles under. After a few miles, you can very occasionally experience feelings of joy, even euphoria; do not worry, this feeling will soon pass.

After a couple of miles in the rain, I had warmed up a little. I can't say it was much fun running in the rain – all that picturesque countryside was rather lost in the cloud and mist. I wished I'd worn my lightweight coat – in fact, I must have been mad to just go out in my wicking shirt. My mesh shoes may have been perfect for overpronators, but they were also perfectly useless at keeping out the water.

What I'd do was run another mile. Then I'd take stock of how I was feeling, and either I'd quit or I would manfully continue with the run. Maybe if I ran faster, I'd get home quicker – now there was a thought! Surprising, frankly, that more runners hadn't cottoned onto this brilliant strategy.

I ran faster, socks and shoes now so totally soaked that I was splish-splashing straight through the puddles, just me alone in the morning rain, the only person in the world mad enough to be running in such a downpour, and as I got to that third mile, and as I took stock, I realised that I was enjoying myself, and was enjoying being hammered in the face by the driving rain, and though I was not quite totally euphoric, the run had taken on its own giddy madness. I could not help myself but continue.

When you run up to a gate, there are a number of things you can do. You can open it; you can sedately climb over it; or, if full of vim, you can vault it. The leading arm flies over and in one smooth, fluid movement, you follow with both legs.

I still don't really know what happened. I'd vaulted at least three gates. I was trotting up this drovers' road, which was very muddy with overgrown hedges, festoons of mistletoe in the tree tops and all overlaid with the lush scent of the countryside. The gate was an old wooden five-bar gate, higher than the others, green with slick lichen. I trotted up to the gate, leaned over and grabbed the second bar. It was so high I couldn't swing my feet clean over. I planted one foot on top of the gate and was following with the other when my foot slipped, and I remember this split second of bemused astonishment as I realised that I was going to hit my head on the gate, and that it was going to be a very hard knock indeed, and that if I didn't look out I was also going to hit my head on the large concrete block on the other side of the gate, and I still don't know if I hit my head on just the gate or both the block and the gate, but the upshot was still the same as I knocked myself clean out, one moment this sleek runner in the rain, and the next, nothing but a dead meat lump lying in the mud.

CHAPTER 11

Now as for our star – the world's hottest star (lest we forget), Tom Cruise – are we allowed to delve into his mind and to see what he makes of Mr Hundred Takes? Are we allowed to know how he feels about Nicole and Elveden and the twelve topless beauties who will be working with him for at least the next three months?

Are we allowed?

Why, of course we are! For this is a fairy story: we may do as we please!

So how is Tom getting on with Stanley Kubrick? Is he, like Glenn, thriving on this never-ending shoot? Does he lick his lips as Kubrick demands that he walk through a doorway again for the ninety-fifth time? Does he enjoy working with the man who is widely acknowledged as the world's greatest living director (and possibly even the greatest director of all time)? Is Tom enjoying all this quality time in rural England with Nicole as they immerse themselves in this great and glorious project?

Well, is he?

No, he is not! He is absolutely hating it – why on earth did he sign up for this project without end when the whole thing was never even remotely his cup of tea? Tom likes running and fighting and killing people, and the stilted, slow-moving (and, dare we say it, dreamlike) choreography of *Eyes Wide Shut* is not really cutting it. He can do it, of course he can do it, because he is, after all, a pretty useful actor. But all this hanging around waiting for Kubrick to make his damn mind up?

Tom. Not. Happy.

Tell you the truth, this shoot (eleven months and counting) has been so stressful it's given Tom a stomach ulcer! Tom hasn't told Stanley yet, because he doesn't want to delay the shoot and the fact is that Tom is in nearly every single scene in the film – save for one, and let's get it out there right now, this big beast of a scene had been hanging heavy on Tom's mind.

The scene was, well, basically, all of Nic's sexual fantasies made flesh. A few months earlier, Tom had been told in no uncertain terms that he was not to go anywhere near the set while Kubrick personally filmed the scene.

Though Nic had been ordered not to talk about what had happened on the shoot, Tom did know a little about it. Nic had been absolutely naked, apart from a lush merkin (a merkin indeed? Before starting out on *Eyes Wide Shut*, Tom had also never come across the word before. It is a pubic wig). The scene had involved a large number of different sexual positions, possibly even as many as fifty, though apparently there had been no oral sex, as Kubrick had (thankfully) deemed it a "cinematic cliché". But still – fifty different sexual positions? That was half the fricking Kama Sutra! Not that Tom was counting, but… he did wonder if he and Nic had even notched up half that number of different positions during the whole of their seven-year marriage.

Oh yes, one last thing: the guy with whom Nic had been partaking in this sexual marathon, one Gary Goba, a supremely hunky Canadian model, not only taller than Tom but five years younger and – ahhh, shall we just say – pretty well put together?

Such hopes he'd had when they'd embarked on *Eyes Wide Shut* just over two years ago. Such dreams! And now, just like a marriage, it had evolved into this never-ending treadmill.

Kubrick had begun his courtship of Tom and Nicole in the spring of 1995. It started with a fax – would Tom and Nicole perhaps be interested in working together on a future Kubrick project? If so, he looked forward to sending them a script in the next few months.

Tom and Nicole nearly bit Kubrick's hand off. Tom was so thrilled that he had Kubrick's fax framed and put in pride of place on his glory wall. Eventually the script arrived. Tom and Nic read it together and, even after the first page, they absolutely loved it. They were in.

A few months later, they met Kubrick for the first time. Nic had been filming *Portrait of a Lady* in London, so they'd taken a helicopter to Childwickbury Manor, Kubrick's sprawling mansion near St Albans. The great man had been out there on the lawn waiting for them, suitably dressed for the occasion in a filthy old blue boiler suit. Nic had been very nervous – this was it! If they kept it tight, they were about to land the big one, and the two greatest actors on the planet would be teaming up with the world's greatest director to create what would ineluctably become (speak it softly) the Greatest Goddamn Movie the World Had Ever Seen!

After they'd climbed out of the helicopter, and clumsily shaken hands, Kubrick led the way into Childwickbury's living room. There were a lot of cats around, lounging on sofas and plumped pillows, but apart from the cats there didn't appear to be a soul in the place.

Even now, two years on, Tom wasn't sure if Kubrick's shyness was genuine or if it had just been part of the game. Very long pauses as he spoke, almost a diffidence. What Tom hadn't realised then (but certainly realised now) was that, though he and Nic had been keen to do the project, Kubrick had been absolutely desperate to have them both on board. Kubrick had been sizing Nicole up for over a year, had demanded showreels and all the rest from her agent before finally making his move.

Kubrick had offered to fix them something to drink, and they'd each had a glass of water. Nic had been too nervous to drink. They'd sat down on a sofa in the living room, and

Kubrick sat on an armchair opposite them, with a wooden coffee table in between. Just as with everything else, Tom only realised much later that it had all been perfectly choreographed beforehand.

Nic and Tom had held hands. Kubrick had initially done most of the talking, like a fat spider spinning its most magnificent web. Tom and Nic had been the foolhardy flies who had delightedly enmeshed themselves in its silken strands. Tom could still remember one of Kubrick's more beguiling lines – "This film is about sexual obsession and jealousy," he'd said. "It is not about sex." Yeah – right. Well try telling that to the porn stars who'd be miming sex in Highclere Castle. Try telling that to Gary goddamn Goba.

After that first meeting, Kubrick could have spun them any baloney he liked. They signed on the line – not bad money, could have made more – but why, why, why had they signed up for a shoot without an end date? Why? Well, because though Tom had thought the shoot might last a year, maybe, tops. It hadn't even occurred to him that they'd be filming for two Christmases straight. One thing he knows for sure: *Eyes Wide Shut* might not turn out to be the greatest movie of all time, but it was sure as hell panning out to be the longest shoot in film history!

Tom knew a little bit about OCD behaviour – though he didn't like to call it that. He liked to call it perfectionism, and Tom was a self-confessed perfectionist. The scientific term for this, as coined by Sigmund Freud, was "anankastic" – and its chief characteristics included, amongst other things, an excessive devotion and indeed extreme conscientiousness towards work, as well as a reluctance to delegate. Not that Tom was anankastic in every aspect of his life, not with the kids, but when it came to his craft and his art, then he liked things to be done perfectly. If things weren't done perfectly, if a take wasn't spot on, then he'd want it to be redone – and redone, and if necessary redone until it was perfect. That's just the way he was.

Tom had met plenty of other perfectionists over the years, had always rather prided himself on seeking a higher degree of perfection than any of his peers. But then he met Kubrick, and realised that he had at last met his match. Kubrick was the king. He didn't just want perfection, he demanded total obedience – both on and off the set. He stipulated when Tom and Nic could spend time with each other. He told them what they could – and could not – talk about with each other. He did not allow either of them on set when the other was filming alone.

He'd even got the set designer to base their *Eyes Wide Shut* bedroom on their actual bedroom! Had insisted that it be filled with genuine stuff from Tom and Nicole's real home. And then, so that they could feel right at home in their film studio bedroom, he'd ordered them to spend a few nights there.

In well over a decade of movie-making, he'd never ever heard of anything like it. It was bat-shit crazy! And there was precisely nothing Tom could do about it, and there was nothing Nic could do about it. They were stuck with this mad genius, and they were stuck with him until the day that Kubrick had had his fill of toying with them.

For the duration of the Elveden Hall shoot, Tom was being put up in a handsome country cottage just outside Bury St Edmunds – always food in the fridge, always spotless when he was chauffeured back home at three or four in the morning. Since Nic wasn't allowed anywhere near the set, she'd taken the kids off to the Lake District – and that meant that, for weeks now, Tom only ever spoke to about four or five people. He spoke to Kevin who drove him back and forth to the set. He spoke to his make-up woman, Terri, who was lovely, and his hair guy, Andy. And of course he spoke to Stanley Kubrick, though you couldn't really describe it as a conversation. Felt like more of a psychotherapy session – in fact, you know what it felt like? It felt like Tom was a fly, and every day, Kubrick would come along and, in the most leisurely fashion, pull his wings off, and then, for good measure, pull off all his legs.

And then overnight, after the whole horror shoot was over, Tom's wings and legs would grow back again Prometheus-like, just so that the next afternoon Kubrick could have the pleasure of pulling them all off again.

Now, not that Tom was ever going to start feeling sorry for himself. He'd gotten himself into this hellfire position – and the only reason he was in this position with Kubrick was because he was the biggest star on the planet. If he hadn't been the biggest star, then, by definition, Kubrick wouldn't have been interested in him.

But sometimes, as he stood there on the set, aloof and alone, not a soul daring to say a word to the great Tom Cruise, he did envy the easy camaraderie of the extras. In between the million and one takes, they'd just be chatting away, not a care in the world, not minding in the slightest whether they were there at Elveden for two weeks or two months. The girls, beautiful, all but naked, would wrap themselves in their blue cloaks and would sit down on the red carpet and sip carefree tea. The crew would banter, Kubrick would be fussing away with Glenn over the lights or the cameras, but as for Tom, he could do one of three things in between takes. He could either stand on his mark; or sit in his personalised canvas chair; or return to his Winnebago, to read scripts of films that one day, when Kubrick gave him his freedom, he might yet be allowed to star in.

The morning, when he went out for a run, was probably his favourite time of the day – just him, alone with his musings. He had quickly learned that it was best to run without a phone, because when he did have his phone, Kubrick could call him, and when Kubrick called, it was never good news. So after a couple of weeks, he'd just stopped running with his phone, and, for an hour or so, he was just a nobody; kinda funny that everybody else wanted to be a somebody, and yet what he sought in those distant greener grass fields was namelessness. Well – not that he'd want it all the time. Being a star did come with one or two odd perks – like, you know, the cash, the clout and the constant adulation – but, for a little while, he wouldn't mind having a taste of this thing that he hadn't tried since he was a teenager: anonymity.

Running gave him a little anonymity. With his hoodie up and his sunglasses, he was just any other runner, though this one particular morning, with the rain, wearing sunglasses would have been patently ridiculous. Not that it mattered – in this rain, in this deep countryside, there was not a soul to be seen.

He was running down an old track, which might have been a drover's road. The drovers, he understood, had for hundreds of years used these old tracks to drive their sheep and their geese and their cattle into the market towns. It was very muddy, overgrown hedges, festoons of mistletoe in the tree tops and all overlaid with the lush scent of the countryside. Not far ahead was a five-bar gate that was green with slick lichen...

CHAPTER 12

The last time I'd been knocked out had been in the Ladbroke Arms in oh-so upmarket Notting Hill. I'd been going down with a cold for the previous couple of days, but, ever the diligent hard-working reporter, I continued to show up at work. All day I'd been scurrying from the hot to the cold, sweltering indoors, freezing outside, must have been into about twenty hot offices in the day, followed each time, by twenty windswept streets. I should have gone straight back home to bed, but instead I went along to the Ladbroke Arms for a sharpener. I ordered a toddy and was sitting at a chair by the bar. The next moment I fainted clean away, giving my head a stout rap on the bar as I slumped to the floor.

At least I'd managed to knock myself out in a warm pub and there was no shortage of people to help me out. (I actually felt a bit hard done by. They thought I was drunk, couldn't get me into a taxi quick enough. Honestly! Do I look like the sort of person who gets sozzled at lunchtime?)

But this time, down that old drovers' road, even as my head was about to collide with that large concrete block, I knew it was going to be bad. It was cold and it was wet and I was at least three miles from civilisation.

Someone was talking to me. At first I couldn't understand what he was saying, but then the words gradually coalesced and I could hear him. 'Are you OK, buddy? Are you OK?'

First I heard the words, calm, reassuring – this guy's got this thing sorted. I might have drifted into unconsciousness again. He kept on talking, his words riding on the cusp of my conscious hearing, 'You hang in there buddy, you're going to be fine.' As I came to my senses, I was thinking to myself, 'That sounds a lot like Tom Cruise. He'll do the business.'

I opened my eyes. I was looking at some grass. He'd got me on my side in the recovery position. My head hurt like hell. It felt like I'd had two big hits, one on each side of my face – as if my head had been sandwiched by a particularly violent cymbal player.

I coughed and spat out a bit of blood. It was still raining. It might even have been sleeting. I was shivering.

'Easy there,' he said. 'Easy.'

'Hiiii,' I said, slurred punch-drunk words.

I rolled myself flat onto my back. The eyes, the mouth, the tousle of black hair under the hoodie. Took a little while to register that Hollywood's biggest star, Tom Cruise, was on his knees next to me. He looked mighty concerned.

'Eyyy,' I slurred. 'Tommmmy!'

He didn't baulk at being called Tommy – frankly I could have called him anything I liked, and I think he'd have stuck with me.

'Hey, how you doing, man?' he said. 'Think you can move?'

'Yeaaahhh Tommy,' I said. I was feeling pretty light-headed. Words were burbling out of my mouth, but I didn't seem to have much control over what I was saying.

'Look, we've got to get you out of the rain. I could run for help, but that's going to be a bad idea. I'm going to try and get you up.'

'Thanksss Tommy.'

'It'll be easiest if you're on all fours. Then I'll help you get up.'

'Sure, Tommmmmy,' I said. 'Loved ya in *Top Gun*! But ya sucked in *Daaays of Thunda*.'

He chuckled as he helped me onto all fours. '*Days of Thunder* was not my finest hour.'

'*The Firm*!' I said. 'That wasssh... that wasssh a good 'un!'

'Loved that one!' He got his hands in my armpits and heaved me up. I was standing now, but pretty groggy on my feet – a dropped boxer trying to beat the count 'Put your arm over my shoulder,' he said. 'We're going to have to walk back.'

'Sure Tommmmy!' I said. We started stumbling off down the old drovers' road. 'Where we... where we going?'

'We're going back to the set – you're a supporting artist, aren't you? You always look like you're having a great time.' We tramped through the mud. I was leaning heavily on his shoulder. No way I could have done it without him.

''At's cos I am having a great time,' I said. 'Love that movie. Love those girls.'

'Those girls are something,' he said. 'I don't really get to speak to them.'

'Heyyy Tommy,' I said. 'You should try it man! They'd love ta chat. No one dares speak to ya!'

'Guess that's right.' I stumbled over a branch and nearly pulled the pair of us over into the mud.

'Easy there, champ,' he said. 'What's your name?'

'I'm... I'm Lawrence,' I said, before suddenly recollecting my manners. 'Hey, is it... s'OK calling you Tommy?'

He laughed again. Looking back on it, I think he was actually enjoying himself. Most of his life was micromanaged down to the last second, and now here he was covered in mud, lashed by rain, and for once in the middle of a genuine adventure. 'Sure, you can call me Tommy,' he said. 'My mom calls me Tommy.'

'Mums – ain't they... ain't they the greatest?' I said.

I can't remember much of the walk. Some of the time I was lucid and some of the time I was like a stumbling sleepwalker. At one stage I was struck by the most astonishing thought. 'I can't... I can't believe it!' I said. 'Tom Cruise saved my life!' I let out a shriek of crazy-man laughter. 'Tommy... Tommmy... ya saved my life, man! What a story! What a great story!'

Thankfully, Tom didn't think to question what I meant by "What a great story", which was lucky, as in my punch-drunk state, I'd probably have blurted out the excellent idea that had already wormed its way into my pea-sized brain: this was one hell of a story! It had splash and a spread all over it – "Tom Cruise Saved My Life!", along with a tasty follow-up the next day of a picture of me cuddling up to my superstar life-saver. It was brilliant! Even if the whole of this *Eyes Wide Shut* story went belly up, I still had more than enough to achieve that one beautiful thing that I had been set on this earth to do: Make. Spike. Happy.

'Ya... ya saved many people's lives, Tommy?' I said.

'No, can't say I have, Lawrence,' he said. 'You're my first.'

'You're my hero,' I said – and I know that generally, when we say "You're my hero", we're being either sarcastic or deeply ironic, but on this occasion, I meant it.

He laughed again. I had a real good close-up of those world-famous teeth and that full throaty laugh. 'I've played lots of heroes —'

'Yeahhhh!' I said. 'That *Mission: Impossible* fella, he... he was a hero. Didn't like all the rubber face masks... them masks was bollocks.'

'I didn't think it was too bad, Lawrence,' he said.

Aware that Tom might have taken offence at me slagging off his latest blockbuster, I tried to make amends. 'Hey but... Hey! Great film though! Loved that film! Good music!' I started singing the Mission: Impossible theme – 'Dum, Dum – Da-Da-Dum-Dum! Eyyyy! Tommy! Aintcha gonna join me?'

'Course I will,' he said, humouring this concussed idiot, and the next moment, the great Tom Cruise was giving me the top notes of *Mission: Impossible* – beautiful moment, wish I'd had it on film, because when I tell people now, they never believe me. But it's true: I sang the *Mission: Impossible* theme with Tom Cruise and he did all the high notes. (Quite melodiously too.)

We stumbled up to another five-bar gate. It was locked.

'Here's a gate, Tommy,' I said.

'Now how, Lawrence, are we going to get you over this?' he said.

'Ah, just leave me, Tommy,' I said. I was suddenly overcome with weariness, and there seemed like nothing on earth that would be so supremely satisfying as curling up in the wet undergrowth and falling asleep.

'Naah, I'm not leaving you,' Tom said. 'I'm loving your chat.'

'Yeah,' I said. 'Me chatty.'

I slumped against the side of the gate, cradling my head on my arms. My head really hurt.

'OK, Lawrence, this is what we're going to do,' he said. 'I'm going to lift you up over the gate, and you're going to perch on the middle. Got that?'

'Yeah.'

'Then I'm going to jump over, help you down on the other side. We cool?'

'Cool,' I said. 'Cool as a... cool as a... cool as a cucumber cocktail.'

'OK, easy does it.' He grabbed me round the midriff, grunted me up and then flopped me half over the gate. He swung a leg over so I was straddling the gate. 'Easy there,' he said. He vaulted over the gate. I started to slip over. 'Easy there!' He lunged to catch me. 'Easy!' He took the brunt of my fall on his back and we ended up in a heap in the mud at the bottom of the gate. He rolled over, and for a moment we were both just flat on our backs staring up at the dripping trees. I think I took his hand. It was quite nice holding hands and lying in the mud in the rain and just staring up at nothing at all.

'Hey T... Tommy,' I said. 'How many more... more gates we got?'

'One or two,' he said. 'Don't think about that.'

'Yeah,' I said. 'Just think about the... the next step.'

'That's right,' he said.

'Cuz… cuz if I thought about all the gates, I might give up.'

'You're funny,' he said.

'Hey, Tommy,' I said. 'Tell us a story. A true story.'

'Sure, I'll tell you a true story, Lawrence,' he said. 'But after I tell you the story, you've got to promise to get up.'

'Me get up,' I said.

We continued to lie in the mud and stare at the sky. 'You know,' he said. 'I'm quite enjoying myself.'

'Me too,' I said. 'Never held hands with a movie star before. I want my story.'

'Sure,' he said. 'Kubrick told me this story last month, so I guess it's true. He was telling me about the first big star he worked with, Kirk Douglas—'

'*Spartacus*,' I said. 'Love that. You're bigger than Kirk!'

'Thanks buddy,' he said. 'Now Kirk was quite a… a randy guy. He loved women—'

'Like his son Michael!' I said. 'He's a sex addict!'

'Quite,' Tommy said. 'So when Kirk was at the studio, he'd eye up all the tourists on the tours, and if there was a woman he took a shine to, he'd get his assistant to ask her if she'd like to meet the great Kirk Douglas. If she said "Yes—"

'Who wouldn't say "yes"?'

'She'd be taken off to meet him. Here's the clever bit. Kirk would chat to her five minutes, and then his assistant would come over and tell him that it was time for his make-up. Kirk would apologise to the woman, and then, on second thoughts, he'd ask her back to his truck so that they could continue to chat over a cup of tea.'

'And that's where he did the deed, the saucy dog!' I said. 'Guess so!'

'Bet you never did anything like that, Tommy?'

'Me? Never!' he said. 'Well… hardly ever!'

'Who wouldn't?'

'Here, let's get you up.'

'Not like it here in the mud?'

'We'll do it again at the next gate.'

He sprang to his feet and hauled me out of the mud. I was much more cold and noticeably more wobbly on my feet. He slung my arm over his shoulder and we tottered off again along the old drovers' road. I was barely capable of speaking. Tommy told me stories to keep my spirits up, sometimes stories about himself, mostly stories about Stanley. I wish I could remember more of what he'd told me, but most of it just went straight into the mulch. I can remember wiping the drool off my chin and realising that it was blood.

We'd got over another gate or two, and now we'd attacked a stile, a slightly different technique from a five-bar gate, but it ended the same way with both of us lying in the mud again, staring up at the scudding rain clouds.

'Hey Tommy,' I said, voice now considerably weaker. 'This is really nice what you're doing.'

'I'm loving it,' he said. 'I am, you know.'

'Thanks,' I said. 'Got any more stories about Stanley?'

'I got a shopful of Stanley stories.'

'I wan'… I wan' my Stanley stories.'

'He told me this really weird one about one of his girlfriends – might have been Ruth, his second wife. He's living in New York City with her, and he's finding the whole marriage thing stifling. It's killing him—'

'Killin' 'im.'

'Yeah, he's bored. He thinks it's all so mundane. So one night, he just packs his bag, packs it with all his gear and he leaves! He's this big tough macho guy and he's fed up, and he's out of there! He's walking down the street with this bag and it's getting heavier and heavier, and after a few minutes it's practically pulling his arm off! Know what he does?'

'Call a cab?'

'Naah,' says Tommy. 'He turns around and goes back home!' Tommy cackled with laughter. 'He just goes back home.'

'That funny,' I said. 'That the same story as what you do

in *Eyes Wide Shut*. You do nothing at your orgy. And you end up back home with your wife.'

'That… That's right!' Tommy said. 'That's right! Never thought about that before!'

'It's *Eyes Wide Shut*.'

'That's why Stanley wanted to make the film! Been wanting to make it for decades! And all because of what happened with Ruth.'

'Thasss right, Tommy.'

He sprang to his feet again. We were on quite a nice patch this time, not mud but wet grass, and the blades of grass tickled my cheeks. He grabbed hold of my hands, both hands this time, and pulled me up. I staggered and he caught me, and I ended up with my arms round him. 'Kimmy want hug,' I said.

'We got plenty of hugs for you,' he said, and even if I forget everything else about that interminable shoot at Elveden, that is one beautiful memory that I will treasure: standing there in the rain having a hug from Tom Cruise, and glancing down at his shoulder and idly registering that I was drooling blood all over him.

On and on we trudged, my head lolling, Tom chatting away, doing his best to keep my spirits up, but nothing was really going in. I remember, of all things, that he'd got on to two-letter words.

'Know what a gi is?'

'Naaaah.'

'It's a Judo garment,' Tom said. 'How about a bo? Know what that is?'

'Naaaah.'

'It's Scottish, Lawrence. A bo is a pal.'

'Yuh ma bo!'

'And you're my bo!' Tom laughed. 'Know why I know all these two-letter words?'

'Naaaah!' I said.

''Cos I'm learning them. There are ninety-seven two-letter words in the English language. I'm learning the lot.'

'Why you wanna do that?'

'I'll tell you, Lawrence.' He pulled my arm a little more over his shoulder so that I was tight in next to him. 'I've been playing a lot of Scrabble with my wife Nic, and you know what, I've never ever beaten her. But when I've learned all the two-letter words, well, then I'll have a chance!'

'Tommy will win!'

'Yeah!' he said. 'Tommy will win! OK – here's another one. What's a xu?'

'I know dat!' I said. 'Vietnam coin.'

'It is!' Tom said, and started giving me definitions of an od and an ai, and though I still have no idea what they are, he certainly succeeded in keeping me conscious, somehow managing to put one foot in front of the other. After I don't know how long, we came to another gate, and this one pleasingly was not chained up. Tom opened it, and we were now off the drovers' road and walking along a track by a field, and in the distance the hall hove into view.

The first person to see us was one of the security guys, and he was in the process of ordering us off the set when he realised that he was talking to Tom Cruise. 'Give us a hand,' Tom said. 'We need to get Lawrence to my trailer.'

I have an arm round each of them, and they are now pretty much dragging me, my feet trailing along the ground. There in front of us is Tom's Winnebago. He pulls me in, blood dripping onto the carpet and the nice creamy chair, and I can hear Tom asking for a car, and now that I'm home and dry I pass out. A vague instinct tells me that I'm in a car, head smacking against the window, and I look over to see that Tom's driving – Tom's driving me to the hospital! That's nice of him. Snapshots of Tom pushing me into the hospital in a wheelchair, and the doctors suddenly galvanised into action as they realise who they're talking to, and then, such a sweet moment, me in a hospital bed with Tom patting my hand and saying, 'You're going to be all right.'

'Thanks, Tommy,' I whispered. 'Thought I was gone.'

'Tell you the truth Lawrence, so did I,' he said and he gave me that legendary smile, the full-focus hundred-watt Tom Cruise beam that can really make your day. I was never sure if he was joking when he said that or if he was being deadly serious, but what else would you expect from one of the world's greatest actors?

CHAPTER 13

Cast and crew had been agog with the news that Tom Cruise had saved the life of one of the extras, the lunatic Lawrence.

It was the second day of the full dress rehearsals, and Mandy and Nina were doing what they had been doing for the last five months, and which in all probability would continue to do until at least Christmas: sitting around, sipping tea, and chatting.

This sort of sitting around time was a little different from the norm, because this time they were on the set, on the red carpet, in nothing but their G-strings, their capes draped like blankets about their shoulders. They were sitting cross-legged opposite each other and were sipping on styrofoam cups of tea that had been brought by an affable runner. It was… fun. Nina didn't mind that they'd probably be filming till spring – because she was there, in the moment, and, oh, by the way, she was also a small cog in creating this magnificent piece of art. Or at least she hoped – blithely presumed – it was going to be a great piece of art. But what if Kubrick's magnum opus turned out to be a complete steaming turkey? Bummerrr!

But in the last couple of weeks, as she'd watched the meticulous Kubrick go about his craft, she'd realised that, in all probability, he knew what he was about. He knew what he wanted (though he hadn't got the faintest clue how to get there): nothing short of total perfection.

Shooting that evening had been delayed by half-an-hour because the star, Tom Cruise, had been tied up at the hospital.

He'd returned so late back to Elveden Hall that even the consistently late Vicky was on set before him. It was Mandy, naturally, who knew exactly what Tom Cruise had been doing.

'He was running down this track and he came across Lawrence out cold in the mud,' Mandy said.

Nina wrinkled her nose in disbelief. There was something ever so slightly whiffy about the story. And Nina's general rule of thumb was that, well, when something sounded like bullshit, it probably was bullshit. 'I'll believe you,' Nina said. 'Thousands wouldn't.'

'Tom certainly took Lawrence to the hospital,' Mandy said. 'He even saw him into a bed.'

'Forgive my cynicism,' Nina said. 'But you are asking me to believe that the bizarre Lawrence just happens to knock himself out on the exact same route that Tom Cruise is running down?''

'Got a better suggestion 'bout what happened?'

'Not yet,' Nina said. 'But what I do know is there is something off about Lawrence. Can't tell you what it is. There is something of the night about him. Look at the hotel he's staying at! All the other extras are staying at the cheapest places they can find – a couple of them are even sleeping in the back of a van! But not Lawrence – he's putting himself up in the most expensive hotel in town! He's in the same hotel as the crew! Nobody else is doing that.'

'Maybe he's rich.'

'Maybe.'

'He's always very generous,' Mandy said. 'Won't even think of allowing anyone else pay for lunch.'

'Haven't you heard there's no such thing as a free lunch?'

'I don't think he wants to sleep with me!' Mandy said primly.

At which, and quite by coincidence, Nina found her gaze dwelling on Glenn, who, yet again, was being hectored by Kubrick. Glenn, in his affable way, was sucking it up – as, indeed was Leon Vitali, who was in his full Red Cloak gear, though with his golden mask perched on his forehead. Neither

Glenn nor Leon looked like sucking-up guys, but for some reason they did suck it up from Kubrick, who now had one of the girls' black G-strings in his hands and was waving it in Glenn's face. Probably not the first time that Glenn had had a G-string waved in his face. Glenn just smiled and beckoned for the costumier; Helena dutifully trotted over. Now that Glenn guy was interesting. Always calm – Nina had never seen him even close to being rattled. The truly amazing thing was that he'd been working on this film for well over a year. Without. A. Break! God he must have some inner steel. She watched him occasionally at the gym, so focused on whatever he was doing. He always showed up, every single day, and always had a good work-out. Took good care of himself. She kind of liked it that they just nodded but never spoke – though she had noticed that he was chatty with the other girls. The previous day he'd even been laughing with Mandy. But for some reason, he chose not to engage with Nina, though perhaps it was she who had made the decision not to engage with him. And being smart, she also realised they were both proud and self-contained, and the one thing that you could never bring yourself to do was stoop to chat to the object of your affections. Perhaps… Did she fancy him? Well, in another life, and if he'd been the only man left on earth, then perhaps it might not have been too much of a chore to have had to have set about repopulating the planet with him – but, as it was, they were working on a movie together, a Stanley Kubrick movie no less, and Glenn was her boss, her highly professional boss, and so it was entirely understandable that on set, at work, he wanted to keep a highly professional distance between himself and, say, the more naked members of the cast. And that was another thing – what was it going to be like at Highclere Castle in the spring when they really would be in the all-together?

One quite funny thing had happened the previous night – and even then, Glenn had maintained his steely froideur, his eyes fixed on their faces and not even once allowing his gaze to drift down to, ahhh, the bounties beneath.

They'd been on about the fifth or sixth rehearsal, when it had all kicked off – and, as ever, there was only one person who could have been doing the kicking: Kubrick the Kicker.

'What are those G-strings they're wearing?' he'd squawked. 'They're so ugly, impossible! Where is Helena?'

Helena the wardrobe woman was called to make her explanation. 'So they're ugly, are they?' she said.

'Yes!' Kubrick said. 'Very!'

'Well, you liked them last month when you picked them,' Helena said. 'Don't you remember telling me to go to London and New York and get photos of every single G-string that was available? And you know what, Stanley – I went to London and I went to New York and I got you those photos! There was not a single G-string in New York or London that was not photographed for you. And you know what happened then, Stanley? You decided which G-string you liked best – and that's the G-string that the girls are wearing now.'

'Ahh, Helena,' he said, momentarily nonplussed. 'Do I contradict myself? Very well then, I contradict myself! I am large! I contain multitudes! Having seen the G-strings in action, I have changed my mind.'

'And that is your absolute prerogative, Stanley. I'll get you the G-strings catalogues and you can decide what else takes your fancy.'

'Very good, Helena,' Kubrick said. 'Thank you, Helena.'

Glenn had then been dispatched onto the red carpet to give the good news to the girls, who, since they'd not been stood down, were all still near naked. The twelve girls, faces inscrutable under their masks, breasts brazenly bare, turned to him as one. Nina was well aware that, masks on, cloaks off, they were a formidable sight. Glenn could see their eyes, but nothing else of their faces.

'Hi team,' he said. 'We're going to be getting you some new G-strings.'

'Why are we getting new G-strings?' said Vicky, the shop steward of the outfit.

'Stanley's not happy with the ones you're wearing,' Glenn said patiently. 'It'll be at least an hour before Helena can get new ones, so you better have your dinner break.'

'Well, at least we won't have the G-string problem at Highclere Castle, will we now, Glenn?'

'We won't,' Glenn said. 'Thankfully you'll all be naked by then.'

'Crew excited?' Vicky said, taunting.

'Doubt they've given it a thought.'

'Pull the other one!' Vicky cackled. 'And what about you, Glenn?'

'Me?' Glenn said, turning away to be admonished again by Kubrick. 'I genuinely haven't given it a thought.'

'You're the only guy on set who hasn't.'

Glenn laughed. 'I don't think Stanley's thought about it,' he said. 'Much.'

Nina had liked the easy way that Glenn had parried Vicky's attack, the jibes gliding past without touching him.

Unsurprisingly, it had taken a deal sight longer than an hour for Kubrick to decide which G-strings he wanted. They'd returned from their dinner (now in the hall, so that they'd didn't have to go outside to the truck), and Kubrick – like some dithering husband in the lingerie department– had still been leafing through Helena's catalogue. It took him the whole night to make a decision, and the next day Helena was dispatched to buy the new G-strings in London; as far as Nina could see, there was precious little difference between the new G-strings and the old ones, the front triangle now perhaps slightly less skimpy – but on this (as on all such matters) Kubrick knew best.

'OK, girls,' Glenn said with a clap of his hands. 'Let's take it from the top again.'

The girls slipped on their cloaks and masks and sidled out of the hall. The extras separated from their huddles and took up their first position – now they really didn't have much to do at all. As far as Nina could tell, the extras did nothing but stand around – in fact, Kubrick didn't want them doing anything *except* stand around. He said they looked more menacing when they didn't move. So all they did was stand there gawping at the girls.

This would be the fifth scenario that they'd rehearsed, with Nina and the eleven other girls processing into the room in double column before forming into a circle.

There was a problem. Nina had known there was going to be a problem, but hadn't really seen it as her place to flag it up. They'd find out soon enough.

'Where the hell's Vicky gone now?' Glenn said.

And again, though Nina knew perfectly well where Vicky was, she did not feel the need to tell Glenn. 'Might have gone to the toilet,' she said.

'I'll bet she's gone to the toilet,' Glenn said. 'And I bet I know who she's with.'

Nina was glad she had her mask on. With mask on, she was world-class inscrutable, and being sphinx-like was, she realised, an utter delight.

As usual, Glenn was spot on – Vicky was almost certainly having sex with Tom Cruise's stand-in, Jimmy. But in such a warren as the hall, the pair would be impossible to find.

'OK, well let's check the lights again, let's check all the masks again.' He called Roddie, the second assistant director. 'Think Vicky needs her own personal walkie-talkie?'

'Tracker device on her cloak might be better.'

'Yeah,' Glenn said. 'Or a tracker on Jimmy, because wherever he is, she's bound to be there too.'

They ran through the lights, and the girls mooched outside the main hall, and Glenn kept the troupe busy with equable good cheer – now wasn't equability an endearing quality? – and in time Vicky clattered down the stairs, cloak billowing about her.

'I'm late, I'm late, I'm late!' She pulled her mask onto her face. 'Sorry sorry! Didn't think you'd need me.'

'Hey Vicky, quick word,' Glenn said. 'I wouldn't mind if you were just keeping me waiting. But as it is, over a hundred of us have been kicking our heels for the last fifteen minutes just because you're late.'

'I got lost, all right?' Vicky said.

It was one of those painful lies which Glenn knew was a complete fabrication, and which Vicky, in her turn, knew that Glenn knew. But since she had the lead role of the Mysterious Woman, Vicky also knew that it would be difficult to continue without her. Difficult, mind – but not impossible.

'Very easy to get lost in the hall,' Glenn said.

'It is!' Vicky said. 'It's so big!'

Glenn was talking into his walkie-talkie, already on to the next thing. For now that the scene was correctly lit, and the cameras were in place and manned, and now that all of the girls and all of the extras had been assembled (with the exception of Lawrence, who was still in hospital), it was time to call for the in-house deity.

'Stanley, we're ready.'

'Good!' Kubrick's crackled. 'I'm on my way.'

A mere ten minutes later, Kubrick bustled into the hall. From the debris in his beard, it looked like he'd been eating a cream cake, probably an éclair.

It was still only a rehearsal, but Kubrick was filming it all the same. He nestled himself into his canvas chair as Glenn set the whole beautiful machine into motion.

'Roll cameras!' Glenn said, and the cameras rolled. 'Background action!' And the seventy extras started doing their background stuff. 'And action!' And in beautiful sync the twelve girls marched into the hall. The men mingled with the girls, who then formed into a tight circle, and knelt down on the ground and went into another of their yoga positions, the upward dog, like a press-up, but with the back arched so that the head is held high. The yoga positions were Nina's favourite part of the whole performance – they had at least seven different positions in their repertoire. Though not so easy on the knees. The red carpet was hard and they'd been doing a lot of kneeling.

'And cut!' Kubrick said. Although it was usually Glenn who set this whole piece of choreography in motion, it was Kubrick and Kubrick alone who could utter that one magical word that stopped everything dead.

'Nice,' Kubrick said. 'Let's do it again.'

They did it again, and they did it again, and the girls tried a variation and another variation, and various yoga positions, and forming in lines and forming in circles, and dropping to their knees and standing up, and dropping to their knees, and dropping to their knees.

'Let's try the first one again,' Kubrick said. It was now well past midnight.

Vicky was the one who revolted. 'My knees are killing me!' she said, feathery mask high on her forehead.

'What did she say?' Kubrick said.

'I said my knees are killing me!' Vicky said. 'Can we have knee pads or something?'

'That's going to be difficult,' Glenn said. 'What —'

'Look Glenn, I've been down on my knees more often—'

'Than when you were a street-walker,' said one of the girls, though it was not quite clear who, as they all had their masks on.

'Who said that?' Vicky said, turning on the girls. 'Who said that?'

'Who said what?' Nina said, pushing her mask up.

'One of you slappers called me a street-walker!'

'Slappers are we?' Nina said. 'That's rich coming from you!'

'Leave it, you stuck-up—'

'Ladies, ladies!' It was Glenn, doing what he did so beautifully – being the peace-maker. Nina had been rather looking forward to a proper spar with Vicky. They'd skirmished over the previous few months, a little sniping, but they'd never engaged. 'Can you save this for later?' Glenn said. 'Look, I'm sorry about your knees—'

'Yeah, what you going to do about my knees?' Vicky said, refocussing her fire back on Glenn.

'We'll get some underlay for the red carpet,' Glenn said.

'When?'

'Tomorrow morning,' Glenn said.

'Well, what about tonight?'

'You don't have to be quite so combative, Vicky,' Glenn said. 'I know it's hard on your knees, but if you could just continue tonight as you were, that would be fantastic.'

'But what about my knees?'

One of the girls piped up again – probably the one who had so insulted Vicky before. 'Shut up, you slapper!'

'Who said that?'

'I did, you slapper.'

Nina wasn't sure who it was, but at a guess, probably Mandy. With their full face masks it was difficult to tell.

Another girl spoke up, still impossible to tell who – 'I did, you slapper.'

And another: 'No I did, you slapper.'

'God, you're all bitches!'

'OK ladies, time for a tea break.' That was Glenn again, bless him – was there nothing he couldn't handle?

'I want it out now!' Vicky said, but she'd lost her audience and the girls were dispersing. For the first time Nina became aware of the effect this small spat was having on the rest of the team. The extras and crew were all watching, rapt, motionless – and fair play, actually, Nina thought, as the girls were only in their G-strings (their new G-strings), and how often did you get to witness a shouting match between twelve beautiful, near-naked women? If only Kubrick had had his cameras rolling... that really would have been something worth filming.

CHAPTER 14

So what to buy the chap who's just saved your life? This delicate question needed some thought, for not only did I wish to say express my thanks to life-saver Tommy, but I was also hoping, in my mild-mannered fashion, to worm my humble way into his affections. Flowers? Food? Some article of clothing, a gadget, a dust-catching bauble? Maybe something for his two kids, like a ton of sweets, or a large box of Lego... now that might work. But if I bought the kids a load of Lego – or indeed, the latest craze of the year, one of those infernal Tamagotchis – then that might make the kids happy, but how it would further my relationship with Tommy? (Imagine the conversation – "How the kids getting on with the Lego, Tommy?" Answer: "Just great thanks, Lawrence, now kindly crawl back under your rock.")

In the end, I went down the journalist's Route One. I bought him some booze. I didn't actually know if Tommy was a boozer (probably not – these Hollywood types tend to take themselves terribly seriously – "my body is a temple" and all that guff), but I figured that if I bought him a tasty bottle of whisky, it would at least show willing. If nothing else, he could give the bottle to one of his superstar buddies.

I'd spent one night in hospital and the next day – face blown up like a football and with one hell of a headache – I wandered into a Bury St Edmunds's off-licence and bought the most expensive bottle of whisky they had, an eighteen-year-old

Macallan Double Cask. It came in at a round £300 and it would be going straight onto my expenses.

Glenn had left a note to say that there was no pressing urgency for me to return to the set, but I was eager to strike while Tommy still remembered who on earth I was.

I wrote him a short letter, quite formal, thanking him for saving my life, and proffering up the bottle of Macallan as a small token of my most humble esteem. I could have delivered the bottle in person to his Winnebago, but it's a big no-no for extras to start banging on stars' doors on set (even if they have just saved your life), so instead I left the bottle on the steps by the Winnebago door.

I discovered that, in my absence, I had become something of a celebrity – well it's not every day of the week that a superstar does something that's genuinely heroic (as opposed to just acting the hero), and everyone, but everyone, wanted to know all about it.

Rather pleasingly, the girls also wanted to hear all about it, and rather than relying on mere second-hand gossip, Mandy and Nina had buttonholed me in the Officers' Mess.

Ah yes... the Officers' Mess. Surprised I haven't mentioned it before.

On a long job, it's most important to have a quiet sanctuary where you can chat and drink with like-minded souls and where you won't be disturbed by the riff-raff. And seeing as we were going to be at Elveden for some time, I had wasted no time in finding a cushy billet for myself and a select group of chums. Fortunately, there was no shortage of rooms.

In the first week on set, when the space-heaters had been warming the place up, I had given Hector, the head of security, a half-case of whisky, and he in his turn had given me the keys to the hall. I only needed them for a couple of hours – just long enough to race into Bury St Edmunds and have a locksmith copy them all.

Then, at my leisure, I explored the hall. It took ages, initially, to find the correct key for each door, but then, holy-moly, I discovered that one of the keys was a skeleton key which opened every single lock in the hall. Enormous rooms which once would have been filled with riches, and now just gloomy echoes of their glory days. For the Officers' Mess, I picked one of the old bedrooms, which was relatively small as there was no electricity in the hall and it would have been tricky to heat (all of Kubrick's electricity was supplied by generators), but it did have an en-suite bathroom.

I'd thought that I might have to furnish my mess with inflatable chairs and the like, but, deliciously, I discovered a lumber room at the top of the house, still filled with a lot of old furniture that had never made it to the auctioneers. One morning, I went up to the lumber room with my new buddy Josh, who'd just graduated from Bristol University, and we carted a number of chairs and a sofa down into the mess room. Then: a few side tables; a couple of old rugs; a tiger skin and a zebra skin; and a bookcase which I would gradually fill up with books. The error was trying to get down the vast mahogany drinks cabinet, which was extremely heavy and extremely ugly. But since it was just rotting away in the lumber room, and since every officers' mess requires a drinks cabinet, I'd decided on dragging it down there.

The cabinet was so heavy, at least quarter of a ton, that Josh had to round up another lanky student, Caspar, to shift the thing. After a lot of grunting and straining, we got it onto one of the set trolleys, and soon had it at the top of the stairs. We had to get it down two flights.

'I think we need a rope, we need a rope,' Josh said.

'Why do we need a rope?' I said. 'The thing's going to whistle down the stairs.'

'That's what I'm afraid of,' Josh said.

'Nah it'll be fine,' I said, with the airy conviction of a someone who hasn't got the faintest idea what he's talking about.

I carefully positioned myself behind the cabinet at the top of the stairs, while the two lads were both at the bottom, acting like human braces. I was sort of holding on with my fingertips – perhaps a rope would have been better…

The lads were doing a lot of grunting and squealing – "Oww, oww it's caught my finger, it got my finger," from Josh, and similar whiny stuff from Caspar.

'Handsomely there, handsomely,' I said.

'What does "handsomely" mean?' Josh asked.

'Make pretty?' Caspar said.

'It's a naval expression, you dolt!' I said. 'It means with a slow, even motion.'

Josh snickered. 'Hate to see what uglily looks…' He turned to look at Caspar, somehow missed his step. The drinks cabinet was suddenly on the move. Josh leapt like a cat – if he hadn't, the thing would have flattened him. I ineffectually grabbed at one of the legs, Caspar cowered, and the whole monstrous piece of furniture was whistling down the stairs. It hurtled across the corridor and boomed into the wall where it was instantly reduced to kindling. The only fortunate thing was that since these sort of crashes were the norm on a Kubrick set, nobody turned a hair and not a single security guard came to investigate.

'That was close, that was so close!' Josh said, quite white at his near miss with the rogue cabinet.

'Hmm,' I said. 'We'll just have to make do with putting the booze on the mantelpiece.'

'But what do with thith?' Caspar squeaked. He was a bit of a nervy one was Caspar, with a very severe lisp. Bizarrely for such a wet blanket, he had a whole rash of tattoos on his back, curling all the way up to the back of his neck, doubtless the better to show that he was a real tough guy.

'It'll be fine,' I said. I unlocked the nearest door. It was another bedroom, a little smaller than the Officers' Mess, but rather handsome, with fine views out over the park. 'We'll just bung it all in here.'

The drinks cabinet had shattered into about eight pieces. We manhandled the smashed wood into the corner of the room. There were still quite a few splinters and bits of detritus on the ground, which I would have swept up in due course, but Josh tore into the room again. 'One of the security guards is coming, one of the security guards is coming!' he squawked.

'It's all right dear,' I said, quietly shutting the door and locking it. We could hear footsteps in the corridor. The guard rattled the doorknob, but had no luck – obviously it wasn't the boss, otherwise he'd have had a key. Josh held his breath. I mooched over to the window to join the bug-eyed Caspar. We gazed out over the wild moonlit lawn with its long grass and its shaggy bushes; what a sight it must have been in its Victorian heyday.

Josh joined us. 'What if they catch us?' he whispered. 'What are we going to do? What will we do?'

'He's not going to catch us.'

'But he'll find the trolley upstairs,' he said. 'What do we do then?'

'We just deny everything,' I said.

'Ohh,' he said, dumbfounded at this revelatory thought. 'Can we do that?'

'I give you permission,' I said. 'Anyway, moving swiftly on, I think now would be as good a time as any to welcome you to The Officers' Mess. You are the founding members.'

'Who elth joining?' Caspar said, for some reason wary.

'The pick of the bunch,' I said. 'Nina and Mandy.'

'Mandy?' Josh said. 'Mandy from Manchester?'

'That's the one.'

'Wow,' he said, suddenly speechless at the news that one of his mess-mates was going to be the most beautiful woman he'd ever seen.

I gave them each a skeleton key and told them they could bring up whomsoever they pleased. Sooner or later we were bound to be rumbled, but, ever the cunning strategist, I already had a fallback plan.

This, then, was the Officers' Mess, our haven from the hurly-burly.

And it was here, an hour before call time, that the girls picked my brains about my new hero, one Tom Cruise. Six candles were lit, various bottles of booze lined the mantelpiece, the door had been locked from the inside and all was snug and secure and pleasingly tranquil, and I, lounging by the fireside, had become the most gracious host since the great American socialite Perle Mesta.

'So what's he like?' Nina said. She was lounging on one of the armchairs with her leg slung casually slung over the side – no starchiness in our Officers' Mess, I can tell you. Both Nina and Mandy had taken extremely well to this Mess life of idle luxury, the lads not so much. Mind you, the lads had never spent so much time with so much beauty. No wonder they were tongue-tied.

'He's a really good guy,' I said. 'Told me some great stories about Kubrick. Personally chauffeured me to the hospital. And when they realised that Tom Cruise, in person, had brought me in, the whole triage unit was flooded with every available doctor in the hospital! After he'd sorted me out, he was posing for pictures and all the rest, just like you're supposed to do if you're a superstar.'

'Hmm,' Nina said. She sipped on her Coke. No booze for Nina – or at least not when she was working. Unlike the rest of us. 'Sounds like he did a good job.'

'Yeah, but he's an actor,' Mandy said. She was lolling on the sofa with Josh, though in the presence of such extreme beauty he was hardly able to say a word. Caspar completed our little circle and was sitting on an armchair. He hadn't said a peep all afternoon.

'Can't an actor do anything nice?' I asked.

'S'pose they can,' Mandy said. 'Thing is, you never know if it's genuine or if it's an act.'

'Must be havoc falling in love with an actor,' I said. 'They tell you they love you and they say it like they mean it – but do they really love you, or are they just putting on another act?'

'One thing I don't understand, Lawrence,' Nina said. 'How

come you were found by Tom Cruise? Did you know his regular running route?'

'What – Nina!' I said. 'Are you suggesting that I found out where Tom liked to run and then accidentally on purpose knocked myself out so that he could come along and rescue me?! That's quite a stretch.'

'It is quite a stretch,' Nina said. She was wearing all black that day, a tracksuit – though with Nina, it didn't make much difference what she wore (or indeed didn't wear). She always looked terrific. Thank the Lord I never fancied her. 'But then it's pretty astonishing that he found you at all.'

'You're a bit of a cynic, if you don't mind my saying so,' I said.

'What are you doing on this set?'

'How do you mean?' I said.

'I don't know what you're doing on this film.'

'Me?' I said, downright flabbergasted that somebody should be calling into question my allegiance to the Kubrick cause. 'I'm just another extra, having fun, trying to do my little bit for a man who is not just the world's greatest living director, but probably, Nina, the greatest director the world has ever seen – in fact, he is more than just a director, he is an auteur —'

'What's an auteur when he's at home?' Mandy said.

'Just a fancy word for a big-shot director,' Nina said. 'It means they've also got artistic vision.'

'Well, he's certainly got something,' Mandy said. 'Can you imagine what he's like at home? "What would you like for supper, darling?" – "Well cook up some spag bol and I'll have a try of that, but maybe put on some fish and chips, just in case that takes my fancy.'

'Or, "Would you like something to drink, dear?"' I continued. '"Yes please," he'd say. "I want a gin and tonic, a cup of tea, a glass of wine and a glass of *crème de menthe* – never tried it before but I might like it."'

Nina was still staring at me, and didn't remotely look

like she was getting into the spirit of things. 'I'm watching you,' she said.

'And to think how we welcomed you into the Officers' Mess,' I said. 'Hey, I've got a question for you, Nina.'

'What's that?'

'When did you start fancying Glenn?'

'I beg your pardon?' She nearly choked on her Coke.

'You heard me – when did you start fancying Glenn?'

'Why should I fancy Glenn?' she said, with lightning-quick recovery.

'Look, Nina, it's a perfectly straightforward question – why can't you give me a straight answer?'

'I'll tell you one thing,' she said.

'What's that?'

'If I did fancy Glenn, you'd be the last person I'd tell.'

'So… a week back? Or when you first saw him in the pub?'

'You're such a schmuck if you think I'm going to fall for your loaded questions.'

'Loaded?'

'It's up there with asking if I've laid off beating my father,' Nina said. 'Whatever I say you'll use to skewer me.'

'What's wrong with that?'

'I think that fall has given you permanent brain damage.'

This affable conversation might have continued longer, except it was nearly 6 p.m. and it was time for us to once again return to our Kubrickian enslavement. Talk about total power! If you've never been on a film set before, you've never seen anything like it – and, actually, even if you *have* been on a film set, you'll still have never seen anything like it. There were well over a hundred of us, what with the crew and extras, and every single one of us had to do just exactly what crazy Kubrick wanted us to do. He decided when our days started and when they were at an end. Tea breaks and meal breaks: all decided by Kubrick. He decided where we stood and what we wore and how we were lit, and of course – his favourite thing on earth – Kubrick also decided how many times we had to run through a particular scene, which was always and without exception *a lot*. Most directors draw up a storyboard before they start filming, which comprises a series of quite elaborate sketches on how they expect the scenes to look. Not Kubrick – because Kubrick had no idea how he wanted a scene to look. He wanted a scene to grow organically – he wanted to be surprised and delighted at how, over time, his cast grew and evolved. Then, after rehearsing for, say, a month or three, he might have got a small feel for how he wanted the scene to look. "Sorry guys, but we're just going to keep on rehearsing this damn scene until I can decide what I want. Might take a week, might take a month – who the hell cares, Warner Bros have made me the boss and I do whatever I want! Do it again!"

It was interesting to see how the crew and the extras took to these rehearsals without end. For the extras, who'd only been on the set for a matter of weeks, it was all still excitingly new. For the girls, who'd been rehearsing the orgy scene for four months, there was a certain friskiness. Some were stoical, some, even, were enjoying the life, and there were some, like Vicky, who had mentally checked out. Since, seemingly, Stanley Kubrick could never be satisfied, then why bother trying to please him?

And then there were the crew, most of whom had been working on *Eyes Wide Shut* for over a year without a single break. A lot of them, like Roddie the second assistant director, had resigned themselves to being nothing more than beasts of burden, just donkeys on a treadmill, put through the same mind-numbing grind every day without surcease. Glenn, on the other hand, whatever Kubrick threw at him just seemed to make him stronger. And, lastly, there was our enigmatic superstar… what did Tom make of it all? He certainly always seemed upbeat and positive, but the thing about superstar actors is that they generally tend to be, well, pretty good at a thing called acting, and so maybe it was all just an act, and maybe Kubrick was driving him certifiably insane. If only... if only he'd had some mild-mannered buddy to confide in...

The girls went downstairs, as it always took them much longer to get ready for the masked ball. True, they weren't wearing much more than G-string and stilettoes, but their hair, in particular, had to be just perfect, not a lock out of place.

I washed the glasses in the bathroom sink, while the two lads plumped up the pillows and set the room straight. I doubt they'd have done this at home or at university, but then I doubt they were in the habit of entertaining beautiful strippers.

'Mandy's nice,' I said to Josh as I blew out the candles.

'She's lovely.' He folded up a rug and placed it neatly over the arm of the sofa.

'Wonder how you're going to win her round,' I said.

'Beats me.'

'I'll think of something.' I followed him and Caspar out of the Mess and locked the door behind me.

'You're not like anybody else on this set, are you?' Josh said, echoing Nina.

'I should hope not!'

'Are you really just an extra?'

'No, Josh,' I said. 'I am much more than a mere extra. I am a match-maker.'

'Like you put people together?' he said. 'Why'd you do that?'

'I am Cupid,' I said airily. 'I am Puck from a *Midsummer Night's Dream.*'

'Doesn't Puck bring the wrong people together?'

'True love is not guaranteed.'

'Why'd you do it?'

'Because, in a small way Josh, I am playing God.'

'Could you play God with me and Mandy?'

By 7 p.m. we were ready for the first run-through. Of all the various scenarios that had been created, Kubrick seemed to be leaning towards having the girls in a circle. Tom Cruise, or his stand-in, lurked near one of the pillars. For this initial part of the orgy, Tom didn't have much to do apart from fix his mesmerised gaze on the girls. The rest of us palookas, meanwhile, were placed all around the hall, while a few of us were up on the first floor. In between takes, we'd chat about this and that; sometimes, if we were eating or drinking, we'd take the masks off, but Kubrick preferred us to keep the masks on. I believe he thought it would keep us all in character, as well as add to the mysterious vibe of the scene. God knows – Kubrick had his reasons, and it wasn't for us menials to question them.

We were rehearsing some of the most eye-popping scenes imaginable. But the problem, at least for me, was how to get a picture of it all. It was all well and good me being on the set but, really, what I needed was pictures, and the real money shot was of course going to be a picture of Tom Cruise surrounded by the dozen topless beauties. If I was caught with a camera on set – let alone taking a picture of Tom with the girls – I'd be out of Elveden quicker than Kubrick could yell "Do it again!" I did have a bit of gossip about Tom Cruise, and I knew what the whole film was about. But no pictures basically meant no front-page splash for little Kimmy, and that in turn would mean a very unhappy Spike.

We'd wrapped for the day, which meant the cast could head back to their beds. The crew still had at least another two hours on set to dismantle all the gear. As for Kubrick, it was said that he often stayed up till 6 a.m. He was nearly seventy at the time. God knows how he managed it.

I hung up my cloak on the hanger and handed my mask into the mask room. This room in the hall was dedicated solely to the orgy masks. At the end of each day, all the masks had to be returned to the mask room, where they were touched up with gold or silver, or paint or plumage, so that by call time the next day, they were all once again pristine. Ditto all the cloaks and the girls' shoes and the girls' G-strings, which were all steam-cleaned every night without exception.

I was just putting on my coat. Perhaps time for one last

drink in the Officers' Mess. One of the runners bustled up. It was Olivia, she of the tattoos, and now sporting a nose ring. 'Excuse me, Lawrence,' she said. 'Tom Cruise wants a brief word.'

'Sure,' I said. 'Where is he?'

'He's in his Winnebago.'

Unbelievable! Of course I'd been hoping for something like this. But for one of my more far-fetched plans to actually come off? I was astonished! 'Tom wants me to see him in his Winnebago?'

'Sure does.'

'Well, ain't that dandy?' With a smile on my lips and a song in my heart, I skipped off to see the great man. Now – keep it tight. But not too tight. Keep it light and breezy – but not too breezy. Keep it deferential. But not slimy. Above all – let's just have fun out there.

A full moon peeped out through the clouds as the hall loomed black behind me. I strolled through the trucks and vans that were parked up in the courtyard, shoes crunching on the gravel, and skipped up the steps to Tom's Winnebago. The bottle of Macallan had been taken.

A light knock on the door and a few moments later Tom opened it, big welcoming smile on his face, delighted to see me. I know, I know – just as Mandy kept helpfully pointing out, he could have just been acting. Can we just take that as read? But there is, also, the possibility that he was genuinely pleased to see me.

'Hi Tom,' I said.

'Hey Lawrence!' He gave me a firm handshake. 'Come in! How you feeling?'

'Pretty well, thanks to you,' I said. I followed him into the Winnebago. It was rather antiseptic, like a five-star hotel room, couple of armchairs and a sofa and a little kitchenette. The only homely touch was the three family pictures on the desk. I quickly observed that in pride of place on the coffee table was the bottle of Macallan.

'We got you back safe and that's the main thing,' he said. He was dressed super-casually, just jeans and a black turtle neck. He was a few inches smaller than normal, because he was just wearing cosy sheepskin slippers rather than the usual elevator shoes that he wore on set. 'Tell you the truth, Lawrence, I quite enjoyed it.'

'At least one of us did.'

'Hey and thanks for the whisky,' he said. 'That was nice. Not at all necessary – but appreciated.'

'You a whisky drinker?' I said.

'Occasionally,' he said. 'Don't think I've tried this one before. Join me?'

'Love to,' I said. I sat on the armchair and Tom fetched a bowl of ice and a small jug of water. He placed them on the coffee table alongside two beautiful cut-crystal tumblers, before pulling the cork of the Macallan and pouring two large slugs of whisky.

We each poured in a little water, and I added a couple of ice cubes – trying to keep it nonchalant, trying to keep it cool, easy-breezy, but all the while very much aware of just who exactly was sitting opposite me. I'm having a drink with Tom goddamn Cruise! Keep it tight and I might even be asked to stay for a top-up!

'Cheers,' I said.

'Cheers, Lawrence,' he said, and we drank the whisky. It was pretty good, though entirely wasted on the likes of me. I doubt I could have tasted the difference between the Macallan and a bog-standard blend.

I wondered if I should start making conversation. Not having chatted socially to a star, I imagined that you let them do most of the heavy lifting.

Tom broke the ice. 'So you do a bit of running?' he said.

'Most mornings,' I said. 'Helps keep me sane on set.'

'Keeps me sane too.'

We had another sip of our Macallan.

'Do you remember how you knocked yourself out?'

'Just about,' I said. 'I'd tried to vault the gate, but my foot slipped. One way or the other, I smashed my head on the concrete block.'

'Still looks painful,' he said.

'It's nothing,' I said. 'I once stood on a six-inch nail and it went clean through my foot. That might even have been up there with childbirth.'

He dutifully laughed. 'We'll never know.'

We each had another sip. It wasn't going badly, but it wasn't exactly going well. It was all a bit clunky. Well, it was now or never to hook him, because if I didn't hook him soon, then it was going to be Goodnight Vienna.

'Every been to Delphi?' I asked.

'Like the Greek Oracle?' he said. 'Never been. Like to.'

'It's got a lot of history, and carved into the stonework are a couple of mottos for life. They're just as relevant now as they were 3,000 years ago. Like to hear them?'

'I would.'

'The first motto is "Everything in moderation".'

'Everything in moderation?' he mulled. 'Not bad.'

'The second is "Know thyself".'

'Know thyself,' he repeated. 'Now that's a good motto.'

'Now, almost exactly a hundred years ago, they discovered a statue of a charioteer in Delphi. I saw him a year ago in the Delphi museum. He's standing up and he's holding the chariot's reins, but there are no horses or chariot any more because they were destroyed in an earthquake. He's made of bronze and he's greenish with wet hair and a soft beard. His eyes are very direct. They're made of onyx.'

'Right.' Tom was giving me full focus, leaning a little forward, hands cupping his tumbler of whisky.

'But the most amazing thing about the charioteer is the expression on his face and on his copper lips. There's a Greek word which describes the look on his face – and that is *arete*.'

'*Arete*.' He savoured the word.

'It means the ecstasy you experience after a job well done,'

I said. 'This charioteer has just won the big race at the Pythian games, and now, on his glorious victory lap, he has a few seconds in that ecstatic place between heaven and earth.' Since I had him hooked, I allowed myself a sip of whisky. Perhaps it was a little better than the regular blends. '*Arete,*' I said. 'Ever experienced it?'

'Maybe once, after we'd done this impossible stunt. It was an impossible stunt on *Mission: Impossible.*' He chuckled.

'I think I experienced it when I was running hard in the rain, just before knocking myself out.'

'Yeah?'

'Yeah.'

He seemed to visibly expand. He was thinking. I had the good sense not to interrupt.

'Would look good in a film,' he said.

'Sure would.'

And the funny thing was that Tom did capture the look of *arete* – in not just his next film, but the very first scene of that next film. It's *Mission: Impossible 2*. Tom is climbing a precipice at Dead Horse Point in Utah. It's a tricky climb, but he's got it all covered. At one point, he's hanging from this overhang, arms outstretched – but he's not facing the rock, he's facing the world, and the look on his face is not quite a smile but something like it… That is *arete*.

'Thanks for that. Like it a lot,' he said, before continuing with four of the most beautiful words I've ever heard. 'Like a top-up?'

'Thank you, Tom,' I said. 'I would.'

CHAPTER 15

The favourite part of Nina's day was being in hair and make-up. Just sitting in the chair in front of the mirror, five other girls next to her and, for over an hour, just sitting there as her tresses were teased and tweaked in contented silence. Since this was a job, and since they'd been at it for over a month, there was none of the usual chatter that you'd get in a hairdresser. Instead, the girls were alone with their thoughts and the hair guys just did their thing. Because of the masks, the girls didn't need much make-up, though their eyes were always finished to perfection with false eyelashes, mascara and smoky eye-shadow.

When the six girls' hair and make-up team were done, they gave their chairs up for the six other girls, and went off to strip and put on their stilettoes and box-fresh G-strings. The girls' dressing room was now so warm that they were near naked as they waited. They only put on their cloaks when they were called onto the set.

By now, Nina knew all the tics of all the main players and could tell at a glance how their days were going. Her gaze as usual lingered on Glenn; difficult to tell what was up, but for some reason he looked a little out of sorts. Not quite as decisive as usual, ordering the Steadicam guy to take up one position, and then a while later, telling him to go somewhere else. Leon Vitali had to remind him which of the myriad scenarios they were rehearsing. Later, after Kubrick had started fussing around, Glenn had slumped in his chair and stared at the ceiling. He looked... he looked completely done in.

The shoot itself was just a repeat of what they'd been doing for the previous three weeks – standing in first positions, putting on their masks and having their hair teased with a last-minute touch-up, and off they'd go to the races again. It was surprising how quickly the extras had got used to the strip show. For the first score of takes, there had been this palpable tension, growing and growing as Leon swung his incense-burner and stamped his staff upon the floor; as the girls' cloaks had dropped to the floor, a ripple of a sigh would stir through the hall. But after a week or two, the extras were as blasé about the strip show as the girls themselves. Or at least most of them were. When Mandy's cloak fell to the ground, Josh, from the Officers' Mess, always looked like a starved mongrel. And what did Glenn look like, she wondered, when the cloaks fell to the ground, and was there anyone in particular upon whom his gaze lingered...

Kubrick called it dinner time at 11 p.m. and the extras drifted off to the catering truck. Nina spent a little while chatting to Mandy. She wasn't hungry. She might go up to the Officers' Mess and read.

Lawrence slouched over, mask in hand. 'Hi Nina,' he said. 'You couldn't take a cup of tea to Glenn please?'

'Err, sure,' she said. 'Where is he?'

'Sitting in the portico, out by the garden.'

'Fine.'

'Thanks.'

He slipped away before she could say more. It was only as she was making the tea in the girls' dressing room that she realised how much had been left unsaid. Like – why hadn't a runner delivered the tea, or even Lawrence himself? Like – why had she, a stripper, been tasked with taking tea to the assistant director? Or even – why couldn't Glenn get his own tea? She stirred milk into the styrofoam cup – Glenn looked like a milk-no-sugar guy – and flicked the tea bag into the bin.

She took the tea through the hall and out the back towards the portico. She didn't tend to go through to the portico as it wasn't part of the set and wasn't used by the crew. She realised that though she was wearing her cloak, she only had on her G-string underneath. She opened the outer door. It was quite still outside, not a breath of wind, crisp but not cold. Glenn was sitting on a bench a little way along staring out into the darkness.

'Hi Glenn,' she said.

He turned, looked at her, wiped his nose. 'Oh, hi Nina.'

'Got your tea.'

'Ohh – thanks.' He stretched for the tea. He'd been crying.

'What's happened?' She sat next to him on the bench, smoothing the cloak along her legs.

'Oh nothing,' he said.

'It's OK, Glenn – what's happened?'

He sniffed, blew into his handkerchief, wiped his eyes. 'My mum's just died.'

'Oh Glenn,' she said. 'I'm so sorry.' She instinctively leaned in to give him a hug, arms enfolding about his waist. For a moment he didn't move, but then he carefully placed the tea on the bench and brought his arms up around her and held her tight, and at first Nina didn't know how she felt about this hug, but after a while she realised that she liked it.

Their heads were touching, her chin almost on his shoulder. He sniffed and held her tighter. She might have said something, but that would have spoiled the moment. A stream of dreamy thoughts – she was hugging Glenn! And she was topless, and her cloak had opened and her bare breasts were pressing against his fleece! And she was liking it!

Glenn pulled away a moment, wiped his wet cheeks, and smiled at her. 'Haven't hugged anybody like that in over a year,' he said, and she smiled at him and he smiled at her, and as one they moved towards each other and they kissed, firmly, sweetly. They could have stopped there, but they did not stop there, and they kissed again, and again, longer, lingering, and, hard to think that just five minutes ago she was making a cup of tea, but now, well, here she was, kissing Glenn, dare we say lustfully kissing Glenn, with stippling tongues, and somehow his arms were no longer outside her cloak but were inside her cloak and his warm hands were on her back, holding her tight, and, what the hell, she returned the compliment, and slipped her hands under his shirt and it all felt right and in the correct order of things.

After some kissing, though it was difficult to tell, because it might actually have been quite a lot of kissing, they broke off and smiled at each other, and, looking each other direct in the eyes, kissed again.

'And have you kissed anybody this last year?' Nina said.

'I have not,' Glenn said and kissed her again. 'Am I rusty?'

'No,' Nina said. 'In fact…' and here she paused to kiss him again, and though the kiss was only meant as a peck, it continued for some time, lips roaming, tongues teasing. 'In fact, quite well oiled.'

'I am very relieved to hear it,' he said.

'Though you do have me at a slight disadvantage,' she said, her hand stroking up his bare spine. 'I'm down to just a G-string.'

'True,' he said, slipping his hand up to stroke her neck, her cheek, as he kissed her again.

'And you've also seen me pretty much naked.'

'Also true,' he said. 'I promise to wear a particularly skimpy outfit at the gym tomorrow – Speedos and a singlet.'

She laughed as she kissed him again. 'That'd be thoughtful of you,' she said, before remembering why it was that they'd started hugging in the first place. 'Hey, I really am sorry about your mum.'

'Yeah,' he said. 'I knew it was coming, but it's still a shock.'

'Must have been tough not seeing her for so long.'

'If I'd known it was going to last quite so long, I might not have signed up for the shoot.'

'Not even with the great Stanley Kubrick?'

He laughed and now, because he could, and because it was permitted, he kissed her again, and now that she had got over the mild shock that she, Nina, was actually kissing Glenn, she was starting to get into it, especially now that he had started to kiss her neck – but where oh where was it all going to lead? They were once again in first positions, looking into each other's eyes, lips within kissing distance. 'Before I signed up, I should have had it carved in stone that I got to see her every three months.'

'Would Kubrick have gone for that?'

'Maybe,' he said in between kisses. 'Before he got me, he was pretty keen to get me.'

'And now?'

'Now that he's got me, he couldn't care less!'

'And I know how that feels.'

'You?' Glenn said. 'How could —' And there he broke off and there the kissing ended, as Olivia the runner had stepped out into the portico, and though she couldn't quite see what was happening, she could certainly see that her assistant director was in a clinch with one of the girls. 'Sorry to disturb, Glenn,' she said. 'Stanley wants a word.'

Glenn laughed. 'Be right with you,' he said, and Olivia discreetly left them to it.

Glenn gave Nina a last long hug. 'Stanley's saved you,' he said.

'Saved me from what?'

'My carnal lusts?'

'That's a shame.'

He gave her a fond kiss and then they separated. 'Of course he wants me,' he said. 'Coming along too?'

'I'll stay a little,' she said. 'Decompression.'

'Thank you,' he said, and with a soft stroke of her cheek he was gone.

Nina brought her knees into her chest and wrapped the cloak tight about her. She realised that Glenn had left his tea (had he even asked for the tea?). She picked the cup up and had a sip. Well...

Well, she certainly hadn't expected that! She'd certainly liked it, enjoyed it, and not that she had – necessarily – wanted a man in her life, but of all the men in all the world, it was pleasing beyond measure that it had been Glenn: bright, reliable and (not that this had any relevance whatsoever) a pretty good-looking guy with a fairly trim body. What if... What if it had been, say, stodgy Roddie, who'd been grieving for his dead mother? Of course she'd have commiserated with him, but certainly would not have responded to his hugs with quite such alacrity...

More teasingly, though, Nina wondered what would happen next. Now that the barriers were down – well and truly – did that mean that there might perhaps be a luncheon date, followed, perhaps, by more kissing, and then... what on earth could more kissing be followed by but, ahhh, further levels of intimacy which might even include Nina being allowed to inspect Glenn's body in just the same manner that he had been looking at her near-naked body for the past three weeks – though he'd probably look better without a G-string, and, not that Nina was a betting woman, but if she were, she'd put quite a sizeable bet on Glenn being just as attractive with his clothes off as he was with his clothes on... Nina smirked at such lasciviousness, but hell, she, like Glenn, had had months on end without a hug in sight, so now that she had been hugged, properly, and with succulent kisses that had also been thrown into the mix, then was it any surprise that she was not just pondering the next stage in developments, but was eagerly anticipating it?

Woahhh, Nina! Let's not get too far ahead of ourselves!

Not that Glenn was anything like any of her ex-boyfriends, but if he was even remotely like any of her ex-boyfriends, then one way or another, it would all end in disaster. (The extraordinary thing being that the disasters were always different, and usually quite unexpected – though on the plus side, this did tend to make them much better fodder for her fiction writing.)

So it might work out; no, she could do better than that, she hoped it would work out. But in the meantime, she would be circumspect and would tread that delicious line between "hungry-for-it" and "couldn't-care-less-for-it".

She was getting a little chilly and went back into the hall which, thanks to the space-heaters, was hothouse hot. She wondered if Olivia would blab. Probably. But in that regard, at least, she really couldn't give a damn. In fact, it might even be to her advantage if the extras knew that she had become the first assistant director's personal squeeze.

Did they have a chance? Could it work – like... really work?

Pah! And double pah! What the hell was she thinking of? She'd kissed the guy, stroked his back – in fact, he might even have stroked her breast, she couldn't be quite sure – but that did not in any way a marriage make! A marriage? Just who on this earth or the next was talking about marriage, or children...

Pah!

CHAPTER 16

I once had a girlfriend who was always late. She was not only always late, but sometimes she didn't even turn up at all. But so desperate was I for her kisses that I ignored this constant tardiness. "No problem at all," I'd say. "What can I get you to drink?" – the only effect of which was that Sibella became even more tardy, and even more likely to not turn up at all. Boy, did she have the whip hand! She eventually dumped me and within three months had married a hedge-fund manager. Dumped for a multimillionaire hedge-fund manager – I ask you! I wonder if Mr Hedgie ever realised that Sibella had been running two horses at the same time, though it probably wasn't just two, more like three or four.

Anyway – the point of this little trip down memory lane is that ever since I've been ever so slightly allergic to people being late. It gets my goat. And now, when people are late, I'm no longer one of those forgiving types who makes them welcome and who springs up to buy a drink. No, in these post-Sibelline days, I generally give voice to my displeasure.

And since we are talking of tardy bastards, I am naturally referring to the tardiest bastard I know: Grubby. Even though we'd arranged to meet up in the Fox at noon, and even though I had actually turned up at 12.30, it was now gone 1 p.m., and I'd just received an uneasy message on my pager – "Running a bit late." If Grubby had sent me a text saying he was running late, then he was going to be really late. Had he even left London? Would he even be in by 2.30, when the kitchens closed?

Well, one thing was for certain, and that was that I wasn't going to postpone my lunch until Grubby grubbed into the pub. I went to the bar and ordered a steak-and-kidney pie, another cup of black coffee and, what the hell, a pint of cider. I returned to my table, my book and my newspapers, and by the time Grubby eventually arrived at 2.30 p.m., I'd not only finished my meal, but it had been cleared away and I was on my fourth cup of coffee. Regrettably, the kitchen was still open. He ordered the usual Grubby staple of ham, egg and chips.

'Made it,' he said as he blundered over to my window table, briefcase in one hand and a dripping pint of IPA in the other. He was wearing his trademark rumpled grey suit, plus grey shirt and food-encrusted tie, the whole look bizarrely capped off with a white plastic belt. 'How you getting on, Kim?'

'I'm getting on just fine considering I've been waiting here for over two hours,' I said tartly. 'What the hell happened this time? Don't tell me – you got stuck in a traffic jam.'

'No, nothing like that,' he said, taking a huge pull on his pint and smacking his lips in the most irritating fashion known to man, and then, perhaps even more irritatingly, wiping the froth off his lips with the back of his hand. 'Slept through my alarm.'

Now I am, as you know, a mild-mannered, softly spoken soul, but this guy was really getting on my wick. He'd kept me waiting two hours and he hadn't even apologised. In times gone by, I might have put up with this sort of behaviour, but there were, obviously, many more reasons for staying civil with Sibella than there were with bloody Grubby. 'Are you even going to apologise?' I said.

'Look at you Mr Hoity-Toity, with all your airs and graces,' he said. 'Fancying yourself as a bit of a superstar now that you're rubbing shoulders with Mr Tom Cruise and Mr Stanley Kubrick?'

'What the hell are you talking about?' I said, and to show

that I wasn't even remotely cowed, I also had a huge swig of my pint, though the cider was a hell of a sight more gassy than the IPA and I had to burp. 'Since when is it hoity-toity to ask for an apology when some oafish git has kept you waiting for over two hours?'

'Oh, poor little Kimmy,' he said, and then he proceeded to finish off the rest of his IPA, all the while eyeballing me through his smudged specs. He slapped the empty glass onto the table. 'Well, if it's going to make you any happier, then I'm very, very sorry. I'm truly sorry. I am pathetically sorry. I am as sorry as you wouldn't believe, and if there's anything, anything at all that would make it up to you, then just ask and it's yours.'

'I don't know why, Grubby, but I detect a slight tingling of sarcasm,' I said. 'Tell me one thing – are you late with everyone? Are you as late with your bosses or your girlfriends as you are with me?'

'Certainly not,' he said promptly, 'particularly not the girlfriends. But you, Kim, well, you're a mate.'

I could have happily dived down this rabbit hole to discuss why Grubby thought it was fine to be late for his mates, but I'd have been wasting my breath. Deep breath in, deep breath out, relax, just let it go. 'Want another pint?' I said.

'Yes, please.'

His lunch had arrived by the time I got back with the IPA and the cider. It seemed that he'd somehow learned to eat without chewing. 'I'm famished,' he said, egg yolk dripping onto his crotch.

'So what's been happening in the office?' I said. 'Anyone miss me?'

'Not really, no,' he said. He'd pronged four chips onto his fork, and was cramming them into his mouth sideways, sort of like a cow eating a particularly stubborn thistle. 'No one really noticed you'd gone, and then one of the news editors wanted you for a job and you weren't there, and they realised you hadn't been in the office for about a month.'

'Oh, that's nice.'

'But it's all been cleared up now,' Grubby said. 'Spike said you'd been sectioned and that you were currently doing time in Friern Barnet loony bin.'

'Sounds plausible.'

'Certainly wasn't a person in the office who didn't believe it.' He'd cleaned the plate in two minutes flat and was mopping up all the gubbins with a slice of white buttered bread.

'Any gossip?' I asked.

'Oh, one fun thing.' He wiped his lips again with the back of his hand, liberally smearing food across his cheek. 'After ten years of happy marriage, Spike's been dumped by his wife. He's currently living in a Travelodge by Tower Bridge.'

'Surprised she lasted one year, let alone ten.'

'Word is that she's going to take him to the absolute cleaners,' he said cheerily. 'Though he's become an absolute menace in the office. You're well out of it.'

'Poor Spike.' We grinned as we toasted the old bastard.

Grubby flopped his briefcase onto the table and clicked it open. He produced a very chunky black pen, some wires, a grey box that was about the size of a pack of butter and a hefty brown envelope. 'The Olympus spy pen!' he said proudly. 'It's digital – cost £15 grand! You better not break it!'

'Excellent!' I picked up the pen. Up close, it did not look even remotely like a pen. 'They'd have done better to disguise it as a cigar tube,' I said.

'So you were just going to have a cigar tube tucked into your breast pocket?' he said.

'Fair enough,' I said. 'So what's the drill?'

Grubby explained how the spy pen worked – and it all sounded spectacularly hit and miss. The idea was that you had the pen in your breast pocket, fingernail lens pointing at what you wanted to photograph. The two wires went from the bottom of the pen to the box which had to be discreetly tucked away into a pocket, and this seemed to be about the only good thing about the plan so far, as what with our cloaks, I'd have plenty of places to hide the box. Of more concern was the pen. Firstly, I'd have to start wearing a jacket, rather than a fleece, and that in itself would provoke comment. Secondly, one of the crew was bound to notice that I'd suddenly started carrying a pen in my top-pocket. Still – couldn't be helped. At least it was better than me trying to snatch a picture with my dodgy Olympus Twin. Grubby pointed out a red button on the side of the box. Press that and I had a picture. So far, so simple.

'The tricky bit is going to be getting the focus right,' Grubby said.

'How do you mean?'

'I had a try-out with it yesterday and it's damn difficult getting the pictures tight,' he said. 'You adjust the focus by twisting the top of the pen. At the moment it's roughly set for ten metres. But the only way we'll know whether it's in focus or not is when you download the pictures.'

'When I download the pictures?' I repeated. 'I haven't got the first clue how to download a picture.'

'It's all in the manual, mate – dead easy. You just plug the box into your laptop, then the wizard will run you through how to set it all up, bish-bash-bosh.'

If ever there were three words to strike terror in the heart of a reporter, it would be hearing a photographer airily dismiss your (justifiable) computer qualms with the words "bish-bash-bosh" – almost as terrifying as "easy-peasy lemon-squeezy".

'I am really bad with computers,' I said. 'They do my head in.' I had visions of three-hour sessions in front of my laptop during which I'd achieve the square root of sod all.

'You'll get the hang of it, bright boy like you.' He stretched over and gave my cheek a particularly irksome pinch between thumb and forefinger.

'Get off me!' I said.

He loafed off to get the next round in. I was inspecting the pen. It didn't look anything like a pen! And most of its pictures were going to be a complete blur! And I'd just have to keep going back onto the set, taking picture after picture, until I had something which was even halfway printable—

'That looks interesting, what have you got there?'

It was Nina, looking like some fresh-faced cheerleader, ponytail, peachy cheeks, pearly white teeth, all that stuff – God, don't you just hate these people who are naturally beautiful?

'Oh this?' I said, hyper-casual. 'Just a pen my mate's bought me.'

'That's a pen?' she said. 'It doesn't look anything like a pen.'

'Yeah, it's a special pen.' I tucked the pen into my trouser pocket.

'And what's this other stuff on the table?' she said, gesturing to the box, the wires, the hefty envelope. 'That going to help fill your pen up?'

'Nah, that's different,' I said, so totally and utterly chilled, but nevertheless mightily relieved when Grubby returned with the drinks.

'Thanks, Grubby.' I said, getting to my feet. It would be as well to make the introductions. 'Nina this is Grubby. Grubby – Nina.'

They shook hands and said howdy-do. Grubby was then given the most rigorous top-to-toe inspection. Before he could completely land me in it, I decided to expand on the introduction. 'Nina's one of the special extras working on the film,' I said. 'Grubby's a used-car salesman.'

'You're a used-car salesman?' she said, barely concealing her incredulity, and I must admit it was a bit of a stretch, since used-car salesmen generally dress like sharp-suited spivs and Grubby was so grubby the binmen would have taken him out, no questions asked.

'You don't look like a used-car salesman,' Nina said. 'What's your best-selling car?'

'Well, that depends,' Grubby said. I could almost see the cogs whirring in his tiny brain.

'Depends on what?'

'Depends on what you're after. Family car, luxury car, sports car or a, er, small car.'

'Family car.'

'Family car, eh?' he said and he dithered for a bit. I was kicking myself for having picked the Fox for a meet-up – what sort of moron fixed up a super-secret lunch at the most popular pub in town?

To my utter astonishment, Grubby actually said something sensible. 'German's usually best, the VW Polo or the Audi.'

'What sort of Audi?'

'My – aren't you the inquisitive one,' I trilled to Nina. 'Anyone would think you were a tabloid reporter... or...' I trailed off. 'Or... a police detective.'

She gave me the most speculative of looks. 'Interesting,' she said. 'Anyone might think that I was a... now what did you say?... a tabloid reporter.'

I bit my lower lip. Nina sniffed. Grubby chimed in again, eager to parade his used-car knowledge. 'The Audi A4,' he said proudly. 'And I'll tell you the second-hand cars to avoid at all costs – Jeeps and anything from Italy.'

'That so?' she said.

Grubby's pager went off – and like the cretin he undoubtedly was, he pulled it out of his pocket and looked at the message. He looked at me, raised his eyebrows – it could only have been the picture desk, sending him off on the next wild goose chase.

'Is that a pager?' Nina said.

'Yeah, it's a pager,' Grubby said.

'Do second-hand car salesmen often have pagers?' Nina asked guilelessly.

'I guess the best ones do,' I said, grinding my teeth in frustration. What a mutant – just gawping at his pager in full view of just about the most suspicious woman I'd ever met. And it was all pretty suspicious. In those days, only doctors tended to have pagers. And scum-sucking hacks. And that even more revolting breed, the scum-suckers' scum-sucker, the paparazzi.

Nina continued to stare. 'Nice to meet you Grubby,' she said. 'I'll leave you to two to your pagers and your, errr, pen.'

We smiled pleasantly at Nina as she sashayed off to the bar and, in silence, took our seats. I took the box and the wires off the table and put them in a Tesco bag. I gave Grubby a foul stare and he tapped the side of his head with his forefinger as if it was me – me! – who was certifiably insane.

'Brilliant,' I hissed. 'Why don't you just show Nina your press card? Would you like me to introduce you to Stanley Kubrick?'

He stuffed his pager back into his pocket and took a long, irritating slurp of beer. 'Look, chummy, you picked this pub, not me.'

'But I didn't think you were going to plonk all this kit right out on the table,' I said.

'Well, how the hell else was I going to give it to you?'

'We could have done it in your car.'

'Your fault for picking the pub.'

'Yes, of course it's my fault,' I said. 'It's always my fault, especially when it's you who's cocked up, and whenever you do cock up, which is often, the very first thing you say is, "It's Kim's fault!"'

'Well, it is your fault!'

I glanced over at Nina. She was leaning back, elbows against the bar, long legs languidly crossed, and she was openly, brazenly, inspecting us as we bickered. I fluttered my fingers and gave her a lovely smile.

'Let's change the subject,' I said. 'I mean, what the hell can she do anyway?'

What the hell could she do?

What the hell couldn't she do?

Grubby did change the subject, and, for once, he moved onto fertile ground. 'So how you getting on with Tom Cruise?' he said. 'You best buddies yet?'

And now it was my turn to have a long, leisurely and indeed irritating slurp of cider. 'You're not going to believe it, Grubby, but yes we are!'

No swanks but... I pretty much sealed the deal on that first night with the Macallan whisky. You wouldn't believe it, but between us we finished the entire bottle, rolling into Tom's Rolls Royce at sunup, before I was chauffeured back to my hotel.

The next day, Tom had given me a wave as he'd come onto the set. Even with the make-up and the eye-whitening drops, he still looked pretty green at the gills – unlike me. He obviously wasn't used to taking the punishment.

Even though we had just polished off an expensive bottle of whisky together, it certainly wasn't for me, a humble extra, to presume to go up to Tom and start making chitty-chat. Instead, I dutifully, diligently went about my business of not getting food on my cloak and not moving when the cameras were rolling. At the close of play I had been expecting to turn in for the night, when the tautly tattooed Olivia sidled up to me again and informed me that my presence was once again requested in Tom Cruise's Winnebago, the only pain of which was that I didn't have anything to give him. It had never occurred to me that Tom might want to see me for two nights in a row, but then it had also never occurred to me that Tom might actually have fallen for my charms.

Tom welcomed me into his Winnebago with a firm handshake, and it was all pretty much as immaculate as it had been the previous night, except there was not whisky on the table but an opened bottle of Chablis. Next to it was a newspaper that looked just a little familiar. It was a copy of the *Sunday Express* that I'd happened to glance over just before I'd set off on my ill-fated run.

'Cheers Tom,' I said. 'How we getting on?'

'A lot better now that I've got a glass of wine in front of me.'

'Never drink when you're filming?'

'No,' he said. 'That would be unprofessional.'

'Thank God I'm an amateur!'

He sighed and sipped and his eyes drifted onto the copy of the *Sunday Express*, which had obviously been left out for my benefit. 'You seen that thing?'

'I'm afraid I did,' I said.

'I mean... I mean who are these people? Why do they make this stuff up?'

'Probably because they think you'll never sue.'

'You know, Lawrence... maybe you're right.'

'It can happen.'

He was swirling the wine in the glass, holding it up to his nose, watching it as it caught the light. Me? I still couldn't believe that I, docile Kimmy, was having a glass of wine with the most famous man on the planet. Never really got the hang of it, even after a month of being his drinking buddy.

'It was a really nasty piece,' Tom said.

'Yeah, a real hatchet job,' I said, instantly kicking myself for using journo jargon.

'A hatchet job?' he said. 'Not heard that one before. But that's what it was – a hatchet job. I don't mind so much them taking me down, but I hate what they've done to Nic. It's just... it's just...'

'Made-up bollocks?'

'Yeah,' he said. 'They just made it up. That... that our marriage is a sham – that I'm impotent and sterile.'

'Vicious lies,' I said.

'These... these reporters. They're—'

'Scum-sucking bottom-feeders,' I said promptly.

'That's what they are!' he said. 'I know I have to deal with them, because that's what you have to do when you want to sell your film, but God, they're just reptiles!'

'The *Sunday Express* reporters are the worst of the lot,' I said with some asperity. 'That damn paper's just a fiction factory.'

'I hear the *Sun* newspaper is pretty bad too,' he said.

'Nothing like as bad as the *Sunday Express*,' I said. 'Or the *Mirror*. Hate that paper.'

'Yeah, but we're just talking about gradations of scum,' he said. 'Like what's worse – leeches or rats?'

'Rats, definitely,' I said. 'I once got into a fight with a rat. He bit me on the nose.'

'Ouch,' Tom said. 'OK, forget leeches and rats. What about fleas and lice – which one's worse? In fact, it's a better analogy because they're both parasites, and that's exactly what these reporters are. Parasites!'

'Parasites!' I said, basking in the warm glow of Tom's love.

'Know what I'm going to do?'

'Astonish me, Tom.'

'I think you're right, Lawrence. I think they only printed this… this crap because they thought I wouldn't sue. Well, you know what, Lawrence? I am going to sue.'

'Carter Ruck are the lawyers you want,' I said.

'Carter Ruck eh?' he said.

'They're the best in town,' I said. 'If you don't sign up with Carter Ruck, then the *Sunday Express* will.'

'I'm going to do it,' he said.

'Good for you Tom.'

'I'll call them up tomorrow, get them to demand an apology.'

'Hmm,' I said. 'Not that I know much about it, Tom, but don't get Carter Ruck to send a letter. That's small beer. Hit them with a writ.' I was barely able to conceal my glee. For us worker-bee hacks, there is no finer feeling on earth than landing your rivals in the ordure. Shame it wasn't Bain at the *Daily Mirror* who had so scurrilously libelled Tom, but, well, you can't have everything.

'Yeah?' he said. 'Like all guns blazing?'

'Writs show you mean business,' I said.

'If nothing else, it'll make the other newspapers more wary about publishing this sort of rubbish in future,' Tom mused. 'How do you know all this legal stuff by the way?'

'My aunt Pat's a lawyer. She's got several big thrills in life, including marrying men and then divorcing them, but her biggest thrill by far is suing people. That's what she really gets off on – getting somebody in the witness box and watching them squirm. She lives for feuds.'

Rather surprisingly, this part of my story was not another Kim fabrication but was actually true. My aunt Pat just lived for divorcing and suing. She died quite recently, and, since she was both childless and husbandless, her seven nephews had fairly been licking their lips for a slice of her multimillion-pound fortune. But when it came to it, the miserable sod left the whole damn lot to the National Trust Southern Coastal Paths. Boo bloody hoo.

'OK,' Tom said. 'Sounds like you know your stuff.'

'Sure do.'

'Carter Ruck?' he said. 'I'll call them tomorrow.'

And call them he did – and in short order the wire services were thrumming with the news that Tom Cruise was suing the *Sunday Express* for libel. He was to develop such a taste for writs that, happy days, he also started taking chunks out of the American rags.

We'd soon polished off the Chablis and, acutely aware that I should not outstay my welcome, I headed for the door. Tom opened it. 'Hey Lawrence, fancy a run one of these days?'

'Absolutely,' I said. 'How about tomorrow morning?'

'See you here at noon?'

'Done,' I said.

He flashed me that great twinkling smile of his. 'I know an old drovers' road you might like.'

'Would that be a very muddy drovers' road with a lot of five-bar gates?'

'It would.'

'Can't think of anything finer,' I said – and I couldn't.

CHAPTER 17

Pumping iron was as good a way as any to grieve. Glenn loaded up the bar with 120 kilos and strapped his weightlifting belt around his stomach. It was made of black leather, eight inches broad; every time he put it on, he always thought of the champions' belts worn by the heavyweight boxers.

He didn't normally deadlift 120 kilos, but he figured that, for a short time, it might take his mind off things. His mum for a start. As usual, he'd made to call her up that morning, had even punched in the number, before it hit him – he wouldn't be calling that number ever again. He rubbed chalk onto his palms, centred his feet, flexed his fingers on the barbell. He'd never got to say goodbye to her; hadn't seen her for over a year. Kubrick was absolutely bound to tell him that he couldn't go to the funeral, but if Kubrick did that, Glenn would walk, no question. And take the strain with his arms, and tense his core, and slowly, slowly lift up this big beast of a barbell, thighs quite quivering with the strain. Even more slowly, return it to the floor. And did it really matter that he hadn't been able to say goodbye to his mother? It would have been nice, but surely the main event was the memories, the walks, the laughs, the life they'd shared together; was it really that important that he hadn't been with her when she'd died? Take the strain again, tight stomach, and ease up the weights off the ground, all but tottering, and return the barbell to the ground, and hell... Not being with her when she'd died had been a big miss, and it would be something he'd regret for the rest of his days. Take the strain again, head up, looking at himself in the mirror – and just off to the side, at the far end of the gym, there really was something to take his mind off his mother: Nina. He, Glenn, had been kissing Nina last night – not just one of the most gorgeous women he'd ever laid eyes on, but sweet-natured and… and… He hadn't had a chance to speak to her after they'd wrapped last night – Kubrick was, as ever, finicking around with the lights, and by the time they'd done, Nina was nowhere to be seen. And now, well here she was, stunning as ever in her men's basketball gear – how had she come by that gear? No, let's not go there – and she was doing, come to think of it, some particularly sexy squats… the beauty of lifting this 120 kilo barbell, was that he could look at Nina in the mirror without her knowing that he was looking at her. Was she looking at him? Difficult to tell. She was looking in his general direction, but was she looking at him? What a kisser! Now that woman, she knew how to kiss… Probably had more than her fair share of kisses – nooo, let's so not go there either. And tense his core, take the strain, rock back and heave that huge weight off the ground, though not nearly so focused this time, he'd been thinking about Nina rather than keeping his back straight and – Jesus – he'd tweaked his back! The whole point of doing these massive weights was to focus, to take his mind off his mother and, well, Nina, and he hadn't been focused and he hadn't kept his mind on the job, and now it felt like he'd done his back in and serve him right!

Glenn gingerly removed the weights from the barbell and returned them to the rack. Had he put his back out? Felt like more of a twinge. Might be best to just take it a little easier today – say, rather than beasting himself, he could spend fifteen minutes in the sauna, come out looking like a fat tomato, an incredibly sexy look, just exactly the sort of thing that would have Nina drooling.

How come she'd brought him that cup of tea the previous night? How had she even known that he was sitting in the portico staring out into the darkness? Glenn had no idea.

Strange to be kissing a woman for the first time when she was all but naked, silken skin under his fingertips…

He went up the stairs with barely a sideways glance – was she looking at him? Might have been – and stripped to his shorts in the changing room and went through to the sauna. He hadn't much liked saunas, but he'd now gradually started to get into them, could now take a full fifteen minutes; what would it be like doing it Finnish style and getting flogged with birch twigs? Pointlessly painful. But what if Nina was doing the flogging? What if Nina, topless, perhaps even bottomless, was doing the flogging – what a thought…

And back to thoughts of his mum, and with a jolt he remembers that he'll never speak to her again, and then there's Nina, who, unless he's very much mistaken, he'll be speaking to in about twenty minutes – and as to that, he still hasn't remotely decided what he's going to say.

Glenn's skin is slick with sweat as he leaves the sauna. He steps into the shower and enjoys the life-enhancing thrill of ice-cold water on red-hot skin, taking it first on his face and his chest, before giving it full play over his back.

He towels down and puts on his clothes and moisturises his face; he takes particular care when he brushes his hair. Though considering what he has to do, and what has to be done, it might be best if he left the changing rooms with hair askew and red leather skin.

He goes out into the reception area, and the café, and there is Nina sitting at a table, where she is sipping coffee and reading a book. She does not look up.

'Oh, hi Nina.' Glenn stands by her table.

'Oh, hi Glenn.' She smiles as she looks up at him. But is it a warm smile – or is it a little fixed?

'Get you another coffee?'

'Another latte would be lovely.'

'Coming right up.' He smiles at her, but he can feel it's way over the top, it's more of a grin. He goes to the counter, pays for a latte and an Americano, returns to Nina's table.

Sits down at Nina's table. She gives him a pleasant enough smile. Glenn has the feeling that the ball is most definitely in his court.

'How are you doing?' he says.

'Very well, thank you,' she replies. 'How are you? I'm so sorry about your mother.'

'Yeah,' he says. 'Thank you.' Another awkward silence, which Nina does not look like she is even remotely tempted to fill. But he knows, and she knows, that, despite his mother's death, there is only one subject on the agenda.

'Hmm, well,' he says. 'I'm very sorry about last night.'

'Are you?' Nina smiled. 'I'm not.'

He stared at the table. The barista brought the coffees over, bought him a little more time. Should he say it? Say it – or go with his gut?

'It shouldn't have happened,' he said. 'I was all over the place.'

Nina was still smiling, but the smile was getting more and more fixed. What spectacularly beautiful lips she had.

'Uh-huh,' she said.

'You see, Nina, I've been in movies all my adult life, and I've got this one fixed rule.' He was almost gabbling – just slow it down. It was easier if he stared at his coffee cup. 'That rule is that, during a shoot, it's best not to get into a relationship with any of the cast or crew. It's just easier.'

Nina brought the latte cup to her lips, eyes unwavering. 'Uh-huh.'

He darted a look at her, reverted to his coffee cup. 'It's just I've seen what can happen on shoots when the crew start having relationships with the cast – it all starts just fine, but then they inevitably break up, and then it all turns horrible, and it's just simpler, easier, not to even go there…' It all sounded particularly lame. But the hell of it was that it was all true. Relationships on set always ended disastrously – as had his one and only foray into these murky waters. It had been about a decade ago, he'd been in the movie business for about five years, and had worked his way up to being the second assistant director on a medium-sized film, budget of about £5 million. There'd been a woman on the set who'd caught his eye, and he had most certainly caught her eye, and one night after a little too much booze they'd ended up in bed, and they'd sort of started dating – which was all well and good, except that the woman, Trixy, wasn't just any old member of the cast. She was the lead and soon enough they'd split up (leading actresses being generally both beautiful and mad as a box of frogs), at which point Trixy not only started sleeping with the gaffer, but had made Glenn's life a merry hell, and had nearly got him thrown off the shoot. Never, ever again!

'Uh-huh,' Nina said. She wasn't helping out much at all, eyes drilling into him and not saying a word.

'I mean, look, Nina, you're a fantastic woman, a wonderful woman. But it's just... Dating people on a shoot is a really bad idea. People talk, people get jealous. Wouldn't be good for you, wouldn't be good for me. It's really a non-starter.'

'That right?'

'But, you know, like, when the shoot's over, and we're done, then, if you're not averse to the idea, then maybe... maybe we could pick things up. Maybe I could take you out for dinner or something like that, see what happens...'

'Uh-huh.' Eyes absolutely glacial.

'Nina, I'm really... really sorry about this. But it's just my one golden rule. No dating on a shoot. But when it's over, you know, we could...'

Nina took a long pull on her coffee, cleared her throat. 'So let me get this straight,' she said. 'For the duration of this shoot, you want to put everything on ice – you want us to return to being our old formal selves, hardly saying a word to each other—'

'No, no, Nina, we can still talk. I'd love to talk to you.'

'I see,' she said. 'So we can talk to each other, but nothing more, and when Kubrick's finally had his fill of us, then we can go out for dinner and the rest, and pick up straight from where we left off? That what you're thinking?'

He nodded. 'That's right.'

Nina snorted – a particularly derisive snort, which may even have included the word 'Pah!'

'Dream on,' she said, getting to her feet. 'Not going to happen. Not ever going to happen.' Her fingers trailed over his shoulders as she walked past him. A trace of the most exquisite perfume. He'd never smelt perfume on her before. 'Good luck with your monk-like existence, Glenn. I want no part of it.' Without a backward glance she walked out of the café and out of the gym – and Glenn was gripped with the most immediate sense of ex-lover's remorse. Not that they'd been lovers, not even close, but it had sure as hell felt like love, and Glenn had the very strong suspicion that, from now on in, for the rest of the shoot, Nina would be giving him the Big Freeze. But... eventually, in time, she'd realise that it was for the best; on-set relationships always, always ended in disaster, that was just the rule of the movie world. They did of course provide a fleeting distraction – a delicious distraction – from the tedium of movie-making, but that only made the subsequent break-up all the more awful and –let's make no bones about it – the number-one rule of movie romances was that they never lasted. They were launched with all the fizzing, crackling energy that comes with a shoot, but, by definition, they couldn't last. And maybe Glenn just had to face it that, even without the shoots, perhaps he just wasn't very good boyfriend material. Shame though. Real shame about Nina. He'd meant every word when he'd pitched the idea of them perhaps dating when the shoot was over. But a go-getting woman like Nina was never going to put up with that... dream on!

CHAPTER 18

Mrs Cocker, owner of the Royal Terrace B&B, tore off another quid of tobacco, gave it a resolute chew and with her tongue deftly tucked it into her cheek; by God, she was irritated. From upstairs, directly above the lounge where she was sitting, there resounded a steady rhythmic thump. It was the disgusting sound of a headboard banging against a wall and was accompanied by intermittent grunts and girlish squeals.

Mrs Cocker spat a jet of tobacco juice into the spittoon three yards away – bang on as always, would have made her old dad proud. There were a number of things that vexed her about this steady thump-a-thump from upstairs. Firstly: it was distracting her from watching the telly. Secondly: it was the sound of that harlot Vicky having sex – and sex, as Vicky had been regularly reminded, was expressly forbidden at the Royal Terrace B&B. Thirdly: as if it wasn't bad enough that Vicky was having sex in Mrs Cocker's B&B, she was having sex at the most ungodly hour of 5 p.m.! Sex, if it was to occur at all, was a night-time activity, best done with curtains closed and lights switched off. And fourthly, and most irritatingly of all, the sound of this couple having sex was a reminder to Mrs Cocker that she hadn't had a sniff of it in decades, not that it had ever been that pleasurable, but, but… Vicky and her lover were clearly making this racket just to irritate her.

Vicky, she knew, had got back to the B&B after what must have been a very boozy lunch with her lover. Mrs

Cocker, snoozling in her armchair, had been woken up as they'd clattered up the stairs. Then, from all the bumping and the banging in Vicky's room above the lounge, they'd immediately stripped and started having sex – but they'd been having sex for over half-an-hour. Who in God's name had sex for thirty minutes? Why on earth prolong the infernal business?

The tempo of the headboard-banging sped up, the yowls got louder; it sounded like the bed itself was jumping across the floor. With one final crash they were done. Mrs Cocker heard something being thrown onto the floor, probably a shoe, and then all was silence. The lovers were asleep.

Mrs Cocker tore off another chunk of tobacco with her brown teeth and pondered what to do. She was going to have it out with Vicky, no question – God, she'd let rip. Of all the girls in the B&B, Vicky was far and away the gobbiest, always had some smart-alec retort. Not this time though – because rules were rules, set by Mrs Cocker herself, and Vicky had broken her number-one rule: no male visitors on the premises. That was the rule. But the real question was whether she wanted to kick Vicky out. She'd had six girls living with her for over six months, a tidy earner; she'd already made double her usual take for the year. Such a tricky line to tread – on the one hand wanting to keep Vicky's custom and yet on the other just thirsting to scream at the woman and tell her she was a complete slut...

Mrs Cocker was watching *Countdown* (that Carol Vorderman, by the way: obviously another hussy) when she looked at the carriage clock on the mantelpiece, and she listened to the upstairs silence, and she realised that there lay in front of her a golden opportunity to really cook Vicky's goose, and probably that boyfriend of hers too, as he was also somehow involved with this pervert film. Because Vicky, if she was to make it to the film set on time, should have already left the house – and yet she was still abed upstairs, doubtless entwined with her lover and sleeping the sleep of the sated.

Some time later, well past 6 p.m., the phone rang. Not wishing to rouse Vicky from her slumbers, Mrs Cocker quickly picked up.

'Royal Terrace B&B,' she cooed.

'Hi, is that Mrs Cocker?'

'It is.'

'Hi, it's Glenn here from the film crew. You haven't seen Vicky, have you? She was supposed to be here thirty minutes ago.'

'I don't rightly know where she is, I'm afraid, sir.'

'Do you know if she's left the B&B?'

'I certainly think she has, sir.'

'Right – thanks very much for your help, Mrs Cocker.'

'I do what I can, sir, I do what I can.'

Mrs Cocker gently returned the phone to its handset, and now, well, there was nothing to do but sit tight and wait – though thinking of it, she did have something to celebrate, and celebrate she would, and she rewarded herself with a large tot of Famous Grouse.

* * *

The mood on the set was mutinous. We'd been rehearsing and rehearsing the girls' entrance for about a couple of hours, but without cameras, because the principal girl, Vicky, hadn't showed up and Kubrick couldn't shoot without her.

Tom Cruise's stand-in, Jimmy, was also a no-show; you didn't have to be Brain of Britain to work out where he was.

Kubrick was exceptionally pettish. The whole thing was perfectly outrageous! It was he and he alone who called the shots! And now, despite wanting to call a shot, he was unable to do so, because this Vicky woman was doing whatever the hell she was doing with Jimmy!

Tom Cruise, having no stand-in, was having to stand in for himself, and seemed to be rather enjoying himself – just standing around as stand-ins do, and chatting to the girls and the extras; for Tom, it didn't make any odds that Vicky was a no-show, as for over a year now he had resigned himself to a life of indentured servitude. His hours were not his own. And for Tom, it made no difference whether he was rehearsing, or whether he was filming, or whether it was Kubrick who was yelling "Do it again", or whether the entire shoot had to be put on hold because one of the girls hadn't turned up.

Of more interest to me was the body language between Glenn and Nina. Having so exquisitely brought the pair together in the portico, and having heard from that tattooed tittle-tattle Olivia that they'd been all over each other, I'd thought my work was done, another happy couple brought together, and all entirely down to me – no please, don't trouble yourselves to thank me. (It is possible, of course, that Nina and Glenn might have eventually found their way into each other's arms – but do me a favour. That proud pair wouldn't have laid a finger on each other if I hadn't nudged them in the right direction.)

Anyway, it seemed that within hours of their marathon kissing session, they'd already split up! What? What the hell had happened between them? I mean I've had a few break-ups in my time, but generally we've lasted a little longer than twelve hours. Maybe... Maybe they'd had a one-night stand! That would've been fast work for Glenn, but I wouldn't have put it past the old dog, especially as he'd been living like a monk for the past year, and what with grieving his mum, maybe some sex was just what he needed, they needed, only for the pair of them to be racked with guilt the next morning. Possibly...

But something was definitely off between them. Glenn was talking with the second assistant director, the porcine Roddie, while Nina was talking to her buddy Mandy, which was all fairly standard, except that I was acutely aware that over the past three hours, neither of them had even so much as looked at the other.

Best, I thought, to find out what had happened – and what,

if anything, I could do to help. 'Hi Nina,' I said. 'Hi Mandy, how's it going?'

Mandy, at least, seemed pleased to see me. 'Loving it,' she said.

Josh oozed over to join us. Josh was as besotted as ever with Mandy, but preferred it when I was on the scene too. 'Hi hi,' he said.

'Hi,' Mandy said, giving him an appraising look. 'Vicky's fairly going to cop it.'

'She sure will,' I said. Mandy and Josh had their masks up on their forehead, but Nina, for some reason, was still wearing her mask. I could see nothing but mascara and black eye shadow and beguiling eyes. 'How you getting on in there, Nina?'

'Just fine,' she said. From the way the words were spat out, she sounded anything but fine.

It seemed to me that, if I were to broach the subject at all, it would be best to arrive at it tangentially.

'This must be really tough on the crew,' I said. 'Bad enough being bossed around by Kubrick, and now they've got to wait for Vicky to show up.'

'She's probably in bed with Jimmy,' Mandy said.

'I'm sure you're right,' I said, before guilelessly continuing. 'I really feel for Glenn, what with his mum dying and... and everything else.'

'He hadn't seen her for over a year,' Mandy chimed.

'Awful for him,' I said, before sending out the most delicate of probes. 'What do you think, Nina?'

'What do I think about what?' she said. Though I couldn't see her mouth, on account of the mask, it sounded like there was a full-fat sneer on her lips.

'What do you think about Glenn?' I said, finally getting to the beef.

'Glenn?' she said, before suddenly snapping to attention. 'Hey Lawrence, I've got a question for you. Did Glenn ask for some tea last night?'

'Glenn?' I said. 'How d'you mean?'

'Did Glenn ask you for some tea last night?' she repeated.

'He was in a bad way. I thought he could use a cup of tea.'

'Thought he could use a cup of tea?' she repeated. 'So why didn't you just take him a cup of tea? Why'd you get me to do it?'

'Well… well…' I was just a little taken aback that, after all my ingenious matchmaking, I was now being given a roasting. I mean, I don't (much) seek gratitude, but I certainly don't expect to be coming under hostile fire. 'I could have sent anybody with the tea, Nina,' I said. 'You happened to be the first person I came across.'

'Bullshit,' she said, face I'm sure now contorted with fury, though I couldn't see it. She gave me a sharp poke with her finger. 'I've got no idea what your little game is, but the very last thing I want is you setting me up with one of the crew.'

'Me?' I said. 'Why… why ever do you think I was trying to set you up with, er, Glenn, or anyone else—'

'You're full of it!' she said. Another sharp poke to the chest. 'You knew exactly what you were doing.'

'Nina – Nina!' I said. 'Is that really fair?'

'Stay out of my life.' Another poke to the chest. My cloak fell slightly open. 'Hey – are you wearing a jacket?'

'I am,' I said.

'Why are you wearing a jacket?'

'Are jackets banned on set?'

Inscrutable eyes stared at me. 'Next thing you'll have a pen in your top pocket.'

'What? What the… What do you mean?' I blustered. She was spot on, as always. God I wish I'd had my mask – so much easier to dissemble. Note to self: wear mask more often, particularly when dealing with Nina.

'You know perfectly well what—' Nina was cut off by the sound of squawking from outside the hall, and then in tripped Vicky. In her wake was the gormless Jimmy, though he at least had the good grace to look a little sheepish.

Kubrick, who was sitting on his director's chair, broke off from talking to Tom Cruise and, in complete silence, coolly surveyed his leading lady.

'Sorry we're late,' Vicky said. 'Overslept.' She giggled.

'You have kept 130 people waiting for over three hours,' Kubrick said.

'Look, I'm sorry, all right?' Vicky said.

Kubrick grunted. 'I'm not sure sorry is going to cut it.'

'What more do you want, Stanley?' she said. 'I've said I'm sorry. And besides, you were just going to be doing more of your rehearsals, which we've done thousands of times already, so does it really make that much difference if I miss a few?'

'I'm sorry?' Kubrick said.

'I'll bet you've just spent the last two hours rehearsing the same scene that we've rehearsed for the last five months. Does it really make any difference if I'm there for one rehearsal more or less?'

'Why indeed?' A small switched flicked in Stanley's head, as, finally, he made his mind up about something. He beckoned Glenn over. 'Glenn, could you get security to escort both Vicky and Jimmy off set. They are not to return.'

'Very good.' Glenn was immediately on to his walkie-talkie.

'Hah!' Vicky said. 'You can't kick me off the film, Stanley – because I'm your principal girl. In the last month, I'm in every single shot that you've filmed.'

The gasp from the cast and crew was audible. The great Stanley Kubrick: being cheeked on his own film set.

'That so?' Kubrick said.

'If I go, you'll have to scrap every second of film from Elveden.' Vicky smiled in triumph as she looked about the hall. 'And you'll be left with only eleven girls.'

'We'll just have to do what we can without you then, Vicky,' Kubrick said. Four of the set security guards bustled into the room.

'Ah gentlemen,' Kubrick said. 'Please remove Vicky and Jimmy from the set.'

'You can't do it without me!' Vicky wailed as the security guards closed in on her.

'I assure you, Vicky, that I very much can,' Kubrick said, before adding. 'Let's break for some tea.'

He had a quick conflab with Glenn and Tom Cruise, peering over at me before clasping his petite hands together. His hands were remarkable, very slim, delicate, almost lady-like – and all the more striking because they were attached to the body of a corpulent slob. Kubrick stared up at the vaulted ceiling and appeared to come to a decision. Glenn peeled off and walked over to our merry little band.

'Hi there,' he said, addressing all of us without looking at any of us. Nina, still with her mask on, gave him a cool glance. 'Lawrence,' Glenn said, turning to me. 'Tom wants you to be his new stand-in, you cool with that?'

'Absolutely,' I said. 'Love to be Tom's stand-in.'

Glenn now turned to the woman who, not twenty-four hours previously, had been the recipient of all his most ardent kisses. 'Nina,' he said. 'Stanley Kubrick has decided you will be our new principal girl. Will you do it?'

A long pause and unblinking eyes. 'Yes, I will,' she said.

'Thank you,' Glenn said. 'Thank you very much indeed.' He all but reached out to give Nina's elbow a squeeze, but she stepped smartly backwards and Glenn was left clutching at thin air.

CHAPTER 19

Perhaps we may allow ourselves another glimpse into the mind of the great Tom Cruise – and why ever not? Who wouldn't want to know how the world's number-one film star feels about being stuck on the world's longest film shoot?

You will be pleased to learn that Tom is feeling much, much happier.

Why is Tom so chirpy?

He's got a buddy, the ever affable, ever cheery Lawrence, who takes Tom on daily runs along the muddy lanes of Suffolk, and who drinks with him at night, and who offers sage advice and wry wit, but who also is very much aware of his place in the pecking order: who never presumes; who teases, but only very gently; who laughs when it is appropriate; and who, when he senses the need, offers up sweet empathy. And now that Lawrence has become Tom's stand-in, they get to hang out a whole lot more; they are even having lunch together in the Winnebago.

Tom was in the toilet washing his hands. He was looking at himself in the mirror, examining the crinkles around his eyes and wondering how much longer he'd got on the top of the Hollywood heap; wondering, in particular, whether a little tuck round the eyes might be good for his career, or whether it might be utterly disastrous. There were some guys out there who'd trashed their careers with a facelift. Top of the list: Mickey Rourke. Mickey had been a big player, had starred in *9 □2 Weeks*. Then he had his face lifted, and now you wouldn't recognise him if you sat next to him in the cinema. Tom might even stick Mickey's picture to the mirror, just as a gentle reminder not to go there. Tom did what he could to look the part, didn't mind make-up and eye brightener and hair dye, and, if it came to it, (though please God it wouldn't come to it), maybe even a hair transplant, but a nip and tuck? Never! Well, hopefully never.

He could hear talking on the other side of the door – it was Lawrence, probably chatting to Julienne, his make-up artist. Though Lawrence was speaking with an American twang. Tom took a moment to place the voice. Lawrence was doing an impression of Tom; he was pretty good!

Tom eased the door open a crack to see what was happening. Lawrence was wearing his stand-in cloak and his stand-in mask. Julienne, meanwhile, was giving every impression that she thought she was talking to the real Tom.

'What you gonna do when this whole thing is over, Julienne?' Lawrence said, lolling back on the armchair, feet cockily kicked up on the table. His accent was uncanny. It was near perfect. Certainly good enough to fool Julienne.

'I'll be going on a long, long holiday in the sun,' Julienne said. She was perched on the edge of the sofa and nursing a cup of tea. 'Might go to Goa, but it gets a bit hot there by March.'

'Reckon we'll still be filming in March?' Lawrence said.

'Course we will, Tom,' she said. 'What are you hoping to do when we finally wrap?'

'Take the kids to Alton Towers,' he said. 'Hear there's a really cool hotel you can stay at there, Splash Landings. Nic's always talking about it.'

'You're going to stay at Splash Landings?' Julienne said. 'You're having me on!'

'Naah, they got this great ride, kind of a squirrel run – the kids are gonna love it,' Lawrence said.

'You have got to be joking!' Julienne laughed. 'You'll get mobbed if you all go to Alton Towers!'

'I'll just wear this mask: no one will know who I am,' he said.

'Have you gone completely mad, Tom?' she said.

It had been fun to watch, but the gag had gone on long enough. Tom opened the toilet door and stepped into the room. Julienne gaped. 'Tom?' she said. 'Who the hell have I been talking to?'

'You've been talking to my twin, Tam,' he said. Tom laughed, a real belly laugh, first time he'd laughed like that in months.

'Fiddlesticks,' she said. 'Who is this joker?'

'It's my stand-in, Lawrence,' Tom said, and at that, the mask was removed to reveal a grinning Lawrence underneath.

Julienne looked from Lawrence to Tom and back to Lawrence again. 'That is unbelievable!' she said.

Tom chuckled. 'That was a great take-off of my voice.'

Lawrence promptly switched to Tom's voice again. 'Maybe, Tom, you're not the only guy who can act round here.'

'You're good, I'll give you that.'

'Reckon I could fool Kubrick?'

Tom put on his best imitation of Lawrence's cut-crystal English accent. 'Reckon I could fool the extras?'

'You guys are not serious?' Julienne said.

'Am I ever serious?' Tom said.

'You're never not serious!'

'If we got a couple of wigs, we'd be in the money,' Lawrence said.

'Really?' Julienne said. 'Are you serious?'

'Let's get the wigs and let's think about it,' Tom said. 'Hey, is there any of that white wine left?'

'I finished it,' Lawrence said. 'Sorry.'

'We'll just have to open another bottle then.'

'Tom!' squealed Julienne. 'What's got into you? You never drink when you're filming!'

'Little glass of wine won't hurt,' Tom said.

Julienne turned on Lawrence. 'This is your doing, isn't it?'

'Me?' said Lawrence. 'I always have a glass of wine at lunch.'

'You're both absolutely mad,' she said. 'Stanley will go mental when he finds out.'

'We'll need coloured contact lenses,' Lawrence said. 'Brown for Tom, green for me.'

'Hadn't thought about that,' Tom said as he went to the fridge and selected a bottle of Sancerre. 'We'll get the wigs, we'll get the contact lenses, and then we'll decide.'

'I'll drink to that!' said Lawrence – and that was the great thing about Lawrence, he just lived for the moment. And maybe that was the right attitude to have on the shoot. Since every single damn day was the same, right through from Monday to Sunday, then you had to find your own fun: might be running in the mud and the rain; might be a little glass of wine at lunchtime – or a bottle of wine after they'd wrapped; might even be… swapping places with the stand-in. Tom tasted the wine and it was delicious – and it was all the more delicious because he was drinking it at lunchtime, and because Stanley would have hated the thought of him drinking at lunchtime. But if, say, just thinking outside the box, Tom were to swap places with Lawrence, then Tom would be able to do something that he had not done in over twenty years – talk to people like a normal human being. He could talk to the girls, talk to the extras, just have a normal everyday conversation… Might be fun.

CHAPTER 20

It's not that Nina was angry with Glenn; she was just a little disappointed. Despite herself, she had allowed her hopes and dreams to turn into that dread thing called expectations. She'd only been and gone and done it again!

How many times? How many times did Nina have to get burned before she realised that having any expectations whatsoever of a guy was just laying yourself wide open to a big fat kiss-off? So, not that she'd known how it was going to work out with Glenn, but after that half-hour of kissing, she'd had that pleasant feeling that a poker player gets when they first take peek at their cards and when they realise that, maybe, with just a little bit of luck, they might be onto a hot one. There were a lot of things that she admired about Glenn – his good cheer, his professionalism, his work ethic; perhaps more importantly, Nina hadn't discerned any deal-breakers. And deal-breakers were just that – they were the red flags that ruled out any relationship whatsoever. All that good stuff like infidelity, and lying, and (at least for Nina) rudeness to minions and dropping litter.

Glenn, then, had no red flags, and quite a lot of green-for-go flags, not least that he was a good-looking guy who could kiss very well indeed, and that, in turn, was indicative of the fact that he might also turn out to be equally attentive in, ahhhh, other areas that might be in need of attention.

So: slightly disappointed. And although not white-hot with rage, it would be fair to say that Nina was pretty damn miffed.

She'd thought/hoped that she and Glenn might have had a good thing going, only to fall at the second hurdle. Dumped after one night of kissing! And though all of Glenn's mealy-mouthed reasoning might have been justified, it was also pathetic – surely if he'd learned anything from this never-ending shoot and, indeed, from his poor mum's death, it was to live in the moment. And though on-set romances might well be disastrous, they could at least have taken it one day at a time, and if things hadn't panned out, then at least they'd have given it a shot. But no, because of Glenn's gloomy principles, then he wasn't even prepared to try – and so he'd once had a dud relationship on a shoot and so what? Over the years, Glenn had probably had a number of relationships, and guess what, one way or another they'd all turned out badly – and given Glenn's reasoning, he should never ever have another relationship. Pah! It was more than just miffing, it was intensely irksome, and the reason it was so irksome was that she'd given him a small slice of her heart.

What about his idea of just putting everything on ice for the duration of the shoot, and then the moment Kubrick called time, then the whole thing could suddenly come purring back to life? That was one of the more lunatic relationship ideas she'd ever heard of: to carry on chatting and tea-sipping with Glenn as if nothing had happened, when (at least for Nina) something very big indeed had just happened, was not in any way going to cut it.

Being as bright as she so certainly was, Nina could admit that pride was also a factor – that she, Nina, had effectively been dumped and she did not like it one little bit, and that, until circumstances changed (i.e. never), she'd firstly be wearing her mask in all her interactions with Glenn, and, secondly, those said interactions were going to be kept to a bare minimum. True, they hadn't really talked very much at all since the very first day of the shoot, but that had been quite, quite different – that had been because they both fancied each other. And she'd had her mask off most of the time.

And what a mask she now had to mask herself from Glenn! Now that Nina was the principal girl, she had the mask of all masks – a beautiful mask, full-face like all the others, with gold trim around the eyes and cheeks, white alabaster from nose to chin and full lips of succulent scarlet. What made the mask a stand-out was that it had a head-dress of black feathers, each at least a foot long, which sprang out from the mask like a lion's mane. It was a mask of great power. When Nina had put it on the for the first time, and when her cloak had fallen to the ground, she'd felt as imperious as a queen; and when Glenn came over after the first take, she had taken especial care to keep the mask on, and it had been brilliantly effective. Never mind that she might be churning up inside: with the mask on, she was untouchable. And when this damn shoot was over – a month, a year, who knew? – she'd keep the mask, see if she didn't, so that she could show it to her grandchildren, and would tell them that one day, once, she had been mistress of all she surveyed.

Taking over from Vicky had been relatively smooth, needing just a small tweak in the timings. Kubrick, it seemed, was happy to go ahead with just eleven girls instead of twelve. He even – daringly – was on the verge of making a decision as to his preferred orgy scenario. Probably be at least another fortnight before he finally committed himself, but the one scenario that he seemed most interested in was when the girls were all in a circle with Leon in the middle thumping away on the floor with his staff. Then – girls down into the child pose, Leon swinging around with his incense-burner, and all the while, this creepy chanting music coming out loud over the speakers; it wasn't going to be the final music, but it was going to be something like it. The girls stood again and, at a signal from Leon, the cloaks fell to the floor and they would be all but naked – disempowering for some, but for Nina and for the other girls, a moment of complete empowerment. At that moment, Nina felt more alive than she'd ever felt at the strip club. The girls then knelt back down on the red carpet (murder on the knees, just like Vicky had said it was!), followed by a part she rather enjoyed, as she exchanged a tender masked kiss with Mandy, before the girls paired off with the masked spectators, and she, Nina, got to pair off with Tom Cruise. They'd chatted a bit. Seemed nice enough. Well, she'd soon find out.

It had been about 4 p.m., a couple of hours before call time. She'd been up in the Officers' Mess with Mandy and a couple of the other girls, Isobel and Evie, as well as Josh, Mandy's hapless hanger-on. There was a coal fire in the grate and Mandy and Josh and the two girls were lying on the floor playing pick-a-stick. Mandy had far and away the biggest pile of sticks; either she was cheating or, more likely, Josh was setting it up for her. Nina, meanwhile, had been reading a heavy-duty book on nineteenth-century Japan, though it wasn't really the correct book to be reading in the Officers' Mess as there was a lot of arguing and scuffling (if not downright flirting) going on on the rug, and it was difficult to concentrate. There was the rattle of a key in the lock and Lawrence came in.

'Afternoon, ladies. Afternoon, Josh,' he said. He was wearing chinos and that jacket of his again – and, what a surprise, tucked into the breast pocket was a pen.

'Hi,' Nina said. 'So you did decide to slip a pen into your breast pocket?'

'Sets off the look nicely, don't you think?'

'May I see your pen?'

'Of course you may.' Lawrence plucked the pen from his breast pocket and handed it to Nina. It was a Parker.

'This wasn't the pen that your friend Grubby gave you though, is it?'

'I've got more than one pen, you know Nina,' he said loftily, before mooching over to the mantelpiece. 'Can I get any of you a drink? Glass of rum? Sherry?'

The girls demurred, though Josh, being a student, accepted a glass of Captain Morgan spiced rum.

Nina eyed Lawrence as he downed his brimful glass in one. 'You're a hell of a drinker, aren't you?' she said.

'Surprised the crew haven't turned to drink long ago.'

'You got Tom Cruise drinking yet?'

'A little,' Lawrence said. 'After we've wrapped, he quite likes to unwind with a glass of Chablis. And, speaking of Tom, I have a little request.'

'Why does my heart sink?'

'Now, now Nina, we can try and be just a little bit more positive, can't we?' he said.

'What is your little request?'

'Quite a nice request, actually,' Lawrence said. 'Tom's got fed up with being in his ivory Winnebago. He wants to start mixing with normal people – normal people like you.'

'He can do that any time he likes,' Mandy said. She flicked a pick-a-stick off the top of the pile, with some skill, actually; maybe she hadn't been helping herself to Josh's pile.

'Tom's problem is, Mandy, that people tend to clam up when they're speaking to him. And Tommy – well, he just wants to have an ordinary everyday conversation without people getting starry-eyed and tongue-tied.'

'So how's he going to do that?' Nina said.

'It's pretty damn simple, Nina,' Lawrence said, pouring himself more rum.

'Uh-huh.' Why, why, when Nina was speaking to Lawrence, did she always feel that he was getting one over her? Granted, he had set up this cosy Officers' Mess, but she always had the lingering feeling that there'd be a price to pay for having this haven – and now, it seemed, this price was about to be extracted.

'Yeah, basically it's like this.' Lawrence took a long pull of his rum. Nobody said a thing. 'If I turn up to the Officers' Mess and I'm still wearing my mask, and my accent is slightly off, then it won't be me – it'll be Tom.'

'Tom Cruise is going to be coming to the Officers' Mess?' Mandy asked.

'More than likely he will, yes, Mandy – and because he's not that great a mimic, it will be perfectly obvious that it's not me. But here's the beauty of it – you will all have to pretend that it is me. That you are talking to your cheery old buddy Lawrence.'

Mandy and Josh gaped. Isobel and Evie rolled their eyes. Nina just continued to stare at Lawrence. 'That is one of the more ludicrous things I've ever heard,' Nina said.

'Come now, Nina – it's not that ludicrous,' he said. 'Is it any more ludicrous than being at the beck and call of our resident lunatic? Is it any more ludicrous than you spending over six months rehearsing an orgy scene which will last barely more than two minutes in the film?'

'It's still pretty damn ludicrous.'

'Nina!' he said. 'It's not remotely like you to be so negative. You're normally so upbeat!'

If the book on nineteenth-century Japan hadn't been such a hefty hardback, she'd have probably ripped it in half. Why did this guy have to be so vexing? What was it about this him that made her want to… to give him a lusty knee to the groin?

Mandy took up the cudgels. 'So if you come in wearing your mask, then it's not you, it's Tom?'

'It'll be Tommy. Just get him a drink and continue chatting to him in the merry fashion that you are now talking to me.'

Nina let out an audible humph.

'Was that a humph?' Lawrence said. 'Did I hear a little humph?'

'What are you going to be doing while we're chatting away to Tom Cruise?' Nina said.

'Me?' Lawrence said. 'I will be minding my own business in my usual mild-mannered way, just chilling in Tommy's Winnebago, drinking his wine, putting my feet up, just, you know, letting the good times roll.'

Josh decided to pipe up. 'Sorry for asking, Lawrence, but is this, is this a wind-up?'

'Nope, Josh, not a wind-up.'

'And he's really going to try and pretend to be you – take off your la-di-da accent 'n' all?

'I don't know if I'd call it la-di-da, Josh. I think I prefer cut-crystal.'

'And you really think he's going to do it?'

'Be surprised if he didn't,' Lawrence said, before grabbing the rum bottle again. 'Gosh it's already empty,' he said, and Nina was now holding her book so tightly that her nails were actually indenting the paper, and then when he added, 'You lot drink like fishes!' she couldn't restrain herself any longer, and hurled the book right at him. Pleasingly, it hit him smack on the forehead.

CHAPTER 21

Taking pictures of the Elveden Hall orgy was just exactly the nightmare I'd known it would be.

Now that Nina had cast herself in this bizarre role as a hyper-vigilant security guard, it proved exceedingly difficult just to get my little pen camera on set. I mean, why was it any skin off Nina's nose if one of the extras just happened to take a few pics of Tom Cruise? As we know, all publicity is good publicity, so running a tasty picture of Tommy and the girls on the front page of the *Sun* could only have whetted the public's appetite for Kubrick's latest masterpiece. Know what I think it was? I think Nina was hurting. She was hurting because she'd had a snog with Glenn and then, for some footling reason, they'd split. Well, was that my fault? It was me who'd actually got them together – and damn all thanks I'd had for it. And now that they'd split, well, *le fromage dur*, Nina, but that's got nothing to do with me. But no, she didn't see it like that, she didn't see it like that at all, and for some insane reason had cast herself in the role of the Elveden Hall snooper – constantly casting dark looks at me and making unsavoury (not to mention unhelpful) remarks about my jacket. If it had been the OCD Kubrick, then I'd have understood. He was a secretive control freak. But Nina? It was like she was really out to get me! And to think of all I'd done for her! I'd provided her with a key to the Officers' Mess! With unlimited alcohol! I'd provided her with a very nice boyfriend! And how did she repay me? By constantly prying and poking, as well as making some simply vile aspersions about my new pen and my friend Grubby, who apparently didn't look anything like a used-car salesman. Not only was she being a pain, she was a total ingrate.

The upshot of having my own on-set security guard was that I had to be much, much more careful when I wielded my Olympus spy pen. I could only bring it out when Kubrick was actually gearing up to shoot, because that was the only time when Nina was otherwise occupied. At least I presumed she was otherwise occupied, but when she had her mask on I could never tell where she was looking. Still, one way or the other I had to get some pictures, and so the spy pen it had to be. The usual drill was that, just before the cameras rolled, the hair and make-up team would titivate the girls' tresses. That would be my cue to contentedly stare up at the glorious ceiling – the pediments! The white marble! The ornate staircase! – while at the same time popping the spy pen into my breast pocket. The wires from the pen ran down the inside of my jacket to the chunky digital box that was strapped to my belt. Then, happy as can be, not a care in the world, so nothing to look at here, I'd open up the front of my cloak and would start snapping away. The difficulty – as Grubby had pointed out – was that I had no idea whether the shots were in focus or not. The solution was to wander around the hall taking pictures of the girls from various ranges, and just hoping that one of the pictures was in focus. This in turn tended to enrage the crew, especially Roddie, the second assistant director – "just stop moving around!" – but what the hell else was a hard-working hack supposed to do? I was just doing my job!

The real money shot, of course, was going to be Tom Cruise, mask off, and surrounded by all the girls in just their G-strings. They looked very nice in their fetching cloaks of midnight blue, but for tabloid purposes they were better by far when they were topless. This money shot was, however, a near impossibility. For most of the scenes in Elveden Hall, it was Leon Vitali who was in the middle of the girls, while

Tom was nothing more than a bystander on the periphery. Still – I'd just have to do the best I could. Besides, in the possible event that I failed to deliver, I was certain that my deputy editor would take it all in good part, giving me a solicitous clap on the shoulder as he said, "Worse things happen at sea." (I jest – Spike was about the most intolerant bastard I'd ever met.)

I'd spent a whole night taking pictures of the girls and had about fifty snaps in the bag. It seemed reasonable to presume that one of them might actually be printable. After we'd wrapped, Tom and I shared a bottle of his new favourite wine, Chateau Musar ("I love this stuff!" I remember him saying. "And it's from Lebanon! It's what Jesus used to drink!"). Bottle finished, I was chauffeured back to my hotel. I could have attempted to download the pictures onto my laptop that night, but sensibly desisted. It was going to be a slightly technical job which called for stone-cold sobriety.

The next morning, Tom and I had our usual run together – that's just what good buddies do. They drink together; they go running together; they spend quality time together, and the reason they spend so much time together is that they revel in each other's company.

As runners go, we were pretty compatible. He could outsprint me but, to my great delight, I could outlast him. During one ten-miler I ran him into the ground. The sheer joy of turning it on as I went up a hill, watching him come panting up after me and hearing him gasp those beautiful words: "Just give me a sec".

We were running in companionable silence along a muddy footpath next to a wood. We were already so filthy that when we came to a puddle we just went straight through it.

'Much happening in the Officers' Mess?' he asked.

'Not much,' I said. I could of course have said more, but, cunningly, I desisted. The less I said about Elveden's most exclusive club, the more alluring it became to him.

'Oh yeah,' he said. 'Mind my asking who's in the mess?'

I dead-balled the question. 'Just some of the guys, few of the girls, nothing much.'

We came up to a kissing gate which I courteously held open for him. He gave me that twinkly smile – boy, could he turn it on when he wanted to; made you feel like you were the very centre of his world.

'And, like, what do you do in the mess?'

'We chat,' I said. 'We hang.' I gave him a bone. 'Sip whisky by the fire. Nice place to relax.'

'You've got a fire in the mess?' he said. 'What do you burn?'

'Found a load of coal in one of the outhouses,' I said. 'I take up a fresh bucket every afternoon.'

'It sounds great.' He pondered this den of Elysian dreams.

'It's OK,' I said with delicious understatement, and, cunning devil that I am, I kept my mouth shut. Soon enough, he'd be gagging for an entrée.

I had a shower and breakfast, though no Glenn in the dining room that day. Much to Kubrick's chagrin, Glenn had actually left the set for the day – well, it would have been slightly churlish to have missed his own mother's funeral. True, Stanley Kubrick skipped both his parents' funerals, but he did send along a family emissary, and he was petrified of flying.

Having had my fill of porridge, coffee and newspapers, I returned to my room, there to do battle with my laptop and the little grey box. I put the box and its attendant wires on the table next to my laptop. I sat down at the table. I poured some more black coffee from the tepid cafetièrc. I made myself comfy. I opened the brown envelope and pulled out a hard disk as well as a finger-thick instruction manual for the spy pen. This would explain, I hoped, how to smoothly and efficiently download the pictures onto my trusty Toshiba.

I riffled through the instruction manual. A whisper of unease. It looked mighty thick for an instruction manual. Still – us worker bees are nothing if not diligent, and, being a certified genius, I was sure that with just a small amount of application, I'd have these pictures downloaded in a jiffy. Like any normal human being, I ignored the introduction and went straight for the good stuff – "Downloading your pictures".

It looked pretty complicated. Before I could even start getting at the pictures, I had to download a program off the CD-ROM. Fiddle-fiddle-fiddle. I found the correct slot in the Toshiba, slammed the disk home. We were on our way!

Fiddle-fiddle. I had to tap in a long sequence of numbers and letters, and this I doughtily did – no slacking for diligent, hard-working Kimmy. After about an hour of tinkering, I'd finally got the disk to start disgorging its beautiful screed. There was a handy percentage bar at the bottom of the screen which showed me just how much of the spy pen program had been downloaded. I watched over it like a mother hen. It was very exciting. In just over half an hour, it had downloaded more than 80 per cent of the program! I treated myself to some now stone-cold coffee. We'd have this thing up and running in no time!

The bar was up to 99 per cent. Nearly there! But it seemed to be stuck there. I waited patiently. Checked my watch. It'd been stuck on 99 per cent for twenty minutes. What the hell was I going to do? Just leave it chewing over this one per cent piece of gristle? Maybe I should go out and have a relaxing walk – and when I returned in, say, half an hour, that final one per cent would have been swallowed, and it'd be tasty pictures, here we come! But I didn't go for a walk. I sat in my hotel room staring at the screen. Nothing was happening. Not that I knew the first thing about it, but at a guess, the thing had jammed. I put my ear to the Toshiba. Not a sound to be heard. What was it doing – what was it thinking? Had it just got fed up and gone to sleep?

I turn on the radio; a tune to soothe, Beethoven's *Pastoral*. I idly glance at the Toshiba. Still nuttin' happening. I try calling up Grubby. He doesn't pick up so I leave a message. I mean, like, how long am I going to give this machine before I give up? It could be stuck like this for hours – for the rest of the day. On impulse, I eject the disk. A message instantly flashes up on the screen – "Download failed".

Oh well – we'll just have to give it another shot. I've only spent the last ninety minutes trying to download the program – no time at all, really – and this time I'll do it right and it'll all work just perfectly. Fiddle-fiddle-fiddle. Tippity-tap at the keyboard. The program starts downloading again. I call up Grubby again. He doesn't answer. A pleasant half-hour passes, the little green percentage chugs merrily on its way, steams up to 99 per cent. And stops.

Since I've been here before, I do at least know the drill. I'm going to chill. I'm going to let this machine just do what it has to do, no hurry at all, old chap, in your own time. I quit my room and pop over to the corner shop, where I buy a Bombay Bad Boy Pot Noodle. When I return, my little Toshiba is still stuck on 99 per cent. I put my ear to the keyboard. Not a sound to be heard. No matter – I put on the kettle, pour boiling water into the Bombay Bad Boy, leave it for a couple of minutes and dig in. Still not a fat lot happening with the Toshiba. Now I know that ejecting the disk isn't going to work. But what if… what if I pressed a button? That might help the machine on its way, just give it a nudge in the right direction. Maybe I should press the Escape button because that, surely, is what I'm trying to do. I'm trying to help my trusty Toshiba escape from this digital quicksand. He's got bogged down. I'm trying to help him out! I press the Escape button. "Download failed".

Hmmm. It's not that I'm aggravated, or even disappointed. I'm just a little concerned. We're now three hours in and, as is my wont with computers, I have achieved precisely the square root of diddly squat. Still – Rome wasn't built in a day, you know. I cheerfully eject the disk, insert the disk, go tippity-tap once again at the keyboard and watch contentedly as the spy pen program disgorges into my machine, up-up-up the little green percentage bar goes, nearly there, nearly there, you can do it old thing! I am a little aware that it is slightly moronic just watching this percentage bar, but it's not like I've got anything better to do.

As assuredly as night follows day, it gets stuck on 99 per cent. Well this time I'm not going to do anything. I'm not going to touch it. We're just going to duke it out, and we're gonna see which one of us has got the stomach for a fight, and this old Toshiba may think he's a toughie, but when it comes to serene patience I'm world-class – hell, I'd spent over a month working with that nutjob Stanley Kubrick!

I look at my watch. I've spent all afternoon on this one job. In another hour, I'll have to leave for Elveden Hall. I know what I'm going to do. I'm going to leave my charming Toshiba to do its own thing in its own good time and I'm going down to the bar to have a refreshing pint of Guinness. I go down to the bar and order a Guinness, and, you know what, I'm also going to have a packet of pork scratchings – cos I'm damn well worth it. Happy in the knowledge that, just like the Little Engine That Could, my Toshiba is even now doing the business, I flick through the local rags, quaffing my beer in a most serene and leisurely fashion, and am so pleased with life and how it's turning out that I don't just stuff the pork scratchings into my mouth, no, I toss them high into the air and, like a circus seal snapping at sprats, I catch the scratchings twixt my sharp little teeth. The bag of pork scratchings eaten, I contentedly continue to sup my pint, so filled with good cheer towards my fellow man that I'm even enjoying the asinine leaders in the *Bury St Edmunds Mercury*. Eventually, though, all good things must come to an end: my pint glass is empty. I trot back up to my hotel room, happy in the knowledge that God's in his heaven and all's right with the world, and I unlock the door, and slip into my room, and see, deliciously, that the per centage bar has disappeared from the screen, which must mean that, Houston, we are a go for pictures, but then, distressingly, I see an all too familiar message on the screen – "Download failed" – and, like the even-tempered, easy-breezy chap that I am, I pick up the Toshiba and, with a howl-at-the-moon shriek, hurl it against the wall as hard as I can, where it pings pleasingly onto the floor. I snatch it up again, start hammering it as hard as I can on the table before, with some effort, wrenching the screen right off from its housing and launching both halves of the infernal computer out of the window.

I was in a perfectly foul mood when I drove to the set an hour later, but this was alleviated, a little, by being provided with a genuine honest-to-goodness news story. It made the splash a couple of days later, and I myself had had a hand in the headline: "The Curse of Kubrick".

CHAPTER 22

As Glenn sips his triple espresso in the departures lounge at Heathrow Airport, he experiences that heady delight of a jailbird who's been released after a year-long stretch in prison. He's free! For one day and one day only, he will not have to be a movie slave – he will not have to reset the lights or shuffle the extras around the hall, or deal with the moans of the shell-shocked crew, and, most gloriously, for one day, he will not have to listen to Kubrick's barked orders. There is one small thing that worries him though, just a little niggle, but this same thought keeps buzzing around his head, a bluebottle bumping its head over and over against the window: is Roddie, the second assistant director, up to the job? If he had to guess, he'd say Roddie was on the verge of a nervous breakdown. Since they'd started filming at Elveden Hall, Roddie was eating more than ever, smelling worse than ever. He looked like a fat wino, a vagrant who'd just mooched in off the street – and, well, there at least he was in good company, as Kubrick also always looked like a wino (though marginally less smelly). Roddie's hands were permanently shaking, he had a nervous tic in his left eyelid, and, most worrying of all, he'd developed this gigantic twitch, his entire body almost going into spasm. There were three words which seemed to trigger this Pavlovian twitch and, during filming, these three little words did tend to ring out fairly often – 'Do it again!'

Still – not much Glenn could do about it now. No, what he can do is savour his coffee and leaf through the book that he's just bought in the bookshop – and even going into a bookshop had been quite a thrill. He hadn't been in a bookshop in over a year; hadn't been in an airport in over a year; had not been in a crowd of strangers for over a year… in fact, quite a lot of things he hadn't done in over a year. Hadn't seen his mum. He'd done his best, called her most days, and now he'd never get to see her again.

He'd gone to Kubrick as soon as he'd known the date of the funeral. He'd knocked on the Winnebago door and, as usual, had been kept waiting for over a minute before Kubrick opened it. 'Oh, hi Glenn,' Kubrick said.

'Hi Stanley, could I have a brief word?'

'Can it wait?' Kubrick said. He hovered by the door. It was clear that Glenn was not going to be invited into the Winnebago.

'Just a quick one,' Glenn said. 'It's my mum's funeral on Thursday. I'd very much like to go.'

'Agh,' Kubrick said, with a rather irritated tone of voice. 'Your mum's funeral?' Kubrick scratched at his neck. Any normal human being might have offered their condolences, but then Kubrick was certainly not a normal human being. 'You'll be back for call time, right?'

'Well, that's just it, Stanley. The funeral is in Aberdeen on Thursday afternoon. There are no flights back.'

'That's a real pain,' Kubrick said. 'Like, d'ya have to go to the funeral?'

'Yes, I do have to go to my mother's funeral,' Glenn said, and though he had long since schooled himself never to be riled by Kubrick, Kubrick was sure as hell riling him now.

'I didn't go to my mother's funeral,' Kubrick countered. 'Didn't go to my father's funeral either.'

'That was your decision,' Glenn said. 'I am going to my mother's funeral.'

'Maybe… maybe a private jet?' Kubrick mused to himself.

'Let me clarify, Stanley. I am going to my mother's funeral. And afterwards, I am going to the wake – I will not be hot-footing it back to Elveden, even if I'm on a private jet. Then, Stanley, I'll almost certainly be getting drunk at my mother's wake, and will be swapping stories about her with my family. At some stage, I will go to bed, and that will also be a bed in Aberdeen, and in the morning, I will get up and I will catch a flight back to Heathrow.' Glenn could feel this white-hot anger pulsing through his fingers. If Kubrick didn't back down, then…

Kubrick's bulbous black eyes flicked over Glenn, peeped over the edge, caught a glimpse of the simmering volcano beneath. 'Yes – yes, yes,' he said.

'Roddie will be fine for a night.' Glenn spoke with much more conviction than he actually felt; he wasn't even remotely sure that Roddie would be fine.

'You think Roddie's up to it?' Kubrick said.

'He's been in movies for over twenty years – he's been on this set for over a year. He knows the ropes.'

'OK,' Kubrick said. 'But you'll be gone for just the one night?'

'Yes, Stanley.' Glenn clasped his hands behind his back, fingers interlocked; what he really wanted to do was punch this man right in the middle of his fat paunch.

'Thursday, right?'

'That's right.'

'Well, I guess you gotta do what you gotta do, Glenn,' Kubrick said. 'You'll prep Roddie beforehand?'

'Yes, I will.'

'OK,' Kubrick said, retreating back into his Winnebago. He was about to close the door when he was struck by a sudden thought. 'Hey, sorry about your mum, Glenn.'

'Thank you, Stanley.'

'It's a tough one when you lose your mum.'

'It certainly is.'

Having almost redeemed himself, Kubrick couldn't stop himself from returning to the main event. 'Hope you're right about Roddie.'

'It'll be fine.'

'I'd still prefer it if you were here,' Kubrick said, and Glenn might have wasted his time explaining just why, exactly, he had to attend his mother's funeral, but by then the Winnebago door had already been shut in his face.

Glenn found the second assistant director eating a sausage sandwich on the top floor of the double-decker, and told him the good news. Roddie didn't look at Glenn, didn't say a word. He just kept on eating his sandwich.

'Did you hear what I said?' Glenn asked. 'I'm going to my mum's funeral on Thursday. You're going to be running the show.'

Roddie's eyes swivelled towards Glenn and then back to his sandwich. He was about to say something, thought better of it, and took another enormous bite.

Glenn took a seat opposite him. Roddie continued to eat.

'It'll be fine,' Glenn said. 'You'll be fine. Just do what we always do. Show the team who's the boss. Don't take any back-chat from the extras. I'll be back by Friday lunchtime.' For some reason, Glenn felt like he was talking to a seven-year-old boy who was being left at the school gates for the first time.

Roddie finished the sandwich. He licked the ketchup off his fingers and looked round the table. His hands were shaking. He clasped his fingers together in his lap. He didn't once look at Glenn. He looked at his hands.

'Did you hear what I said, Roddie?' Glenn said. 'I'm not going to be here on Thursday. You'll be running the show with Stanley.'

The tic had started on Roddie's eye again. Glenn realised the eyelid only ever really stopped twitching when Roddie was eating.

'Yeah,' Roddie whispered.

'You're going to be fine,' Glenn said.

Roddie continued to stare at his lap. 'Yeah,' he said again, though in such a manner that Glenn was left with the irresistible realisation that Roddie was going to be anything but fine; he remembered Sven the Steadicam operator, who'd gone clean off his rocker. But Roddie wouldn't do anything like that. Would he? It would have been better if Roddie had had a competent Number Two, but they'd lost the third assistant director to the Steadicam, and anyway going down that route was a sure path to madness: might as well say that it would have been better if Kubrick had not been a demented control freak; or that it would have been better if Tom Cruise hadn't been quite so passive; better, even, if Glenn hadn't signed up for this stinking project in the first place – but then, hang on, if he hadn't signed up for the project, then he'd never have got to know Tom or Nic, would never have worked with the great Stanley Kubrick. Certainly wouldn't have kissed Nina.

Speaking of Nina, he still hoped that, somehow, he might be able to pluck something out of the fire. True, it did seem that, for the moment, he'd royally screwed things up with Nina. But she might relent when they were finally done filming – might appreciate that his "no-sex-on-set" rule had been implemented for the very best of reasons. It was possible. Give her enough time and she'd surely come round to the idea of putting their fledgling relationship on ice, just for a little while. But they could still chat together, have coffees together, do all that good stuff that couples do for the 99 per cent of time that they're together but not actually having sex.

To that end, Glenn, when he was in the Heathrow bookshop, had by chance found himself drawn to the history section. Lots of interesting books there, and, oh look, there was the book that Nina had been reading. He'd picked it up, given it a flick. It was about the Japanese samurai. Looked pretty interesting – in fact, what the hell, he'd buy it. Might give him something to talk about with Nina – just in case she continued to give him the cold shoulder. Yes, he could see it right now – sitting in the gym café, quietly reading his book, and Nina would see that he was reading very same book that she herself was reading and would be completely unable to resist coming over to have a chat about it. Got to be worth a shot, anyway.

He felt comfortably numb on the flight to Aberdeen. His sister picked him up at the airport. The only part he really remembered of the day was lowering his mother's coffin into the ground. There'd been a posy of roses on the coffin. He'd tossed on a handful of claggy earth. A single bell had been tolling – and he immediately thought of that magnificent call to arms from the poet John Donne: "Send not to know for whom the bell tolls – it tolls for thee." What a wake-up call! The bell that tolled for his mother was ever so succinctly telling him, yelling at him, "Get it while you can." Pertinent, obviously, to Nina, but also to this never-ending film shoot, but that then raised the unholy question of how he could possibly change Kubrick? Screaming at him, pleading with him, that'd never work. Kubrick, he realised, was on one long ego trip, not just lording it over cast and crew and his two superstars, but also royally stiffing all the otheer film studios who'd had to put their own movies on hold (most particularly *Mission: Impossible* 2) until Kubrick deigned to release Tom Cruise.

But how to chivvy Kubrick without the despot knowing that he was being chivvied? Kubrick sure as hell wasn't listening to his crew or his stars, but he might possibly be swayed by his wife or his daughters. How, how, to get some leverage over the man?

CHAPTER 23

With Glenn away for his mum's funeral, the second assistant director, Roddie, was having to step up to the plate. But where Glenn had been all affable, controlled calm, Roddie was a juddering bundle of nerves, pettish with the crew, shouty with the extras and, when it came to dealing with Kubrick, just utterly hopeless. He had the fearful air of somebody who had resigned themselves to always getting it wrong. True, I didn't help matters – but then it's not in my nature to be helpful. I was put on God's earth to lark around and to dig up stories – which, finally and at long last I managed to do. I believe that, for at least ten minutes, Spike was very happy.

Since Tom Cruise still hadn't plucked up the courage to do the great switcheroo with your humble narrator, I was actually having to do the job that I was being paid to do: be Tommy's stand-in. Most of the time this didn't involve anything more than what I'd been doing as an extra, just standing around watching the girls do their stuff. But, deliciously, I did get to kiss Nina a lot. Well not really kiss her, because my name didn't happen to be Glenn. But sort of kiss her. And I did get to spend a lot of time having Nina's beautiful bare breasts nudging against my cloak, so I guess that just about made up for it.

As ever, Kubrick had still not made up his mind over what he wanted, but whatever he eventually decided, one way or the other Nina was going to have to end up paired off with Tommy. But when she paired off with Tommy, what was she going to do? In true Kubrick fashion, the possibilities were limitless! Should she get down on her knees and make an obeisance? Or tap him on the chest and tell him he'd pulled? Or take his hand? Well, these were, of course, all possibilities, and I'm sure they'd have all been just great, but one of the scenarios that Kubrick was experimenting with was to have Nina kiss Tommy. Several times. And that meant that, for several hours a night, she'd be kissing Tommy's preternaturally handsome stand-in. (Some said, by the way, that Tommy's stand-in was actually more handsome than the star; it happens.) True, we were both wearing full face masks, so it wasn't actually lip to lip, but quite intimate all the same. It's not often that I've spent hours on end with a near-naked woman, and I'm sure that Nina enjoyed it just as much as I did.

The call-time was, as usual, 6 p.m., and while Tommy and Kubrick chillaxed in their separate Winnebagos, the crew and the cast went through the same old routine, cloaked girls in a centre circle with Red Cloak, Leon Vitali, in the middle with his swinging incense-burner. What with the lighting and the girls and the extras, it always took ages to set the scene, which was fine, and we humble extras did what we always did and chatted to each other.

Roddie was fussing around on the red carpet with the girls. Since Vicky had left, they were down to eleven, which meant they'd had to slightly alter their positions – not by much, but enough to stress Roddie out.

Josh had sidled up to me and, as ever, had only one subject on his mind: 'How d'you think I'm doing with Mandy?'

'Very well indeed,' I said. 'Just keep doing what you're doing, keep it nice and tight, and one day an opportunity will present itself.'

'Like what sort of opportunity?' he blurted, tiny mind completely unable to fathom the meaning of that dread concept "opportunity".

'Dunno,' I said. 'But one day she might be in need of a hero, and when that day comes, let's hope you can do the business.'

'You don't... you don't think I'm punching too high?' he said.

'Punching high doesn't begin to do justice to what you're attempting with Mandy,' I said. 'You are the equivalent of a cruiserweight taking on Mike Tyson!'

'Oh,' he said, and even though he'd got his mask on, I could tell he was pretty crestfallen.

'Look, chin up, Josh,' I said. 'Ah, but a man's reach should exceed his grasp, or what's a heaven for?'

He was about to say something boneheaded (such as – "what does that mean?") except that Roddie suddenly lost his rag. 'Will you all just shut up?' he shouted. 'I can't hear myself think. Just shut up! All of you!'

For a minute or two, we were all quiet as wee dormice, still chatting to each other – obviously – though only in a whisper. Roddie was in a huddle with Red Cloak and Nina talking about some great matter of moment. After about ten minutes, normal volume had been restored, and the hall sounded like just your average Millwall football match.

'Will you shut up!' Roddie shouted, face like a great fat tomato. 'Just shut up! Shut up!' I'd had a hapless Latin teacher like him once, barely out of teacher training – he'd lost control in the first week, and after that, it didn't matter how much he hollered, he never got it back. Same, I'm afraid, with Roddie. Didn't matter how much he screamed and spluttered, he'd lost us. There were some people we'd pipe down for, notably Glenn and Kubrick, but Roddie had no natural authority. There was a momentary lull and then we were back to chatting at full volume. Now that Glenn, effectively our regimental sergeant major, had gone for the day, the hall crackled with an air of frisky rebellion.

Roddie swore a bit more and went off to get Kubrick and Tom Cruise. Tom came straight in, followed ten minutes later by the other two, and because Kubrick was there, we did pipe down a bit. There was a bit more faffing about as Kubrick arranged his plump bottom on the director's chair and, then, just like we'd been doing for well over a month, it was masks on, and a small smoke canister was triggered in Leon Vitali's incense burner. Kubrick was most particular about this incense burner. Not to mention all his dicking around over what he wanted the girls to do, we'd spent a solid week filming the incense-burner and how the smoke trailed through the room. Ain't got a damn clue what Kubrick was looking for – but neither, obviously, did Kubrick.

Now that the incense-burner was properly smoking, it was just the usual roll cameras and action. Now – once this elaborate machine had been set into motion, the cameras would continue to roll and the girls would continue to do what they had been trained to do until that single guillotine word had been uttered: Cut! And to be clear – on the entire set, there was only one person who was authorised to use this one magical word, and that was His Majesty Stanley Kubrick.

But as I've mentioned, without Glenn at the wheel, there was a topsy-turvy mood to the hall; a mood, perhaps, for hijinks. The girls' cloaks had just fallen to the floor, shoulders squared, toned torsos, bare breasts jutting. God, they looked awesome. What was supposed to happen next was that Leon Vitali would hammer his staff on the floor and one by one the girls would leave their circle and pair off with various lucky extras. The whole scene normally took about two minutes, but this time, just as Vitali was about to start banging his staff, somebody yelled "Cut!" – and it certainly wasn't Kubrick.

Kubrick went mental. He and he alone was allowed to say that one magic word and he took very grave offence at anyone else using it.

'Who said that?' he said. 'Who said that?'

Kubrick's problem, of course, was that everyone was wearing a mask, and it was absolutely impossible to tell who'd said "Cut!" He didn't even know which part of the hall it had come from. No one owned up (who on God's earth would?), and though there was a bit of a huffing and puffing, there wasn't much Kubrick could do.

'OK, we'll do it again,' he said. 'No more funny stuff.'

It took about ten minutes to reset and then we were off to the races again, Leon Vitali swinging the incense burner, girls in their yoga child's pose, but this time, the girls' cloaks had only just fallen to the floor when the magic word "Cut" was uttered. And once again, it wasn't Kubrick.

'Which one of you bastards did that?' he said. 'Roddie – find out who did it and throw them off the set.'

Roddie set to work, haranguing us and telling the miscreant to 'fess up – as if any of us would voluntarily get thrown out of Elveden Hall. What did he take us for – a bunch of seven-year-olds? Roddie's task wasn't helped by the fact that most of us still had our masks on, so he had no idea if we were laughing at him or quaking in our boots. 'Just tell me who did it!' he screeched. 'Tell me!' There was a long silence. No one came forward. Roddie wasn't looking too good, very sweaty, his entire body trembling; he looked like he was on the verge of a heart attack.

'Let's do it again,' snarled Kubrick. 'And I'm warning you, if anyone but me says the word "Cut", then the consequences will be dire.'

We had another take. It appeared to be going very well – that crazy music blaring over the speakers, Vitali banging on the floor, girls pairing off. 'Cut!'

'Which one of you bastards did that?' Kubrick shouted. He'd levered himself out of his chair and was strutting around glaring at his cohort of extras. 'Roddie!' he shouted. 'Find that man!'

'Who did it?' Roddie shouted. 'Who did it?'

Complete silence. Seemed like he was going to have as much luck as he'd had the previous time. Then some idiot piped up – 'I am Spartacus'.

A long pause. And somebody else yelled out – 'I am Spartacus'.

To explain: you've probably never seen Kubrick's first big-budget film *Spartacus*, but in the 1960s it was huge.

It's the story of the Roman slave rebellion, which was led by Spartacus – played by that dimple-chinned sex addict Kirk Douglas. At the end of the film, all the rebel slaves have inevitably been rounded up. The slaves are offered a free pardon – on condition that they identify Spartacus. What happens next is one of the most memorable moments in cinema history. One slave calls out, "I am Spartacus!" And then another, and another, until every single one of the captured slaves has bawled out "I am Spartacus!" Didn't do them any good – the Romans had the whole lot crucified, 6,000 of them strung up on either side of the Appian Way. Me? If I'd been one of those slaves, I'd have shopped Spartacus first chance I got – "It's him!"

Anyway – here, now, on the set of *Eyes Wide Shut*, Kubrick was having his own Spartacus moment. More and more of the extras were getting in on the act. Everyone was calling out that they were Spartacus. But unlike the Roman general Crassus, Kubrick was not capable of having us all crucified.

Someone had to be blamed for all this cacophony of catcalls, and Kubrick obviously picked on Roddie. 'Just sort this shit out!' he said.

'Shut up!' Roddie howled. 'Everyone shut up.'

We all simmered down for a bit, but then somebody had to go and do it again – 'I am Spartacus!' – and the whole hall reverted to bedlam. I think even some of the girls were claiming to be Spartacus.

Roddie was near hysterical as he tried to regain control. 'Shut up!' he squawked. 'Shut up, shut up, shut…' Roddie suddenly clutched at his chest, staggered a couple of steps and keeled over onto the edge of the red carpet. He'd only gone and had a heart attack!

He was sprawled on the floor quite close to me and I was the first to react. I took off my mask and knelt next to him: he had no pulse. I started giving him chest compressions, firm and solid. I looked up to see the rest of the extras just gawping. One thing I didn't fancy was giving Roddie mouth-to-mouth.

'Here, Josh,' I said. 'Tilt his head back. Check his mouth for blockages. Then breathe into his mouth, long and slow. Two breaths every thirty compressions.'

'Are you sure?' he said.

'Just do it.'

Josh's face was a picture of distaste. He opened Roddie's mouth to check that he hadn't swallowed his tongue, then wiped away most of the spittle round his bristly lips. He was still dithering – and I could see why. The prospect of giving the sweaty ashen-faced Roddie an open-mouthed kiss was singularly repellent.

'Just get on and do it!' I said. I, at least, knew what I was doing, still remembered my boy-scout training, heel of my left hand just below the nipples, arms locked straight, and keeping my tempo by humming 'Stayin' Alive' by the Bee Gees.

Josh pulled one last face – it was like he was being force-fed a bowl of congealed vomit – and then dived in to give Roddie the kiss of life. Two full breaths – God it looked disgusting, those blubbery lips and great wattles of fat around his neck. Kubrick was clearing the room, though some of the girls were lingering by the door for a last glimpse of our little cameo. As for me, I was doing everything I could, pumping away, regular as a metronome. I suppose I did feel just a little bit guilty about what had happened, as 'twas me, I'm afraid, who'd been the first person to yell "Cut", and it was me, also, who'd been the first to call out, "I am Spartacus!" – but I had nothing whatsoever to do with the two subsequent "Cut" calls, let alone the ensuing "I am Spartacus!" revolt, and it was those unedifying incidents, surely, which had pushed fat old Roddie over the edge. Mind you – he took so little care of himself that maybe it was only a matter of time before he had a heart attack.

Josh was looking at me glassily as I continued to pump away at Roddie's chest. 'How we doing, Josh?' I said.

'OK,' he said. He was kneeling by Roddie's head, hands clasped in his lap.

'You looked like you were really getting into that kissing,' I said. 'Hope you don't get too turned on.'

'Are you completely mad?'

'Some say,' I said cheerily. 'Now pucker up and give him another kiss on those fat bristly lips.'

'Why can't you do it?'

'Because I'm doing the chest compressions,' I said with some asperity. 'Just kiss him! We're trying to save his life!'

'Do I have to?'

'Mandy's watching you,' I said. 'She'll think you're a real hero.'

'OK.'

'And no tongues this time.'

Josh scowled at me and then locked lips with Roddie again; as for me, I was feeling cheerier by the minute. It was exciting, it was different from the usual on-set monotony and, quite apart from anything else, it was not a bad story. Hell – if he died, it might make the splash! I was already pondering when to call the story through to Spike. Call it in too early, and Kubrick would know for sure that there was a mole on the set. But leave it too late, and some other scumbag might flog it, and that would be Kimmy's world-exclusive scoop gone up in smoke. Such a ticklish problem to conjure with. I figured I'd just have to sit on it until I knew whether Roddie was going to live or die. It'd be an OKish story if he ended up in hospital, but better by far (news-wise) if he ended up in a box. May sound callous – but it's true. Of course we can empathise with the victims and their families, but there is also a part of our dark journalist hearts that always hungers for the story.

Tom Cruise bustled back into the hall with the on-set medic. The medic had a kit-bag full of equipment but no defibrillator. He cast a professional eye over my technique. It seemed to pass muster. 'You doing all right there?' he asked.

'I'm fine.'

'Keep doing what you're doing.' He turned to Josh and

pulled what looked like a white tissue out of his pocket. 'Here's some gauze to go over his mouth.'

'Thank you.' Josh snatched at the gauze and placed it over Roddie's lips; still pretty repellent having to give Roddie the kiss of life, but just not quite as repellent.

The medic clucked around, kneeling down next to me. I could see he was itching to take over my role as the chief heart-pumper, but I was having none of it. 'Why don't you take over from Josh and give him mouth-to-mouth?' I said.

He gave Josh a lairy look but was not tempted. 'He's doing great,' he said.

I glanced over at Kubrick, who was plumped on his director's chair and watching us like a fat stoat, chubby little fingers interlocked over his pot belly. It must have been very, very annoying for him. It was Kubrick and Kubrick alone who got to call the shots on set, and now this damnable second assistant director had had the sheer effrontery to have a heart attack! And right in the middle of the shoot! Now, thanks to Roddie, the whole night was probably going to be a wash-out! What the hell's a director supposed to do?

Eventually, about ten minutes later, we could hear the ambulance sirens. Two paramedics trotted into the hall, and I was unceremoniously shifted off Roddie's chest. I sat cross-legged on the red carpet next to Josh. They slapped the defibrillator pads onto his chest and gave him a shock to wake the dead, but it was a no-go. There was no waking Roddie. They heaved him up onto a gurney and in very short order he was done, and we were done, and Kubrick had wrapped for the night.

It was all very quiet, very still on the set – and to think that only half an hour earlier we'd all been yelling out, "I am Spartacus." I'd dropped off my gown and mask and was just getting ready to drive back when, slightly to my surprise, Olivia told me that Tom Cruise wanted to see me.

I knocked at his Winnebago. The door was promptly opened.

'How we doing, man?' he said.

'It's a bad do,' I said. 'A bad do.'

He was still in his black tux and trousers. He gestured for me to sit down and pulled a bottle of white wine out of the fridge, thought better of it and grabbed a bottle of Glenfiddich. He popped a few cubes of ice into two tumblers and, in silence, filled the glasses to the brim. We chinked, looked at each other. 'To Roddie,' he said.

'To Roddie.'

We sat and we sipped, and I knew better than to break the silence. I already had an inkling of what he was thinking. He was slouched back on the sofa, just staring up at ceiling.

'That's a hell of a wake-up call,' he said. 'Gotta live every moment.'

'That we do,' I said.

He leaned forward, elbows on knees. 'Hey, you know that idea we had?'

'What idea was that?'

'We were just goofing around, you know, and we talked about maybe switching jobs. I'd be the stand-in.'

'Oh yeah,' I said, as if somehow dredging up the memory. 'I remember.'

'Why don't we do it?' he said. 'I want to do it.'

Now that I had him hooked, I could play devil's advocate. 'Is this really a good idea, Tom?' I said. 'What if Kubrick finds out? Are you even able to mimic my voice?'

'Stanley will never find out,' he said in a ridiculous hoity-toity accent. I suddenly realised that this was his impersonation of me.

'You don't sound anything like me!' I said.

'I sound exactly like you,' he said, again putting on this pseudo-posh accent. But he just sounded like a Yank pretending to be a toff – and absolutely nothing like the roaring Sloane that I genuinely am.

'You're cracked,' I said.

'Maybe I am,' he said, now thankfully reverting to his normal voice. 'Come on, Lawrence, it's a great idea.'

'I just don't know.'

'C'mon,' he said. 'It'll be fun.'

I shrugged before bowing to the inevitable. 'I guess you've got much more to lose than I have.' I raised my glass. 'To the great switcheroo!'

'To the great switcheroo!' he said. 'So – tell me about this Officers' Mess. Where is it and how do I get in there?'

CHAPTER 24

The Officers' Mess was rather subdued that evening, everyone silently sipping their tipples, staring at the coals glowing golden in the grate. Not that any of them had been much of a fan of Roddie, but he'd been another of Kubrick's troops, expected to obey his orders without complaint, and they were the lesser without him.

Nina was sitting on the sofa examining an old photo that Lawrence had dug up from the attic. The photo was of Elveden Hall's most famous owner, Duleep Singh, the Indian Maharajah who'd handed over the Punjab and the Koh-i-noor to Britain, and who for a short time had hobnobbed with the British aristocracy. The photo had been taken just in the portico of Elveden Hall – the same place, actually, where Glenn had kissed her. She wondered how he'd been getting on at his mum's funeral; it had certainly all kicked off without him.

The photo, anyway, was of one of Singh's shooting parties, the rather tubby Maharajah sitting at his leisure in the middle and surrounded by not just dukes and earls but the Prince of Wales. In his heyday, Singh had thrown the most lavish shooting parties. They'd lasted for days, and the weekly bag had consisted of thousands of pheasants and partridge, as well as scores of deer, hares and rabbits, along with any other wild animal that was worth having a pot at. Singh had not only provided his blue-blooded guests with top-notch shooting, but also board and lodging. Perhaps, a hundred years ago, the Prince of Wales had slept in this very room that they now called the Officers' Mess, and had placed his glass on the same mantelpiece, and had warmed his capacious backside at the very same hearth. How ridiculous those shooting parties now seemed – and then Nina smirked at herself, because in the entire history of Elveden Hall, nothing could ever top the wholesale ridiculousness of *Eyes Wide Shut*.

Nina returned the photo to the mantelpiece and went over to the window, where, in black silhouette, she could just make out the local church. She'd have to pay it a visit before she was finally done with *Eyes Wide Shut* – if only to see Singh's grave.

Nina had just returned to the sofa. There was a rattle of a key in the door, and a moment later Lawrence came in – still with his cloak on, still wearing Tom Cruise's mask, a sinister latticework of gold about the eyes, and cheeks and chin of alabaster white. She suddenly recalled one of Lawrence's more bizarre conversations earlier in the week, and realised that, in all probability, this whole surreal month was just about to get even more surreal: it seemed that Tom Cruise was now masquerading as Lawrence. Though that in itself begged another question – what, exactly, was Lawrence's masquerade?

Might as well try and make Tom feel at home. 'Hi there,' she said. 'Grab a seat.'

'Thanks, Nina,' he said with a cough. 'Got a sore throat.' The accent was a slight approximation to Lawrence's la-di-da voice; it was Tom Cruise, no question. He sat next to Nina on the sofa.

'I sometimes like to keep my mask on,' she said. 'Though it plays havoc with my drinking.'

'I'll bet,' Tom said. His accent was decidedly off, and put Nina in mind of Eliza Doolittle in *My Fair Lady*.

'Pretty bad what happened with Roddie,' Nina said. She looked over at Mandy, jerked her head as if to say, "Give us a hand."

Mandy, like Nina, was wearing the black tracksuit that the girls tended to wear when they weren't stripped to their G-strings. 'Awful,' she said. 'Hey, Lawrence, how you enjoying this shoot?'

'Loving it,' he said. 'We're working with a genius.'

And that confirmed it in spades that this guy was definitely not the flaky Lawrence – because Lawrence would never have said that he was loving the shoot, and he certainly wouldn't have called Kubrick a genius. Still, not every day that you got to sit next to a superstar who was pretending to be a nobody. Who knows where it might lead…

Tom Cruise picked up her book, the one on the samurai, and had been just a little intrigued. 'Don't know much about the samurai,' he'd said. Nina told him a little about this Japanese warrior class. 'For a long time they outlawed guns,' she'd said. 'Know why they did that? Keep the lower classes in their place.' Tom liked that, liked that a lot. 'They only fought with swords?' He mulled it over, as if tucking away a useful piece of information.

That was one of the highlights of the evening. Then, because they were only talking to the world's most famous movie star, Mandy pinned him down about his favourite films. Tom started banging on about how he loved watching the movies in the cinema, before eventually admitting that he adored the entire oeuvre of one Stanley Kubrick. They were all incredulous. No one had understood the supposedly "brilliant" *2001: A Space Odyssey*, and every one of them concurred that (much like his shoots) most of Kubrick's films banged on a bit. 'I once tried to watch *Barry Lyndon*,' Josh said, by now well pickled on rum, and therefore less tongue-tied when in Mandy's company. 'Gave up after an hour. God, it was boring.' Tom/Lawrence sprung to Kubrick's defence: 'It was fresh, so beautifully filmed' – but the team were having none of it.

The final highlight of the evening was an absolute zinger. Before that night, she'd never told a soul, not even Mandy. It was just a question that you never asked – just as you should never ask a soldier how many people he's killed.

But Josh was full of bravura after a half-bottle of rum, so he asked the unaskable question. 'Hey Nina,' he said. 'Mind my asking you how you became a stripper?'

'I don't mind,' Nina said.

'And will you…' Josh slurred. 'Will you answer my question?'

Nina was going to duck it, just like she usually did, parry it with another question, but then she happened to glance at Tom Cruise, and even though he was masked up, he looked interested, leaning forward, legs crossed, hands clasped round his knee. 'Like to hear my story?' she said. Tom nodded. 'Please.' She stroked the back of her hand. She glanced over at Tom, as ever pretending to be something he was not. 'OK, I'll tell you,' she said. 'And I can tell you one thing – it's not your usual stripper story.'

Nor was it.

And so the story began, and no one interrupted, and for a full fifteen minutes Nina had the floor.

'I had quite a square upbringing,' Nina said. 'My mum and dad were both civil servants. By the time I turned eighteen, I'd hardly even drunk alcohol, let alone been into a night club. I did OK, I guess, at school, could have had a gap year, probably should have had a gap year, but as it was, I left Leigh-on-Sea to go straight to Manchester University – and it was there that I met my best friend, Clara. We were in the same hall, we were both studying English, and during our first term we read books and we talked books, and we gradually dipped our toes into the seamier side of life – boyfriends and drinking and clubs and sometimes drugs.'

That first Christmas, when she'd gone back home to Leigh-on-Sea, her parents could barely believe the transformation that had occurred, their bright, biddable daughter, now with sauce and attitude, as well as a tongue stud and a ring on the top rim of her ear. In the spring term, Clara had upped the ante, by proposing that they form the Extreme Picnicking Society, which they did, and since the girls had no shortage of admirers, most weekends they could be found picnicking in ever more extreme environs – the middle of a roundabout, a church crypt (twenty minutes before they were thrown out), behind a church altar (they'd lasted slightly longer here, twenty-five minutes), and, Nina's idea, most creative of all, they'd set up their picnic, wicker basket and all, right at the front of a cinema, just a few yards from the screen. (They'd lasted seven minutes. The film had been *The Silence of the Lambs* – and ever after when Nina saw the film, it always gave her a kick.)

Other dares and adventures had followed – probing, and exploring, and generally seeing whether their partner in crime had got the bottle. Sometimes it worked out brilliantly – they'd gone along to a Christian Union meeting, and Clara had picked up a rather nice boyfriend, a little staid, but very generous. (They'd lasted a month, Patrick's aversion to premarital sex proving to be a fatal flaw.) Some, not so well – like the time that Nina had been on a second date with a guy, and they'd been in a club, and on Clara's whim she had urged Alfie to see if he could get into a fight with the guy at the next table; Alfie had been more than up for it, had gone over to the guy at the other table – "Are you looking at my bird?" – and, for his pains, had been knocked out cold. After he'd got out of hospital, Nina had felt obliged to go on one more date with him, but his smashed nose and his lack of teeth had proved insurmountable.

This, then, was the position that Nina and the also extremely leggy Clara found themselves in towards the end of their second year at Manchester. They'd been out clubbing, just the usual dozen or so besotted suitors chatting them up, buying them drinks, sending them flowers – but if you were a guy trying to attract these girls' attention, you were going to have to do a lot more than just buy them a drink.

They'd been walking past a strip club. And since they'd

never been into a strip club before, and since Nina had pointed out that they'd never been into a strip club before, they had no option but to go into the strip club. It had been a Friday night, the place had been heaving. Nina and Clara had taken up station at a small table towards the back; they were just about the only women there who still had their clothes on, Nina in jeans and a beautiful brown leather jacket. Their complete absence of bare flesh meant that they became even more beguiling to the clientele: within five minutes, two bottles of champagne had been delivered to their table, followed in short order by the rather oily manager, who had first inquired whether they were enjoying themselves, and had then had the nerve to ask if they'd like a job.

How they'd laughed! Them, Nina, Clara, working as strippers!

Clara, of course, had made the obvious suggestion. 'I think you should try it,' she'd said.

'Me become a stripper?' Nina said. 'Why don't you become a stripper?'

More laughter, quite hysterical laughter, more booze, and by 4 a.m. they were back at the flat. By lunch the next day, Nina had forgotten all about it.

Three days later, they'd gone out to their local wine bar; Clara had been absolutely euphoric – giddy with her news. She'd bought a bottle of Sancerre (paid in cash), filled their glasses.

'What have you done?' Nina asked.

'I did it,' Clara said, eyes twinkling as she gave Nina the most puckish of smiles. 'It was the best night ever.'

'What did you do?'

'I went along to that strip club,' Clara said. 'I am a stripper.'

'You're joking.'

'Got the money to prove it.' Clara produced a wodge of £20 notes.

Nina could never remember her friend on such a high, gabbling away about how empowering it had all been, how the other girls had been great, how she'd loved every moment. Another bottle of Sancerre had been ordered, and Clara had thrown down the gauntlet ("your turn now"), and Nina had duly demurred, because being a stripper did not wholly take her fancy, but anyway, on Clara's earnings they'd had one hell of a night of it, and all the pestering men had been sent packing, and there it might have all ended, just another one-off adventure, except that the next day, at teatime, Clara had been crossing the road and had been hit by a police car, who'd had his lights on but perhaps not his siren; she'd clung on for a week, and then her organs were harvested and she was gone. Nina, devastated, had not gone out for a year, confining herself to her books and her essays – if nothing else, and to her parents' astonishment, it had helped her notch up a first-class honours degree.

A year to the day after Clara's death, Nina had been toasting her memory with a bottle of chilled Sancerre. She'd been drinking at home with an on-off boyfriend, and had wryly told him about Clara's turn at the strip club.

The guy, straight, square, dependable David, had all but tutted. 'She was a stripper?' he'd said incredulously.

'She loved it.'

'I'm so glad you weren't tempted.'

'Why's that?' she'd said.

'Well, it's a bit, you know, seedy.'

'How do you mean?'

'I guess sluttish – being paid for men to ogle at you.'

'That so?'

'It's only a short step to outright prostitution.'

'Uh-huh.'

Had David's antennae been more acute, he might have realised that her temper waxed as her answers waned. And then, being the idiot that he undoubtedly was, David said the one thing that would absolutely certainly send her clean over the edge: 'Thank God you weren't tempted,' he'd said. 'But you'd never do anything like that.'

He sat back, this self-contented smile on his fat smug face, contentedly sipping at his glass of Sancerre, safe in the knowledge that sex was soon in the offing – and was rather taken aback when he found himself not just dumped, but immediately bundled out of the flat (without even finishing his Sancerre!). He'd barely been outside for more than two minutes, still wondering whether to whine over the intercom, when a taxi had drawn up, and Nina had herself bowled out of the flat, and without even so much as glancing at the hapless David had slipped into the taxi, thence to be taken immediately and without delay to the Red Coat strip club.

That first night when she'd been about to strip, Nina had been nervous and mildly stunned that she was doing what she was about to do, but with it there was also this thrilled excitement that, a year after Clara's death, she, now, was about to pay the only tribute that she could possibly pay – and if there was one thing of which she was absolutely certain, it was that Clara, wherever she was, would be utterly delighted.

The manager, Ali, was seedier than she remembered – and, as she got to know him better, would become seedier yet. But Mandy had taken her in hand, and – a little to her surprise – she'd enjoyed herself, peeling off her clothes and pole-dancing, and the gibbering menfolk who were nothing so much as patsies in the palm of her hand. She had not perhaps been quite as ecstatic as Clara had been after her first time, but it had given her enough of a buzz to want to do it again, and then again, and along with the excellent money (at least compared to any of the other student jobs she'd tried), Nina had come to relish her nights at the Red Coat.

At the end of Nina's tale, there followed a long, long silence in the Officers' Mess at Elveden Hall, which was eventually broken by the man himself, Tom Cruise.

'Why did you love the Red Coat?' he asked.

'I'll tell you,' she said. 'Because every time I went there, I was tipping my hat to my dead friend Clara – and even now, here in Elveden, every time that my beautiful blue gown falls to the floor, I think of her.'

'What a beautiful story,' Tom Cruise said. 'Thank you,' and he took her hand, and he held it, and he looked at her, and behind his golden mask, his glistering eyes revealed that he was crying.

CHAPTER 25

Hwaet! That is Old English and means "So!" (Don't we just love these little digressions, by the way? I think they add tone to a book, above all showing that you are reading high-quality literary fiction.) It is the first word of Beowulf. As Seamus Heaney explains in his translation of the epic poem, the word "So!" operates as an expression that obliterates all previous discourse and narrative, and at the same time functions as an exclamation calling for immediate attention. But *hwaet* means so much more than just "so"! It is nuanced – it can also mean "lo!" and "hark!" and even "what ho (Bertie)!" There are several other famous first-word "So"s, including at the beginning of Alfred Tennyson's Morte d'Arthur – "So all day long the noise of battle roll'd", as well as Lord Byron's "So we'll go no more a roving." The Irish, however, use the word "So" in the opposite manner; it does not begin sentences, it ends them. As in: what with Tom Cruise gone, I finally had his Winnebago all to myself, so.

So! I did think that Tom's great switcheroo venture was just a little cracked, but who was I, your humble narrator, to contradict such a heavyweight superstar? If he wanted to toddle off to the Officers' Mess and chew the fat with Nina and Mandy and the gormless Josh and the even more gormless Caspar, then good luck to him.

First things first, I knocked back the glass of white wine that I'd been drinking, and had a look for more booze. Just the one bottle of white wine in the fridge – I'd have to remind him to stock up – but tucked away above the sink was a decent bottle of malt, so I cracked it open, poured myself a healthy slug, and turned on the telly. Then – to business! To do not just what I'd been trained to do but what, I believe, I'd been set on God's earth to do: rifle through all of Tom Cruise's private papers and the like and see if I could find anything at all that was remotely newsworthy.

Such a lot of film scripts he had! Tons of them! It seemed to me that he didn't actually read books, he just read film scripts: sci-fi scripts, action scripts, thriller scripts, all of these benighted writers just hoping, praying, that Tom might be turned on enough to express an interest, because once you had Tom Cruise on board, then your film was as good as made. But Kubrick's interminable shoot was causing a bit of a logjam in the whole process. The scores of scripts kept coming through to Tom, but not a single one of them could be actioned until Tom had been released from his indentured slavery. Until that happy day, all that Tom Cruise could do was read his scripts, and express vague interest in projects but he could never sign on the line.

He had two cupboards full of scripts, all fancy bindings and covers and all utterly unreadable. Most people don't read film scripts, but I've read a fair few and I can tell you one thing about them – they certainly ain't meant for pleasure. Though a film itself may be beautiful beyond belief, its film script is just a boring blueprint, entirely shorn of colour, vim and, indeed, humour; they are dead, huskless embryos waiting for Tom and the director to breathe life into them.

I had a flick through a few of the scripts, but seeing as I wasn't in the movie business, the writers' names went clean over my head. Screenwriters, eh? I doubt you could name a single one of them.

I had more luck in one of the drawers in the kitchenette. It was filled up with page after page of Tom's handwritten scrawl. They revealed that, having learned all the ninety-seven two-letter words in the English language (complete with meanings), he'd now moved onto the 974 three-letter words. He must have been really, really hungry to beat Nicole at Scrabble.

Also in the drawer were some cute drawings by his kids and a few notes from Nicole. Nothing too juicy in them, nothing for me to get my teeth into, but I did notice a certain *froideur.* Definitely no kisses or hugs at the end, definitely no mention of that dread word "Love". They seemed more like lists of chores, and the ever-diligent Tom had doubtless performed all these to-dos, as they had all been handily ticked off.

At the very bottom of the drawer was one of the most bizarre documents I've ever read, comprising fifteen pages of closely-typed Kubrickian drivel. It was Kubrick's bonkers instructions on how to look after his animals. The 37th instruction read thusly: "If a fight should develop between Freddie and Leo [his father and son tomcats], the only way that you can do anything about it is to dump water on them. Try to grab Freddie and run out of the room with him. Do not try to pick up Leo. Alternatively, if you open a door and just let Freddie get out, he can outrun Leo. But if he's trapped in a place where you can't separate them, just keep dumping water, shouting and screaming, jumping up and down and waving shirts and towels, and doing anything you can to distract them. Just try to get them apart and grab Freddy.'

It was a bit of an eye-opener. I'd realized long ago, of course, that Kubrick was on the eccentric side. But these care instructions were way more than mere eccentricity. He was nuts! In fact, he was the nutjob's nutjob; even Spike, my deputy editor, would have been forced to bow down at his feet and concede that he was in the presence of a greater power.

Tom Cruise's papers duly sniffed through, I poured myself another large malt, and wondered what the hell else to do. Answer: not much! I had a brief nose under his mattress, just to check that he hadn't been hiding anything from mild-mannered Kimmy, but no, straight-up guys like Tom Cruise have no need for squirrelling away private papers under mattresses. I watched a bit of telly, helped myself to some cheese, and then, not just bored but epically disappointed, I caught a cab back home. There was no one in the hotel bar, so I had no option but to go to bed – the unheard-of prospect of bed before midnight on a Stanley Kubrick production!

I curled into my pit and slept the sleep of the just, to be woken at around 9 a.m. by an obnoxious banging on the door. Not a little knock or a discreet tap, no, it sounded like a yeti pounding the door with his fist.

'All right!' I said. 'I'm coming!'

The yeti continued to hammer on the door. I pulled on a dressing gown and opened the door. His Serene Scrofulousness, Prince Grubby, was standing outside – standing on the newspapers that had been dropped off outside my room, no less – and in his regulation stained grey suit, egg-spattered shirt and limp rag of a tie.

He gave me an appraising once-over, bush-baby eyes behind thick grimy specs. 'It's all right for some,' he said.

'What do you mean by that?' I said.

'It's 9 a.m. and you're still in bed.' He mooched into the room, dumping his holdall on the table. 'I've been up three hours.'

'Yes, Grubby,' I said with infinite patience. 'But you have not been working with the world's most OCD director till five in the morning.'

He lumped himself down at the table. 'Can we order some breakfast? I'm starving.'

'Yes of course we can order some breakfast,' I said. 'What would you like me to order you?'

'Full English,' he said promptly. 'Though I don't like black pudding. Can they give me an extra sausage, instead?'

'One extra sausage for Grubby,' I said. 'I daresay you'd like coffee and orange juice with that.'

'Yeah,' he said. A please might have been nice.

I phoned the order through to room service, a full English plus extra sausage for Grubby and toast and coffee for my abstemious self. I was still on the phone when, to my absolute horror, I saw Grubby making his way to my bathroom. He'd locked himself in before I could stop him.

He didn't even have the good manners to give the toilet a courtesy flush. I went and picked up the papers from outside the door and turned the TV up as loud as I could, but nothing could mask the grotesque trumpeting from behind my bathroom door. He was in there five minutes, as I fruitlessly tried to distract myself by reading the papers, and when he finally came out he was still doing up his belt buckle. I had to breathe through my mouth.

I gave him a sour look. 'Tuck your shirt why don't you?' I said.

'That's better,' he said, inconsequentially stuffing his shirt into his underpants.

'You couldn't have done that downstairs?' I said.

'It's just a toilet,' he said, lumping himself next to me at the table. 'What's the big daddy?'

'You've stunk the whole room out.' I got up and opened the window.

'Well, pardon me for living,' he said. 'If you're so uptight about it, why don't you go and spray some air freshener in there.'

'You know what – I will.' I went into the bathroom and though I didn't have any air-freshener, I sprayed half a can of deodorant. Ominously, the lid to the toilet was closed.

When I returned to my room, Grubby was scratching his armpit. 'What happened to your laptop then?' he asked.

'Got stolen,' I said smoothly.

'How did that happen?'

'Took it on set,' I said. 'Some bastard pinched it.'

'Yeah?'

'Yeah.'

'So where's the program disc?'

'That got nicked too.'

'I'll believe you.' He gave me a lairy eyeball roll. 'Thousands wouldn't.'

'Well, why shouldn't you believe me?'

'The way you just covered your mouth with your fingers,' he said. 'Total giveaway.'

'I've never heard such bollocks.' I swiftly dropped my hand. 'Just had an itch on my lip.'

He gave me another of those nasty eyeball rolls and pulled out his own laptop from the holdall. 'Whoever's nicked it will have a nice surprise when they find that program disc,' he said. 'They might even be able to work out that one of the extras has got a spy pen.'

'We'll just have to see.'

'Yeah,' he said, before suddenly scrutinising the table. 'Lot of dents and chips on the edge of this table, if you don't mind my saying so.'

'Are there?' I said, super-casual.

'Looks like somebody's been hitting the table.' He glanced at the wall, just happened to notice a squareish dent near the ceiling. 'Somebody, say, with one hell of a temper.'

'I don't know what you're talking about,' I said primly.

'Your fingers are covering your mouth again.'

'Now where is that spy pen?' I said, bouncing up from the table and rummaging through the bedside drawers. 'Here we are! And here's the lead!'

Grubby plugged the spy pen into the laptop, and as I flicked through the papers he busied himself with downloading the pictures. It took ages, just as all computer-related activities used to do in the 1990s. I was trying to read, but it wasn't easy – it was like sitting next to some stinking silverback gorilla who spends its entire time scratching himself and eating his own fleas.

It was a small relief when the breakfast arrived and, knowing as I did Grubby's disgusting drill, I poured myself a coffee and stood at the window, gazing out at the tranquil grey sky, and doing my level-best to ignore all the scrunching grunts that were coming from the table.

'God, you're a noisy eater.'

'I'm just eating.' He crammed an entire sausage into his mouth (it had to go in sideways).

'Yeah, you are just eating, and you're the noisiest eater I've ever met.'

'Get you, Mr Fancy Manners,' he said. Bits of sausage sprayed over the table.

It was so revolting that I had to turn away and look out of the window again. Scrunch-scrunch-grunt-burp. I wondered how it was humanly possible to make so much noise when you were eating – and then I twigged it. The bastard was doing it on purpose. He was making as much noise as was humanly possible, the sole purpose of which was to irritate me.

It was actually making me feel ill. I went through to the stinking bathroom, slammed the door shut and had a shower, and for a few blissful minutes I didn't have to listen to the sound of Grubby masticating all over my bedroom, and then I went to have a pee, and in my vexed state I'd forgotten all about that particular piece of unpleasantness, recoiling in horror as I lifted the lid. I could have just meekly scrubbed it all up, but since I was seething, I opened the bathroom door and let the coffee-slurping oaf have it – 'Why don't you learn to use a toilet brush, you inconsiderate cretin!' – and slammed the door shut. I shaved and brushed my teeth and then dressed, so by the time I quit the bathroom ten minutes later, I had calmed down a little. As for Grubby, there was no apology, no anything – I might as well have been remonstrating with a sow in its sty.

He was scrolling through the blurred pictures on his laptop. If I hadn't taken them myself, I'd have had no clue that they were from the set of *Eyes Wide Shut*.

Grubby continued to scroll. You could just about tell that they were pictures of naked women, but beyond that, nothing.

'That's not bad,' he said.

'Hmm.' I looked at the picture. It was pretty grainy, but I could at least tell that it was a picture of Nina and Mandy, both of them topless.

'And that's not bad either,' Grubby said. This was a picture of Red Cloak swinging his incense burner with Nina kneeling beside him.

'I suppose it's OK,' I said. Well, it was sort of OK – if you were absolutely desperate, it might have made a very blurred splash picture.

'These are the best we've got,' he said. 'You'll just have to keep on snapping away with the spy pen.'

'Suppose I will.' The prospect of wearing my ludicrous jacket and taking more spy-pen pictures did not entirely fill me with glee.

'Better send them over to Spike,' Grubby said. 'Let him see what we're up against.'

'You don't think it'd be better to leave it until we've got something decent to show him?'

'Nah,' Grubby said, as he dialled up the *Sun* picture desk. 'They're fine.'

* * *

By lunchtime, I'd perked up a little. Grubby had thankfully left the building. The two pictures, perhaps a tad grainy but still eminently usable, had been sent over to the *Sun*, and were doubtless even now being pored over by the picture editor and the deputy editor. And, last but by no means least, I had rather a tasty story for the *Sun*, which with just the tiniest bit of titivation might make a splash. I was just mulling over whether to call the story in or whether to save it for a rainy day, when – happily – my mobile phone trilled and my dilemma was resolved.

Not for Spike the usual pleasantries such as 'Hi Kim' or 'How's it going, Kim', or even the common courtesy of announcing just who the hell was calling me. Even an 'It's Spike!' might have been nice.

But no, I got none of that – and all I in fact got was somebody yelling into my ear at the top of his voice, 'They're shit!'

'Who is this?' I said.

'It's me, you idiot,' he said, before once again repeating his stock line. 'They're shit!'

'Oh hi Spike,' I said. 'How's it going?'

'Don't you give me that shit!' he said. How pleasant it was, after a month of working with that despot Stanley Kubrick, to be having a chinwag with my avuncular *Sun* boss. 'These pictures are completely unusable! Why did you send this crap over? What do you think I'm going to do with them – use them to wipe my—' As ever and as always, Spike's conversation has been heavily redacted.

'Oh,' I said, honeyed words on a troubled sea. 'I'm sorry to hear that.'

'What the hell have you been doing for the past month?' he said. 'You haven't filed a word, and the only thing you have sent over are two pictures which were so blurred I didn't even know that they were upside down.'

'Oh I'm sorry,' I repeated, the ever-emollient super-reporter. 'I'll just have to have another crack and hope for better luck tonight.'

'Really?' he said. 'What's the point? You're just wasting your time and my money! Your expenses alone are running at damn near two thousand quid a week!' From the way he was rabbiting on, you might have thought that Spike was personally funding this whole mission, paying my expenses out of his own bank account. Sadly, this was not the case. No – in those days, in the mid-90s, The *Sun* was making over £1 million a week, and you'd have thought that most of this money would have been ploughed back into the paper, to pay, say, for top-notch reporters, but not one little bit of it. Most of the loot just went straight back into News International, where it was used to prop up Sky TV (then in its infancy) and the thundering cash sinkhole otherwise known as *The Times*.

'Sure, sure,' I said. 'But actually, I do have quite a tasty story for you.'

'What you got?' Deep suspicion.

'The second assistant director had a heart attack on set last night,' I said. 'He's dead!'

'The second assistant director died on set?' Spike repeated. 'So what?'

'It's part of a pattern, Spike,' I said.

'Yeah?' Less suspicious now, more dubious.

'Yeah!' I said enthusiastically. When pitching a story to an editor, it's best to do it *con brio*. Sometimes it can be catching – not always, but sometimes. 'The shoot's already lasted a year, it's gone way over budget and way over schedule! One of the stars, Harvey Keitel, got so hacked off that he quit the movie and had to be replaced by Sydney Pollack! And just recently we lost the principal stripper. She was shagging Tom Cruise's stand-in! And he's gone too!'

'Yeah?' he said. He might have moved up a gear from "Dubious" to "Ever so slightly interested".

'Yeah!' I said again. 'It's a great story. It's… it's… It's Kubrick's Curse!'

'Hmmm,' he said. 'The Curse of Kubrick…'

I kept my mouth shut. When you're fishing, and when the trout has finally taken the fly, you must not strike too soon. You have to count to three, slowly intoning, "For what we are about to receive." Strike too quickly and you'll flick the fly out of the trout's mouth; bide your time and the hook's barbs can begin to bite. And so with Spike. Having taken the bait, he had to be allowed to swallow of his own accord.

'Hmmm,' I echoed.

'Might work,' he grunted. 'File and I'll have a look.'

'Sure,' I said, not remotely nettled at the lack of a "thank you", or a "nice work", or a "good job, Kimmy".

'And for Christ's sake get some decent pictures,' he said. 'We need the pictures!'

'Yes, Spike.'

'Are these women really stunners?' he said.

'They're the most beautiful women you've ever seen in your life, Spike,' I cooed. 'And every one of them is buck naked.'

'Well, it's no good you telling me that,' he said. 'Get me my pictures!'

So back off to Elveden Hall I went, the hard-working scribe going about his diligent business, with no thought for thanks or plaudits, merely revelling in the pleasure of his craft. Problem was, since Tom Cruise had now decided to be his own stand-in, I wasn't getting nearly as much time on set. No – while Tom was gabbing away with Nina, Mandy et al., I was stuck in Tom's Winnebago. The only time I actually spent on set was when Tom came back to the Winnebago (as his own stand-in), to return five minutes later back into the hall as himself. I, meanwhile, would go back onto set with my original mask and take up my station with the rest of the extras.

We were filming the most unbelievably tortuous part of the orgy. By now, we were coming to the end of the first half of the scene, and the girls, naked but for their G-strings, had all been pairing off. As the principal girl, Nina got to pair off with Tom. All she had to do was step off the red carpet, sidle up to Tom and then kiss him – mask to mask. To anyone else this might have been fairly simple, but – as you will by now be well aware – Kubrick just loved to spin things out. On this one kiss scene, he spent over three days, just your usual hundred-plus takes, and though Tom Cruise had been broken in long ago, I could see that it was starting to get to Nina. They'd do a take that was not just usable but 100 per cent perfect, and yet all Nina got at the end of it was Kubrick growling, "Do it again".

The upside of this ten-second kiss was that I had a chance to take more pictures with my trusty spy pen, and for three days solid I was happily snapping away from my first position at the side of the hall. There wasn't much science to this picture-taking – just open up my cloak, press the button and hope for the best. (My kinda photography!)

Just after the 6 p.m. call time on the second day of Nina's kiss scene, Kubrick called the whole team, cast, crew and caterers, into the hall. We were all scattered about the hall on the red carpet, while Kubrick addressed us from the first-floor balcony. He'd never done this before. There was an expectant hush. I was just my usual bland, benign self, not doing anybody any harm, just being a good mousey extra, just getting on with my mousey business of the day.

'There's been a story about us on the front page of today's *Sun*,' Kubrick said into his microphone. 'Now I just hope to God it's not one of you guys selling that story. We're a team – we're a family.'

Since we weren't wearing masks, I nodded in happy agreement, like some mad cult groupie. It seemed the right thing to do.

Kubrick glared at us through his round glasses. 'What I'm hoping is that one of you talked to a friend, and it was maybe one of them who sold the story. So look – what happens on this set stays on this set. We're family, right, and family don't tell stories on each other.'

Well, I don't know what sort of family Kubrick came from, but most of my family could sing like canaries. If you told my blabbermouth uncle Gervase something in the "strictest confidence", you could be utterly certain that in under two hours he'd be broadcasting it from the rooftops.

When Kubrick had finally finished chuntering, we all sidled off to get our gear on (or off in Nina's case). Josh, like the rest of them, was squawking away – 'Who could it be, who could it be?'

It's always like this when there's a hunt for a tabloid mole. I saw it when I had a stint at Buckingham Palace as a footman (*Palace Rogue*), and I saw it again when one of my snouts was flogging me stories from Eton (another zinger, *Eton Rogue*). When the stories first start appearing in the *Sun*, there's this extraordinary moment of amazement as the main players realise they've got a mole on board. They can't believe it! They've hitherto imagined that everyone's on the same team, everyone's pulling together, and it suddenly dawns on them that they've been harbouring a scum-sucking viper. Then, invariably, they start berating the entire team in the vain hope that the mole will either a) confess, or b) desist from scum-sucking. Some hope! Me desist from scum-sucking? It is in my nature! Just as the great René Descartes said, I scum-suck therefore I am.

At Elveden Hall the extras were all abuzz with scandalised chatter and speculation about who it was who might have blabbed – and, such sweet ecstasy, dear old Josh was even beginning to blame himself!

'I told one of the barmaids at the Fox about Roddie's heart attack,' he said. 'I know I shouldn't have, but I was a bit in shock.'

'You told one of the barmaids?' I repeated. 'Jesus! Well that's just great! You better go and tell Kubrick.'

'What?' Josh said. 'You think I should?'

'Course you should,' I said. 'Especially if you never want to see Mandy again.'

'Uhhh?' he said, little cogs whirring, denser than a block of tungsten. How on earth he got into Bristol University, I have no idea.

'If you tell Kubrick, you'll be kicked off the set in five minutes flat.'

'Well, why would I want to tell Kubrick then?' He stood there in front of me, mouth vacant as a goldfish, tiny little mind trying, trying to make sense of it all.

'I'm pulling your leg, you wally!' I said. 'Of course you shouldn't tell Kubrick!'

'Uhh, OK,' he said, vacuously. 'And what should I say if Kubrick asks me if I talked to the barmaid?'

'You deny it, you complete idiot – what do you think you do?'

'Yeah that's right, I deny it!' he said, comprehension finally dawning.

'You say this magical phrase – "I don't know what you're talking about". Say it!'

'I don't know what you're talking about.' He said it in a flat monotone, a dullard schoolboy reading by rote.

'And again!' I said. 'Say it like you mean it!'

'I don't know what you're talking about,' he said. A bit better but not much.

'And again!' I said. 'What we want is hurt outrage!'

'I don't know what you're talking about!'

'Better,' I said. 'And —'

'What's going on here?'

I turned. It was the fragrant Nina.

'Oh, hi Nina,' I said. 'How we getting on? Tommy behaving himself, not being getting too fruity with you?'

'Yeah,' she said dismissively. Like the other girls, Nina was wearing her black tracksuit. 'What have you got Josh parroting?'

'Oh that,' I said. 'He's the blabber. It's thanks to him that the story got into the *Sun*.'

'Don't tell her!' Josh blurted, before turning pleadingly to Nina. 'I told a barmaid,' he gabbled. 'She might have sold the story. Please don't tell.'

'Of course it wasn't you,' Nina said, haughty as a duchess. 'It wasn't?' he said.

'Couldn't have been you,' she said. 'It was Lawrence.'

'*Me?*' I said. 'What the hell are you talking about?'

'You flogged the story,' she said. 'It's written all over your face. The only wonder is you didn't flog the pictures too.'

'Pictures?' I said, genuinely outraged. 'How the hell am I going to get pictures? This set is as tight as a gnat's chuff!'

'With that rotten pen camera of yours,' she said promptly.

'You've got a nerve!' I said. Jesus, she was good! She was brilliant! How... how did she know? How had she sussed me? Had she got some sort of witchy sixth sense? 'I've never heard such claptrap!'

'Say what you like, Lawrence, it's still you,' she said.

'What – what??' I said. If she carried on like this, then Glenn or Kubrick might take an interest, and then I would be royally skewered. 'What ever happened to innocent until proven guilty?'

'This isn't a court of law,' she said dismissively. 'You're full of it.'

I had to change tack. 'Nina, dear,' I said soothingly. I gave her my biggest puppy-dog eyes. 'I am shocked, shocked that you could even think that I'm some of sort of stooge for the *Sun* – it's just not what I'm about. It's not what I do. I'm a pretty straight kind of guy.'

Nina gave a snort of derision. 'Enjoy snooping through Tom Cruise's Winnebago.'

'I beg your pardon!' I said, but Nina was already striding off to wherever the hell she was striding off to.

I thought she was being a little unfair, because I hadn't actually flogged the story. No, indeed not – just like any other self-respecting staff reporter would have done, I had *given* the story to the *Sun*. And besides that, Nina had no reason whatsoever to believe that I was a scum-sucker. Why – while I'd been at Elveden, I'd been positively good as gold, hadn't stepped so much as an inch out of line. Frankly, I thought Nina was being a bit unsporting; that she was spot on the money had nothing to do with it.

I mooched into Tom Cruise's Winnebago. As expected, Tom was not there. Tom was not there because he was having a good time with the girls and Josh and all the other palookas they'd invited along to the Officers' Mess (the Officers' Mess that *I* had initiated through the kindness of *my* heart).

I helped myself to a glass of wine and had a quick forage through the kitchen drawer, but there was nothing new there. There were also no fresh scripts in the screenplay cupboards. Nothing on the telly either. For a few minutes I contented myself with doing a few anagrams from the Scrabble board. I may not be much good at remembering all the two-letter words in the English language, but I have got a knack for anagrams. I pulled out seven letters from the Scrabble bag, scanned them, and the word popped out in five seconds – "LEISURE". And another seven letters, and there's the word just begging to be played, "CRETINS", and actually there's another one! ("CISTERN.") God I'm good at this, and I happily contented myself with solving anagrams for all of fifteen minutes before I got bored. Fortunately, I had brought along a thing called "a book". I kicked my shoes off, put my feet up on the sofa and, taking an occasional sip of white wine, I read my book, and it was all just as cosy as can be, not just downtime, but me time. Really, when you've got a good book for company, then who needs to be roistering with piss-head extras? It's a complete no-brainer.

I'd just poured myself a second glass of white wine when there was a light double tippity-tap at the door. 'Hi Tom?'

Ooooh. This could be nasty.

I soundlessly set my glass upon the table.

Another knock at the door. 'Tom, I know you're in there.'

It's a woman's voice. It's a voice that I rather recognized.

'Tom, I know things haven't been great between us, but just open the door.'

It's Nicole.

I'm not at all sure how to play this one.

CHAPTER 26

Glenn has been barely away from Elveden Hall for thirty-six hours and returns to total bedlam. Roddie, his second assistant director, is dead, and the feeling among the cast is, if not mutinous, at least frisky. The crew also have a strange vibe, as if they're done with Kubrick and his million and one takes. Roddie's death has been a stark reminder that, for over a year now, they have all been stuck as Kubrick's cat's paw, there to comply with the tyrant's bidding.

Glenn can sense it also among the extras as they start dribbling onto the set in the late afternoon. It's almost a defiance, like "You want to make something of it?" Well, what could Kubrick do about it? Short of firing every one of the extras, there was very little Kubrick could do. Though best not go there, best not even suggest the idea to Kubrick; he might even act on it, can a whole month's worth of filming and start again from scratch, just for the sheer hell of it.

The previous night, during his mother's wake, Glenn's phone had fortuitously been turned off, and when he had stumbled to bed at two in the morning, he hadn't bothered to check his messages. This was a good thing. If he'd had his phone on, and he'd actually accepted a call, he'd have had to listen to two hours of Kubrick wittering when there was nothing to be done about it.

Glenn had got up at 8 a.m., had showered and got dressed with only a mild fizz of a hangover, and only then had turned on his mobile phone. "You have 21 new messages."

The first ten, at least, were from Kubrick, demanding, insisting, that Glenn get straight back to Elveden, his tone getting more and more furious and peevish, before eventually hinting at a very light degree of concern: "Glenn are you OK? Call me when you can." The rest of the calls were from the runners and various secretaries who'd been tasked with tracking him down.

Glenn left a very brief message for Kubrick, who in turn had switched off his phone. Glenn was so very sorry to hear that Roddie was dead – and he'd be back at Elveden at around 1.30 p.m., just exactly when he said he'd be back.

He had breakfast at the airport and mulled over who to draft in as the second assistant director. Get in someone new, or bump everyone up the ladder, promoting the third assistant director to second assistant director and so on. That said, the third assistant director was currently serving time on Steadicam duties after... after Sven had gone mad. Poor old Sven, hadn't thought about him in weeks, just another one of Kubrick's victims.

Such a flux of thoughts trickling through Glenn's head as he stared at the thundering planes. And it was rather nice, sitting there at a table, without pen or notepad, and without feeling any especial need to act upon his thoughts, as his mind drifted from Kubrick and the film, and then onto his mum, and how all his daily phone calls with her were so suddenly over; it was a fresh jag to the heart every time he thought of her.

And then – not that this was the primary thought in Glenn's head, but it certainly cropped up every so often – there of course was Nina. For any lover on earth, was there anything so beguiling, so bewitching, as a fledgling love affair which has been nipped in the bud? Not that Glenn was assuming anything, or indeed presuming anything, but if he were to, ahhh, *infer* anything at all from not just Nina's kisses but her conversation, then he might deduce that she was a keeper, and also, in all probability, one hell of a lover. With one hell of a body!

Another plane landed, another plane took off. What would it be like dating a stripper? Would she continue to be a stripper after Kubrick was done with them, or had she perhaps moved on from that? And – just another ludicrous thought in a morning of ludicrous thoughts – would he, Glenn, get jealous, if Nina, potential girlfriend, continued to ply her trade as a stripper? How would he feel if, say, after a congenial lunch together, and, perhaps, a sniff of love-making, Nina had given him a smacker on the lips and said she was just pottering off for a stint at the Red Coat, there to be drooled over by a score of piggy-eyed strangers...

Glenn did realise that he was rather jumping the gun. Though talking of love-making, he'd been on very short commons for well over a year now; he was nigh on a virgin!

And back to thoughts of his mum, and Kubrick, and the thousand and one things that would have to be attended to, and soon enough they would be attended to, but for now it was glorious just to sip coffee and to attend to nothing at all.

He switched off his phone for the duration of the flight, and Kubrick called him when he was driving back to Elveden – "See me the moment you get in."

And see him he had.

He'd knocked on the door of Kubrick's Winnebago and, as always, there'd been an immense kerfuffle inside, the sound of shuffling and a door banging, before, perhaps a minute later, the door was finally opened. Kubrick was wearing one of his green tunics from *Full Metal Jacket*, pockets stuffed with pencils and notebooks; he'd gone full hobo.

'Hi Glenn,' Kubrick said. 'Good to have you back.'

'Good to be back,' Glenn said, lying through his teeth.

He followed Kubrick inside. The Winnebago was humming, a mix of sweat and cigarettes. Even an open window might have helped, but Kubrick loved a warm fug. Over in the corner, the rock tumbler was still dutifully grinding away. Glenn saw that a few more shiny pebbles had been added to

Kubrick's collection; they looked very nice and smooth, with not a hard edge between them.

Glenn was given a can of Coke, and Kubrick poured out his tale of woe. 'They were all yelling "I am Spartacus", and the next thing Roddie was down and dead!' Kubrick said. 'Nothing we could do about it.'

'Christ!' Glenn said.

They discussed at length who would be promoted to second assistant director – answer: the new third assistant director, who would in his turn be replaced by... the fourth assistant director – before Kubrick eventually changed the subject.

'When do you think we'll be finished here?' he asked Glenn.

'Maybe a couple of weeks?' Glenn said, instantly kicking himself.

'Two weeks?' Kubrick hooted. 'Not a chance! We're just getting comfy here!'

Glenn said what he should have said first time round. 'When do you think we'll be finished here, Stanley?'

'Way past Christmas, I know that.'

Past Christmas? By that reckoning, Kubrick wouldn't be finished by the summer. That'd be another seven or eight months of shooting! And though Glenn was well schooled in Marcus Aurelius's philosophy of the obstacle being the way, he did, on occasion, allow himself to size up the obstacle in front of him – and, from where he was sitting right now, Coca-Cola in hand, it looked like not just a massive obstacle, but also a particularly painful one.

But on the upside (and Glenn was always about the upside), he'd get to spend more time with the crew, as well as, ahhh, being snubbed by Nina – so all good stuff and he couldn't wait to crack on. With another seven months with Kubrick. Seven more months! With the biggest control freak in history! Notwithstanding all the perks (more time with Nina, more time with Nina with no clothes on, more time with Nina not talking to him), that was a middling tough obstacle. Scratch that. This was a man-sized obstacle.

Kubrick had started to look covetously at his magazines; the latest issue of *The Lady* had arrived that morning.

As Glenn got up to leave, he suddenly realized that he hadn't had a pee since breakfast. 'Mind if I use your toilet, Stanley?'

Kubrick had already flicked back his La-Z-Boy chair, like a luxury reclining seat on a private jet. Thin fingers already stretching for his magazine. 'What was that?'

'Mind if I use your toilet?'

'What?' Kubrick said. 'Oh no!' He shot out of the chair. Glenn had never seen him move so fast. 'You can't go in there. Problem with the sink.'

'Oh,' Glenn said. 'I'll get one of the lads to fix it.'

'It's all in hand, thank you, Glenn.'

With beetling eyebrows, Kubrick watched him out of the Winnebago. It was odd behaviour, very odd – but then, every single thing about Kubrick was odd and eccentric. Maybe he was one of those anal types who couldn't bear for his toilet to be sullied by anyone else; the comic actor Kenneth Williams, who'd died nearly a decade ago, had been another. Maybe it just went with the OCD turf.

Back on set that first day, Glenn had felt like a lion-tamer returned to the cage after his pets had made a meal of one of the stagehands. What had gone wrong? How had Roddie let it get so out of hand? And with just the smallest crack of his whip, discipline was restored and all was as it once was.

He couldn't be sure, but maybe the reason why Kubrick had Cruise repeatedly kissing Nina was that he just wanted to remind them, once and for all, that he was the boss. He was the guy who, if he felt like it, could get the biggest star on the planet, Mr Tom Cruise, to kiss Nina a thousand times over. Because he could! Cos he felt like it! And, hell, if he felt like it, he'd have Cruise kissing Nina for a whole month, and there was not a damn thing that Cruise, Nina or anyone else could do about it. Do it again!

Kubrick had Nina and Tom Cruise doing their damn kiss for three days – every conceivable variation of kiss, and always with their masks on. Cheek to cheek, mouth to mouth, lip to neck and hand to head. Glenn had long ago ceased to wonder why Kubrick was so keen on his repeated takes, but it sometimes felt like he was just doing it for the sheer fun of being the boss. He could ask them to do whatever he liked, and like the whipped dogs that they were, they did what he wanted.

On the third day, then, Glenn had arrived at Elveden at about three in the afternoon, had picked up a coffee and had taken it to the top deck of the double-decker. Before the extras and the girls arrived, this top deck was his little haven; no one knew he was there, no one would even think to think that he was there. He liked to tuck himself away at the furthermost table. It was the perfect place to sit in silence and to plan his order of campaign.

Now – he wasn't sure whether Mickey was up to the job of Steadicam operator; maybe give him another day on it, and if it still wasn't working out, they could give Olivia a try. Though was Olivia even strong enough to wield the Steadicam for eight hours a night?

He heard a sniff on the stairs of the double-decker, and, a moment later, Nina walked onto the top deck; she was wiping her nose with a tissue, though it might have been her cheek. She didn't seem to have noticed him. She slumped down at the first table she came to, head in her hands. She didn't move for quite a while.

Glenn busied himself with his oh-so-important plan of campaign, flicking the occasional glance at Nina; she really hadn't noticed him. And the longer he left it, the more difficult it would be to suddenly announce that he was there, on the top deck, with Nina.

He darted another glance at her – and, oh Christ alive, she

was crying! Her elbows were on the table, head in her hands. He could see the tears trickling steadily onto the tabletop.

What to do, what to do? What the hell should he do? Give a delicate cough to alert her that he was there? Immerse himself in his notepad and pretend that he wasn't even aware of the snuffling at the other end of the bus?

And quite apart from all that… why was she crying?

Well, he did at least know the answer to that – Kubrick, the bastard, had finally broken her. And he'd done it by the simple expedient of ordering her to kiss Tom Cruise a thousand times over – and kisses, mind, which were just play kisses, with masked lips being pressed to masked lips.

Stay – not stay? Busy himself with his note-taking – or get stuck in? But be damned to artifice! He wanted to get stuck in! Nina was crying. He wanted to help her!

Smooth and agile, Glenn stepped out from his table, took fifteen quick steps down the aisle, and slipped onto the banquette opposite Nina.

'Hi Nina,' he said.

Red eyes flicked up. A flare of surprise, then rage, to be quickly followed by resignation. She reverted to her first position, head held in her hands, elbows on the table. After a long silence, the tears continued to drip onto the table.

And then, beautifully, Glenn remembered what his mum had used to do, when he'd been a kid, and when he'd hurt himself, and when she was trying to take his mind off things. She'd tell him a story. 'A few years ago, I was working on a film with Steven Berkoff,' he said. 'Just like now, I was the first assistant director – and Steven was in his usual role as the villain.

'Well, let me tell you one thing about Steven: he looks like one tough *hombre* and this is absolutely what he's like on the inside. He doesn't take any shit from anyone – ever. He exudes menace. He's not somebody you muck around with. And that's why the casting directors just love him – he doesn't have to act tough. He is tough! Tough as teak!'

Glenn had his hands clasped in his lap. Nina hadn't moved. The tears had stopped; probably a good thing.

'He's played so many villains – and he just adores it! Says he finds it extremely flattering. He was a Soviet general in one of the James Bonds, a corrupt art dealer in *Beverly Hills Cop*, a bad guy in *Rambo*, another bad guy in *The Krays*. He only really does the movies to pay for his first love, which is theatre. I guess that he's played every single one of Shakespeare's baddies. If you want a villain, then Steven is your go-to guy.

'So you will not be surprised to hear, Nina, that Steven quickly came to the attention of your friend and mine, Stanley Kubrick – and the reason, of course, why Stanley was interested in Berkoff was because he wanted to tame him. He wanted to see if he could tame the toughest, hardest actor on the block – and that was Steven Berkoff.'

Nina sniffed and wiped her nose, and after a while her eyes slid from the table up to Glenn, and, unblinking, she looked at him.

'Berkoff first came into Kubrick's orbit when he had a small role in *A Clockwork Orange*, but he had a much bigger part in *Barry Lyndon*, when he played the role of this gambling aristocrat, Lord Ludd. Berkoff must have been in his mid-thirties at the time.

'A lot of the shoot was in Ireland, and Kubrick did what he always does – and what he is now doing to you. He tried to break Berkoff, and the way he did it was, naturally, to order Berkoff to repeat the same scene over and over again.'

Glenn smiled to himself. Berkoff had told him the story when they'd been having breakfast together in a Los Angeles café, basking in the sun on the pavement, fruit and muesli for both of them, and Berkoff getting more and more into the story, until by the end, he was giving it everything he'd got. Glenn had had the supreme luxury of witnessing the full Berkoff, maximum energy, maximum power, searing blue eyes on full lock.

'Berkoff knew instantly what Kubrick was about – "He

was trying to break me, Glenn, the swine was trying to break me!" That's what he said to me. He even tapped me on the chest when he said it, just to make sure that I'd got the point. Just like I'm doing to you now.'

Glenn stretched over and tapped Nina lightly on the chest bone, grinning as he did it. She allowed herself to smile back; he hadn't seen that smile in a long time.

Nina sniffed. 'So what happened?'

'He changed his attitude,' Glenn said simply. 'And that changed everything. Instead of letting Kubrick wear him down, Berkoff decided to feed off it. He'd done about twenty-seven takes for a scene, and every single time that Berkoff heard those three beautiful words "Do it again", it made him stronger. And he got stronger and stronger and tougher and tougher, and this strength is just shining out, it's dripping off him, he's loving it; above all he's thinking not just that Kubrick's not going to break him, but that he, Berkoff, is going to break Kubrick.'

Nina chuckled. 'And how did it all end?'

'Berkoff beat him hands down,' Glenn said. 'Kubrick had given him another ten takes, and with every take, he could see his star's power increasing, and he even realizes that Berkoff is enjoying himself. His star's loving it! And that was never ever supposed to happen. The point of doing hundreds and hundreds of takes was to get his stars to submit. For them to be enjoying themselves was completely intolerable. Berkoff even goaded Kubrick a little, saying, "Can we do it again?" with a big fat smile on his face, but Kubrick knew he was beaten. He folded. "I think we're done," he said, and off he wandered to his caravan. And that, Nina, is how to do it. You're not looking to survive this. You're looking to beat him – and you will, because you, Nina, are one tough *madre*.'

Nina leaned back and stared at the ceiling. 'One tough mother,' she repeated.

'Go the full Berkoff,' Glenn said.

'I'm going to channel my inner Berkoff,' she said

decisively. 'When Kubrick starts to rattle me, I'll just think, "What would Berkoff do?"'

'I reckon you could probably out-Berkoff Berkoff.'

'Thanks for that, Glenn.' Nina smiled and got up. 'Sorry I've been so snotty.' Ever so lightly, her hand touched his shoulder. 'You're one of the good guys,' she said, and with that she was gone.

CHAPTER 27

The time has finally arrived for us to be introduced to Stanley Kubrick's heroine – and that would be the one and only Mrs Tom Cruise.

So how's Nicole been enjoying this whole laborious journey with the manifest genius that is Stanley Kubrick? Answer: not so very much.

The whole thing has been dragging on for over a year now, most of her scenes are done, and while it's been great having all this time with the kids and touring Ye Olde England – just *loved* the Lake District! – and it's been fun learning Italian, but, can she allow herself to admit this? She's bored.

Aside from the monumental Kubrick problem, there is one other tiny problem with the shoot: things are not going that well with Tom. He's been working every single night, back to back, for over a year now, and the only time that he had had off had been the six days when – how can we delicately put this? – she'd been filming explicit sex scenes with the Canadian studmuffin Gary Goba. Nicole doesn't really like to dwell on those six days, but since the subject has come up, we may as well deal with it: in a long career of working with handsome brutes, Gary Goba was just about the most handsome brute she'd ever laid eyes on. And she'd spent six days absolutely naked with him. Even a few months on, she still found it just so *bizarre*! One moment, she's being introduced to Gary, is shaking his hand, and they're both uttering the usual pleasantries – "really looking forward to working with you" and such like – and the next moment, Gary's stripped naked, she's stripped naked, and Stanley's holding the camera, and ordering them to, ahhh, do this and that to each other. It honestly could not have been more graphic if it had been just your average porno film. Fifty different sexual positions they'd done – fifty! – some of which Nic had not only never partaken of before, but had never conceived that they even existed! How did Stanley know all these positions? Was he some kind of porn junkie, or had he just spent a lot of time leafing through the Kama Sutra? (Fact: Kubrick was actually the former – a porn junkie.)

For the six days, Nicole had had to wear a merkin (that is, a pubic wig). It had been strawberry blonde to match her hair, and at one stage, Kubrick had ordered the divine Gary Goba to, ahhh, to satisfy her orally, and had been yelling at him, "You've got to really get in there, Gary!" And when Gary had finally been allowed to come up for air, he'd started plucking at his teeth with his fingernail – "Got a pubic hair stuck there," he'd said. Just a little turned on? Just a small smidgeon of desire trickling up her spine, as the most beautiful man she'd ever seen manhandled her about the bedroom – and though she was married, happily, happily married, to Tom, you'd have had to have been a cyborg not to feel a bat-squeak of desire as you looked down and watched your breasts being caressed by the beautiful hands of Gary Goba. And as for Gary, naked but for his "modesty pouch", she did sometimes wonder whether the desire was mutual, and, hell, why not just admit it, that if she had been single and he had been single, when Stanley was finally done with them, she might have enjoyed sharing a little drink with Gary, and maybe a meal, and maybe, just, you know, getting to know him a bit better, and if, say, his character had been even half as handsome as his body then... well it might have been fun to see if this simulated sex could ever, ever match up to the real thing. Well... Maybe. But these illicit thoughts are not something that Nicole likes to dwell upon. She's a married woman! And has a very nice husband, a bit of a star of a husband, thank you very much indeed, one Tom Cruise.

It would be fair to say that, well, things haven't been going that great with Tom at the moment. It's partly the film, partly the kids, partly the sex (or lack of same), but mainly it's just down to that simple thing called connection. It's gone. They go through the motions, they express interest in each other's lives, they discuss the children and the movie, but there's not a whole lot of fun there any more. It's just, you know, hard work. Friends say that all marriages get like that after a while, and that you just have to soldier on and that in time it'll get better, the prospect of which doesn't exactly sound thrilling.

Still – here she is, back from the Lake District, giving it yet another try. How many more tries has she got left in her? She does not know. But what she does know is that she's here, now, at Elveden Hall, and that she's going to go into Tom's Winnebago and she's going to see if she can reconnect with him again – and if they can reconnect, they might even reconnect physically (get back, you evil thoughts of Gary Goba!). Well, who knew how it would all turn out, but she sure as hell was going to give it her best shot.

She dithered in the dark. She could just glimpse Tom through the Winnebago blinds. He had his feet up on the sofa and – odd – was reading a book and – odder – appeared to be drinking a glass of white wine.

She knocked at the door, and he wouldn't open. What was he playing at? Was he going to pretend he wasn't there?

She knocked on the door again. 'Tom, I know things haven't been great between us, but just open the door.'

And the door opened. Tom was wearing not just his cloak, but his mask. He gave a courtly bow and with his right arm gestured for her to enter. '*Buonasera*,' he said. '*Vieni nel, mio amore.*'

Quite a lot of thoughts running through her head at the same time – Tom – speaking Italian! (and pretty good Italian too – his accent was spot on) Tom – being rather charming, for once! Tom – who somehow in the last month had contrived to have a hand transplant! (what long fingers he now had). She didn't know who it was. But it sure as hell wasn't Tom.

Still – when in Rome…

'*Grazie, gentile signore*,' she said, offering her hand up, and Tom 2.0 took her hand and brought it to his masked lips. So definitely not Tom!

With a waft of his hand, he offered her a seat and, again in the most perfect Italian, though perhaps rather formal, asked her if she'd like a drink. (For ease of reading we will translate into English.) 'Glass of white wine, madame?' he said. 'A dram of whisky?'

Nic replied in kind. 'That very kind of you,' she said in her not-so-perfect Italian. 'I like a glass of white wine.' Pretty sure that she'd got the tense wrong, but still – not too bad.

She appraised Tom 2.0 as he opened the fridge. He looked taller, maybe six inches taller – he wasn't wearing Tom's usual heel inserts. And graceful, actually, the way he twirled the bottle in his fingers, pouring the wine with a flick of his wrist.

So if not Tom, who was it? Almost certainly his body double, the one he'd started jogging with. Tom had done pretty much the same thing with his last body double on the first *Mission: Impossible*, which had also just happened to have involved a lot of mask-wearing – and now, surprise, surprise, Tom was up to his old tricks, wearing a mask so that he could slum it with the supporting artists. Everyone of course knew it was Tom with a mask on, but they all dutifully went along with the charade of pretending he was just another nobody.

But Tom's *Mission: Impossible* double hadn't been nearly as confident as this guy – well, apart from anything else, he hadn't had the nerve to pretend to be Tom Cruise! But Tom 2.0 – he was chatting away in fluent Italian about how lovely it was to see her, and how were the kids and, much more to the point, how was she doing?

Of course she knew it wasn't Tom; in a moment of sweet

clarity she realised that he knew that she knew that it wasn't Tom, and, just for the fun of it was going along with it anyway. *Just for the fun of it.* Now there was a phrase she sure as hell hadn't used in an aeon. And certainly not with Tom, for whom everything tended to be just a little on the serious side – and while Nicole was also eminently serious, there was a side of her that, on occasion, liked to let her hair down and do things, even quite weird things, just, say… for the fun of it.

Like, for the sake of example, playing along with this charade that this, this exotic chap was actually her husband.

Well… she'd give him one glass of wine, which, if he had panache, would be opportunity enough to beguile. And – not that she would ever, ever have been unfaithful to Tom (Get behind me, you Gary Goba satan!) – after seven years with Tom, she was just a little itchy, and, what the hell, right here, right now, she was in a mood for that soothing balm of beguilement.

Tom 2.0 handed her a glass. "*Saluti!*"

She accepted the glass, took a sip – an extremely expensive Pouilly-Fumé, from the taste of it; well, say one thing for Tom 2.0 – he certainly had good taste in wine.

So there she was, having a drink with this man who was pretending to be her husband, wondering how it was all going to pan out, and she happened to notice the book that Tom 2.0 was reading. It was a romance, and not just any old romance – 'twas the queen of romances, the very *urtext* of vibrant womanhood. She'd watched the mini-series only two years ago, and had duly drooled over Colin Firth. But she'd never seen a guy reading the book before – ever!

'*Pride and Prejudice*?' she asked (as ever in her best Italian, though not knowing an exact translation of Jane Austen's book, she just had to give it her best shot).

'*Ahhh – Orgoglio e pregiudizio!*' Tom 2.0 clapped his hands with delight, before continuing in his deliciously husky Italian. 'It is my favourite romance, and shall I tell you, darling Nic, why it is my favourite?'

'*Per favore fallo.*'

'It is because we have not just one romance, but several, and by the end, everyone is happily paired off, and everyone, but everyone, gets their just desserts.'

Nicole mulled this over and decided that, on balance, Tom 2.0 was probably right.

'I have read it now six or seven times,' Tom 2.0 said. 'But there is one part of Austen's beautiful book that I am still not quite sure about. It is towards the end, after Lizzie Bennett has finally fallen for her Darcy. Lizzie's sister Jane asks her when, exactly, she first fell in love with Mr Darcy, whom hitherto she had wholly detested, and Lizzie replies, "I believe I must date it from my first seeing his beautiful grounds in Pemberley." So what she wanted was not the man, but his Derbyshire mansion.'

'Is that so?'

'Yes it is very much so, darling Nic, but what I wonder is whether Lizzie is stating the truth, or whether she is in fact being dreamily ironic.' Nicole had some difficulty in catching up with this flurry of fluent Italian, but she got the gist of it.

'I think a little of both,' Nicole said.

'Tell you one thing, Nic – Lizzie certainly wouldn't have fallen for Darcy if he *hadn't* had the mansion! Would you have fallen for me if I hadn't been the world's number-one superstar actor?'

'Would you have fallen for me if I hadn't been the most talented actress on earth?' Nicole countered.

'Would you have fallen for me if I hadn't been so devastatingly handsome?'

'Would you have fallen for me if I hadn't been such a brainbox?'

He chuckled and offered up his glass in toast. '*Touché!*' he said, and a small squeak of a shiver went up Nicole's spine as she realised that, with this strange masked man, she was enjoying herself. For the first time in a long time, she was... larking around.

'So how's your Scrabble?' Nicole asked. 'Learned all those two-letter words?'

'My Scrabble?' Tom 2.0 said. 'My Scrabble is excellent – easily good enough to beat you, darling Nic. But I must warn you… we're going to be playing with new rules.'

'Oh, are we now?' she said, and looked at her glass and saw, to mild surprise, that it was empty. Tom 2.0 filled it with alacrity.

'Yes, Nic, there are going to be some new rules in town.'

'Tell me.'

'See this rotten Scrabble dictionary that I've been wasting my time with for the last two months?'

'I was very touched,' Nic said. 'I'd no idea you were so desperate to win.'

'One win would have been nice,' he said. 'Know what I've realised about this dictionary and all your two-letter and your 974 three-letter words?'

'I love my three-letter words!'

'Well, this is what I think of the Scrabble dictionary that you gloatingly gave me!' And with that, he ripped the book in half, right down the spine, and tore it again and again, and then, with great finality, tossed all the torn pages over his shoulder, where in a wordy confetti they fluttered to the floor.

'Now how will you even begin to learn all the words that have no vowels—'

'Or, indeed, all the words that have a Q but no U?'

'Quite so.'

'I'm not going to learn them, Nic, because I have no need of them. We have the new rules.'

'Uh-huh.' Nicole was not overly sure whether she was going to enjoy these new rules – because, truth be told, she rather enjoyed beating her husband at Scrabble. In this one respect, at least, she was his master. And she had a small hunch that, if Tom 2.0 was suggesting a rule change, then it would not be to her advantage.

'Let me explain, Nic,' he said, lolling back on his armchair and cockily crossing his ankle over his knee. 'This game, when it was first invented, was about the joy of anagrams. It was about getting seven tiles and working out the various wonderful anagrams. What the game was so not about was learning all the ninety-seven two-letter words in the English language, followed, then, by the 974 three-letter words.'

'Oh yes?'

'And what I am proposing, my lovely, beautiful, exquisite Nic, is that in future, you can only put down words of which you know the meaning, and which you would also use in everyday English.'

'That's quite a rule change.'

'It is taking the game back to what it was meant to be. It is how Alfred M. Butts envisaged the game when he invented it in 1931.'

'So no more OE?' Nic said.

'No, there will be no more whirlwinds from the Faroe Islands,' he said. 'No more UTs (musical tones), no more EMs or ENs (printing letters for M and N).'

'Very well,' Nicole said magnanimously.

'But on the other hand, Nic, and because you are my jo (sweetheart), and because I have just used that word, I will allow you JO.'

'Thanks,' she said. 'And when are we going to start?'

'Now, now, very now,' he said. (In Italian – was it Shakespeare? Was it *Othello*? How, how did he know this?)

The Scrabble tiles were returned to the bag, and he offered it to Nicole and she drew a Y, and he picked an A, which meant that he would begin. He drew seven tiles from the bag, proficiently placed them on the rack and, with great dexterity, started to switch the tiles round on the rack (again something the real Tom would never have done). In under a minute he had placed four of the tiles on the centre of the board – "MONK".

'Very good,' Nicole said, aware that she might have sounded just the tiniest bit patronising.

'Very sweet of you to say so,' he replied, before reaching

for the remaining three tiles on his rack. 'But I have not quite finished.' He set the three remaining tiles on the board, with the Y on the double letter, to give "MONKEYS". With the bonus 50 that was 90 points right off the gun!

Nicole hunkered down over her rack, not a great lot of letters, only one vowel. She went into the tank for a couple of minutes; the best she could come up with was PHONY.

'Very good – well done you,' Tom 2.0 said, patronising as hell, just as if he were talking to a seven-year-old. He wrote her score down on the paper and then started doing his rack thing with arranging and rearranging the tilers.

'Ah,' he said, before putting down four of his letters to give the word "TROUS".

Nicole humphed. 'Since when was that an everyday English word?'

'Oh, sorry,' he said, before reaching for the remaining three tiles and placing them on the board to give the word DEXTROUS, and that was damn nearly another 70 points.

'Are you going to do that every single time you get a bingo?' Nicole said. 'Put down half the letters, fumble around, and then, a minute later, stick down the rest of your letters?'

'Might do,' he said. 'I like to watch this furious flurry of emotions cascade over your beautiful face.'

'You're a swine.'

'Thank you.'

He didn't just beat her – he wiped the floor with her, and as the game had progressed, she went through the whole gamut of emotions, at first disbelief, then outrage, until ultimately she was resigned to her fate, and though Tom 2.0 had changed the rules, she still very much doubted whether, even with her armoury of two-letter words, she could have beaten him.

She had not enjoyed losing – well who does? But that night, after drinking far more wine than was good for her, and after she'd popped in to her sleeping angels and given them each a peck on the forehead, she realised that in the last two hours she'd thought about a lot of things, but there was one thought that repeatedly popped into her head: who was that guy? Who was Tom 2.0 whose Italian put hers to shame, and who read Jane Austen, and who could thrash her at Scrabble, and who had such a vexatious sense of humour, which did indeed vex, as it was supposed to do, but which was also impishly funny. At one stage in the Scrabble game, she had laughed out loud, long and loud, drinking wine and chuckling at the ridiculousness of it all, and wondering, wondering, about the face behind the mask.

The next day, Nicole returned to Tom's caravan at the same time, though now she had spent just a little more time on her hair and her make-up and her lipstick also, and as for the dark-green dress that she was wearing, it was certainly not her husband's favourite, but it was Nicole's favourite, and this was because (she'd been told) it showed her figure off to its best advantage. The same man was there in the caravan, still in his cloak, though now wearing a different mask, a mask of gold that covered most of his face, but which left his mouth free – and this, she was sure, was so that he could drink white wine, which he did, like a fish. Quite nice lips, she decided, with very nice teeth; his hazel eyes also pleased. They talked about Jane Austen and George Eliot, and other female writers of note – what guy did that? – and they had another game of Scrabble, and she took her beating with good grace, because Tom 2.0 was fundamentally a better player. But what she remembered most about that night and the nights after it, was sitting at the coffee table, the both of them staring at their Scrabble tiles, and her knee nudging against Tom 2.0's thigh, only for a moment. Then, by chance, it had happened again, light, companionable, such that by the end of the evening, Nicole was pondering that age-old question that we all of us have asked ourselves: what would it be like to kiss those lips?

CHAPTER 28

Nina wakes with not just a feeling of steely inner resolve but a smile on her face: she's going to do way more than just suck it up from Kubrick. She's going to beat him. For tonight's shoot and for ever more, she will be a beautiful Berkoff, and when Kubrick growls, "Do it again," she will not only say, "Yes please!" but, with every fibre of her being, she will believe it. That which we are we are, made weak by time and fate, but strong in will to strive, to seek, to find and not to yield.

And she has new purpose, also, as Mrs Cocker grumps around the breakfast room, for having breakfast with Mrs Cocker is an occupation that blights her soul and is a chore which in future she will forgo – she will eat anywhere else, and she will eat anything at all, but she will never again be eating with Mrs Cocker.

'So you don't want any breakfast?' Mrs Cocker asked – though it was not really a question, more of a challenge.

'No thank you,' Nina replied. 'Not today, not ever.'

'You don't want any more of my breakfasts?' She scratched at her chin, and then, as if limbering up for a fight, started cracking her knuckles.

'No thank you,' Nina said.

'Why not?'

'I've found somewhere more congenial to break my fast.'

'And where's that then?'

'Never you mind.'

'You'll still be charged for your breakfast, even if you don't 'ave it.'

'And there was me imagining that I might be able to claim it in glasses of wine.'

'You'll do no such thing!'

'I am joking, Mrs Cocker,' Nina said as she swept out of the B&B. 'Thank you for all your many kindnesses' – and that last jibe must have really stung, because Mrs Cocker had never knowingly offered up a single kindness to any one of her guests, least of all Nina.

As Nina sauntered to the gym, she wondered just how long this new mindset would last – perhaps just a day, a night, though she had the feeling that, after Glenn's pep talk, there had overnight been some chemical reaction within her. Strong, but flexible with it, and above all grateful – hell, she was working on a movie with the two biggest names in the business! And no matter if it took another year or two years, she would love it, and she would continue to thank her stars for that chance meeting in the Red Coat with the great Leon Vitali.

Nina puts on her gym gear, and that is the basketball gear, the baggy shorts, the pumps, the man-size Chicago Bulls shirt. Why does Nina wear men's basketball gear? Well perhaps, later on in our story, we will come to this.

On the gym floor, after warming up, Nina tasked herself with doing her least favourite exercise – the plank, which involves turning yourself into a human plank, with just your toes and your elbows in contact with the ground, with the rest of your body suspended straight, a few inches above the ground. The plank position, so very perfect for the body's core (and, indeed, for keeping Nina in trim fettle for the camera), is held for one minute, two minutes, as many minutes as you like, and is a most unsatisfying exercise to perform. There is no blessed release as there is with weights, and instead the plank is just a long and tedious exercise in pain, as your stomach muscles burn and burn and you watch the clock and wait for the seconds to tick down.

But on this occasion, and with this new-found resolve, she asked herself what Berkoff would do – and Berkoff, of course, would have enjoyed the exercise, and taken pleasure from his perfect form and from knowing that he was even able to perform the plank, and this is what Nina does, for three minutes, arms shaking, stomach quivering, but holding the position for three minutes, until she collapses onto her front, lying there like a fallen giant, smelling the gym smells, and idly watching Glenn over in the corner doing some pull-ups, and from that thought, by chance, she idled over the shocking realisation that she'd not had sex in some considerable time...

It was debatable, actually, whether the plank was Nina's least favourite exercise on earth, as there was another exercise which was right up there – the chair. You sat against the wall, knees at a right angle, thighs parallel to the floor, arms outstretched – exactly as if you were sitting down, except without the benefit of a chair, and you sat there and you sat there, counting your breath and trying to ignore the pain as the minutes ticked by, just as excruciating as the plank. But the distinct advantage of the chair was that, for three minutes, you were able to survey your fellow gym rats – speaking of which, there was Glenn again, on a rowing machine now, sweat dripping off him, and had it been wholly necessary to be so damn rude to him when all he'd done was hurt her feelings a little by asking if they could leave off the snogging until the shoot was over?

When Nina finishes her chair, her thighs are so sapped of strength that she just slides down the wall till her bum hits the floor, sitting there in partial collapse, arms easy on her knees, feeling the blessed relief of the blood flowing into her legs again – and where's Glenn gone now? Why, the cheeky sod is also doing the chair, doing the chair right opposite her on the far side of the gym, and just as she is staring at him, he is doubtless staring at her. She makes a gun with her fingers, fires at him, and then, because she feels like it, and because this is exactly what Berkoff would do, she strolls over to

Glenn, and joins him in his chair, so that, side by side and with arms outstretched, they are both chairing it together.

'Hi Glenn,' Nina says.

'Hi Nina.'

'Having a good time there?'

'I'm having a great time – the more it hurts, the more I like it.'

'That some kind of sado-masochism thing you got going?'

'Naah, nothing like that, Nina.' From looking straight ahead, they both turned inwards so that they were both looking at each other. 'I take this punishment the better to deal with Kubrick.'

'That's why I like hitting my head against the wall,' Nina says. 'Kubrick looks good by comparison.'

Glenn laughed, 'Oww,' he said. 'You're making my stomach muscles hurt.'

'How much longer we doing this for?'

Glenn looked at his wristwatch. 'Another minute, if that's good for you.'

'That'll be perfect for me.'

Nina did not have the breath for any more words, and when they were done, they silently slid down the wall, and took pleasure in a chair shared and an exercise over. Nina had never exercised with anyone else before in her life; it was a first and she liked it.

'Thanks for your Berkoff story,' she said.

'Looked like you needed it.'

'I did,' she said, and there was something lovely about sitting slumped against the wall with Glenn next to her. 'Now I've got a story for you. Shall I tell it to you as we do the plank?'

'Is there any other way?'

'How long we doing it for?'

'Maybe two minutes, if that's all right by you?'

'Two minutes is perfect.'

They went to the mats and Glenn took off his watch

and placed it on the mat in front of him. They took up their positions and the story began.

'My favourite grandfather was called Terence,' Nina said. 'He was always full of songs and stories and great belly laughs – he was a guy who loved life and who enjoyed every moment of it. Know why that was? Because he'd been caught in Singapore in the war and had been forced to work on the Burma railroad; and after that, every single day was a bonus.'

'I'll bet it was.'

'I'll finish the story when we're done.'

In shivering silence, they held their planks for another minute, and then, as before, Nina collapsed onto her front, and when she turned her head to the side, she saw that Glenn had mirrored her: they were looking at each other and, at the same time, they smiled.

'The odd thing about the Burma railroad was that the officers had a much better chance of survival than the men – not because they had better food or better living conditions, but because every night, without exception, they were playing bridge with each other. It was the high point of their days, when fortunes were won and lost to be paid once the war was over and they were back home in Britain.'

'I'll bet.'

'About a decade ago, Terence was in hospital and I went to see him with my dad. We took along a bottle of chilled champagne, and Terence insisted that then and there we open it, and we drank the champagne and Terence was just as jolly as ever and the next day he was dead.' Nina sighed, and remembered kissing her grandfather on his dry parchment cheek as she'd said goodbye. As she'd left the room, he'd been crying and she'd been crying, and if she had it all over again, she'd have spent the night with him, would have been with him right to the very end, but she hadn't and it had been a miss.

Glenn stretched over and took her hand and gave it a squeeze. 'Thank you for that.'

'I'd forgotten all about it,' Nina said. 'Might have lost my way a little doing all this stuff for Kubrick.'

'Easily done.' Glenn was still holding her hand; how nice and effortless it was to be lying next to him on the mats, almost as if... ridiculous thought!... they were sharing a moment of post-coital bliss.

'So, Glenn, savouring the moment, trying to live each day as if it were my last, and since you happen to be the person who I respect most on our film set, I would like to spend more time in your company – though with the very strong proviso that there is to be no hanky-panky whatsoever until this blasted film has finally wrapped. How's that sound?'

'I like the sound of that very much indeed,' Glenn said. 'Now holding your hand like this obviously doesn't count as – now what did you call it? – hanky-panky.'

'No this would be handy-pandy, and it was done in an emotionally supportive manner, which is of course entirely acceptable.'

'Sorry about the no-sex-on-set rule,' Glenn said. 'I realise I could have put it better.'

'I was bitterly disappointed, I can tell you.' Nina laughed.

'I think I worked that out.'

'Buy you a coffee later?'

'I'd like that.'

'Just don't you be getting any ideas, Glenn,' she said.

'Me?' he said. 'Let's keep it friendly, above all businesslike.'

'Platonic and above all with no thoughts of sinful kissing.'

'And certainly no thoughts of lustful love-making.'

'That goes without saying,' Nina said. 'Are we doing another plank?'

And they did another plank, side by side, sweat dripping from their noses and onto their mats, and the mood was comfortable and affable, and for a moment Nina was almost minded to make a confession, but the confession died a death on her lips, though if the words had been spoken, what she would have said was that, some of the time, while they were doing their planks (which, in her defence, do bear a passing resemblance to the missionary position), Nina would fantasise about Glenn having no clothes on. But she could never have uttered this thought because they were now both firmly, solidly, in the friendship zone, and – just as Glenn had requested – hand-holding was out, and kissing was out, and all else that she so desired was out. It was all so utterly infuriating, but if she'd learned anything at all from grandfather Terence, the key was not just to endure these footling reverses but to enjoy them, to revel in them; and besides, the Victorians, the Hindus, the Muslims, they all of them seemed to have thrived on their lack of premarital sex, and it was possibly even all the sweeter for the wait – and at that Nina chuckled to herself: yeah, right, just keep on telling yourself that, darlin'!

CHAPTER 29

Moving on, I had some chores to do at Elveden, the first of which was to deal with the remains of the drinks cabinet that, you may remember, we'd been hauling down to the Officers' Mess, but had contrived to smash into kindling. All the bits of the drinks cabinet had been dumped into quite a pretty room near the staircase. I had decided that this room had better uses than as a repository for our smashed furniture.

Josh and Caspar had been summoned early to Elveden to help me out, and, as we lugged all the bits of smashed furniture up the stairs and dumped them in the lumber room, Josh was doing one of my very least favourite things on earth (almost up there with being sworn at): he was being whiny.

He'd started before we'd barely even got the second tranche of splinters upstairs. 'Why are we taking this all upstairs?' he said. 'Why can't we just leave it in the room?'

'Like I've told you, Josh,' I said. 'I need the room for something else. It's got some of the best views in the whole hall.'

'What are you going to use it for?' he said. Obviously.

'Patience, pumpkin,' I said. 'All will be revealed.'

'What's in it for us?'

'What's in it for you?' I repeated. 'There's lots in it for you! Look, have a little tot of De Kuyper cherry brandy, that'll perk you up.'

'I don't like cherries,' the ingrate said, ever the mule.

'Get you,' I said. 'All right, have some Captain Morgan spiced rum, will that will all right for Sir?'

'All right,' he said, a bit churlish. I stupidly gave him the whole bottle. He immediately started chugging on it, a calf at a cow's udder.

"Hey, hey! What are you doing? Leave some for Caspar!' I said.

'Caspar doesn't mind cherry brandy,' Josh said, wiping his lips. 'I like this stuff!' he said, and continued to pour the rum straight down his throat.

'What about me then?' I said, grabbing the bottle straight out of his hand. 'You are one greedy bastard.'

'Well, what about Caspar?' he said, and, what with being distracted by Josh, I'd taken my eye off Caspar, who had also upended the De Kuyper bottle, and I had no option but to grab that straight out of his hands too. He looked at me like some pathetic puppy that's had a dog chew snatched out of its mouth.

'Jesus, do you two clowns know nothing?' I raged. 'Why can't you drink this stuff in moderation?'

'What – like you?' Josh said.

'Do I detect a certain level of sarcasm?' I said.

'Well, it was you that got us onto Captain Morgan spiced rum in the first place,' Josh said.

'Dat true,' Caspar said.

'You two have got a damn nerve!' I said. 'You were both complete lushes long before you met me!'

'And we're running low on booze in the Officers' Mess,' Josh said, as if that was somehow my problem. 'Tom Cruise is a nice chap 'n' all, but he does bang on. We've drunk all the rum and all the whisky, and do you know the only thing we've got left? That foul dry sherry, Tio Pepe!'

'Me hate Tio Pepe,' Caspar said.

'I am so, so sorry to hear that,' I said, practically grinding my teeth in vexation. What an utterly thankless task it had been setting up the Officers' Mess, and now even though I was getting damn all use out of the room, I was still supposed to keep it topped up with booze.

What I could have done was tell those two useless gits that if they were so unhappy with the alcohol situation in the Officers' Mess, then they knew what they could do: buy their own.

But since I still needed Josh and Caspar on side, I smiled pleasantly and counted to ten. 'Tell you what, guys,' I said. 'Help me out with this little task and I'll give you a hundred quid and you can get whatever booze takes your fancy.'

'Well… OK,' Josh said, ever the charmless oik.

'Anyway!' I said brightly. 'Come with me, come with me! I've got something amazing to show you!'

The boys followed me through to the far end of the lumber room, weaving our way through all manner of bric-à-brac, bedpans, carpets, pig-stickers, polo mallets, battered travel trunks and a trove of dusty brown furniture. I gestured grandly with a waft of my hand.

'Duhh,' Josh said. He had the sort of blank face you see in dogs when you show them a card trick.

'Ever seen one of these before, Josh?' I said. 'It's called a four-poster.'

'We can't move that, we can't possibly move that!' he said. 'We won't even be able to get it out the door!'

'We take it to bits, you wally,' I said.

Now, since this bed has some little bearing on our story, I'd best describe it. It was a king-size four-poster, perhaps seven feet by eight feet, black with age and at least 600 years old. The posts, twelve inches wide in parts, were largely square, with intricate floral patterns etched into the old oak. The headboard had carvings of Adam and Eve in the half-round, while on the pelmet rail were carved three coats of arms – royal coats of arms no less. When I had first espied this four-poster, two weeks earlier, it had had rich crimson hangings, but these had been so dusty that I'd stripped them off and taken them to the dry-cleaners.

One part of the bed was invisible to the eye – but, because I knew the story behind this particular four-poster, I knew all about this extraordinary detail: the bed had a false bottom, the better for hiding that which needed to be hid. I might have told the story to Josh and Caspar, but seeing as it would have been entirely wasted on them, I didn't bother.

While the lads sat on the horsehair mattress and tippled at their booze, I went downstairs to retrieve my tool bag. It contained a couple of wooden mallets, a hammer, two punches, three chisels and, just for old time's sake, a sledgehammer and a hefty crowbar.

Dismantling the four-poster was, as expected, a caper. Even though I'd read up on it at the local library, and so actually knew what I was doing, Josh and Caspar were just a couple of handless halfwits. If there was something that could be bodged, they'd bodge it. It was fortunate the bedposts and struts were all but unbreakable.

At top and bottom of the bed were four carved joists which were connected to the four bedposts by simple mortice and tenon joints. These joints had been locked into place with cylindrical wooden pegs. It was these pegs which were holding the whole thing tightly together, and all we had to do was knock them out. It was quite good fun. We'd locate the pegs, and then tappity-tap-tap with the mallets and the punches, and out the peg would pop – and, being smart as a whip, I didn't just leave these pegs lying around on the floor, oh no, I picked them all up and placed them in my tool bag.

Trickier by far was separating the posts from the joists. At first, we tried kicking them, but when that didn't work, I got going with my trusty sledgehammer, and, true, we did smash up some of the more detailed carvings, but frankly the oak was so black you wouldn't have known the difference. With a satisfying boom, one whole side of the bed toppled onto the floor, and there in all its glory was revealed the bed's false bottom, six inches high and stretching the full length of the bed.

We carried on happily hammering and clattering away – destruction being so much more primally enjoyable than creation – until, two hours later, we'd battered the thing into submission.

'Job done!' Josh said, jubilantly dusting his hands together as he reached for the Captain Morgan spiced rum. 'I am outta here!'

'Hang on!' I said. 'Hang on!'

'What do you mean?'

'Aren't you forgetting something?'

'Errr – don't think so.'

'We've got to take the whole thing downstairs and put it back together in that room we've just cleared out.'

He gawped at me like a fish on the slab, moron eyes and mouth agape. 'But... why?' he said.

'Because we need a bed downstairs!' I said.

'But who's going to use it?' Josh said.

'Not me,' said the unhelpful Caspar.

'And not me either!' said Josh.

'Guys!' I said. 'After all I've done for you!'

'Done for us?' Josh said. 'You said you were going to fix me up with Mandy!'

'I got you together in the Officers' Mess, didn't I?' I said. 'I've filled the room up with a constant supply of booze! And now you want me to get Mandy to actually fall for you??'

'Yes!' he said. 'You said you would!'

Caspar decided to get in on the action. 'I want girlfriend too!' he said.

'Oh, so, you want a girlfriend too, do you Caspar?' I said. 'What – one of the hotties? Would that be all right?'

'Yeth,' he said, utterly complacent, as if I'd offered him nothing more than a cup of tea.

'Well, that's quite an ask, lads,' I said. 'For a kicker, whenever one of the girls comes within three yards of you, you both get completely tongue-tied!'

'But you said!' Josh said.

'OK, fine,' I said magnanimously. 'If you help me rebuild

the four-poster downstairs, I will do what I can to get you both girlfriends.'

'So you will get us girlfriends?' Josh said.

'Yes,' I said – God dealing with these two was like having a tooth extracted – no, worse than that, because at least when you have a tooth out, there's some little light relief at the end of it all, whereas with these two gimps there was no respite, ever.

'Hottie for me?' Caspar said.

'No offence, Caspar, but that might be difficult,' I said. 'What about one of the runners – they're lovely.'

'I want hottie,' he said, crestfallen, a five-year-old tyke told he's not getting any more ice cream.

'They're out of your league, Caspar.'

'OK,' he said, lower lip trembling. 'Runner for Caspar.'

'Done!' I said. 'Now let's get this stuff downstairs, and let's build ourselves a four-poster!'

The bedposts alone were at least a hundred kilos, and while we heaved it all downstairs into the master bedroom, Josh had obviously been doing some thinking.

'Hey Lawrence,' he said. At the time we were struggling with the vast Adam and Eve headboard, and there might have been better occasions for a chat, what with us all straining and grunting, but this trivial detail was, as ever, lost on Josh. 'Can I use the bed with Mandy?'

'Well, let's not get ahead of ourselves,' I said loftily. 'But if Mandy wishes to use the bed with you, then of course be my guests." Well, you know, *noblesse oblige* and all that.

'And there will be booze?' he asked.

'Yes,' I said, so very grateful for having spent so many months with the Kubrick, because if the crazy old sod had taught me anything at all it was the gift of eternal patience. 'There will be booze.'

We hammered and grunted away, with the occasional squeal from Caspar when he missed the wooden pegs and contrived to hit his thumb with the mallet, but by 6 p.m. we had, rather unbelievably, reconstructed the four-poster in my room of choice. It just needed a few more choice items from the lumber room, as well as some little goodies that had been ordered along the way, and the Sergeants' Mess would be complete. The Sergeants' Mess?? Indeed so. Non-military types might imagine that the Officers' Mess is classier than the Sergeants' Mess; this is not the case. The sergeants, who have grafted their way up through the ranks, look after themselves far, far better than any greenhorn subalterns, and as a result the Sergeants' Mess is much better appointed than the Officers' Mess: hence the four-poster and… and its other accoutrements.

What with all this toing and froing up the stairs, not to mention having to deal with Josh and Caspar for six hours straight, I was in sore need of not just a drink but a shower. In all likelihood Nicole would be paying me another visit that evening, and – just a small tip here – when you're entertaining one of the world's superstar actresses, it's best not to stink like a badger.

Nicole and I had been getting on mightily well as I'd blathered away in my most lavish Italian. I was never sure if she could understand even half of what I was saying; maybe, strange thought, she just liked the sound of my voice. Thankfully, I now had a half-mask that covered most of my face but which left my mouth free, because, nice though it was flirting with Nicole, knees occasionally nudging as we lingered over the Scrabble board, fingertips touching as we dipped for more tiles, it was always more enjoyable when alcohol was added to the mix. Why, the previous night, I'd even thrown a game of Scrabble; you should have heard her excited squeals as she placed down the winning tiles and then – and I promise I'm not making this up – she started doing a celebratory cha-cha, twirling round and around, rhythmically clapping her hands above her head. As she'd left, she'd leaned on me lightly, her hand easy on my elbow, and had given me a kiss, though not on my masked cheek, but, erotically, on the tip of my chin. Then, at the door, she said something which set my mind awhirring: "I much prefer you with your mask on." But what did that mean? Did it mean… merely that she preferred my company to that of her dry old stick of a husband? Or did it mean… No! Let's so not go there!

I let myself into Tom's Winnebago; Tom, as usual, was not there. He'd already have got his magic mask on and would be on set schmoozing with the extras as Glenn set up the scene and the froward Kubrick grunted his favourite three words on earth: "Do it again". Still, Tommy could do as he pleased and, by the same token, I could do just as I pleased. I had a shower, much classier unguents and creams in Tom's bathroom than I ever had in the hotel, and after putting on my tux and tie, I was more than ready for a drink. I'd developed quite a taste for Pouilly-Fumé since I'd been getting to know Nicole, but damn me, if there was any wine in the fridge. What the hell was going on? True, we had drunk all the booze the previous night, but, as per Tom's standing instructions, the fridge should have been properly stocked up that morning! It was not only sloppy, it was exceedingly annoying: how the hell was I going to be able to entertain Nicole without any booze? At a pinch, we could have had a try at the Grand Marnier, but it gets a bit sickly after the third glass.

There was only going to be one place at Elveden which had any more wine, and that was going to be Kubrick's caravan. Since he was otherwise engaged on set, I mooched over to his Winnebago to pinch a few bottles.

Kubrick was not only hugely secretive but also utterly chaotic, which, practically speaking, meant that although he always liked his Winnebago to be kept locked up tight, he was forever fearful that he'd lose the key. As a result, he always kept a spare key under a plant pot close by to the door. I picked up the plant pot. There was nothing there. The old fool had forgotten to lock up.

I trotted up the steps, opened the door, took a spritely step into the Winnebago – and there was Kubrick. He was in his usual blue dungarees and was lounging back on his La-Z-Boy chair, little feet lifted, dainty fingers holding up the latest copy of *The Lady* magazine.

He pistoned in his chair. 'What, what?' he said.

'Oops!' I said. 'So sorry! Didn't realise you were in.'

To have said anything more might have compounded the offence, so, after a brief wave, I backed out of the Winnebago, quietly clicking the door behind me.

Well… just a tad embarrassing, setting out to swipe some of Kubrick's booze, and finding the man himself already *in situ*. I plodded back to Tom's Winnebago, there to contemplate my misdeeds. Seemed like Nicole and I would just have to make do with the Grand Marnier after all.

My steps get slower and slower. I stutter to a dead-stop. Because… because they're already filming in the hall! Kubrick is in the hall with Glenn and the rest of them!

Maybe… maybe he was having a time out. I slipped on my cloak and trotted over to the hall. The security guys gave me the nod and I poked my head round the door. It was all very much going on. Pook's music banging away over the speakers, the girls stripped, ready for action. Leon Vitali was there, Tom was there as his own stand-in, and there, lounging close to the camera was… the great Stanley Kubrick. Or, if not Kubrick, then certainly his exact double. My face hidden by my cowl, I eased round the edge of the room. It certainly looked like Kubrick – and sounded like Kubrick. I looked and I looked; it was like one of those spot-the-difference pictures. You can tell something's wrong but you can't quite put your finger on it. The similarity was uncanny, but there was something just a little off, and then I spotted it and all was revealed. Kubrick, as I may have mentioned, may have been a rotund slob but did have the very daintiest of hands, with sensitive, artist's fingers; this guy's fingers were of a match with the rest of his corpulent body, great pork sausages attached to flabby-boy mitts.

As quietly as I had entered the hall, I slipped out. I returned to Kubrick's Winnebago and breezed straight on into the festering honk den. Kubrick was still on his La-Z-Boy. *The Lady* had been discarded. He was looking pensive – as well he might.

'Oh hello there, Stanley,' I said. I went over to the fridge, pulled out a bottle of Chablis, and as Kubrick goggled at me, I busied myself with the corkscrew. 'Just helping myself to a glass of wine,' I said. 'Like one?'

He played the only card he could – complete outrage. 'Get out of here!' he said. 'How dare you!'

I poured myself a good glass of wine and had a delicious sip before taking a seat opposite Stanley. I had another sip of wine and, what the hell, kicked my feet up onto the coffee table. I gave Stanley my very warmest, loveliest smile. 'It's a no-go, Stanley.'

'What?' he said. 'Get out! Get out!'

'What – to go and join your fat-handed doppelgänger on the set?' I said. 'I've just seen him – and now I've just seen you. If it weren't for his fat fingers, he could have been your clone.'

'Oh,' he said, the wind well and truly taken out of his sails.

'That's right,' I said, chirpy as an early-bird sparrow who's found his first worm. 'You been rumbled.'

'Oh,' he said again. 'Perhaps, then, I will join you in a glass of wine.'

'Excellent!' I leapt up to pour him a large glass of wine. 'I think that, for my discretion to be assured, Stanley, we need to have a little chat.'

Kubrick accepted the glass of wine. 'Very well.'

'OK, Stanley,' I said. God, it felt good! I nestled into the armchair and took another languid sip of wine. I'd got him, I'd got the fat despot bending, and there was damn all he could do about it – and that, my friends, is just precisely my favourite position on earth. 'Why don't you tell me how long you've been using this double?'

Kubrick grunted and started polishing his glasses with an old hankie. I did not feel any especial need to fill the silence.

I drank some more wine. Kubrick continued to polish. It seemed he required a little chivvying. 'Let me put it another way then, Stanley,' I said. 'You better start talking or I'm going straight back into the hall where I will immediately expose Mr Fat Fingers as a fake.'

'Very well.' He eventually finished with his glasses and perched them on the end of his nose. He took a sip of wine before lolling back in his chair. 'What is it you wish to know?'

'I want to know everything,' I said. 'What do you take me for? So let's start with you telling me how long you've been using this double.'

He sniffed. I thought he was going to try and weasel out of it again. 'About a year,' he said.

'Why do you want a double?'

'Oh – you know…'

'No I don't know!' I said. 'You tell me!'

'I needed a double because… because it was all so exhausting! I wasn't capable of putting in the hours, and then… it just came to me. I'd met this guy a while back. Why not get him to do the legwork?'

'I'm not with you,' I said. 'What is "the legwork"?'

'You just don't get it!' he said. 'With these actors, you must exert your authority! You must break them in! They are like wild stallions which can only be tamed once you have completely and utterly broken their will.'

'OK…' I said, just a little doubtful. 'So how did it work?'

'We'd start off, I'd run through the scene a few times, just to make sure everyone knew what they were doing, and then, well, I'd come back here, and we'd swap over, and Larry – my double – would put them through their paces for the next day or three, you know, getting Tom to do the same thing over and over again.'

'But why not just use the second or third take?' I said. 'He's a pro: all of the takes are pretty good.'

'Like I said buddy, you gotta break them. It's only when you've broken them that you can start getting something good out of 'em.' Kubrick was getting more than a little excited with his exposition, leaning forward and fixing me with his beady black eyes. 'Look Lawrence, you know what a metaphor is?'

'No,' I said, curious. 'What is a metaphor?'

'A metaphor is, like, kinda like a symbol—'

'Of course I know what a damn metaphor is,' I snapped.

'Well, why d'ya say you didn't know what a metaphor was?'

I held my hand up to cut the blather. 'What's your point?'

'Look – see that stone tumbler grinding away in the corner?'

'What – you're going to tell me it's a metaphor for your mad film-making?'

'That's exactly what it is!' Kubrick exclaimed, little feet drumming up and down in excitement. 'It's a metaphor. It grinds and grinds away for weeks on end, knocking all the edges off the stones, and if you leave it for long enough it'll grind 'em to dust!'

'And this is how you see yourself – grinding Tom and Nic?'

'That's me!' he said. 'I'm a human rock tumbler!'

'You're stark staring mad.' I helped myself to more booze.

Clearly imagining that I still hadn't yet fully understood the beauty of his film-making methods, Kubrick continued his exposition. 'Look, Tom's good, no question,' he said. 'But I had to get him to walk through that doorway ninety-five times – I had to! And what I got at the end of it was something truly exceptional—'

'And there was me imagining it was just Tom walking through a door,' I said. 'So did you do the same thing with Nicole and that guy Gary Goba?'

'Sure I did,' he said. 'Had to! They're actors! You gotta break 'em! Though, tell you the truth, I was more than happy for Larry to sit most of that one out – Nicole with no clothes on is something else, I tell ya!'

'I see,' I said, and by now I certainly needed something a little stronger than white wine. I mean I knew the guy was certifiable, but this took crazy to a whole new level. 'What about the crew and the extras? You've broken them too.'

'They're getting paid, ain't they?' he said. 'Besides, they're getting to work with the great Stanley Kubrick—'

'Or at least his fat double.'

'Most of 'em are so keen to work with me, they'd do it for nothing!'

'You're crackers,' I said.

'Ain't it just great?' he said, and I'm sure he'd have continued to chunter on, except that at that moment there was a slight tap at the door. I looked round to see Molly, the caterer, backing in through the door with a tray in her hands.

''Ow's my big baby?' she called over her shoulder. 'Who's ready for his liver and onions?'

Molly turned round, first saw Kubrick and then saw me. 'Oh,' she said. 'You got company.'

'It seems that I have, Molly dear,' Kubrick said. 'If you could just leave the tray on the side, that would be most kind. I'll be with you in a moment.'

'Don't be long!' Molly quit the caravan.

A speculative silence. I let Kubrick continue to stew; since he was so very keen on breaking in his stars, not to mention his crew, I was keen to see just how well he himself took to being broken in.

'Soooo,' I said. 'Molly's big baby?'

'Oh, it's just a little name she has for me,' he said with a flick of his fingers. 'She means no harm.'

'Of course not,' I said. 'But if it's all the same to you, Stanley, I'd like to hear all about it.'

'Ah, well.' He was squirming in his seat, a scrofulous baby who'd been caught with his mitts in the jam jar. 'It's, ahhh, it's like this...'

CHAPTER 30

It is 3 a.m. and after a surprisingly pleasurable shoot at Elveden, Glenn is abed, and for the first time in over twenty years, is reading poetry; more than that, he is whispering the words out loud. He is trying to learn the poem by heart. 'Twas Nina's wish; he has no option but to comply.

'Out of the night that covers me,

'Black as the pit from pole to pole.'

He's said the opening line to William Henley's 'Invictus' at least ten times over to himself, and it's only just beginning to sink in. Until now, he'd never realised that learning lines was so difficult – but day after day the actors somehow managed to do it, and that was because if they didn't know their lines, then Kubrick would sack them on the spot. On *Barry Lyndon*, Glenn recalled, Kubrick had done just that, replacing four guys one after the next, and all of them fired for the unforgivable crime of not remembering their lines absolutely word for word.

Glenn thought he had the first line off pat. Now for the second.

'I thank whatever gods may be

'For my unconquerable soul.'

As he learned his lines, Glenn was also evaluating the ebb and flow of the night's work at Elveden. When they'd resumed filming after dinner, there had been this frisky tension in the hall, and it had seemed to be emanating from the director himself. Then, incredibly, by 1 a.m., Kubrick had called it a wrap and they'd all gone back to their beds. Glenn didn't know what had happened, but something had most definitely happened.

The next morning, at the gym, Glenn was pleased to find that he had memorized the first two verses of 'Invictus'. Nina was already there, as always, in her man-size basketball gear, too big, too baggy by far, but on Nina, it all looked just incredibly, well, sexy. Glenn sort of wanted to ask her about the outsize clothing – like, of all the things she could wear at the gym, why, why was she so hooked on these various basketball shirts and shorts? But... Nina was an intensely private person. Did he dare?

Since their rapprochement, they now exercised together; no bones about it, this hour in the gym was the very high spot of his day, pumping iron together, rowing together, and all underlaid with this teasing tension of sexuality. Their conversation and their entire body language was poker-straight, not the slightest hint of innuendo; he could have had the same conversation, almost, with any other member of the *Eyes Wide Shut* team. And yet, dripping through it all, slicing its way through their every interaction, was the memory of that night – the Night of the Long Kissing, with Nina entwined on his lap, lip to lip and his hands comfortably caressing her bare skin. No, they did not mention that night, nor allude to it in any way, nor talk of all that was ahead of them when Kubrick was done. No, they looked neither to the past nor the future, instead just savouring the sweet moment.

The poetry, Glenn discovered, was to be recited when they performed their planks together. Side by side and on elbows and on toes, they'd taken up their planks, legs and torsos straight as the proverbial plank.

'Do you want to start or shall I?' Nina said.

'You start,' Glenn said. He didn't know what they were starting, so it was probably best if she began.

She recited the first verse of 'Invictus'. 'Your turn,' she said.

Glenn was pleased indeed to have done the previous night's homework; lots of guys wouldn't have bothered. The second verse was recited nearly off pat, just a mild fumble. 'Over to you,' he said.

Without missing a beat, Nina trotted out the third verse. 'You going to finish it off?' she said.

'I'll try,' Glenn said, but he hadn't properly got round to learning this last verse – well, in his defence, he hadn't known just why he was supposed to be learning this poem – and he muffed the last two lines.

Nina completed the poem – 'I am the master of my fate, I am the captain of my soul,' she said, and they collapsed to the floor and rolled onto their backs.

Nina turned to Glenn. 'How come you forgot that line?' she said. 'It's the best line in the whole poem.'

And Glenn in his turn turned to Nina. 'I think I had a visceral reaction to the line – as it's so palpably not true. I am anything but the master of my own fate – Stanley Kubrick is.'

'Maybe you're right,' she said, delectable hand propping up her delectable cheek. 'I'd forgotten about your PTSD.'

'Is poetry now going to be part of our gym routine?'

'If it's all right by you,' she said.

'Very much so,' he said, truthfully, as who would not have wanted to exercise side by side with Nina as she recited beautiful poetry? 'What's our next poem?'

'You may decide the next poem.'

'I'll let you know later then.'

They resumed their planks and recited their poem, and when they were done, they stared at the ceiling in silence, so many thoughts left unsaid, and Glenn was, among other things, thinking about the Long Kissing, but he couldn't talk about that, could never talk about that, so instead he blurted out the first thing that came into his head: 'Hey Nina, bet there's a story behind all that big basketball gear you wear.'

She gave a wry smile to the ceiling. 'A small, boring story, in fact,' she said. 'You don't want to know.'

'Uh – OK,' Glenn said. Now what to blazes did that mean? A small, boring story which he so didn't want to know – but those very words meant he wanted to know all the more about the origins of the basketball gear. Maybe they'd belonged to an old boyfriend, which would mean, could mean, that she was trying to protect him. Would he be jealous if it was all the gear of a boyfriend past? How could he possibly be jealous – they weren't even dating! Scratch that, he'd be jealous as hell. God, she looked amazing when she was holding her plank position, made it look so effortlessly easy when he knew for a fact it was anything but.

Later that day, then, Kubrick had demanded that the initial scene be shot from a new angle, this time with the camera up top on the first-floor balcony, and, like the whipped dogs that they were, everyone duly complied. They'd had eight takes and then Kubrick had called time for the requisite hour-long dinner break.

The girls and the supporting artists had disappeared, and the crew also were wending their way to the catering trucks. Glenn had been talking about the light set-up with one of the grips, when the peculiar Lawrence had wandered over. His mask, the angry red mask, was perched on the top of his head. He did not join in Glenn's conversation with the grip, but patiently waited for them to finish.

The grip nodded his agreement to Glenn's suggestion and went over to join the rest of the crew at the trough.

Glenn turned to Lawrence. 'Hi Lawrence,' he said.

'Hi Glenn,' Lawrence said. 'How's it going?'

'Very good, thank you.'

'Got a message for you from Nina.'

'Oh yeah?' Glenn's interest was more than a little piqued.

'Yeah,' Lawrence said. 'First though, I heard the most amazing story about a bed, a four-poster, actually – thought you might like to hear it.'

'Er, yeah,' Glenn said. 'Sure.'

'It's a great story, Glenn – you're going to love it!'

'I am?' Glenn said. 'But what about Nina's message?'

'All in due course, Glenn,' Lawrence said. 'But first let me take you back to the year 1485. It's the 21st of August, and King Richard III has arrived in Leicester in preparation for a great battle – the battle that we would come to know as the battle of Bosworth Field.' His royal retinue have already set up his running wardrobe in the best suite at the Boar's Head inn, and this includes a huge four-poster bed, with rich crimson hangings, and carvings of Adam and Eve on the headboard, and the King's own crest on the pelmet. Most deliciously of all, this four-poster has a double bottom, only accessible through a secret hatch, which popped open when you pressed the serpent's eye—'

'Forgive me, Lawrence, but what has this got to do with Nina's message?' Glenn said.

'Patience, Glenn dear – I'd have thought that, if nothing else, you'd learned about this from our great director,' Lawrence said infuriatingly. 'Richard III spent his last night on earth in that bed, and the next day was killed at Bosworth.'

'Really?' Glenn said.

'Yes, really,' Lawrence said. 'As for the bed, well, it was so heavy that it couldn't be moved, and, over the next few decades became the star attraction at the Blue Boar. People from all over Britain, nay, the world, would pay good money to spend the night in it.'

Lawrence paused and smiled, obviously well pleased with his story.

'And?' Glenn said. Without even so much as a hint of impatience. What in God's name was Nina's message?

'And, the Blue Boar passed from tenant to tenant until, more than a century later, in the reign of Good Queen Bess, it was being run by a publican called Mr Temperley, and one day, Mr Temperley's wife Joanna happened to be giving the bed a shakedown when an old gold coin tumbled to the floor. Mr Temperley was promptly called in to the master suite, where, upon close examination, the serpent's eye was discovered, and the false bottom was revealed, and in it was King Richard's hoard – enough gold, it was said, to pay for a king's ransom, and though we do not know what happened to the hoard, what we do know is that was the last day that Mr and Mrs Temperley ran the Blue Boar; it's said that they went off to the theatre, where they spent the rest of their lives listening to music and happily watching the latest works by one William Shakespeare.'

'Great story,' Glenn said. But now that – surely – the story was at an end, he'd be damned if he'd beg for Nina's message.

'And it's true,' Lawrence said, turning away before suddenly smacking his forehead. 'Oh – I had a message for you,' he said.

'What – the message from Nina?'

'Yeah, that's right,' Lawrence said. 'She wants to see you. She's up in the Sergeants' Mess. Here's the key.'

Glenn took the large, elaborate key. 'Where's the Sergeants' Mess?' he said.

'Upstairs,' Lawrence said. 'First floor, just past the Officers' Mess. There's a sign on the door. You can't miss it.'

'There's an Officers' Mess?'

'The Sergeants' Mess is much nicer – don't you worry, ,Glenn – and, just by chance, there's a piece of furniture in there you might recognize. I believe it was purchased from the Blue Boar by Maharajah Duleep Singh.'

'I better go and see Nina then.'

'Good luck, my friend,' Lawrence said, and after a resounding clap on his shoulders, Glenn was alone in the hall. Quite a lot to take in. Summoned – by Nina! To the Sergeants' Mess, no less, and its vast bed with an improbable history. How come he'd not heard of this room – or, for that matter, the Officers' Mess? He was supposed to know everything that went on within this shoot. But... but that didn't matter a damn! Nina awaited. And he did not know why she was waiting for him, but if she wanted him, he wanted to be with her.

He took the stairs two at a time and strode briskly along the gloomy corridor. He'd never really explored up here before – since he'd always had a million and one tasks to do on the set, he'd just never had the time.

From one room came the sound of raucous music and chanting. The door opened and Josh blundered out. A glimpse of masks and cloaks and flashing lights – it was a full-on disco, at least a dozen people writhing and jiving. 'Oh, hi Glenn,' Josh said. 'Coming in?'

'Err, no,' Glenn said. 'Though thank you.'

Glenn continued down the corridor. Past another room and another room and then, unbelievably, there it was – a brass plaque screwed into the door which read "The Sergeants' Mess". There was the keyhole, so very receptive to his long key, and the key turned and the tumblers dropped and the lock clicked open.

Glenn gave a light double tap on the door, waited a second and, when there was no response, entered the room.

He hadn't known quite what to expect. He was ready for anything – or, perhaps, almost anything. He had just about conceived that there might be a four-poster in the room. But no, he had not thought it would be anything at all like this.

First, though, to Nina. She was standing by the window, long straight hair tumbling over the collar of her cloak of midnight blue. He could not tell if she had on her black tracksuit or if she was just wearing… just wearing her G-string. She was drinking a glass of champagne. She turned, and smiled.

Glenn gradually took in the rest of his surroundings: the four-poster with its black posts, its opulent red hangings, and with what very much looked like fresh white bed linen, with four plump pillows and a king-size duvet. Directly opposite the four-poster, a fireplace steeped with glowing coals, and on either side of the fireplace, two comfortable-looking armchairs upholstered in green grey velvet, each with its own side table. Next to the window, a chair and writing bureau, on top of which was a cork coaster and a silver ice bucket which contained the opened bottle of champagne. Else, else? Three matching candelabras in pewter or perhaps tarnished silver, two on the mantelpiece and one on the table by the four-poster; also on the mantelpiece, a selection of hardback books between two cast-iron bookends, and above the mantelpiece a large oval mirror; on the floor, a lush Indian carpet with elaborate swirls of red and black. The ceiling was high and in perfect proportion to the room, and though a stickler might have cavilled at the peeling paint and at the echoes of the old walls, Glenn thought the piebald patchwork worked well, indeed would not have changed it.

'Quite a room,' Glenn said.

'Just so,' Nina said. 'Glass of the Widow?'

'Thank you.' She poured the Veuve Clicquot; toned arm, bare skin, which probably indicated… that beneath the cloak she was all but naked.

They toasted each other with their eyes and then Nina walked back to the window and Glenn followed, and there they stood for a while, looking out over the wild garden and to the silhouette of the black church, their elbows easy against each other.

'I hoped it might be you,' Nina said.

'You didn't ask for me?'

'No, I did not ask for you.' Nina laughed. 'That was the work of our resident matchmaker – he told me to wait in here and, lo and behold, ten minutes later you walk through the door.'

Glenn also laughed as he took another sip of champagne; he never, ever drank on the job, but on an occasion such as this, he was more than prepared to make an exception. 'Lawrence is certainly keen to get us together.'

'I'm in two minds about it,' Nina said. 'On the one hand, the thought of being manipulated by someone like Lawrence does very much stick in the throat—'

'And on the other hand?'

'And on the other hand, Glenn, well it is you, and there is

no one in this world who I would rather have seen walking through that door five minutes ago.'

'There is no one I would have preferred to find.'

They coolly inspected each other, shadows flickering in the candlelight and the moonlight, and not that they either of them needed it, but the light could not have been more flattering. What is it that happens when, close up, you look someone in the eye? You look and you look, and then for no discernible reason there is a mutual green light; Glenn could not resist himself. With the glass of champagne easy at his side, he moved in towards Nina and kissed her on the lips, and to his great delight (not to mention relief) her lips responded with a pulse of pressure.

They were standing now not a foot apart, Nina smiling, cat-like and inscrutable.

'Do you know, Nina, that there are some nincompoops who believe that it is madness to form a relationship during a film shoot?'

'Are there now?' Nina took a sip of champagne, bubbles lingering on her lips.

'Yes, there are, Nina,' Glenn said. 'These blockheads believe that film sets are sacrosanct and that they must on no account by sullied by such a thing as, say, a crew member entering into a relationship with, say, a senior member of the cast.'

'I see,' Nina said. 'And what, pray, is your position on this all-important matter?'

'I think these dimwit prigs know nothing!' he said, and, just like that, he leaned in again and kissed Nina on the mouth again, tarrying a little longer as lips glided against parting lips.

'That so?' Nina said, arm tracing up from her cloak – she really did have no clothes on – and cupping his cheek.

'And what I was wondering, Nina, on the very off chance, and no pressure at all, none whatsoever, was whether you might consider embarking on a, ahh, relationship with me?'

'When?' she moved in to kiss him; with her in her stilettoes they were very much a match for each other. 'Like you thinking about embarking on a relationship when the shoot ends a year or two from now?'

'If it's all the same to you, Nina, I would like to set sail immediately.'

'Like now, now?' She unzippered his fleece, easing him out of it, and the fleece fell to the floor.

'Like now.'

'One more thing, Glenn.' The buttons on Glenn's shirt were unbuttoned, and this also was discarded onto the floor. 'How long's this relationship going to last? For the duration of the shoot?'

'I was hoping quite a bit longer,' Glenn said.

'And will it include love-making?'

'Wouldn't be much of a relationship if it didn't,' he said.

'Then I approve,' she said, and led the way to the bed, where shoes and belt and trousers were also abandoned, and for a while there they sat on the edge of the bed with its ten-tog duvet and its four fine-feather pillows, lips kissing and hands stroking with unfettered caressing, and eventually the chain of Nina's cloak was unclipped and that joined the other discards on the floor. 'How nice it is to be touching your bare skin rather than merely looking at it,' Nina said.

'Not as much sweat as when you usually look at me at the gym.'

'But deliciously scented – were you expecting me?'

'No!'

Now, they might have made love then and there, but oftentimes, and particularly after so many months of waiting, these matters are the better for being teased out, and in between kisses and other such acts of delicious foreplay, Nina posed Glenn a question. 'Did Lawrence spin you a yarn about this bed?' she said, rolling from top to underneath.

'He did,' Glenn said. Not that it mattered, but how was it that he was now naked while Nina still retained her G-string? With quick fingers he made amends.

'Do you think the story's true?'

Glenn kissed the thin black G-string before tossing it to the floor and, with his arm easy on her stomach, he slipped his other arm around her neck. 'Know what I know about Lawrence?' Glenn said as he kissed her. 'Half the stuff he tells you is true – and half of it is just so much made-up bollocks. But you never have any idea which is which.'

Nina turned her head to look up at the headboard, where, just as described, Adam and Eve had been carved in the half-round, and where a fine serpent was wrapped around an apple tree.

'Excuse me one moment,' Nina said, disengaging slightly. She stretched up and pressed the serpent's red eye. There was the sound of a distinct clink from beneath the mattress. 'We should investigate,' she said.

Abandoning their sweet caresses, they quit the bed to kneel on the floor. Nina tugged at a thin six-inch panel beneath the mattress. As it opened, a small silver coin fell to the floor. She examined it. 'What do you think?' She passed the coin to Glenn.

'A silver groat,' he said, turning the coin in his hands as he inspected the curly-haired king with a crown on his head. 'Almost certainly Richard III.'

'How on earth do you know that?'

'It could be from Richard's original hoard.' Glenn tossed the coin in the air, caught it with his other hand and returned it to Nina. 'But my guess is that the coin was put there by Lawrence – and since he has been most peculiarly attentive to every last detail of the room, from the bed to the armchairs, not to mention the fire in the hearth and the Veuve Clicquot on ice, then if Lawrence put this coin there, then he might have sourced an original.'

Taking Glenn's hand, Nina pulled him back onto the bed. 'Or he might not.'

'That is also true,' Glenn said.

Nina carefully placed the coin on the bedside table.

'But I have more than had my fill of talking about this mad Machiavellian schemer, and now I would very much like to have my fill… no, let me rephrase that better, I would, ahhh, very much like to consummate my love with my love.' Her eyes glanced at Glenn's wristwatch. 'We're not due back for half an hour, and if at all possible, I would like to spend the entirety of that time making love with you. How does that sound, Glenn?'

'You are the mistress of my fate, you are the captain of my soul,' he said, and she giggled.

'The Dear Leader would not at all happy at how you have mangled your line,' she said. 'But for myself, I think they are very pretty words to mark… ahhhh-haaaa… the start of our relationship.'

CHAPTER 31

In some respects, at least, the owner of the Royal Terrace Bed and Breakfast, the widow Cocker, was not so very different from Kim the reporter from the *Sun*: they were both out-and-out snoopers who loved nothing more than prying through other people's most personal papers and pictures. Though the difference was that Kim, at least, was poking around other people's private papers for purely professional reasons: to dig up the dirt and, if at all possible, slap it all over the front page of the world's biggest-selling English language daily.

Mrs Cocker's nosey motives were more obscure. Primarily, she wanted to know every last smidgeon of gossip about her lodgers, but – if pushed, and if, indeed, she'd even heard of Francis Bacon – she might have also acceded to the maxim that "Knowledge is power".

To that end: it is when her lodgers have left for the day that Mrs Cocker likes to go about her business. Whilst ostensibly making up the beds, cleaning the sinks and getting the rooms *all-a-tanto* (as her merchant-seaman husband, God rot him, used to say), Mrs Cocker also likes to ensure that all papers and such like are put into good and respectable order. Naturally, this could only be done properly once every letter and scrap of paper had been most thoroughly scrutinised. Some of the girls did not tend to write so much, but Nina – she used to be a stripper, you know! – not only wrote and received letters, as well as scribing at some unreadable manuscript, but also had a diary. The diary had been kept most well-hidden, in a small leather case which had contained, outrageously, a false bottom, such that it had taken Mrs Cocker a full two months to discover the thing, but once the secret pages had been discovered, it became Mrs Cocker's daily delight to peruse them. The shocking awfulness! The stunning depravity! The stories of long-lost loves and lusts – and there was, even, a current one! It was completely unputdownable!

So Mrs Cocker was already well apprised of Nina's rollercoaster relationship with Glenn, and of the first kiss, and – *bliss!* – the crushed hopes and dreams, but since the inconsiderate Nina had not written up her diary for the past three days, Mrs Cocker had yet to be apprised of the recent change in Nina's circumstances.

This morning, then, the widow Cocker has two reasons to be pleased. The first is that the previous night, Slut One, Mandy, returned home with a young man in tow, some slack-jawed student, and it had given Mrs Cocker the very greatest of pleasure to send him packing. The second cause of Mrs Cocker's joy is that Slut Two, Nina, did not return at all to the Royal Terrace B&B the previous night – doubtless making the beast with two backs with some movie scapegrace – when if Nina had had any consideration *whatsoever*, she would have called up Mrs Cocker, the better to inform her that she would not be coming back to her bed that night. It was a matter of manners. And common courtesy. And was just exactly the excuse that Mrs Cocker had been looking for to tear Slut Two – Nina – off one almighty strip, just see if she didn't! And she would like tearing Nina off a strip! She would enjoy herself! The widow Cocker loved nothing more than putting tall, beautiful women in their place – just see how she'd got that slapper Vicky fired! – and she was thoroughly relishing the thought of putting Nina back into her box. Relishing it? She was licking her scaly lips!

Mrs Cocker heard a key in the front door. She let herself out of Nina's room, locking the door behind her, and stood atop the stairs awaiting her victim.

Nina, coming up the stairs, did not at first notice Mrs Cocker. She looked up – 'Ah, morning, Mrs Cocker,' she said, with a huge cat-who's-had-the-cream smile, and Mrs Cocker well knew what *that* meant.

'Don't you good-morning me, you little madam.'

'Is it already gone noon?' Nina checked her watch.

'You've got a nerve!' Mrs Cocker said. 'You didn't come back home last night – and you never thought to call! I was worried sick about you! Worried sick about you! You could have been dead in a ditch!'

'It must have been awful for you,' Nina said lightly. She reached the top of the stairs and just walked straight past Mrs Cocker. 'Did you bother to lock the door or is still open?'

'It is still very much locked.'

'Did you return my diary to its case?'

'Yes… no! What are you taking about?'

Nina laughed as she unlocked the door. 'I hope you've enjoyed my little stories.' Then, without so much as a backward glance, she went into her room and closed the door behind her. The sheer effrontery of the woman! This was not how it was meant to be!

The widow Cocker hammered at the bedroom door. 'You, Nina, I want a word with you!' She tried the door but, damnably, it was locked from the inside and the key was still in the door.

'Just give me a moment, Mrs Cocker.'

Mrs Cocker put her ear to the door but could only hear the excruciating sound of Nina singing to herself. What to do, what to do? Stay here and wait – no, that could not possibly be right. She would wait downstairs in her parlour in order to beard this madam when she came down the stairs – and that is what she did, viciously chewing her quid of tobacco and expectorating so very violently that she altogether missed the spittoon and the brown globule of spit spattered into the wall.

From upstairs, Mrs Cocker could hear what was perhaps the sound of drawers being opened; was it drawers being opened? Was it something else? Then, suddenly, the patter of footsteps on the stairs, the sound of the front door being opened, and before Mrs Cocker had even launched herself out of her armchair, the sound of a man – *a man!* – entering the Royal Terrace B&B.

'All set?' Mrs Cocker heard him say.

'Come on up!'

Mrs Cocker scuttled to the parlour door, but 'twas too late, too late, as Nina and the man – tall, broad shoulders, simply awful – were already upon the staircase. If Mrs Cocker had been at the top of the stairs, as she had been the previous night with Mandy and the purulent student, then she could have headed them off at the pass, but this was altogether more difficult now that they were ahead of her.

'You!' Mrs Cocker shouted. 'What are you doing? Men are not allowed!'

Nina turned cheerily at the top of the stairs. 'Oh, there you are, Mrs Cocker,' she said. 'I wondered what had become of you.'

'No men in the house!' Mrs Cocker screamed. 'Rules is rules!'

'Don't worry yourself, Mrs Cocker,' Nina said.

Don't worry herself? The widow Cocker was not so much worried about having a man in her house as most extremely vexed. 'I want him out now!'

'Absolutely.'

The man was by now at the top of the stairs. He gave Mrs Cocker a wave and followed Nina into her room – and though Mrs Cocker remained resolutely at the bottom of the stairs, she was still able to hear what the male creature said: 'Just the charmer you said she was!'

Well! Well! Mrs Cocker flew up the stairs in a fury, only to find that the door to Nina's room was once again locked. 'Open this door!' Mrs Cocker hollered. 'Open up now!'

'Coming,' Nina said. 'Just coming!'

The sound of another drawer being opened, a laugh, and

then, repellently, the distinct sound of a kiss, and the good widow Cocker well knew what came after a kiss: frottage! 'Stop that!' she said. 'Stop that right now!'

Mrs Cocker put her ear to the door. Some muttered conversation which she could not quite make out, and then, just like that, the door swung open, and she was literally caught bending. Nina, briefcase in hand, was standing in the doorway. 'I do so hope, Mrs Cocker, that you weren't too disturbed by the sound of our kissing,' she said.

The man strolled towards the door. He had a suitcase in each hand and a bag slung over his shoulder. ''Scuse me,' he said, and though Mrs Cocker would have liked to have bearded the both of them together, it looked like the man was coming on through anyway, so she had little option but to step aside. Nina, on the other hand, was deserving of the full treatment – and she was gonna get it! Mrs Cocker blocked the doorway; Nina was briefly stalled.

Nina did the most irritating thing she could have possibly done: she smiled. 'I'm moving out,' she said. 'May I thank you for all your many kindnesses.'

Having been brought to a rolling boil, Mrs Cocker exploded: 'twas nothing less than Mount Vesuvius pouring its bile over the luckless Pompeiians on the day of August 24, 79 AD.

'Do you have any idea what I have done for you these past six months?' Mrs Cocker spat, face contorted in hellcat rage. 'Do you have any idea of the hell that you and those other bitches have put me through? You come in at all hours of the night, you with your fluttering eyelashes and your cheap tart clothing, and half the time you've got a man with you – don't tell me you didn't – and you couldn't care less about me or my peace or everything I do for you. Know what you are, you are just an easy-lay slattern – oh, I've seen you, a'wiggling your scrawny-bitch buttocks – and let me tell you that soon enough you'll be a washed-up witch and mad with it, and not a single person, man or woman, will touch you with a bargepole, and that's how it's going to be for the rest of your days, and as for this ridiculous movie that you're filming, you still haven't got it, have you, because you really think it's some big-shot arty-farty flick, but it's nothing like that, nothing at all, it's a porn film, haven't you got it yet, and that is what you are and that is what you have become, you young madam, you were a cheap stripper and now you're nothing but a common prostitute, so be damned to saying you're leaving my bed and breakfast, you're not quitting here, I am kicking you out, and you, you harlot, are out of here now and you're never coming back, not even if you beg me on your knees – so be off with you. Get out of my house!'

There was much, perhaps, that Nina could have said to Mrs Cocker. She could have corrected Mrs Cocker on her misapprehension that *Eyes Wide Shut* was a porn film; she could have argued the toss about the various night-time prowlers that had supposedly been whisked into the Royal Terrace B&B; she could, even, have returned fire with fire with a few choice insults of her own. All these thoughts tripped through Nina's head as she stood on the threshold of her room. Mrs Cocker, craggy face still red with rage, was blowing quite hard, almost dancing on her feet; she looked like she was on fire for some kind of response, willing Nina to say something, so that she, in her turn, could come out with some absolutely zinging, stinging response.

Nina side-stepped through the door, past Mrs Cocker, and took herself to the top of the stairs, and started going down, and had been intending to say nothing at all, but when she was halfway down the staircase, Nina paused and looked up at Mrs Cocker through the bannisters and said that one simple word that is so utterly enraging to a person who is athirst for a fight: 'Goodbye.'

* * *

She settled herself very nicely in Glenn's room at the Angel hotel, and they – naturally – christened Glenn's double bed. Very comfy indeed, but not in the same league as Richard III's four-poster – though that said, both Nina and Glenn had been carnally abstinent for some quite considerable time, so it was also possible that the four-poster's beauty was entirely entwined with the satiation of their quite ravenous appetites for each other.

They both showered – together, of course – and, do you know what, they then made love again, right there, in the shower, such silk-smooth soapy skin, so that by the time they eventually made it out of the bathroom and into their clothes, they were sharp-set, and walked down to the restaurant for lunch, holding hands and not giving a damn who saw them.

Owing to the various events in the Sergeants' Mess the previous evening, they had neither of them had dinner; Nina ordered smoked salmon to start and a ribeye steak (medium rare) with chunky chips and a Caesar salad, and, pleasingly, Glenn did not bother to look at the menu but ordered the same; and, onto the question of what to drink – booze or no booze? – and to hell with it, booze it would most definitely be, as she, they, were in love and most definitely had something to celebrate.

With knees easy next to each other, and sitting at right angles rather than the more formal adversarial position, they discussed that most intriguing of subjects with which all new lovers so love to while away their time – when did they first fancy each other, when did they know, what might they have done so very differently? The answer, at least for Glenn, was not to have been such a stuck-up nincompoop and started dating immediately after that first especial kiss.

They had finished their starter, their steak, and as they nibbled at their salads, they stared in into each other's love-drunk eyes and wondered if there was room for more (yes, indeed, *that* kind of more). Lawrence then happened to sidle into the restaurant, newspapers tucked under his arm. A pause, barely but a moment, as he spotted Nina and Glenn together, and after giving Nina the very glibbest of winks, he sauntered to his table.

Glenn signed the bill and they were about to leave the room when Nina decided on a detour to Lawrence's table.

Lawrence, papers spread all about the table, took a leisurely swallow of black coffee and patted his lips with the white linen napkin. 'Good afternoon.'

'And good afternoon to you, Lawrence,' Nina said; Glenn contented himself with a 'Hi'.

'Hey, Lawrence, got a question for you.'

'Fire away – though I may not answer it.'

'Why did you decide to set us up?'

'Felt like it,' Lawrence said, hand stretching out for his coffee cup. 'And didn't it turn out well?'

'It certainly did,' Nina said. On the one hand, Nina was exceedingly happy; on the other, Lawrence's general smugness was peculiarly irksome.

'Come on – why d'you do it?'

'Ah, Nina, Nina,' he said. 'Why do you need to know the mechanics of matchmaking? Is it not enough that I thought the pair of you were a match – and that, frankly, if I hadn't got stuck in, the pair of you would still be stuck on your ivory pedestals, and probably would still be stuck there even after the wrap party? So to sum up, Nina – I, like my heroine Jane Austen, make matches because I enjoy making matches, and not just you two either – later, on the set, you may observe that our Mandy is much enamoured of our Josh—'

'How the hell did you pull that one off?'

'A magician, dear Nina, does not reveal his tricks.'

Glenn did not really know what to make of it all – and nor did he much care. What did it matter whether they'd been manipulated, match-made, or whether, indeed, Lawrence simply had a God complex? 'Thanks anyway,' he said.

'A pleasure, Glenn.'

Nina was on the verge of saying something barbed, but

realising, perhaps, that Lawrence might have had a point about the two of them remaining for ever stuck on their ivory pedestals, she leant down and gave Lawrence a small squeeze of his earlobe. 'Thanks,' she said.

'You're so very welcome – and please don't forget to invite me to the wedding.'

Nina and Glenn strolled back to their room. 'Think we'd have got it together without him?' Nina mused.

'Not for a long time.'

'I was going to ask him about the Sergeants' Mess and the bed and all that, but he'd never have told us a thing.'

'Hmmm.' Glenn pondered the point. 'Maybe it is better to leave the magician with his tricks.'

'Very good point, darling,' she said, and with that they had reached their room, and the door was speedily unlocked, and in a trice their clothes were off and they were back doing what they had been yearning to do for the past half-hour – and though this may seem like overkill, in their defence, they were in love and they had both of them spent over a year of going without.

Glenn drove Nina to the set and, after a kiss and a caress, Glenn went off to attend to Kubrick's needs and Nina was left alone to revel in the amazing occurrences of the previous twenty-four hours. It was dusk as she strolled around the Elveden grounds, feasting on her memories – most particularly of entering the Sergeants' Mess for the first time, the coal fire ablaze, the set of Jane Austen books upon the mantelpiece, the beautiful bed and the ever-so-slight hope that Glenn might come up to join her, and then, indeed, he had come up to join her – this time, thankfully, with his head properly screwed on, so that they had finally made love, just as they were so meant to do.

She wandered back to the trucks and the Winnebagos, the whole village bright with arc lights, and in front of her she espied another couple, both in nothing but tight T-shirts which revealed tantalising glimpses of the most elaborate tattoos, and as she came closer to the loving couple, she recognised them as Caspar and Olivia, no less. As she made her way to the hall, she thought that the day could not get any more extraordinary when, deliciously, it did: whilst she was weaving through the Winnebagos, she heard the sound of shouting and swearing from Kubrick's caravan. The shouting stopped and there was a loud, crisp slap and, like some mad jack-in-the-box, Lawrence's face was being mashed up hard against the Winnebago window.

CHAPTER 32

Imagine, if you will, a jaunty mongrel scavenging amongst the dirty dumps of Mumbai city. This dog is a cross between a silk-smooth Labrador and a pye-dog (that is an Indian pariah dog, free-ranging, half-wild). It has erect ears, a wedge-shaped head and a spriggish waggy tail, so far, so pye-dog, but this mongrel is different because it has a lush coat of dirty golden hair. This delightful dog is up of a'morning, and is just going about its regular duties at its home dump, a little sniff here, a pee there, nosing through the old nappies and champing down on the mutton bones. This friendly mongrel, beloved by 'most everyone, may not be the king of the dump, but it knows its place in this world, and every day is a fresh delight.

At Elveden, then, I was that perky mongrel – arriving early, leaving late, mischief-making, match-making, drinking myself senseless and, as best I could, getting all the gossip that was fit to print.

That last Sunday started exceedingly well – and the day just got better and better!

As usual on a Sunday, Tom and I had met up for a long run, and just for old time's sake, we were trotting down our old favourite, along the muddy drovers' roads, through the puddles and the mulch, the wet trees now leafless and the five-bar gates as slippery as they ever were.

Tom was, for once, keen to chat.

'Meeting you was the best thing to happen to me in years,' he said.

'Very sweet of you to say so,' I said. 'Been pretty good for me too.'

'Those guys in the Officers' Mess, I really like them – that Nina, she's always reading, always writing, fascinating stuff about nineteenth-century Japan.'

'Japan, eh?' I said. 'Don't know much about it.'

'I love it!' Tom said in his usual, gushing way. 'Incredible!'

We'd arrived at a five-bar gate, our favourite five-bar gate as it happened, the gate with the concrete block, the gate where it had all started.

'You want to take it easy going over here,' Tom said. 'Otherwise you could really do yourself a mischief.'

'Thanks for the tip,' I said and we continued on our way, me mostly in silence, while Tom chirruped away about this and that. I'd been taking in the sights and the smells of the mud and the wet wood, only half paying attention to Tom's prattle, when I realised he was talking about his wife.

'Don't know what's happened with Nic, but she seems a lot happier,' he said.'

'Oh yeah?' I said.

'Yeah,' he said. We jogged on in silence as he marshalled his thoughts. 'As you know, Lawrence, we haven't really been getting on that well for over a year now, but... but in the last few weeks, she just seems a lot happier.'

'That's nice.'

'Yeah.' He mulled the matter over. 'She's really working hard on her Italian. Think she might have something going with her Italian teacher?'

'So what if she does?' I said. 'You're happy – she's happy. Why rock the boat?'

'Maybe...' he trailed off. 'Maybe you're right.'

'Can I offer you one small piece of wisdom, Tom?' I said. 'Sometimes you can ask one too many questions.'

'You can?'

'Yeah Tom,' I said, warming to my theme, because us hacks, we know all about asking too many questions. You ask and you ask and you pry and you probe, and then, to your horror, you realise that you have asked one too many questions and that the whole edifice of your story has collapsed like a sandcastle in the face of a spring tide. And as it is with journalism, so it is with those equally complex things called human relationships. 'If you're both happy then that's the only thing that matters. Start digging and you might well hear something you don't want to hear.'

We ran down the drovers' road as the splendid rain spattered our heads and our legs.

'You're saying is it's better to be in blissful ignorance?'

'One thousand per cent!' I said. 'What is this need to know everything, to get to the bottom of everything, to have the truth, the whole truth and nothing but? That's not how relationships work.' I said it, and I believed it, and fortunately he did swallow it, as the one thing we did not want was for Tom to start grilling his darling wife – or, indeed, myself.

'Never thought about it like that before,' he said. 'You might be right.'

'I am certainly right!' I said. 'Happiness is a very fleeting thing, and what I do know is that there's no quicker way to making yourself unhappy than to start picking at old scabs, and ripping them off, and all purely for the pleasure of experiencing all your old hurts.'

'Yeah?' Tom said, letting the idea swill inside before it chimed. 'Yeah!' he said. 'Do you want to be blissfully ignorant, or, or—'

'Insightfully unhappy.'

'Give me simple and happy any day!'

'That's the spirit!' I said, and we continued to run, and when we reached his Winnebago, we high-fived and he gave me the full hundred-watt Tom Cruise smile – quite something to be on the receiving end of it, I can tell you – and though I'm not sure, I think that was about the last time I saw him.

Then, like the dear little mongrel scavenger that I had become, I visited all my other regular haunts on the shoot

– a chirpy word at breakfast for Nina and Glenn, who were both very much in love and who tended to eat with Nina's leg delightfully slung over Glenn's thigh, but who, for some reason, did not give their matchmaker his due, and in fact generally tended to treat me under sufferance.

A slightly warmer reception, however, from Josh and Mandy, who were also unable to keep their hands off each other. The most amazing thing was, of course, that I'd actually managed to get them together in the first place – or, as the clodhopping Josh had demanded: 'What have you done, what have you done?'

'It's perfectly simple,' I'd replied. 'I told Mandy that you were the sole son and heir of that particularly wealthy Scottish laird, the Duke of Buccleuch.'

'What?' Josh had said. 'Why did you say that?'

'Because I'm smart!'

'But I'm not the son of the Duke of Buccleuch!' he wailed.

'Oh really?' I said in mock astonishment. 'Listen! It was the only way I could think of to get the two of you together, you daft muppet,' I said before adding, 'You better start brushing up on your colloquial Scots.'

'But... but...' he said, wholly confounded that his entire relationship with Mandy was based on a lie.

'Look, it'll be fine,' I said. 'You're here under cover. I've said that under no circumstances should she ever mention that your dad's a multimillionaire.'

'But what when she finds out, what then, what then?'

'Look, when that happens, if that happens, you just blame it all on a misunderstanding – but hopefully by then you'll be so in love that it won't make any odds.'

'Humph,' he said, typically – but us humble matchmakers rarely expect much in the way of gratitude, and nor, indeed, do we get it. No matter – 'tis enough, generally, to see a couple in love and to know that we have had a hand in it.

And there on the set, also, were another match-made couple, one Caspar and Olivia – and this had been altogether easier to effect: I had simply instructed the Caspar bonehead to start wearing tighter, skimpier shirts on set, the better to show off the enormous tattoo on his back that stretched from his buttocks to the nape of his neck, the better to be espied by Olivia, who, as we know, already had some large tattoos of her own. For if there's one thing I've observed about people with tattoos, it is that they don't half fancy other people with tattoos, and so it was with Olivia when she saw the monster dragon tat on Caspar's back, and within days the pair of them were, err, christening every nook and every cranny that was to be found in Elveden.

Since the night's filming was still a way off, I amused myself by going off to Molly's canteen to get a bacon roll.

'How's your big baby?'

'Big and getting bigger,' she said, huge breasts quivering as she slathered butter onto the roll. I could certainly see why Kubrick adored her, but as to what she saw in Kubrick, I have no idea – though I daresay multimillionaire men do have their charms, or what's a heaven for?

'Shall I take him his liver and onions?'

'Could you?' she said. 'Bit up against it.'

'A pleasure.'

So that is how I found myself, feet up on the table, in Kubrick's Winnebago – a.k.a. The Honk Den. It was just the two of us, as Larry the body double was yet to arrive for another hour, and while I delicately ate my bacon roll, Kubrick champed his way through his liver and onions – God it was the most repugnant sight, what with bits of gravied bacon getting caught in his beard, and his fat toes on full display not six feet from my face. Frankly, in the disgusting stakes, Kubrick could have given Grubby a damn good run for his money.

I had learned by now not to attempt a conversation with Kubrick while he was eating – it only made everything worse, his mouth sort of turning into a human muck-spreader.

'There!' he said, licking the last of the gravy off his knife before lightly tossing the plate and cutlery onto the floor.

'Hey Stan,' I said. 'You couldn't wipe your beard, could you? You got a whole load of liver and bacon stuck there.'

'Sure, sure,' he said. 'Throw me that towel.'

Kubrick mopped at his beard with the towel – imagine a fat baby trying to clean its face, but instead of cleaning itself, it's just smearing the muck everywhere – and then, believe me, he inspected the towel and picked off the tastier bits of bacon for reingestion.

Over the previous week or so, Kubrick and I had had a number of conversations, of which the most fruitful by far had been when he'd been talking about the stars he'd worked with. He'd had a fair few of the big ones, including, of course, Kirk Douglas, Jack Nicholson, Peter Sellers and Malcolm McDowell, but that evening I was keen to press him on his second-tier stars.

But before the confessional could begin, I first had to open a bottle of wine. Glasses were filled, the bottle of wine was placed conveniently close on the table and, lastly, I ordered Kubrick to either put some socks on or to take his fat pink toes out of my face. He obediently put on some slippers.

'Let's talk about Shelley Duvall,' I said. 'Is it true you really monstered her in *The Shining*?'

'Well, maybe a little,' he said. Know what he reminded me of, lying flat-a-back on his La-Z-Boy? Like a huge gannet chick, sitting in its nest, entirely unable to move and complacently waiting to be fed.

'What does that mean, Stanley?'

'She just…' he said. 'She just didn't get it. She wasn't doing it right.'

'OK.' I didn't need to say any more. I just had to shut up and then, given enough time, the story would begin.

'Shelley was good, no question, that's why she had the part,' Kubrick said. He slurped a bit of wine, half in his mouth, half going into his beard. 'But she wasn't giving me what I wanted. It just wasn't there. She didn't have it! And so, you know, I had to break her.'

'How d'you do that?'

Kubrick cackled at the memory – God, he was a mad one. 'First, I got Duvall real isolated on the set. Didn't allow anyone to talk to her – not the runners, nor any of the crew; she's completely ostracised, and she's trying to work out if it's her or if it's something she's done.' Kubrick let out another mad chuckle. 'Truth was, it was me – they weren't talking to her because I wouldn't let them talk to her! Must have driven her half mad. So that was the first thing I did. Second, I had her crying a lot. I had her crying twelve hours a day for weeks and weeks on end. Get up at seven in the morning and switch on the waterworks. My own version of the Japanese water torture.'

'What fun,' I said, which Kubrick took entirely at face value, as if it was, indeed, great fun to drive his star to the brink of madness.

'Yeah, great fun!' Kubrick said. 'Loved that. And the last thing we did, obviously, was the good ol' multi-take routine! Boy, did we make her sweat for that one! There was one take, sort of close to the climax of the film, when Duvall is in the big hall and it suddenly dawns on her that she's married to a psycho. So there she is, on the stairs, and her nut husband is coming at her on the stairs, and she's fending him off with a baseball bat, sort of poking him away, that kinda thing, but pretty ineffectually, and the whole thing isn't really doing it for me. So ya know what I did?'

'Quite a few takes?' I needed more wine. I topped myself up.

'I'll say!' Kubrick guffawed. 'Up until that scene in the hall, I'd only been playing pat-a-cake with Duvall, sort of fifteen takes, tops. But when it came to that scene on the staircase, I got my all-time record – even beat young Tommy Cruise walking through that doorway. How many takes, d'you reckon?'

I pondered the matter. 'Got to be well over a hundred,' I said.

'You bet your sweet ass!' he said. 'Made Duvall do the

scene 127 times! Boy did it work out well,' he said, tittering to himself before adding, 'Completely broke Shelley, nearly made her give up acting, that's how bad it was, but so worth it!'

'Perhaps,' I said – for there indeed is a question for the ages: when creating a great masterpiece, is it OK if, along the way, a few people just happen to fall through the cracks? If, for instance, a few bit-players happen to end up completely broken? If, because of you, they end up giving up their careers, if not their sanity? What if, for the sake of example, you are directing two superstar actors who are not only very much in love but who also happen to be married to each other – and who then, precisely because of your insane film schedule, happen to fall out of love and get divorced? What price art? Well, all I can say is that if you're a dictator director who's hell-bent on bending his stars to your will, then you sure as hell better produce one blockbuster of a movie. And as for *Eyes Wide Shut*… Well soon enough we will come to that.

We had started talking about another of Stanley's second-tier actors, Leonard Rossiter, when there was a knock at the door. We didn't normally get visitors at that time, in fact, the only three people who ever really came to visit Kubrick were Glenn and Molly and Olivia.

Stanley flipped down the foot-rest and squirmed out of his chair, polishing off the last of his wine before he waddled to the door.

Since I had my back to the door, I couldn't see who it was. But I could certainly hear him.

'Sir James, ya old dog, finally here to inspect my lovelies?'

'If that's all right, Stanley,' the man said. It was a voice that I well remembered. I heard the man step into the Winnebago.

'Hey Sir James, come meet my pal Lawrence.'

I only had a couple of seconds. I lurched to the ground, grabbed Kubrick's beard-mop towel and pretended to be sick. I wasn't sure it was very realistic. 'Sorry, sorry,' I said. 'So sick.'

With the towel wrapped about my mouth, I made to totter

out of the Winnebago. As I had suspected, it was indeed the executive producer, one Sir James Hutchison, who, when last we saw him, had been flat on his back after I'd upended him in the lavatories of the RAC. He was in his usual pinstripe suit, just as big and brawny as ever.

He was standing right by the Winnebago door. I was letting out the low feeble moans of a man suddenly struck down by the most terrible gastroenteritis.

I was all but at the door when, instead of staring dully at my feet, I made the mistake of looking at Sir James. I looked him in the eye. Nothing much, barely a moment, but it was, nevertheless, eye contact.

Now – I wonder if you've ever done any big-game hunting. I know a little about it and I'll tell you one thing that sometimes happens. You wing a leopard but you don't quite kill it. You and the guide then have to track the beast down until you can eventually shoot it dead. You follow the paw prints and the blood trail until eventually you come up to a bush or a thicket, and this, in all probability will be the place where the wounded animal has holed up. You survey the bush, you look at it from all sides, and though you're pretty certain the leopard is in there, you're not quite sure. As for the wounded leopard, it will sit tight and it will do nothing, and it will do nothing, until quite suddenly it will spring from the bush and leap straight at you – and that is the moment that you have looked it in the eye. Once you have looked a cornered leopard in the eye, no matter how briefly, then you know he's there and he knows you know, and now the only thing for certain is that within one second you'll both be fighting at very close quarters, you trying to bring your rifle to bear, cursing yourself for not bringing a revolver, and all the while the leopard is atop you, trying to bite your jugular and rake your guts out with his rear claws.

And so with Sir James. Just the very briefest of eye contacts. I'm stepping out of the Winnebago door. And then this animal roar and the monster has grabbed me by my collar, dragged me back inside and thrown me to the floor. I hit the ground with an oomph that took the wind out of me. I still had the towel clutched to my face.

'Sir James, Sir James!' Kubrick whinnied. 'What are you doing?'

Sir James ripped the towel away, glared at me. 'What are you doing with this pond life?' he yelled. 'He's a *Sun* reporter!'

I put on my stoutest East London accent. 'Not me, guv!' I said. 'Don't know what you're talking abaht!'

Kubrick was dickering around near the sink. 'A *Sun* reporter you say?' he said. 'But Lawrence has been working here for months! He's Tom's body double. He couldn't be!'

I groggily got to my feet. 'Sorry mate, must be some mistake.'

'Of course he'd say that!' Sir James said, surveying me with distaste. 'Every time you open your mouth another lie pops out – *Capisco, capisco?*' He inspected the towel and tossed it to Kubrick. 'Where's all the sick that he's supposed to have thrown up?'

'I ain't ever worked for no *Sun* newspaper.' I made to walk past him – if I even got close to the door then I was out and on my way, and not even Tom Cruise would have seen me for dust.

The besuited yeti grabbed me by my lapel, slapped me and then face-planted me into the plate-glass window. 'I've had enough of this sham,' he said. 'You're going nowhere.'

It felt like he'd broken my nose. I sat down on a banquette. 'I want an ambulance,' I said. 'I'll 'ave you for assault.'

'Dear oh dearie me,' Stanley said. 'I don't know what to think.' He started squawking into his radio – called up security, called up Glenn. The security guys arrived first, took a look at me, and were then posted on sentry duty outside the Winnebago. Glenn arrived about ten minutes later. I was still on the banquette and was drinking wine in sulky silence as Sir James glowered from the door.

Glenn cast a glance at me before turning to Kubrick. 'So he's a *Sun* reporter, is he?'

'That's right,' Sir James said. 'I came across this reptile about six months ago.'

'Don't know what you're talking abaht,' I said.

'Well, there's one very easy way to find out,' Glenn said. 'Apparently he likes to keep a spy-pen camera in his breast pocket. If he's got the pen, then he'll have a lot of explaining to do.'

Oh. Dear.

Sir James speedily pinned my shoulders. The pen was discovered.

'Looks like a camera to me, Mr *Sun* reporter,' Sir James said.

'I was being blackmailed!' I said. 'They had my sister, my sweet, sweet sister, they made me do it—'

'Oh, for God's sake!' Sir James said. 'If you don't stop talking I'm going to gag you!'

'It was for my sister!' I said. 'I had to—'

The next moment, a tea towel was being stuffed into my mouth, where it was kept in place with one of Kubrick's enormous belts. I was sat by the sink, mutely simmering, not even able to have any booze, as they had a conflab about what to do next. Why, why, had I kept on going with the spy pen? Well, true, I had got a few OKish pictures in the bag but, ever the keen, go-getting reporter, I was looking to get some *better* pictures. That's just the kinda journalist I am: I'm not just content with "good", I want "brilliant". And God, I'd been unlucky to be caught in the Winnebago with Kubrick – any other time and I'd have had my mask on. And, and... well thanks a bunch, Glenn! After all I'd done for him! And thanks, Nina, also, for blabbing in the first place, no it really was my absolute pleasure to set up – not to mention stock! – the Officers' Mess and the Sergeants' Mess, and to get the two of them together, and all they do, first chance they get, is throw me under the bus. My kinda guys!

Eventually, they decided to imprison me somewhere in Elveden Hall – and that, at least, I couldn't complain about, as they chose to lock me up in the Sergeants' Mess.

Glenn and Sir James and two security goons frogmarched me up the stairs – and here, at this complete cliffhanger, it feels right to have a short interlude.

* * *

There is a small interesting fact about news stories that your average punter is not even aware of: why does a particular story happen to break at a particular time? Is it just happenstance that, say, a political sex scandal happens to break on any given day? Or are there, perhaps, other forces at work?

Well, my friend – I will tell you the answer! There are a lot of stories, like deaths and natural disasters, which break just as soon as the news filters out there. If a news reporter gets wind of some star's death, then they're not going to hang around with that story – they'll file just as quickly as they can, because red-hot scoops about a star's death or a star's arrest tend to have very limited shelf lives. Reporters won't waste a moment in filing every word that they've got.

But there are other stories, particularly those stories which involve politicians, where the timing is much more Machiavellian. What I'm saying in essence is this: a lot of stories will have been sitting on the books for weeks, months even years; these stories are ready to go, but they are just waiting for somebody, some malign force, to pull the trigger. But until that trigger has been pulled, the story has been put on ice – and sometimes, perhaps, it will always be kept on ice, just a useful threat for a chief whip to have dangling over some loose-cannon backbencher.

There are other reasons why stories might break – and I well remember this from my (short) stint as a lobby correspondent in Westminster. It'd be a Sunday morning and you'd call up some low-life minister. (Is it possible that politicians are even more low-life than journalists? Quite possibly so – though I realise I am merely talking about gradations of scum-suckery.) You'd gently quiz the minister about whatever was the *scandale du jour*, and they of course would be doing everything in their powers to hush it all up, because at best they'd be getting a bollocking, and at worst they'd soon be languishing on the backbenches. A very beautiful dance is performed in which the reporter pushes harder and harder, and the minister (perhaps even the cabinet minister) tries to pour cold water on the story, until eventually the reporter flops down his cards. "I think we'll be running with it anyway," he says.

The minister usually responds thusly: "Please, please don't run it, it's just not true. It'll finish me – have a heart!" The reporter, also playing his part in this delicate minuet, then sucks on his teeth, and says the immortal words, "I just don't know – if we pull this story, it's going to leave a big, big hole in the paper. Know of anything else we could fill it with?"

And at that, the minister leaps at the bait and offers up the story that he's been sitting on for the last three months, and which will, firstly, get him out of a deep hole and which will also, with luck, land one of his rivals right in the ordure. Such is the way of political stories. Remember that one about Matt Hancock canoodling in Westminster with his glamorous mistress? The timing of that story stank to high hell. Don't know what happened there, but what I do know is that there must have been *a lot* of dirty work at the crossroads.

Anyway – 'tis not just the politicians who keep stories back for a rainy day. Stars in all their forms have plenty of skeletons, and when these skeletons come tumbling out of the cupboards, the stars need some other titbit to assuage the hordes of ravening reporters. (Though the problem here is that the skeleton still very much exists. You might for a short while be able to repack it back into the cupboards, but one day, some day, it'll come tumbling out again, just like they always do. Still, you'll have survived another day at the top of the heap, and that's all that counts.)

And as it is with stars, and as it is with politicians, so it is with us humble hacks who do not reveal our exclusives quite as quickly as our mad masters might like us so to do. To wit – some great pictures of Tom Cruise, Nina and Mandy on the set of *Eyes Wide Shut*.

After weeks and weeks of diligent snapping with my trusty spy pen, I finally had some half-decent pictures. This was the photographic equivalent of the thousands of monkeys tapping away at typewriters until they finally ended up with, say, a Shakespearean sonnet. I'd been snapping away (happily) for about a month and had become so technically proficient that I could even download the pictures onto my new laptop. Every morning, I'd download the previous night's snaps, and every morning, I'd be staring at a load of grainy blurred pictures, which, even with the best will in the world, were completely unprintable. And then, each night, I'd go back to the hall and have another shot with my spy pen – paying most particular attention to steer well clear of Nina, who had become most unnecessarily suspicious. I'd try to change the range and the focus, but it didn't seem to make much odds, because the next day, I'd end up with just another batch of blur, until one day, and to my complete astonishment, I realised that I was looking at some OKish pictures. Photos of Tom Cruise chatting to Stanley Kubrick, Cruise sitting on his chair reading a script, and – hallelujah, come home to daddy! – several pictures of Tom with his mask off chatting to the girls (with their bras off). In terms of splash pictures, there was one beauty of Tom chatting to Nina, she in just her mask, stilettoes and G-string, but side on, so that her breasts were only in profile. In terms of front-page pictures, this was important, as although the *Sun* in the 1990s was more than happy to have bare breasts on the inside pages, they were not in the business of splashing bare boobies on the front page.

In all, there were about ten usable pictures, of which four

were crisp and clear and enough even to make that hellhound Spike punch the air with glee and shout ,"You little beauty!"

Now, you would have thought that, being the keen diligent reporter that I am, I would have filed the pictures *prontissimo*, along with all the reams of copy that I had cobbled together over the previous few weeks – for after all, my job was now complete. I had the story and I had the pictures to go with it: my work with Stanley Kubrick and Tom Cruise was done.

But on the other hand… what was the big hurry? Number one, I wasn't in the *Sun* newsroom, there to be abused by Spike et al. for the non-production of stories, and number two, I was having a high old time at Elveden Hall with Tom and Nina and Josh and, ahh, Nicole, so why, oh why, would I be in so much of a hurry to scurry back to the *Sun*, where, like as not, I'd just get a brief pat on the shoulder and a "Nice job, Kimmy" before normal service was resumed the next day with Spike swearing at me at the top of his voice.

So, no, I most certainly did not file those pictures, nor my thousands of words of blistering copy, though nor did I just leave them languishing on my computer. No, like the cunning weasel that I am, I had emailed them to myself (God, it took *hours*! Welcome to emailing pictures in the 1990s), where, like all the best political stories, my scoop was safely tucked away until the time that I was good and ready to use it, which would be… whenever the hell I decided.

* * *

Where were we? Ah yes – Glenn and Sir James and the guards were about to imprison me in the Sergeants' Mess.

We were halfway down the corridor when who should I espy being turfed out of the Sergeants' Mess but Josh and Mandy – doubtless having put Richard III's four-poster to good use. The pair of them gawked at me as I walked past. 'What's happening, what's happening?' Josh said. I would very much have liked to tell him, but the tea towel was still stuffed in my mouth.

I was led into the room by Sir James, who was still holding tight to my elbow. 'What the hell's this?' he said. 'Why are we keeping him here? He should be in the cellars!'

'It's fine,' Glenn said. 'I'd like a word with him please – in private.'

After a lot of huffing and puffing, and after I was stripped of phone and skeleton key, James left the room with the two security guards.

Glenn unhitched Kubrick's belt and pulled the tea towel out of my mouth. I was parched. There was a bottle of chilled champagne by the fire. I poured us a couple of glasses, knocked mine straight off and poured another.

'I'm very sorry about all this, Glenn,' I said. 'I'm sure it'll be sorted out soon enough.'

'I doubt it,' he said. 'Anyway – I'll send up some food for you later.'

'And a bottle of wine?'

'And a bottle of wine.'

'Thank you!'

'Best make yourself at home,' he said. 'You'll be locked in here and there's a guard below the window. You're not going anywhere any time soon.'

I turned to the hardback books that, only a few days ago, I had so lovingly left on the mantelpiece. Who ever would have thought that I myself would be getting the most use out of them?

'A fire and Jane Austen and a bottle of booze,' I said, standing by the grate as I flicked through my old favourites. 'Does it get any better?'

Glenn was already at the door letting himself out. 'Perhaps someone to share it with? What do they say? Here with a loaf of bread beneath the bough, a flask of wine, a book of verse and thou beside me singing in the wilderness – and wilderness is paradise enow.'

'That's a very pretty line,' I said. I decided to plump for my very favourite favourite, *Pride and Prejudice*.

'My girlfriend's got me learning poetry.'

He was just leaving the room, but on a whim, and because he'd only quoted me the greatest verse from Omar Khayyam, I called him back. 'Hey Glenn,' I said. 'Got something to tell you.'

CHAPTER 33

Glenn had been ninety-nine per cent sure that Lawrence was, in fact, a *Sun* reporter – it all stacked up: the leaked story; the dozens of newspapers that he read at breakfast, the spy pen – and let's not even get started on Lawrence's swaggering cockiness.

The laptop sealed it. Glenn had used a maid's passkey to let himself into Lawrence's hotel room and there had found all manner of incriminating evidence, including a laptop which was so new that the reprobate Lawrence – or whatever the hell his name was – had not even bothered to set a password. Within five minutes of walking into the room, Glenn had discovered not just pictures, hundreds of pictures, but also story after story detailing every last smidgeon of gossip from Elveden, quite a lot of it from Nina and Mandy, as well as from the movie's star, Tom Cruise. Was that why Lawrence had set up the Officers' Mess?? What a schemer! Just get people drunk and get them talking and scribble your notes as fast you can. Glenn chuckled – he liked the guy, found him quirkily amusing, and had a lot to be grateful for, not least for his sterling work with Nina… but this! This! What a complete low life!

Glenn took the laptop back to Elveden Hall, where filming had been suspended for the night. No one knew what exactly had happened, but the set was awash with whispers, especially as Josh and Mandy had actually witnessed Lawrence being locked up.

What Glenn would have liked to have done when he returned to the set was to have had a talk, and perhaps even a drink, with Nina, but he'd been given the role of Kubrick's first assistant director for a reason – and that was largely because he was diligent, hard-working and thoroughly professional; his new and highly desired girlfriend would just have to wait.

He knocked on Kubrick's door and was called in. Kubrick was drinking whisky with Sir James Hutchison; Glenn knew that Sir James Hutchison had helped finance the film, but that did not in any way mean that he liked him. Glenn also found it peculiarly distasteful when Kubrick's middle-aged horndogs turned up on the set in order to leer at Nina and the rest of the girls.

'Get yourself a whisky, Glenn,' Kubrick said. 'Tell us what ya got.'

'I've got his laptop.' Glenn poured himself a large slug. 'He's got a lot of pictures from the set. Thousands of words of gossip.'

'Christ!' Sir James said. 'We got the rat just in time.'

They spent the next hour working their way through the whisky and making interminable calls to lawyers. After the initial excitement, Glenn found it all rather a let-down. It was all so tawdry. He had no idea what the lawyers would do, but they'd certainly be keeping the laptop and the phone and the spy pen.

What a relief, finally, to go back to the hotel, and to find Nina warm and drowsy in bed, drowsy but not asleep, and certainly not too drowsy to listen enthralled to Glenn's stories of the night while obviously also doing… that which had to be done.

The next day, as the lawyers wrangled, Glenn was on set just before tea. Filming was to resume that night. When Glenn had completed the various chores that are the bane of a firsrt assistant director, he had a coffee and then another coffee and, when he was ready, he went to Kubrick's Winnebago.

As usual, after he'd knocked on the door there was a bit of

shuffling and a long wait, and, now that he was listening for it, a discernible door click.

Kubrick opened the door. 'How are ya, Glenn?' he said. 'Come in! Jesus! A *Sun* reporter – here! Makes ya sick!'

'Yes.'

Kubrick flopped back into his La-Z-Boy. Glenn also took a seat, the sound of the stone tumbler grinding away relentlessly in the background.

'So all set on the set?' Kubrick said. 'Ready to go?'

'We are, Stanley.' Glenn looked out of the window, studying the arc lights as he weighed his words. 'Though things are going to have to be a little different from now on.'

'A little different, Glenn?' Kubrick said testily. 'Like how d'ya mean?'

'Like I know about Larry.'

'Larry?'

'Yes, Stanley, your lookalike, who is currently hiding in your lavatory.'

'Oh… oh,' Kubrick started to fiddle with his beard.

'He better join us.' Glenn knocked on the lavatory door. 'You can come out now, Larry.'

The door opened and Larry came out – wearing the exact same clothes as Kubrick. Save for Larry's fat fingers, the pair were all but identical.

Glenn looked at the two Kubricks, and Larry and Kubrick sullenly stared back at him.

It was Kubrick who broke the deadlock. 'You gotta understand, Glenn – the hours were just crucifying me! I couldn't do it! It was killin' me!'

'I see,' Glenn said, though he didn't really understand, and nor did he even bother to try, because how on earth could you ever hope to understand the mind of a complete lunatic? He stood up, went over to the corner of the room and turned off Kubrick's stone tumbler. The silence was magical. 'Now you'd better listen to me, Stanley,' Glenn said. 'Because I think there's something that *you'd* better understand.'

CHAPTER 34

You might not believe it, but it is possible to tire of Jane Austen. I'd read *Pride and Prejudice* and *Emma*, and was trying to tackle *Persuasion* when I realised that my attention was wandering. What the hell were they doing and why was I being kept locked up in the Sergeants' Mess for so long? As already mentioned, it was a very beautiful room, but being cooped up in there for two days was doing even my tiny little head in, and the stinking commode in the corner (retrieved from the lumber room) certainly didn't help.

My food was brought to me on a tray by a surly security guard who would not even engage in the very lightest of conversation. Perhaps he'd been warned that I had supernatural powers and that even to look at me, let alone talk to me, would cast him under my spell.

So: I read a lot, I slept a lot, I ate my meals with a hearty appetite, I drank my grog, and I wondered and I wondered how it would all turn out for little me. Sir James, of course, would have liked nothing more than to have sunk me in the nearest pond with a millstone round my neck – but though I probably deserved it, killing me might raise awkward questions.

Short of killing me, however, how was Kubrick going to shut me up?

I would soon find out.

I'd spent two nights in the Sergeants' Mess – there was a hell of a smell, even with the window open. Any civilised captors would have emptied my commode, just as I'd asked, but no, they wouldn't do that, so I was just left in the room with my mouldering effluvium.

It was late afternoon on, I think, the Tuesday, when the door was unlocked by one of the security guards. I'd hoped he might be bringing me an early cocktail, but no.

'Good afternoon,' I said from the comfort of my fireside chair. 'What's cooking?'

'You're out of here.'

'Excellent!' I said. 'Like – right now?'

'Yes.'

'Well, let's go!' I said, and without so much as a backward glance I waltzed out of my prison – no matter how luxuriously appointed, a cell is still a cell. I thought that I'd be escorted to Kubrick's Winnebago for another dressing-down, or maybe another bear hug from Sir James, or maybe even legal papers, but there was none of that. The whole place was pretty much deserted apart from a few of the crew tinkering with some gear. No star, no girls, no director, no first assistant director. I walked through that giant deserted hall for the last time; what a time we'd had together.

Outside, I'd expected some sort of formal reprimand, such as the military traitors used to receive when they were drummed out of the army – epaulettes hacked away, buttons cut off, sword snapped in half and then the entire army turning its back on you as you were escorted off the parade ground. But no, there was nothing like that; it was all weirdly anticlimactic. I'd spent the previous two day polishing up some of my very choicest barbs for Sir James and the rest of them, only to discover that no one was even remotely interested.

We wended our way through the trucks and the Winnebagos, and when we reached my car, the guard simply gave me my keys and, without a word, walked off.

Of all the many scenarios that I'd been conjuring with, this particular one had not featured. They'd just taken me to my car! Before they thought better of it, and without so much as a backward glance, I was on my way. I went straight back to the hotel and packed my stuff, and in under five minutes I was out of there, out of Suffolk, out of Kubrick's clutches, and on my way! Freedom! And with a great story to boot!

So Kubrick had got my laptop and my spy pen and good luck to him, because, as you will recall, I had already emailed the stories and the pictures to myself, where they quietly languished in my private email account, awaiting the moment when they would be forwarded to the *Sun* newsroom.

Back at my London flat, I made myself a gin and tonic, a stiff one. Duly fortified, I called the newsdesk. I'd not spoken to any of them in well over two months. After a lot of squeals (of delight), I was eventually put through to that wholesome avuncular chap, my deputy editor.

'You took your time,' Spike said, ever the charmer.

'I did take my time,' I said. 'And I've now got the pictures and I've got the story.'

'OK,' he said, with about as much interest as if I'd brought him in a packet of stone-cold fish and chips. 'Send them over.'

'I'll do just that,' I said brightly – you know me, ever eager to please.

'Right.' And then the charmless bastard just slammed the phone down. Without even a goodbye or a "Well done, Kimmy". Talk about bad manners!

I sent my various bits of copy over to the newsdesk, and when that was done I got to work on the pictures. It took ages, and it was well past 10 p.m. before the tenth and tastiest picture had finally chugged its way out of the outbox.

My story was filed, my pictures were filed, the *Eyes Wide Shut* job was done. I called up Spike to tell him the good news. He was already scrolling through the pictures.

'Some of these pictures are OK,' he said (high praise). 'Why didn't you file these the moment that you had them?'

'Got them on the very last day just before I was rumbled,' I said stoutly.

Spike sighed. 'What about the copy? Why didn't you file that?'

'I was going to file the copy with the pictures,' I said. 'Didn't seem any point in filing the copy until I had the photos to go with them.'

'Hmmm,' he said. I could hear him tapping away at his computer. He was probably reading my copy. Though he might just as easily have been emailing his latest lover.

I let him tap away for about a minute. Maybe he'd forgotten I was there. 'So what do you think?' I said.

'You should have filed this stuff when you had it.'

'Well, anyway, now you've got it,' I said. 'When do you think you'll run it? Day after tomorrow?'

'The day after tomorrow?' he said. 'The day after tomorrow?' He burst into this mad cackle of crazy laughter. 'You just don't get it!'

'Errr,' I said, fast playing catch-up. 'What don't I get?'

'We're not running this story in two days' time, or two weeks' time, or ever! They've served us with a super-injunction!'

I certainly knew what an injunction was – had had a few of them in my time, including one particularly spiteful one from Buckingham Palace, but that, though, is another story. (Indeed so: *Palace Rogue*.)

I asked the obvious question. 'What's a super-injunction?'

'It's an injunction with all the bells and all the whistles, you imbecile!' Spike said. 'We can't even write about the injunction, let alone who's behind it.'

'What?' I said. 'I've never heard of such a thing!'

'Well, you better get used to them, sunshine,' he said, 'because within two years, every celebrity on earth will be using them to shut us up.' (True.)

'Oh,' I said. 'So there's nothing we can do?'

'Not a damn thing,' Spike said. 'This whole movie stunt of yours has been a complete waste of time. It's a fiasco!'

'Oh,' I said.

Worse was to follow.

The next morning, after more than eighty days on set back-to-back, I was more than ready for a day off. It was all a quite staggering let-down, my epic movie career careening into the buffers and only the one "Curse of Kubrick" story to show for it. I mooched about in the morning, tried to call Spike, but he was otherwise engaged. I'd had a run round Hyde Park and had gone out to the shops and had bought myself a bunch of flowers – well, sure as hell nobody else was going to buy them for me.

It was gone 5 p.m. when Spike eventually called. He sounded pretty well oiled, which was unusual for him. He did not often drink at lunchtime.

'Got any more pictures?' he asked.

'No,' I said. 'They took my laptop.'

'So let me just get this right,' Spike said. 'You just happened to get these pictures on the Saturday night, and then you emailed them to yourself on the Sunday morning, and then, just a few hours later, they rolled you over.'

'That's right!' I said.

'Bit of a coincidence,' Spike said. 'Oh well.'

If I'd had my wits about me, I would have smelt a very large rat. What Spike would have normally done, under such circumstances, was scream at me at the top of his voice and call me all manner of sulphurous four-letter words. But for Spike to emolliently end our conversation with the words "Oh well"? Inconceivable!

It had been a very, very trying time of things. I made myself some beans on toast and went to bed – to be woken by a midnight phone call. It was Seb, the editor. Now Seb hasn't really featured in many of my tales, mainly for the reason that we never crossed swords that much. Seb was the titular head, the man who glad-handed the politicians and who dined with the stars, but it was Spike who was the power.

I couldn't even remember the last time that the editor had called me up – least of all at midnight. He was howling with rage.

'Your story's a world exclusive in the *Mirror*!' he shouted. 'All your copy, all your pictures – everything!'

'Duhh – what?' I said.

'It's all over the first fifteen pages of the *Mirror*!' he yelled.

'What… What… Who wrote it?'

'It's Charlie Bain's story!' he shouted. 'You are coming in here first thing tomorrow and you will explain to me exactly how this happened!'

Bain? Charlie Bain? Cannot compute!

'My story is in the *Mirror* under Bain's byline?' I repeated.

'That's just what I said!' he said. 'How did it happen?'

'I don't know how it happened!'

'My office, 9 a.m.!'

I appeared in the *Sun* courtroom at 9 a.m., dressed sharply, soberly, in a blue suit with a blue shirt and a grey tie. Seb and Spike were already in Seb's office, in shirtsleeves, coffee in hand, each reading a copy of that day's *Mirror*.

Seb was a bit of a hefty guy – all those expense-accounts meals – with an uncombed and unkempt thatch of straw hair and some rather rough-looking stubble. He peered at me through his steel-rimmed glasses. 'What have you got to say for yourself?' he said.

'Morning, Seb, morning, Spike,' I said – it never harms to be courteous. 'What have I got to say for myself about what?'

'Selling this story to the *Mirror*!' he said. 'You were one of the few people who knew that it was just us who'd been served with the super-injunction! You flogged it to Bain!'

'Don't be ridiculous!' I said. 'Firstly, I'd never deal with the *Mirror*, and secondly, I hate Bain!'

'Well, who did it then?' Seb's eyes drifted back to the centre spread; both Nina and Mandy were looking at their most beguiling.

'How do I know?' I said. 'Could have been anyone in the newsroom!'

I looked over at Spike, who for some reason was strangely silent. Normally, he'd have been up and screaming like the best of them, but all he was doing was sipping his coffee and leafing through the *Mirror*. Eventually, he looked at me. He had this odd expression on his face, not quite a smirk, not quite a smile, but most definitely not neutral.

'So you didn't sell the story then?' Seb said.

'I did not sell the story! I promise I didn't sell the story!' I said hotly. 'But Bain knows who sold the story. Why not ask him?'

'Maybe,' Spike said, and, having lost complete interest in my interrogation, he leaned back in his chair and turned to look out of the stormy skyline, dreaming, perhaps, of sun-drenched holidays yet to come.

Seb, however, was still very cut up. 'This is bad!' he said. 'This is very bad! We have a mole in the newsroom!'

'I guess we have,' I said.

'But we'll catch him – we'll catch him!'

'Sure,' I said, though in my experience moles were very difficult indeed to catch, most particularly the ones who worked for tabloid newspapers.

'Well, off you go then,' Seb said.

Spike got out of his chair. He not only escorted me to the door but opened it for me. 'Thank you,' I said.

'You're welcome.' As Spike closed the door behind me, he gave me a full-fat wink – and though I didn't know for sure what it meant, I certainly had my suspicions and, a month later, I was not remotely surprised to learn that the hitherto impoverished Spike had whisked his new *inamorata* – Stella the newsdesk secretary, damn him – off for a luxury trip to the Seychelles.

Still, it's only the hacks who care whether a scoop breaks in one paper or another. As for the general populace, no one either knows nor gives a damn who gets a scoop – and anyway, what do these scoops matter when within days the newspapers will all of them have been consigned to their usual fate as the next week's lining for the hamster cage. And as for me, well, I'd had a good time, a great time at Elveden, and so Bain had got the picture byline that should have been coming to me – and so what? Bain had done nothing more than lounge on the sidelines. I had actually been on the pitch. I'd got to meet Kubrick and Cruise and Nicole; I'd chatted and boozed with some of the world's most beautiful women; I'd met some amazing people – Nina and Glenn, and Molly the cook, and even, I guess, Josh and Caspar. So did it really matter that it was the Mirror who'd had the scoop, because it was me who'd dug up the story, and it was me who'd had my petty revenge on Sir James Hutchison, and it was me, also, who'd had all the fun.

CHAPTER 35

In short order, normal business was resumed, and I was back at the daily grind in the *Sun* newsroom, with one despotic boss now replaced by another despotic boss, the latter slightly less unhinged than Kubrick, but a lot more shouty.

I wouldn't say that I was shunned for the first week, but most of my colleagues – especially the chief reporter, John-Henry – tended to treat me as if I had a mild dose of leprosy. But after a week, two weeks, and the Christmas parties and Christmas itself, all was as it once was, back to the glorious business of getting my byline into the paper.

As for *Eyes Wide Shut*, I was, as best I could, keeping tabs on anything and everything that was going on with the shoot. I had all the local agencies on the case. They didn't have much to report about the second half of the orgy scene – that is, the really, *really* spicy part of the orgy where everyone was naked but for their masks and half the male cast were going at it like jackhammers.

Given what I knew about *Eyes Wide Shut*, I'd expected the shoot to take another year or so – and knowing the priapic director as I did, I thought he was certain to have milked the Highclere scene for six months minimum.

But no, Kubrick did not do that. Principal photography was wrapped up within a matter of weeks, and although Tom and Nicole were called back to redo a couple of scenes, by June 1998, Kubrick was finished.

Kubrick then went into cinemagraphic purdah, just him

and one obedient editor, as they set to work on sorting all the thousands and thousands of takes and knocking them into some kind of shape. By March 1999, Kubrick had finished his film and copies were sent to Warner Bros and to Tom and Nicole. Tom and Nicole watched it twice over and adored it. Warner Bros was also very happy.

For three days, Kubrick basked in the warmth of their general affection, delighted that his final project was destined to be yet another blockbuster, and then promptly dropped down dead. The cinematic world went into mourning. Tom and Nicole couldn't stop crying; Tom was a pallbearer at Kubrick's low-key funeral in Hertfordshire.

As for me – I didn't really know what to make of Kubrick's death. I do remember feeling that his timing was impeccable: he delivers his movie, it gets a resounding thumbs-up from the principal players, and then he's gone, and all the marketing and all the circus that surrounds the launch of a new film (which Kubrick loathed) was now somebody else's problem.

I could have gone to the London premiere of *Eyes Wide Shut* at the Warner cinema in Leicester Square, perhaps catching the eye of Tom or Nicole, or maybe even Nina, if she'd been invited, but I wanted to see the film solo, and so one rainy afternoon in September, I took myself off to the Gate Cinema, an appropriately magnificent cinema in Notting Hill.

Three things I loved about the film.

Firstly: the music that bookends the film, Dmitri Shostakovich's Waltz Number 2, which switches from the major to the minor key: this gives it a distinctly dark edge. The tune is beautiful and light and romantic, but it drips with this melancholic uneasiness. You can't put your finger on it, but it's there.

Secondly: I loved – no, I adored the orgy scene with Jocelyn Pook's crazy music, and watched the film five times over just to see this scene again. I myself featured in it for approximately one second.

And lastly: well, I really liked the final scene in the film, and most especially the last word, for it so beautifully sums up what is and has always been the key ingredient to a long-term relationship. This last scene was almost entirely written by Stanley, and mighty proud of it he'd been too.

Tom and Nicole are in a big toy shop with their daughter, and are mundanely chit-chatting about this and about that. But then Nicole suddenly changes gear. She tells Tom, 'But I do love you… and you know… there is something very important… that we need to do as soon as possible.'

Tom says: 'What's that?'

And Nicole is gifted with the last line of the movie. What is it that this glamorous couple so urgently need to do together, and what is the mortar that binds most marriages?

'Fuck,' she says.

So those were my favourite bits of *Eyes Wide Shut*, but as for the film itself, well… rather like Schnitzler's original novella, it seemed to drift a bit. Didn't overly do it for me. But then I'm a philistine, so what would I know about high art? The critics, who'd been waiting agog for Stanley Kubrick's Last Great Movie, eventually came round to the film; it dusted its feet at the box office.

And that was the end of that, another story over, another day done. Or so I thought.

Years later, some several years later, I was on a job on the island of Nevis, in the Leeward Islands of the West Indies. A football club owner, let us call him Freddy, Freddy Shepherd, had been having a trying time of things in the media. He'd called his female supporters "dogs" and had dubbed Newcastle United's star striker (Alan Shearer) as the "Mary Poppins of football". After one day of the ensuing hoo-ha, Freddy had decided to lie low in the Caribbean. Grubby and I had been sent to follow him. The drill was for me to lurk in the background while Grubby got the pictures of Freddy in the bag; what we needed, most particularly, were pictures of fat Freddy sunning himself on the beach and drinking a pina colada. When – and only when – Grubby had filed his pictures, I would then front Freddy up and ask him how he felt about bad-mouthing his fans.

We'd been there about five days, and though we'd spotted our quarry in his car, we'd yet to get the money shot of Freddy on his sun lounger. Grubby had gone off for the day, chasing Freddy over the hills. I had been left to my own devices. I decided to spend my day on a beautiful but little-known Nevis beach, Pinney's Beach – named, as it happens, after one of Nevis's slave-owners.

There weren't many people on the beach at the time. I had slathered on my factor 30, was drinking my first rum punch of the day, and was mightily enjoying myself – because although Pinney's Beach is a beautiful beach, it's all the sweeter when you're there on company time, when they're paying for not just your flights and luxury accommodation (we had to stay in the same five-star hotel as Freddy, obviously), but the drinks also. And, the final bonus, normally on these foreign jobs, reporters can start to get a little tense, as they fret over whether they'll actually be able to bring the story in, but not this time, no sirree, as the onus of this job was very much on Grubby to deliver. All I then had to do was front Freddy up, and I certainly knew what was going to happen then – he'd swear at me, would possibly try to hit me, and would then storm off in a huff. (As did the pint-sized pop star Chris de Burgh after the second time we caught him trysting with his nanny – but that, though, really is another story.)

I was worming my toes into the Pinney sand, not just delighting in being by myself, but also especially thrilled to have been freed from Grubby for the day; after six days' together, including six breakfasts and six suppers, his company was wearing thin.

As you do on the beach, I looked to left and right, scanned the other holiday-makers; on the sun lounger next to me, about five yards away, was some fat bearded bloke in a Panama hat and Hawaiian shorts. He needed a bit of suncream on his shoulders. He was reading a copy of *The Lady* magazine.

Not a magazine that's often read by men.

Interesting.

I turned onto my side and, hidden by mirrored sunglasses, inspected him. At first I thought it might have been Larry – but the fine, delicate fingers did not tally.

Five minutes later, a tall, glamorous woman came over with a couple of ice creams. Pneumatic curves. She was wearing a white swimsuit and had a quite spectacular *embonpoint*.

''Ow's my big baby?' she said. 'You're burning! Let's get some oil on your shoulders!'

Very interesting indeed.

I wished that Grubby had been there to take a few pictures, but Grubby was not there. I, of course, had my mobile phone, but we were still then in the Neanderthal age when phones were not even capable of texts, let alone pictures.

I waited for half an hour until Molly had made another expedition to the bar. I'd pondered how best to tackle it. By nature, I prefer coming in from the side, tiptoeing around the subject before revealing my hand at the very last moment. I didn't think that would work this time.

I just strolled straight over. 'Hi Stanley,' I said. 'How's it going?'

Stanley nearly shot out of his sun lounger, hands jerking up as his magazine fell to the sand. I settled myself down nice and easy on Molly's vacated sun lounger.

'I... I...' Stanley said. 'I think you must have the wrong person.'

'Don't think so Stanley,' I said, cheery as anything. I took a long cool suck on my crispy cold rum punch. 'What you been up to since you dropped dead in the spring of 1999?'

'I... I...' He looked me at furtively, like a fat sun-burned baby who's soiled his nappy. 'I don't know what you're talking about.'

'I know it's you Stanley!' I said. 'Cuckoo! And I think you

probably remember me too – Elveden Hall? Ring a bell? Your favourite *Sun* reporter?'

'It… what… Just…'

'You can think all you like, Stanley, but if you don't start talking, I'm going to start writing! I can already see the headlines! Kubrick's Alive! And maybe with a fat subdeck that would read something like, "Crazy Director Faked His Own Death!" How d'ya like them apples, Stanley?'

'Oh no, oh no!' he said.

'Oh yes, oh yes!' I said. 'Tell Kimmy everything!'

'Well, OK, maybe,' he said – and tell he did.

He hadn't planned it, but then, quite out of the blue, Larry had let Kubrick know that he was dying of cancer. Kubrick then had six months to get his affairs in order – first of all finishing off the edit of *Eyes Wide Shut*, which by now was hanging round his neck like an albatross, and then liquidating enough of his assets to see himself and Molly off into the sunset. Finally, after a very large payment to Larry's family, all he had to do was wait for Larry to meet his maker. At dead of night, Larry's body was deposited in Kubrick's bed at Childwickbury, while Kubrick himself made off for Southampton docks with Larry's passport. Kubrick – still just as terrified of flying as ever – got on the next ship out to the Caribbean, there to be joined by Molly, and the Great Switcheroo was complete.

As Kubrick finished his story, Molly came over to join him. They sat together holding hands on the sun lounger.

'So there ya have it,' Kubrick said. 'Whatcha gonna do?'

'I don't know,' I said.

'Please don't tell,' Molly said. A single tear rolled down her cheek. 'I'm very 'appy. We're very 'appy.'

And, like the soft touch that I always am, I just rolled over. 'All right, fine,' I said.

'You won't tell?' Molly said, absolutely amazed, swimsuit quite rippling with the strain of staying in one piece.

'No,' I said. 'Besides, no one would ever believe it.'

And that was true, actually. Without any pictures, the story would have been dismissed as just another of my confected fairy tales.

'Thank you,' she said, and she leaned over, hand on my knee, and kissed me on the cheek, and though it might have been nice to reminisce about *Eyes Wide Shut*, Kubrick, the old dog, was yearning to get her back to his bedroom.

'See ya!' he called over his shoulder, positively tugging at Molly's hand as he led her back to their honeymoon suite.

And with that, we have tied up almost all the loose strings in our tale, though there are two final strings that I would like to attend to: Tom and Nicole.

After *Eyes Wide Shut*, Nicole had certainly developed a taste for Arthur Schnitzler, as within weeks of the film being wrapped, she'd signed up for another Schnitzler adaptation. It was a play called *The Blue Room*, directed by one Sam Mendes, and co-starring the supremely hunky Iain Glen. The show was notable for Glen's astonishing full frontal (whilst performing a cartwheel!), as well as a brief flash of Nicole's pert rear. The *Daily Telegraph* dubbed it "pure theatrical Viagra", whilst the *Sun*'s theatre critic (your humble narrator), handily detailed the best seats in the house from which to view Nicole's bare bum.

Apparently, Nicole and Iain Glen never had an affair, though there was a lot of speculation. Affair or not, within two years of the *Eyes Wide Shut* premiere, Tom and Nicole had split. The reason why was never really clear – though to my mind, it was entirely down to Kubrick. He was mad and he'd driven them half-mad, and filming *Eyes Wide Shut* had completely broken them.

After the break-up, they went off to do whatever... they went off to do. Tom speedily moved onto another red-hot star of the day, Penélope Cruz, and as for Nicole, well, I was never quite sure, perhaps she fulfilled her Gary Goba fantasies, perhaps she did not.

It is so many years after my *Eyes Wide Shut* experience

that sometimes I can go days at a time without even thinking about it.

I'm in the *Sun* newsroom again, hell to some people, heaven for me, as this is where my friends are, this is where we banter and tell stories and occasionally get screamed at by our despotic mad masters; above all, this newsroom is at the very heart of the action. It is in this room, at these keyboards, that the news is manufactured. It gives a voice to those who do not have a voice; it is the place where the great and the powerful are held to account. (Or so I tell myself on a good day.)

I'm sitting at my desk in the early afternoon, perusing the *Evening Standard* as John-Henry quietly fumes at his desk: he's still not been allowed back into the RAC and he's still not forgiven me.

The phone rings. I love it when my phone rings in the newsroom, as this, usually, is how a story begins.

It's Stella, the newsdesk secretary, thankfully come to her senses after her dismal trystings with the deputy editor. 'Call for you.'

'Who is it?'

'Wouldn't say.'

And with a click, the caller is through. 'This is Kim.'

A pause. Quite a long pause.

'*Mi mancano i nostri giochi di Scrabble,*' she says. ('I miss our games of Scrabble.')

I give a sharp snort as my skin stipples to quivering attention. '*Mi manca il tuo ballo di cha-cha,*' I say. ('I miss your cha-cha dance.')

'*Hai la maschera?*' ('Do you have the mask?')

'*Lo faccio certamente.*' ('I certainly do.')

'*Voglio vederlo!*' ('I want to see it!')

'*Più eccellente!*' ('Most excellent!')

CHAPTER 36

We are five years on from the crazy Kubrick universe of Elveden Hall, and much has changed for Nina – not least that her life is now not entirely her own and she is contemplating that greatest of maternal conundrums: the work-life balance.

As best she can, Nina strives to divide her time fairly equally between her twins (Poppy and James) and her writing, while also factoring in enough time for herself and, lastly (but by no means leastly), her dear husband, and on that latter account she hasn't been doing too badly, as her toddler twins are soon to be joined by yet more pattering feet.

But enough of such idle daydreaming! Nina has got a goddamn job to do, and she has just fifteen minutes to do it, and though some writers might crumble, Nina loves nothing more than a nice, tight deadline. It sharpens the wits and gets her creative juices a-tingling.

She is sitting on a cheap canvas chair in front of a cheap Formica table, on top of which is her laptop, though this is certainly not cheap, and is in fact the most state-of-the-art laptop that money can buy. There is also a large sofa in the bell tent, but Nina tends to find that the muse is more receptive when she is at the pit face of the Formica table. She's wearing khaki shirts and a khaki shirt, all very loose, very comfortable and actually rather fetching. Was there ever a more comely screenwriter? Well, if there was, I have yet to hear of her.

Around her neck dangles an old silver groat from the era of Richard III, while hanging above the bell tent entrance is another nod to her old life – that gorgeous black-feathered mask from *Eyes Wide Shut*. As for her stilettoes, her G-string and her cloak of midnight blue, they are all safely stored away at home, there to be worn on high days and holidays.

Incidentally, her old outsized basketball shirts and shorts, which Nina had used to wear to the gym, those are also stored away at home, though not in the bedroom, but instead are tucked well, well away in the attic. And are we, perhaps, allowed to know their provenance? We most certainly are! The shirts and the shorts were indeed a gift from an old boyfriend, a very rich boyfriend who had once played for the Chicago Bulls with Michael Jordan. Astutely, Nina had never told a soul, not even the love of her life – a woman must be allowed her secrets.

Though the views outside Nina's tent are perhaps the most extraordinary she's ever seen – they're in the most verdant summer countryside in New Zealand – Nina has closed the tent flap, the better to concentrate on the script. And when, in fifteen minutes' time, she has done with her dialogue, the view will be her reward; there may be other rewards, including perhaps time with the twins, who at this moment are probably barefoot foraging through the woods with their nanny.

Tom Cruise, who is, of course, the hero of the film, has asked, very prettily, if a couple of the lines for his next scene can be tweaked. He says that his lines are already "just great", but he'd prefer them to be "brilliant".

'No problem at all,' says Nina, who, along with being the most beautiful screenwriter you've ever come across is also the chirpiest. 'Just give me fifteen minutes.'

The film – well, you may have heard of it. It was *The Last Samurai*, and it was Tom Cruise's first big project since *Eyes Wide Shut*. It was the perfect all-action role for Cruise, and, indeed, the ultimate antidote to his two years of complete inaction with Kubrick.

But what, what, is Nina doing on the set?

To explain: Tom Cruise had been expecting to spend at

least another year on the set of *Eyes Wide Shut* – and then, quite out of the blue, the whole dang shoot was wrapped in a matter of weeks. Most bizarre of all, Kubrick was limiting himself to a maximum of six takes per scene.

This was all thanks to Glenn, who had somehow acquired some sort of leverage over Kubrick – Cruise was never quite sure what – but whatever the leverage was, it must have been most potent. Tom had once asked, but Glenn had never told. The upshot was that, during the wrap party, Tom Cruise had happened to mention that he was much beholden to Glenn, and that if, perhaps, Glenn had any projects in the pipeline, then Tom would very much like to see them.

By very great good fortune, Glenn did indeed happen to have a project that he'd been working on with his screenwriter girlfriend – the pair of them had dovetailed together quite beautifully, Glenn with the story arc and the structure, and the things called beats (that is, a shift in the narrative), while Nina did the detail and the dialogue, and she was rather brilliant at it.

The screenplay that Nina and Glenn eventually served up to Tom Cruise was the script for *The Last Samurai*, about a nineteenth-century US army veteran who goes off to Japan to fight with the ancient samurai. Cruise was already smitten with the subject, and having read the script, he signed up on the spot – not just to star in the film, but also to co-produce it, and let me tell you that when you've got Tom Cruise on board, then your money worries are over.

It had taken some little while, of course, to get all their ducks lined up, especially as an entire Japanese village had been constructed on the hillside of the Uruti Valley in New Zealand, with Mount Taranaki having to stand in for Mount Fuji.

Then, well, there was merely the simple matter of uprooting the entire family to New Zealand for six months – but if you've got a chilled husband, not to mention an affable nanny, then you take such moves in your stride.

As far as Nina could tell, the shoot was going fairly smoothly. And though the structure of the movie was now set, Tom occasionally liked his dialogue to be tightened up, though always cast in the manner of a most deferential suggestion.

These little tweaks were Nina's absolute forte, which was fortunate, as her co-screenwriter was generally otherwise engaged.

So – to business! Although *The Last Samurai* was undoubtedly an action movie, it also had a sniff of a love story. Tom's character, Nathan Algren, was slowly falling for a beautiful samurai woman, Taka, but the romance had not got off to the best of starts: Taka was a widow after Algren had killed her husband.

That very often tends to be the way of these movie romances, with the two love interests initially at loggerheads until they're eventually ready to be won over. A screenwriter, however, needs great dexterity in bringing their two lovers together. It cannot be hurried; it is like the slow unfurling of an orchid.

And so it is with Algren and Taka. At first Taka loathes Algren, can hardly bear to have him in the house, but gradually he wins her round with his old-school charm.

The problem for Nina is that the movie needs a sort of linking scene. What she's got at the moment doesn't quite cut it. What Tom wants, and what Nina has got to write, is just a few lines to show that the couple are well on their way to falling in love.

Algren, who has taken the time to learn Japanese, has already told Taka's young son that he'll defend their little community to the death. And why will he do that? Because he loves the place.

The boy storms out of the room. Algren and the beautiful Taka are suddenly alone. They look at each other. They're both a little in love. But how to reveal this without revealing too much?

Nina twirls a pencil in her hand, doodles on a scrap of paper. She coils her hair and fetchingly pins it up with the pencil. What about…Taka saying to Algren: 'The way of samurai is difficult for children. He misses his father.'

Better. Much better.

Algren, of course, will have to take this the wrong way. For that is the first rule of the love story. Putative lovers must always get the wrong end of the stick.

So Tom's character will think that the boy's left the room because he's still sore about his dad being killed.

Nina taps out a line, another line, works at it, titivates it – and then there it is – a nice, solid line for Tom: 'And he is angry because I am the cause of that.'

Now all it needed was a wry look from Taka and then she gets the zinger. She has to set Algren right about her boy, while also revealing that she is also just a little in love.

Nina taps out a few sentences, melds them, blends them, and then there it is – the end of the scene: 'No,' Taka says. 'He is angry because he fears you will die as well.'

Not bad – not bad at all! After Tom Cruise and Koyuki, the actress who played Taka, had worked it up together, they'd make it sing.

At that, there is a call of "knock knock" from outside (actual knocking being impossible with a bell tent) and Tom Cruise himself walks in. He's wearing the uniform of a US Army officer who's killed a lot of Indians. His hair's longer and he now has a beard; an improvement on his *Eyes Wide Shut* look. 'Hi Nina,' he says. 'How's the scene shaping up?'

'Just finished, Tom.'

Tom pulls up a canvas chair next to her, stares at her laptop. As he reads, he's mouthing Nina's words. It's an extraordinary thrill. The world's biggest superstar is sitting next to her, is reciting her words, will soon be bringing them to life.

'Love it,' he says. 'Print it and let's go.'

Nina speedily prints off ten copies and, not twenty minutes

since she first entered her writing tent, Nina's work for the day is all but done. She gives the new scene to the third assistant director, one Olivia, she of the tattoos (though sadly pining after her tattooed boyfriend), who speedily has them translated into Japanese.

Tom is rehearsing the lines with Koyuki; Nina is still astonished at how quickly they can learn new lines. They're word-perfect in under five minutes.

Screenwriters don't often hang around for the filming, but Nina always stays; she loves the entire craft of film-making from the first concept to the final cut.

Tom and Koyuki take up position under the arc lights. They're in Taka's house. A couple of the make-up guys touch up the stars' make-up, remove every last speck of hair and dust from their costumes. All is still – and then, from behind one of the two cameras, a voice, a very gentle voice which is still capable of turning Nina's heart to mush, says simply, 'In your own time…'

And the pair deliver their lines over long, lingering glances and after a few seconds of silent perfection, a single word breaks the spell – 'Stop.'

Tom and Koyuki get into a huddle, and Nina already knows what they're saying – and already knows how it's going to turn out. Tom will, as usual, be asking for another take, but the director will very nicely and very sweetly tell him that he's had his one take and that it's perfect.

Besides – the crew are already setting up for the next scene.

Having received a sufficiency of praise, Tom and Koyuki retire to their caravans, and the director, the mild-mannered rather handsome director, has a brief word with his most capable first assistant director, before strolling over to join Nina on the edge of the set.

'Nice job you did there, Nina,' he says. He smiles as he cups his hand round her waist and gives her a kiss.

'Thank you, darling.' Nina returns Glenn's kiss with interest. For if Nina has learned anything at all from the ending of *Eyes Wide Shut*, it is that there is a certain mortar that binds married couples together, and that if they are to remain happily married, then this mortar must be liberally applied. 'You know you could occasionally allow Tom to have a second take.'

'He does it perfectly every time – so what's the point?'

'Stroke his ego?'

'True – but Tom's ego gets stroked plenty already. And anyway...' Glenn's hand has snaked round her waist and is cupping her firm, full belly.

'And anyway?'

'The fewer scenes we have, the more time I get to spend with you.'

Hardly even aware of where they'd been heading, they find themselves next to Nina's bell tent, Nina's slim fingers slip by his belt buckle to touch bare skin. 'That is a very good point and well made,' she said.

'Don't get me wrong, Nina.' Glenn removed the pencil hairpin. Her hair uncoiled clean about her shoulders. 'It also gives me more time to spend with the kids. But within a marriage, I think it's important for parents to carve out some quality time for each other.'

Letting her hands glide from Glenn's shoulders to his biceps, she tugs her husband towards the sofa. 'Just so,' she said, and who would have thought that so much love and so much happiness could have come from a *Sun* reporter inserting himself onto the set of the longest movie shoot in history, but that, my dears, is just the way it happened.

HISTORICAL NOTE

Though much of this novel has been made up, a surprising amount of it is true – not least the small matter of a tabloid reporter infiltrating the set of *Eyes Wide Shut*. As to whether this reporter ever became friends with Tom Cruise, well, we can't know for sure, but… more than likely he did.

In late 1999, soon after I'd returned from New York to be the *Sun*'s political correspondent, I had a drink with one of my old Sun compadres, Sean Hoare. I'd first met Sean in 1993 when we'd worked together on Piers Morgan's *Bizarre* column.

The conversation turned to *Eyes Wide Shut*, which had just come out the previous month.

To my utter astonishment, Sean claimed to have been one of the extras in the orgy scene.

I was sceptical, but Sean assured me that in 1997 he'd been at Elveden Hall for several weeks, there to do just exactly what tabloid reporters were put on this earth to do: get all the gossip and every picture that was fit to print.

Sean did not succeed because, as usual, he'd been taking enough drugs to stun an elephant. He was eventually thrown off the set for being a disruptive influence. (It was indeed Sean who drove Kubrick mad by yelling out, "Cut!")

Among other things, Sean also claimed to have become pretty pally with both Tom Cruise and Stanley Kubrick. This was more than possible as Sean was the complete charmer.

But on the other hand,… it must also be conceded that Sean was partial to, ahhh, embroidery.

So this conceit of a tabloid reporter befriending Cruise and Kubrick on set is more than just possible. It's actually quite probable. I'd put it at about 70–30.

Sean died in 2011 at the age of forty-seven, largely rolled over by alcoholism. He'd just become a whistle-blower in the phone-hacking scandal, all very drear. But for me, the way I remember Sean best is as a raconteur, and as a teller of stories, and for his infectious Sid James laughter.

Most of the details about Stanley Kubrick are all spot on, from his obsession with porn to his love of *The Lady* magazine. Kubrick loved having hundreds and hundreds of takes, somehow seeing it as a means to getting something extra special out of his stars. He did dress like a shambolic wino, and would indeed go into total apoplexy if his stars weren't word-perfect with their lines.

The incidental stories about Kubrick's stars – like Kirk Douglas, Ryan O'Neal, Steven Berkoff and Shelley Duvall – are all true.

As for the stories about Tom and Nicole, well, a few of the details are true, and some are the product of my most impish imagination; personally, I think they both come across as thoroughly endearing, fun and wholesome to be around.

Various other genuine facts have been woven into the tale. Once, when I was a *Sun* staff reporter, I was duty-bound to stick to the facts and nothing but the facts (though a little light massaging was occasionally permitted). But now that I am a novelist, I love nothing more than blurring fact with fiction.

The details of the Elveden Hall shoot are largely accurate, including how Kubrick's factotum, Leon Vitali, recruited most of the girls from a variety of striptease parlours. The girls were trained for months and months before being set loose on Elveden Hall, where they had so many takes that they were indeed complaining about their aching knees. The lead girl was fired for being bolshy, following Harvey Keitel, who'd walked out a few months earlier; it was a very unhappy set.

As already mentioned, the 400-day shoot went on to garner

the world record for the longest continuous shoot in history. Though one oddity of the shoot was that after Elveden Hall the whole film was wrapped up astonishingly quickly (at least by Kubrick's standards). Who knows why Kubrick suddenly got fed up with his usual hundred takes. Maybe he realised that Tom Cruise and the crew had already been thoroughly broken in. He'd beaten them – soundly. Perhaps he was hungry for fresh meat. Or perhaps, just possibly, some senior crew member had discovered how to twist Kubrick's arm...

It's never really been clear why Tom Cruise and Nicole Kidman divorced – though for myself, I think it's highly likely that it was *Eyes Wide Shut* that did for them. Kubrick completely got into their heads, had them both leading these most secretive lives. It certainly wasn't conducive to marital harmony.

Incidentally, the strange details of Nicole's dreamy sex shoot with Gary Goba – including the merkin, the fifty different sexual positions, and Gary getting a pubic hair stuck in his teeth – are all well documented. Kubrick himself was the man who was wielding the camera, cackling away as he ordered Goba to "really get in there".

The particulars of the life of a movie extra are fairly accurate – and I can say this because I have well and truly paid my dues. I've been a movie extra (or supporting artist as we luvvies now like to style ourselves) for over seven years. I've been in *Fast and Furious 9* (for about one second), *Batgirl* (for no time at all, as despite over $90 million being spent on the film, the entire movie was cancelled), *Good Omens 2* and *A Castle for Christmas* (with Brooke Shields, who I nearly managed to take out during a country hoedown). So yes, I do know a little of what it is to be a movie extra. It is certainly not to everyone's taste, but I just love it, and still occasionally turn up on set for the ungodly 5 a.m. call times. There's a lot of hanging around and there's a lot of being bossed around, but, my particular delight, there's also a lot of time to talk; you hear the most amazing stories.

As for my two leads, Nina and Glenn, they are both composites of people I've had the luck to work with. Though Glenn is named after my favourite assistant director, Glenn Whelan, who is forever upbeat and who possesses the most uncanny ability to remember people's names. Even though Glenn deals with hundreds and hundreds of extras, even months afterwards he'll still remember who you are.

The *Sun* newspaper is pretty much as I've described it, from the large windowless newsroom to the banging out of journalists as they leave for the last time. *Sun* reporters were forever trying to infiltrate the places where they were least wanted – places such as Buckingham Palace, or movie sets, or even Eton College.

Tabloid reporters have also always been partial to selling stories to rival papers. Journalists may have a great time of things but they certainly don't get paid a lot. Stories that were spiked by one editor were frequently passed on to a rival newspaper; the *Sun* even had a mole on the *People* newsdesk.

Super-injunctions? This term hadn't quite been coined in 1997, but it was certainly the stars' default when dealing with tabloid newspapers. If you didn't like the look of what was about to be printed, then ankle-tap them with an injunction.

The tasty tale of the Newcastle United boss Freddy Shepherd calling his female fans "dogs" happened in 1998. I was the reporter who was tasked with fronting Freddy up, though he was staying not on Nevis, but at Barbados's most exclusive hotel, the Sandy Lane. My photographer at the time was not Grubby (Phil Hannaford) but Shannon Sweeney. She got some great shots of Freddy on his sun lounger, as well as some pictures of the singer Luciano Pavarotti, who just happened to be staying at the Sandy Lane at the same time; Luciano was wearing, as I remember, the most immense kaftan.

Tom Cruise did produce *The Last Samurai* in 2003, though it was directed and co-produced by Edward Zwick, who also co-wrote the screenplay with John Logan and Marshall Herskovitz. I, however, needed a suitable pay-off for Glenn and Nina after their purgatory with Stanley Kubrick. *The Last Samurai* fitted the bill very nicely. (Glenn's one-take style of film-making is actually based on that of Clint Eastwood.)

The *Sun*'s chief reporter in the 1990s was a former journalist of the year, my friend and mentor, the great John Kay. I occasionally accompanied him to the RAC where he wined and dined his most secret sources; it all ended in disaster.

After the phone-hacking scandal that shut down the *News of the World*, the police started a separate investigation at the *Sun* in 2011. Specifically, they were looking into reporters giving money to police and civil servants for stories. Scores of police officers trawled through hundreds of thousands of emails and all the rest, and eventually, twenty-nine of my former colleagues were put up for trial at the Old Bailey, including John Kay. They were accused of bribing cops and civil servants – a charge that was entirely denied by the *Sun*'s journalists, who said they'd merely been paying off whistleblowers. A number of police officers and civil servants were sent to jail, but every single *Sun* journalist was acquitted (one after appeal). The whole sorry saga completely broke John Kay. He never returned to the *Sun* newsroom and died in 2021 at the age of seventy-seven. The five-year police investigation had cost over £14 million. By a bizarre quirk the name that the police gave to this investigation was eerily familiar to me. It was called Operation Elveden.

And finally… some people might think that, in Kubrick's final act, I must have taken leave of my senses. How utterly preposterous to have Kubrick faking his own death and then turning up on the paradise island of Nevis! Now, in general, I absolutely detest conspiracy theories. But in the case of Kubrick's very sudden death, there was a huge amount of speculation that he'd had a body double and that he had indeed faked his own death. Well, when you're a novelist, and when you hear something like that, it's just too good *not* to use.

William Coles, Edinburgh. 2025

ACKOWLEDGEMENTS

The best part of being a movie extra is getting to meet all these highly unusual cats on set. These are a smattering of the friends I have made in the movie world. (My humble apologies to anyone who feels they've been left out. If you do feel you've been snubbed, then do please drop me a line and I'll vilify you in my next book.)

I would like to thank: Aaron Aitken, Tony Atherton, India Brown, MaryAnne Hunt, Asia Hutchinson, James McIntosh, Dàn Mac Tire, Miranda Maxwell, Max Maxxa, Nikki Miller, Flora Munro, Stephen Sharp and Glenn Whelan.

I'd also like to thank my extras agency, the BBB Talent Agency, most especially Iain Wilkie and David Rapp, as well as Callum Donald at Social Mouth Media, who has taken on the burdensome task of turning my books into blockbusters.

In my novels, I love to name characters after my friends – particularly the villains. The general of thumb is that the worse they come across, the higher that I hold them in my esteem. These include: Charlie Bain (who really was a staff reporter on the Mirror); Hannah Cocker; John-Henry Cugley; Phil Hannaford (a *Sun* staff photographer, who was indeed known as "Grubby"); and Sir James Hutchison. I hope that I have done you all justice!

I'm also especially grateful to the team at Legend Press - always such a pleasure to work with. These include Lucy Chamberlain, Olivia Le Maistre, Ditte Loekkegaard, Liza Paderes, Sam Rennie, Cari Rosen, and Lauren Wolff-Jones.

And then of course there's the boss Tom Chalmers, and my editor Christian Müller who had the Herculean task of knocking my manuscript into shape. (Christian only hacked away 5,000 words; he said it was less than he'd expected.)

And lastly we come to my greatest cheerleaders, my mum and dad Bob and Sarah, my brother Toby, my sons Dexter and Geordie, and my wife Margot; they make the whole damn thing worthwhile. I thank you all!